Cult
& SF

TERROR'S REACH

TERROR'S REACH

TOM BALE

preface
publishing

Published by Preface Publishing 2010

10 9 8 7 6 5 4 3 2 1

Copyright © Tom Bale 2010

Tom Bale has asserted his right to be identified as the author of this work under the
Copyright, Designs and Patents Act 1988

First published in Great Britain in 2010 by Preface Publishing
20 Vauxhall Bridge Road
London SW1V 2SA

An imprint of The Random House Group Limited

www.rbooks.co.uk
www.prefacepublishing.co.uk

Addresses for companies within The Random House Group Limited
can be found at www.randomhouse.co.uk

The Random House Group Limited Reg. No. 954009

A CIP catalogue record for this book is available from the British Library

ISBN Hardback 978 1 84809 074 3
ISBN Trade Paperback 978 1 84809 075 0

The Random House Group Limited supports The Forest Stewardship Council (FSC),
the leading international forest certification organisation. All our titles that are printed
on Greenpeace-approved FSC-certified paper carry the FSC logo. Our
paper procurement policy can be found at www.rbooks.co.uk/environment

Typeset in Electra LH Regular by Palimpsest Book Production Limited
Grangemouth, Stirlingshire
Printed and bound in Great Britain by
Clays Ltd, St Ives PLC

For Ann and John Harrison

One

They sent the first man in at midday. His job couldn't have been more straightforward. All he had to do was sit on the beach. Watch, listen, wait, and not be too obvious about it.

The target was Terror's Reach, a stunning accident of geography nestled within the dazzling surroundings of Chichester Harbour. One small island: five homes, nine residents and combined assets that ran into billions. It was a gold mine, practically begging to be plundered.

But the remote location posed its own challenges. The options for reconnaissance were limited, long-term surveillance all but impossible. There was no passing traffic, no way to go unnoticed. Here amongst the super-rich, anyone seen loitering was liable to be challenged or reported to the police.

The solution, on the day, involved a gamble, but the good weather helped to minimise the risk. It was an easy enough gig, and Gough was pleased to be assigned the role. He could sit on his arse as well as the next guy.

But it also carried serious responsibility. As first man in, his actions had a direct bearing on the whole operation. Get it wrong and he was in big trouble.

He was under no illusions about the kind of people he was working for. If he screwed up, they would probably kill him. Simple as that.

*   *   *

Two in the afternoon: siesta time. With the temperature pushing ninety any sensible person would be glad to lie in the shade and have a doze. But Jaden, at six years old, didn't see it in those terms. Bursting with restless energy, he had no intention of taking a nap, and he was making his feelings known to his mother.

Joe Clayton was aware of the protests coming from the other end of the garden, but he wasn't really listening to them. He was sitting on the broad stone terrace, finishing a lunch of cold meats and salad.

'I want to go to the beach.'

'Not now, Jaden. Sofia has to sleep, and so should you.'

'I'm not tired. Sofia's a baby. I'm six.'

'Well, go in the pool, then. But only for a few minutes.'

'I don't want to go in the pool. I want to go to the beach.'

'It's too hot. And I have to stay here and watch Sofia.'

'I can go on my own.'

'No, Jaden.'

'It's not fair. You don't let me do anything.'

There was a thud, followed by a loud crack. Joe looked up and saw something skidding across the grass. The boy had thrown one of his cars to the ground. It must have ricocheted, hit another toy and broken.

Jaden glowered at the tiny die-cast models, furious with his mother, and himself, and the whole world. It was a state Joe keenly remembered: the terrible aching frustration of childhood.

'I hate it here,' Jaden shouted. 'I wish we still lived with Nanny and Grandad.'

Joe winced. He had already decided to intervene when a first-floor window was thrown open and a voice above him roared: 'Cassie! Do something about that boy!'

The window slammed shut. On the lawn, Jaden scooped up the broken car and fled to his refuge: a sun-proof beach tent that was variously a cave, a fire station and an enemy camp. His mother called him back, but Jaden ignored her.

Maybe it was the heat making everyone so fractious, Joe thought.

Not that Valentin Nasenko ever had much patience with his stepson. It was little wonder the boy missed life with his grandparents.

Joe drained his glass of water, tipping the remnants of several ice cubes into his mouth. As he stood up his chair scraped on the stone and he almost expected another tirade from above. When Valentin was preoccupied with something, he demanded absolute peace and quiet. *And what Valentin Nasenko wanted . . .*

Joe had been working for the Nasenkos for just over nine months. He'd met them the previous September on the Greek island of Naxos. Having concluded a summer-long stint as a deckhand on a chartered yacht, he'd picked up some casual bar work in Naxos Town.

Valentin's principal adviser, Gary McWhirter, had been in the bar when a fight broke out between rival football fans during a televised Champions League game. Impressed by Joe's adroit handling of the mini-riot that ensued, McWhirter had invited Joe to meet Nasenko. One of his security team had resigned at short notice, and Valentin wanted an extra body to watch over his wife and newborn daughter during a three-week cruise around the Aegean.

At first Joe had been reluctant. The thought of babysitting a young mother and her child didn't hold much appeal, but inevitably the money on offer made the decision for him. One thousand euros a week, available in cash if he wanted it.

Cassie Nasenko had seemed equally unhappy with the arrangement. She rarely made eye contact with Joe, and was constantly ill at ease in his company. The situation didn't improve when Joe overheard her singing some cheesy ballad and quipped that, with a bit more practice, she could make a decent karaoke singer. He later discovered that at the age of seventeen Cassie had reached the final stages of a TV talent competition and had gone on to enjoy a brief career as a pop singer.

It wasn't until the third week that she grew accustomed to his presence, and he came to see that what he'd perceived as arrogance was actually shyness. She was from an ordinary lower-middle-class background, very similar to his own, and she was still coming to terms with the idea of having staff at her beck and call.

When the cruise ended it was Cassie, rather than Valentin, who suggested that Joe should stay on the team. Joe suspected it was largely because of Jaden, Cassie's son from a short-lived relationship with an actor in a TV soap. Jaden was often quiet and withdrawn, but Joe seemed to have struck up a rapport with him in a way that few others had.

Returning to the UK posed another dilemma. In many ways he was in no hurry to go back, and yet he couldn't deny his fascination with the idea. It was there constantly in his dreams, when the past could be effortlessly unrolled and reworked.

Joe had often agonised over the *if* and *how* and *when* of his return, always careful not to dwell on the resultant question: *What then?*

The answer, as it turned out, was simple. Just go to work and get through the day. Go to work and never think about where you might be instead.

Joe descended the half-dozen steps from the terrace. The middle section of the garden was effectively a large playpen, a neat square of lawn fenced off for safety from the swimming pool and the jetty beyond. It was littered with trikes and footballs, and Jaden's current favourite diversion: a giant game of Connect 4 that was taller than he was.

Cassie Nasenko was sitting on a picnic blanket, staring pensively in the direction of Jaden's hideaway. Next to her, ten-month-old Sofia was stripped to her nappy and lay fast asleep beneath a large parasol, her pudgy white limbs contrasting with her mother's deep tan.

Cassie was a small, slight woman with an almost boyish figure: narrow hips, bony shoulders and thin arms. At first glance you could mistake her for a teenager, rather than a woman of twenty-five, a wife and mother of two children.

Throughout the present heatwave, unseasonable even for June, she'd maintained a uniform of flip-flops, denim shorts and cotton shirts, with a bikini in place of underwear. Her sun-bleached brown hair was tied up in a ponytail, her green eyes clear and bright against the tan. A sprinkle of freckles over her nose gave her a pretty, tomboyish look.

At Joe's approach she put on a brave smile. Close up, he was struck by the weariness in her face. Sofia was teething at the moment, and having a bad time of it. Despite the sleepless nights, and contrary to her husband's wishes, Cassie remained determined to bring up her children without the help of a nanny. Joe admired her for that.

He said, 'I'll take him to the beach if you want.'

'We shouldn't give in to him when he's had a strop.'

'I know. But for a quiet life.' Joe nodded towards the house. 'Just this once.'

'All right. Only for ten minutes or so. Then he really must get out of the sun.'

'You okay if I have a swim while I'm there?'

'Fine,' said Cassie. 'But keep an eye on him. He's being a little monster at the moment.'

'Jaden's a good kid at heart. I'm sure he didn't mean what he said about living here.'

As soon as the words were out he knew he'd overstepped the mark, but she just gave him a curious, slightly sad smile.

'Oh, I think he meant every word.'

Two

Terror's Reach had captivated Joe from the moment he'd first set eyes on it. He wasn't familiar with the area, and had imagined Chichester Harbour to be a man-made construction, with a sea wall and all the accoutrements of a commercial port: quays and cranes and slipways, and maybe a yacht marina.

In fact, it was a vast natural harbour, straddling the counties of Hampshire and West Sussex. Eleven square miles of water in a tidal basin of mudflats and salt marsh. There were three main channels and countless other inlets, creeks and waterways around half a dozen peninsulas of varying size and shape.

The Reach was a small island on the eastern side of the harbour, once joined to the mainland by a narrow causeway, accessible on foot at low tide. Its name derived from a Victorian working boat, the *Terror*, which had sailed around Chichester Harbour, transporting oyster catches from larger offshore vessels. The Reach marked the furthest southerly point on its route.

Although uninhabited until the 1890s, the island's sheltered coves and woods had been used by smugglers for centuries. When coastal erosion finally destroyed the causeway in the mid-1930s, a chain ferry was installed, jointly funded by the residents and by the War Office, which had acquired two-thirds of the five-hundred-acre island for use as a training camp.

The ferry was superseded in the 1960s by the construction of a road bridge, and while the Ministry of Defence still maintained the training camp, its lack of use in recent years had led to fevered speculation about its future. In the meantime, the only private dwellings were spread in a graceful arc on the south-western corner, with views out to sea and across the bay towards Hayling Island.

Originally there had been eleven relatively modest houses on the island, but in the past two decades all but one had been demolished and replaced by much larger, architect-designed mansions. Now there were just five in total, with an average value of four million apiece, making property on the Reach almost as expensive as that in the more famous resort of Sandbanks, about seventy miles to the west.

Joe had spent every spare moment exploring his new home, and it had brought him up short when he first caught himself thinking of it in that way. This felt like home – or at least the nearest thing to a home that he could hope for.

Jaden's whole demeanour was transformed once he stepped through the gate at the bottom of the garden. It was as though he'd been granted an unexpected release from prison. His shoulders lifted and he grinned, whooping with pleasure as he broke away from Joe's grasp and tore off along the timber decking. Joe had to jog to keep up.

The decking was about five feet wide, forming a communal walkway that ran for some three hundred yards along the rear of the properties. Each home had a private jetty that branched out from the deck and extended fifty or sixty feet over the water, though today there were only a couple of small craft moored here. For most of its length there was no fence or safety rail on the seaward side of the deck, so Joe had to watch that Jaden didn't trip and fall in.

Nevertheless, he couldn't help admiring the boy's daredevil streak, perhaps because he recalled a similar quality in himself at that age. It meant Jaden was straining for independence at every opportunity and, to his mother's continual despair, angrily protesting whenever limits were imposed on him.

Joe could see both points of view. To a restless, energetic six-year-old the island must have seemed like a personal adventure playground. And in many ways the Reach was the safest place imaginable in which to grow up. Only a handful of residents. Minimal traffic. No strangers passing through.

But Cassie, like many parents where their first born was involved, saw danger lurking around every corner. That was all the more reasonable, given her husband's wealth: it was why Joe had been employed, after all. For weeks Jaden had been pleading to be allowed to go to the beach on his own, and Cassie had steadfastly refused.

Valentin's property was furthest from the beach, so their route took them past the other four homes. Three of the four were imposing buildings in vastly different styles: mock-Georgian, ultra-modern and faux Gothic. The gardens were a little more uniform in design: all terraced, with a mix of lawns and paved areas. Most had swimming pools. All were scandalously under-appreciated, in Joe's opinion.

It was Friday afternoon, a truly glorious summer's day, and yet there was no one outside to enjoy it. Joe and Jaden didn't see a single resident until they reached the last house, owned by a retired couple: Donald and Angela Weaver. Theirs was the only remaining original property, and even though it had a substantial ground-floor extension it was modest in comparison with its neighbours.

Donald Weaver was just visible amidst the mass of sweet peppers and tomato plants in his greenhouse, a small red watering can bobbing about in mid-air as if of its own accord. Jaden spotted him first, broke his stride to call and wave, but there was no response. Either Donald hadn't noticed him, or he just couldn't be bothered to acknowledge the boy. Joe had a feeling it was the latter.

A few yards beyond the Weavers' home the deck ended at a tall gate, marked with a warning on the opposite side: RESIDENTS ONLY. In case anyone should disregard the sign, one of the residents, Robert

Felton, had paid to install a basic combination lock, as well as adding several yards of fencing to prevent intruders from simply climbing around the gate. It hadn't been a universally popular addition, but as owner of two of the island's five properties Felton's wishes often tended to prevail.

Jaden had already fumbled the gate open by the time Joe caught up with him. They stepped down onto a gravel path, fringed by wild grasses bleached almost white by the sun. Less than ten yards away was the narrow shingle beach that ran along the island's southern shore, facing the open sea.

It was a beautiful, solitary location, neglected by the residents and little known to the outside world. Visitors weren't prohibited on the Reach, but nor were they encouraged. There were no parking areas, and the asphalt road gave way to a narrow track of beaten earth for the last thirty yards between the Weavers' home and the beach. By way of further deterrents, nettles and brambles had been allowed to encroach on the track, and a sign marked PRIVATE PROPERTY had been erected – illegally – by Robert Felton.

Today, however, those deterrents had failed.

There was a stranger on the island.

Gough heard them coming before he saw them, but only by a second or two. He didn't have time to react, and he was professional enough to know that sudden movements attracted suspicion. So did furtive ones, in a situation like this. Better not to move at all.

He ignored them for a moment, then realised it would be unnatural to show no curiosity. He turned and gave them a glance. A man and a boy, dressed for the beach. The man had a couple of towels rolled up under his arm.

They were from the Nasenko house, he decided. The kid must be the wife's bastard offspring. And the man was a bodyguard. Had to be.

Gough made eye contact with him, noted the man's surprise, and maybe something else. Something harsher. To counteract it he gave the sort of quick nod that said: *Hello* but also: *Yeah, I'm here, too. Get over it.*

Then he went back to ignoring them, hoping that they would ignore him in return. He gripped his fishing rod and stared at the sea and worked very hard not to look at the rucksack by his side. But he was acutely aware of what it contained.

If they left him alone, all well and good.

If they didn't, there was always the gun.

Three

The fisherman was in his thirties, Joe estimated. Wearing an Arsenal shirt and three-quarter-length trousers. He had a good physique and a hard face. Short dark hair under a black baseball cap. He was sitting close to the shore, holding a cheap-looking fishing rod with the line cast out fifteen or twenty feet. There was an open rucksack next to him, a half-empty bottle of Evian water propped against it. A couple of tabloid newspapers lay folded next to him.

As they crossed the beach Joe glanced back towards the road and saw a motorbike parked on the track. A mid-sized Honda road bike, perhaps 500cc, with panniers for storing the fishing gear.

Joe's first reaction was disappointment, and he scolded himself for it. He'd always been disdainful of the idle rich, living in splendid isolation, and now here he was falling prey to the same selfish impulse.

It was the first time he'd seen someone fishing at this spot. The island occasionally played reluctant host to birdwatchers, wildlife photographers and hikers, but the sheer size of the harbour meant there were always plenty of better-known and more accessible sites to attract them.

Jaden ran to the shoreline and began searching the beach. Joe followed him and sat down a few feet away. The sea lay flat and calm, sparkling beneath the white-hot glare of the sun. The only sound was the chittering of unseen crickets in the grass behind him, and the distant trilling of a curlew. The tide was gently advancing, filling the harbour basin, but the rich sulphurous scent of the mudflats lingered in the air. At first Joe had found the smell distasteful; now, in an odd way, he savoured it.

'Only ten minutes, remember,' he said. 'Are you going to swim?'

Jaden, distracted, shook his head. He picked up a stone, examined it, tossed it over his shoulder.

'Can we do skimming instead?'

Joe smiled. He might have known that Jaden would change his mind. It was breathlessly hot and Joe would have liked a swim. But if Jaden wasn't going in, neither could he.

'Okay. Find me some flat ones.'

Gough kept his eyes on the sea, but his attention never wavered from the other occupants of the beach. They were about ten yards away, standing close to the shore. The boy was gathering stones and trying to bounce them on the water.

They talked while they did it, and Gough overheard their names: Joe and Jaden. The kid's technique was improving, with the bodyguard demonstrating how to hold the stone between forefinger and thumb, the flick of the wrist and the low-angled release that produced the best results. When Joe managed five, then seven bounces, Gough was tempted to have a go himself.

Bad idea, he thought. Befriending them ran the risk of inviting awkward questions, and his cover story wasn't detailed enough to withstand that.

He remembered that he was supposed to report any developments. There was a mobile phone in the rucksack. He couldn't talk while they were in earshot, so he sent a text. *Man and boy on beach. Man is called Joe & kid maybe belongs to Nasenko wife. Trouble?*

The reply was almost immediate: *No threat to us. Relax.*

Gough snorted when he read that. Easy for you to say, he thought.

It seemed an age before they grew tired of the game, although it was actually less than fifteen minutes. Cue some bratty whingeing from the kid when the bodyguard said it was time to go, but Joe was having none of it.

'Your mum will give me hell if we don't go now.' The bodyguard turned towards Gough and added, for his benefit: 'Anyway, this poor man can't wait for us to leave. We're scaring his fish away.'

Gough acknowledged the comment with a disinterested smile, then saw to his horror that the kid was heading towards him.

'Have you caught anything?' he asked.

'Not yet.'

'How long is the rod?'

Gough, mystified, began to stutter a reply, but Jaden beat him to it.

'I think it's about six foot. And it's telescopic. They're not very strong. For beach fishing you need something longer.'

Gough glanced at the rucksack. There was a Browning semi-automatic pistol tucked between a bait box and a folded-up jacket, just the grip visible. The boy was two or three feet from it, and edging closer in that fidgety way kids had. Another couple of steps and he'd see the gun, even if he didn't recognise what it was.

The bodyguard called: 'Jaden!' But the kid didn't seem to hear.

'I've got a ten-foot rod, with a Shimano reel,' he declared, his eyes shining with pride. 'My grandad has to help me with casting, but what I catch is mine.'

'Nice. Perhaps you took all the fish, eh?' Gough tried a light-hearted chuckle, but the boy just stared at him as though he was mad.

'There's *loads* of fish left.' Jaden was still shifting nearer. 'You just need more practice. And a better rod.'

'Okay. Thanks for that.' Gough casually tipped the rucksack towards him, disguising the movement by grabbing the bottle of Evian and taking a long drink.

'Jaden! Come on. *Now.*'

This time the kid reacted, gave him an apologetic smile, turned and ran off.

Thank Christ for that. Gough finished the water and tossed the bottle away. Much as he'd have enjoyed wringing the little brat's neck, it was better for them all if the encounter passed without any trouble.

Then he heard a crunching of footsteps on shingle. He looked round and saw the bodyguard approaching. Jaden was hanging back, uncertain, like he'd been told to wait where he was.

What now?

Joe saw the fisherman tense, as though he knew what was coming. He shifted round, moving the rod to his left hand. His right hand came to rest, almost protectively, on the rucksack.

'Beautiful beach, isn't it?' said Joe.

'Suppose so.' The man's voice was gruff, with an estuary accent. He had a tattoo on the side of his neck: a crudely inked serpent, poking up from the collar of his football shirt.

Joe gestured towards the Evian bottle. 'No bins here, I'm afraid. You'll have to take your litter with you when you go.'

The man seemed confused, then belligerent. 'What?'

Joe kept his voice friendly, but his eyes stayed cold. 'It's a bugbear of mine, people coming to enjoy a place like this and then thinking it's okay to leave their waste behind. I hope you're going to clear up after you.'

The man looked away, grinning as if at a private joke. 'Is that a threat?'

'Do you need it to be a threat?'

'I don't like being told what to do, I know that much.' He stared at Joe, his eyes narrowed.

'Consider it a suggestion, then. Or even a polite request. *Please take your litter with you.*'

The man snorted. There was a long pause, of the kind that sometimes precedes an outburst of violence. Joe readied himself for it, while the fisherman stroked the top of his rucksack as if it were a pet.

Then he gave a sudden conciliatory smile.

'Sure, I'll clean up,' he said. 'You won't even know I was here.'

Boiling with suppressed fury, Gough leaned over and retrieved the water bottle. He felt Joe's gaze on him for a few more seconds, then the bodyguard turned and crunched his way over the stones. He rejoined the kid and they walked towards the boardwalk, chatting quietly, not hurrying.

Joe's broad back made a perfect target. Gough longed to pull out the gun and bring the fucker down. Shoot the kid too, for that matter. He stuck his hand in the rucksack and felt the comforting solidity of the Browning's grip. Joe was punching in the code to open the gate. There was still time to do it. Empty the magazine into them both, then run for the bike. He could be out of here in seconds . . .

And then what?

He thought about the text: *No threat to us. Relax.*

'Yeah, right.' He dropped the fishing rod, grabbed the phone and made a call. Joe and the kid were through the gate now, all but out of sight.

'They've gone, but the bodyguard was suspicious.'

'Why? What happened?'

'Nothing.' Gough knew he sounded too defensive. 'I just think I should pull out. I can't see fuck all from here.'

A moment's deliberation. Then: 'All right. We'll be coming in ourselves soon enough.'

Four

Joe and Jaden were almost at the house when they heard the distant roar of the motorbike. Joe was surprised that he might have scared the fisherman away, but he wasn't particularly sorry about it.

He resolved to wander back to the beach later and see if the man had made good on his promise; maybe get a swim at the same time. He had protection duties this evening, when he had to take Cassie and the children to Brighton, but the next few hours were his own.

It wasn't until he'd delivered Jaden back to his mother that Joe realised how restless he felt. The run-in with the fisherman had got his adrenalin pumping. He had a lot of energy to burn off, and he knew just how to do it.

Valentin Nasenko's house sat on a large plot: some two-thirds of an acre. The frontage was a hundred feet wide and eighty deep, enclosed within a rendered brick wall. Most of the space was paved driveway, with decorative shrubbery along the borders. A month ago Valentin had decided that the greenery served no useful purpose and should be paved over.

Joe thought this was a shame, especially as it involved ripping out plants and trees that had been planted at great expense just two years before. But rather than bring the landscaping firm back, Joe had offered to do the work himself in his spare time. It kept him busy, and it kept him fit.

And sometimes it served as a kind of penance.

He'd completed one side of the driveway, and the other side was coming on well. He'd excavated the land to the correct depth, laid weed fabric and hardcore. The next task was to add a layer of sharp sand and compact it to form a bed for the block paving.

Earlier in the week ten tonnes of sand had been delivered in bulk bags and stored just inside the gates. Now, fetching a wheelbarrow and a shovel from the garage, Joe began to transport the sand across the drive and spread it over the hardcore. The ninety-degrees temperature made it punishing work, but that was good. That was what he wanted.

Within a few minutes he'd settled into a pleasing rhythm. What he found most satisfying was the simplicity of the task and the immediacy of the results. He liked the solitude and the fresh air, and the fact that he could go anywhere in his mind while he worked – or he could just let his mind go blank. Forget everything.

More than once Joe had reflected on the path his life might have taken had he opted for a trade like this: a life of good honest labour. If he'd chosen that route he might now be enjoying a happy, uncomplicated existence with his wife and daughters; instead he was marooned here, in a seductive illusion of paradise.

He was running the wheelbarrow back for another load when he caught movement beyond the gates. Angela Weaver was walking past, pushing her sturdy mountain bike. With her wide-brimmed hat and floral summer dress she resembled a character from *Miss Marple*, but her legs were as slim and toned as an athlete's, and she had the kind of deep natural tan that came from years of outdoor living.

She was a familiar and treasured sight, sailing past with her long grey-blonde hair whipping out behind her and Brel, her elderly yellow Labrador, hustling in her wake. But Joe wasn't accustomed to seeing her like this, trudging by on foot, head down and face hidden.

'Angela?'

She didn't respond. Joe left the wheelbarrow and walked across the drive. He saw she was hobbling slightly, and the bike's front tyre was flat. Her Labrador looked every bit as tired and dispirited as she did.

'Angela? Are you all right?'

Now she glanced round, her face creased with pain. 'I'm fine.' She gave an unconvincing smile. 'I just took a tumble.'

'Let me see.' Joe hit the button on the post that opened the wrought-iron gates. 'Come in for a minute.'

She angled the bike towards him, the flat tyre splaying on the ground. For all her stoicism, Joe had the feeling she was actually quite glad to see him. Brel escorted her through the gates, accepted a quick rub around the jowls in greeting, then trotted off to investigate the pile of sand.

'Donald's always cautioned against my "reckless" cycling, and now he has irrefutable proof,' Angela said. She had a clear, well-modulated Home Counties voice; the sort that Joe's parents would have teasingly summed up with the word *frightfully*. But it fitted her age and appearance so aptly, Joe couldn't imagine how else she might sound.

'Did you hit something?' he asked.

She shook her head, slightly ashamed. 'I'd just come over the bridge when I heard an engine. I looked up and found a motorcycle haring towards me in the middle of the road. Taking the racing line, I suppose.'

She sighed. Joe felt a twinge in his jaw and realised he was gritting his teeth.

'Goodness knows what speed he was doing,' Angela went on. 'Anyway, in my panic I swerved towards the verge, while also looking round for Brel. I hit a fallen branch, burst the tyre and went flying.'

'What about the motorbike? Did it stop?'

'Sadly, no. And I didn't recognise him. One of Oliver Felton's friends, perhaps. I shall have words with that young man.'

Joe held her gaze for a moment. Her eyes were cornflower blue and very clear, with a vitality that made her look thirty-something rather than in her sixties. Of all the island's residents, Angela was the only one Joe really trusted, the only one he'd come close to confiding in.

'It's nothing to do with Oliver,' he told her. 'In fact, it's probably my fault.'

He ran through his brief conversation with the fisherman and concluded by spreading his hands in an expression of guilt. 'If I hadn't been playing the eco-warrior, this wouldn't have happened.'

'Nonsense. For all you know the man always rides like a maniac. Besides, you're quite right to challenge litter louts.' She gave a mischievous wink. 'If I had my way, I'd kneecap the halfwits who throw cigarette butts from their cars. Polluting beaches should be a capital offence.'

He grinned. 'Well, I'm still sorry it happened. Are you hurt?'

'Not really.' With no hint of bashfulness, she hoisted the hem of her dress to mid-thigh. There were grass stains on her shins and a large graze oozing blood on her right knee. Joe was surprised to hear a cheerful laugh.

'A schoolboy wound. I look like something out of *Just William.*' She refused his offer to fetch the first-aid kit. 'I'll clean it up when I get home. And then try to get this damn machine roadworthy again.'

'I can help you there,' Joe said. He raised a hand even before she spoke. 'No arguments. I'm doing it.'

'Very well. But you don't have to.'

She stood back as he turned the bike upside down, resting it on the handlebars and saddle, then fetched a box of patches from the garage. He'd used one a few days ago for an emergency repair on a big inflatable crocodile that Jaden had burst while playing in the pool. There were no tyre levers, but he had a Leatherman multi-tool. The file, wrapped in a handkerchief to stop it scratching the rim, would do the job just as well.

Joe rolled the tyre off the rim on one side and the inner tube flopped out like a dead black eel. He used the bike's hand pump to inflate it and locate the puncture: a single tiny hole.

'There we go. Shouldn't take long to fix.'

'Actually, I'm not sure if I do have a repair kit at home,' Angela said. 'I'm very grateful to you.'

'It's nothing. As a kid I spent half my life messing around with bikes.' Joe grew wistful. 'When I was promoted to detective sergeant I treated myself to a Marin. First brand new bike I'd ever had. I did the whole South Downs Way a couple of times, before the girls were born.'

'You should get one now.'

'Hmm.'

Angela smiled at his non-committal response. She knew he wouldn't buy a bike because that would feel too much like putting down roots; and Terror's Reach wasn't his home, not really.

Although retired, Angela did voluntary work as a counsellor for a charity in Portsmouth, helping young people with a range of issues including drug and alcohol dependencies. Consequently she was a good listener: one who knew when to intervene and when to say nothing.

Hunched over the bike, Joe found the truth easier to tell. 'Even if it didn't cause your accident, I overreacted. It was bloody stupid, risking a fight over a discarded water bottle.'

'But there wasn't a fight. You might have felt aggression, and that's perfectly natural. All the more so in your circumstances. The crucial thing is that you controlled it.'

'Only because he backed down. I didn't even think about Jaden in that moment. And I'm there to protect him.'

'I can't imagine Cassie's children being safer with anyone else. Don't forget, a healthy dose of aggression is what the family are paying you for. It's part of the job description – as long as it's channelled correctly.'

'Maybe that's the thing. It's so peaceful here, there's nowhere to channel it.' He waved towards the wheelbarrow. 'Except for work like this.'

'From what you've told me, the crux of your problem is practically irresolvable. There's really no alternative to what you're already doing. Getting through it, one day at a time.'

Joe pushed his hand through his hair. 'I suppose so. I just thought I'd gone beyond wanting to settle disputes with my fists. Now it seems like the impulse was just lying dormant.'

Angela considered for a moment. 'Well, then perhaps you have to accept that it's part of who you are. That means coming to terms with it. Living with it when it's dormant, *and* when it's awake.'

He looked up at her. Her face was solemn, even vaguely sad.

'At the risk of sounding terribly mystical,' she added, 'I'd suggest it might be there for a purpose.'

After patching the hole in the inner tube, Joe checked for other punctures, then ran his hand round the rim to make sure there were no thorns or grit left inside. He replaced the inner tube, worked the tyre back into place and finished inflating it.

Angela beamed at him. 'Thank you, Joe. I was dreading what a drama Donald would have made of this.'

'Least I can do.' He spun the wheel and heard it rub against one of the brake blocks. 'It's a bit buckled. Might need straightening.'

'Oh, I'm sure it was like that before. It's an ancient, creaking old wreck.' She laughed. 'Just like its owner.'

Joe shook his head, unsure what to say. He could see Angela reddening slightly. He turned the bike the right way up and rolled it forward, testing the brakes. They squealed a little, but worked fine.

Angela climbed on and adjusted her sunhat. She called to Brel, who trotted over, happier for having had a rest. Joe accompanied them to the gates. There was a car approaching from the north, a sleek-looking Renault with a man at the wheel. He was doing about forty: not a crazy speed, but still too fast for the island.

'Rather than tempt fate, I'll wait for him to pass,' Angela said.

'That's the guy who's trying to sell Felton's place, isn't it?'

'The estate agent. Yes.' There was a wry note in her voice, for which she offered no explanation. Not in the mood for gossip right now, Joe surmised.

The Renault slowed for a left-hand bend just beyond the Nasenko property and disappeared from view. Angela pushed down on her right pedal and wobbled out onto the road.

'Thanks again, Joe. I owe you a favour.'

'No, you gave me some good advice. We're quits.'

He watched her pick up speed as she cycled towards home. Already he could feel the negativity returning, seeping through his mind like a stain. For no matter what Angela had said, he *did* bear responsibility for her accident.

It was a salutary reminder to Joe that it wasn't only good deeds that were paid forward, but bad ones as well. Another tiny measure of guilt; another bitter taste in his gullet.

Five

Liam Devlin couldn't bear inactivity. After meeting the others at the staging post on an industrial estate south of Havant, there had been a couple of hours with little to do but check over their equipment and wait. The whole time he was aware of a manic energy surging through his body. He felt like an overcharged battery, leaking heat from his pores like acid.

Then came the bad news from Gough. Liam had had concerns about surveillance from the beginning. Although the beach wasn't an ideal vantage point, it was the safest place they could find. The trees opposite the homes would have been perfect, but all it took was someone's dog sniffing them out . . .

On the plus side, Gough's early retreat gave Liam good reason to bring the operation forward. Only the first stage, and only by an hour or so, but at least he'd be moving. There was plenty of waiting still to come, once they were in place, but that would be easier to handle. For one thing, he'd have a distraction.

Priya had arrived late for the rendezvous. She was polite but aloof. She kept to herself during the afternoon, ignoring the repetitive small talk and jittery gallows humour. A frosty little bitch: that was the consensus Liam picked up from the others. They were knuckle draggers, mostly; the type of men who hated authority in any form. The idea of a woman as second-in-command wasn't just alien, but repugnant. The colour of her skin didn't sit well with some of them, either.

For Liam, it was different. He was top dog on this mission and he made sure everyone knew it. Also, his background was white-collar, so he was used to dealing with snotty bitches in all shapes and shades. Priya's typically female air of superiority didn't threaten him in the slightest. On the contrary: it gave him a thrill.

From the moment he first set eyes on her, he knew he had to have her. With a bit of luck and a lot of willpower, he might be able to keep that desire under control till the job was done. But if not . . .

If not, he'd do it whenever he got the chance.

Liam looked like a bandit in an old-fashioned western. He'd grown his dark hair to shoulder length. He had a long, drooping moustache, modelled on the one sometimes sported by the singer Nick Cave, and he'd gone without shaving for a couple of days. The combination of the moustache, the stubble and the granite-grey eyes gave him exactly the right persona: he was one mean sonofabitch. Not to be messed with.

The new look worked equally well as a disguise. He was dressed like a builder, in heavy boots, jeans and a tight black singlet. When the job was done he'd shave and cut his hair short. With a good suit and a neat side-parting, no one would connect him to the grubby desperado who'd raided the homes of some of the wealthiest men in Britain.

If there was a drawback, it was that 'grubby desperado' didn't seem to do it for Priya. So far she'd hardly spared him a glance.

That was okay, Liam decided. He liked a challenge. It made the eventual conquest all the more satisfying.

With Angela's misfortune weighing on his conscience, Joe worked furiously for thirty or forty minutes. When he finally paused, the muscles of his arms and back were screaming for relief and his body was dripping with sweat. But he felt a lot better.

He peeled off his T-shirt and mopped his face with it. The sun was high above him, mercilessly hot. A couple of black-headed gulls drifted silently overhead. There was almost no birdsong, he realised; just a distant forlorn chirping from the woods across the road.

Joe walked over to the pallet of paving blocks, where he'd left his watch for safety. It was three forty-five. Time to get that swim he'd promised himself.

He was putting on the watch when the sound of an approaching vehicle made him look up. With traffic so rare on the island, he had spent enough time out front that he could recognise most of the local cars by their engine tones. This one was unfamiliar.

It was a white Ford Transit, two years old, the bodywork faded but clean. A sign on the side in plain black lettering said *CC Construction*. Below that, in a font too small to read quickly, an 0845 number. No web address or trade-association logo.

There was only one man in the cab: slim, youngish, with unruly dark hair and a gunslinger's moustache. He gave Joe the briefest of glances, then turned his attention back to the road, his brow furrowed with intense concentration. Either deep in thought or pissed off about something.

Probably the latter, Joe guessed. Builders' vans weren't a particularly unusual sight on Terror's Reach, but at this time on a Friday he'd have expected to see them heading in the opposite direction, back towards the mainland and the nearest pub.

Joe was turning away when an audible thud from the rear of the van caused him to hesitate. The Transit veered slightly, as if the driver had been startled by the noise. Then the van straightened up and accelerated away. Before it disappeared around the bend in the road Joe memorised the registration mark. No real reason, but old habits died hard.

He went on thinking about it as he tidied up. The likeliest possibility was that some equipment had shifted or fallen over. But the thud hadn't sounded hard and metallic; it had been soft and muffled.

Yielding, like flesh. It reminded him of the noise a disruptive prisoner made, throwing himself against the side of a police van.

Except that didn't make any sense. If there was someone else in there, why weren't they sitting up front with the driver?

As Liam drew alongside the Nasenko house, his attention was caught by a man on the driveway. Late thirties, dark hair, tall and muscular. He was staring straight at the Transit. Liam focused on the road, sneaking another look as he drove past.

A thump from the back echoed through the van. The shock made him jerk the steering wheel.

'Shit,' he muttered. *Sit still, you silly bitch.*

He corrected the steering and checked the mirror. Saw the man watching as the van rounded the bend and the Nasenko house slipped out of sight. That must be the fella on the beach who'd rattled Gough. Seeing him, Liam could understand why.

Easing up on the accelerator, he grabbed his phone and pressed the speed dial.

'What?'

'Just passed some big bastard, paving the driveway. That's the other bodyguard, I take it?'

'Yes. But you have no need to worry about him.'

'You sure? He looks pretty handy.'

'Don't worry, I tell you. Soon he will be gone from here. The others are ready, yes?'

'Oh, yes. Everyone's ready.' Liam smiled. 'Ready and raring to go.'

Six

Angela Weaver freewheeled onto her driveway and half dismounted, balancing gracefully on one pedal as she rolled along the path at the side of the house. She felt tremendously relieved that Joe had come to her aid. It meant she didn't have to mention the accident to Donald at all. Her only regret was making that clumsy joke about her similarity to the bike. *An ancient, creaking old wreck.* What had she been thinking?

She regularly encountered Joe on the beach, usually reading or sketching with pencils. Over a period of months, as they'd sat and talked, he had gradually revealed more about himself and his chequered past. She was flattered that he'd taken her into his confidence. He was a lovely man, who for the most part endured his suffering with good grace. He didn't deserve the fate that had befallen him.

Then again, Angela thought, who did?

She propped the bike against the fence and turned to make sure Brel had followed her into the garden. Before going in she checked the graze on her knee. It was drying up nicely, but cleaning it out with witch hazel could wait. First she needed a cup of tea and a sit-down.

She took a couple of deep breaths to compose herself. Rubbed her hands over her face, took off her hat and patted her hair into some kind of order. Silly, really. She could stroll in wearing clown make-up and a bright orange fright wig and Donald would be hard-pressed to notice.

She opened the back door and stepped inside, and as she crossed the threshold a familiar melancholy descended.

Angela had once watched an intense, beautiful film called *House of Sand and Fog*, and it had inspired her to christen her home in a similar fashion. For the past two years this had been the *House of Sorrow and Fury*, and although she could never countenance leaving it, she also knew she could never quite feel happy here any more.

Donald was sitting at the scarred pine table in their large old-fashioned kitchen, engrossed in a recipe book. Impervious to the heat, he was wearing his favourite gardening clothes: old brown cords and a threadbare check shirt. He didn't acknowledge Angela's presence until the dog padded over and collapsed, panting, at his feet.

'Nice ride?'

'Lovely,' she lied. 'Though it's sweltering out there. Poor Brel was labouring.'

Donald bent down, stroking the Labrador's head. 'You go far too fast, that's the trouble. It's not the damn Tour de France.'

'It keeps me fit. I wish you'd exercise more often.'

'No point,' he said, licking a finger and turning the page. 'See anyone?'

'Not really. Just that chap who works for the Nasenkos. Joe.'

Angela saw her husband flinch. His body tightened, his head dipping closer to the refuge of the book. She grabbed the kettle and tipped the dregs into the sink.

'That's his *name*, Donald. He's called Joe. I can't help that, and I can't not say it.'

'Yes, you can.'

'Oh, Donald.' Her exasperation blew out on a sigh, lost in the gurgling rush of water as she refilled the kettle. Here was a man who decidedly did *not* bear his suffering with good grace.

So many times she had resolved to confront him, try and bring this nonsense to an end. But always she found herself putting it off. Today her justification for doing so was slightly more impressive. The accident had left her weary and shaken, and a lot more upset than she'd dared admit to Joe.

Because the truth was that the motorcyclist had seen her in plenty of time, and yet made no attempt to correct his position.

If anything, he'd been aiming right at her.

The first thing Liam noticed was that the gates were open. A second later he spotted a car on the driveway. It must have come in after Gough had left the island.

He let the van roll past the entrance, coming to a halt alongside the perimeter wall. The neighbouring property was partly obscured by a screen of mature fruit trees, and there were no buildings at all on the opposite side of the road. Plenty of privacy, at least.

He turned off the ignition and thought about what to do. Almost immediately he was interrupted by a rapping on the bulkhead. A wary voice called his name.

'Yeah, all right.' Liam slipped out of the cab, wiping his face with his hands. He checked the road was clear, then opened the rear doors. The wash of hot stale air made him recoil.

The van was loaded with equipment, which included eight large propane cylinders. Squashed amongst them, Priya should have looked grimy and dishevelled, but there didn't seem to be a trace of sweat or dust on her.

'Welcome to Terror's Reach,' he said, and as she stepped down it was all he could do not to gasp.

Even in blue jeans and a plain black top, she looked like an Indian princess. Or maybe a Bollywood star, playing the part of an Indian princess. She was tall and slim, with broad shoulders and a narrow waist. Her hair was dark and lustrous, as light and fine as smoke. She had milk-and-honey skin, every inch of it utterly smooth and unblemished.

No sense denying it to himself, Liam thought. He was hooked.

While Priya took in the magnificence of the building, Liam studied her face. He saw her eyes widen, then narrow again with concentration. He noted the way her lips came together, leaving just a tiny hole in the centre.

The house was called Dreamscape, and to Liam it resembled a dozen gigantic Coke cans, stacked in two layers of six. It was a monstrosity: eight thousand square feet of prime real estate. The curved exterior walls were clad in red and white glass ceramic panels, while the interior featured huge open-plan rooms and a wealth of solid oak and marble.

The current price tag was six and a half million, and it had been on the market for nearly two years.

'The design's too idiosyncratic,' Priya said at last. 'That's why it hasn't sold.'

'That, and the fact it's overpriced by about three million quid.'

She turned to him, frowning. 'Why are the gates open?'

Joe finished clearing up while debating whether to walk along the road to the beach and see where the mysterious van had gone. At the same time a voice in his head told him to leave it. His job was to watch over Cassie and her children, not patrol the island for rogue builders and potential litter louts.

He was still undecided when the front door opened and Cassie Nasenko appeared, carrying a tall glass of water.

'Thought you needed a drink,' she said. 'You'll give yourself a heart attack, working so hard in this heat.'

'I quite enjoy it,' said Joe. The glass was slippery with condensation. He was careful not to drop it, or let his fingers brush against hers.

He drank gratefully, while Cassie turned and inspected his handiwork. 'It's coming on well,' she said, without much enthusiasm. He knew she'd have preferred to leave the shrubbery untouched.

'Thanks. Is Jaden okay?'

'Yeah. He still wouldn't have a nap. And Sofia didn't have long enough, so they'll probably end up being grumpy tonight.'

Joe tutted. 'I bet you're looking forward to seeing your friends?'

'Yes, I am.' Her gaze flickered towards the house. 'Oh, and there's been a change of plan. Yuri wants to see you.'

'He didn't send you out here, did he?'

It was a curt response, enough to make Cassie blush.

'I was bringing you the drink.'

'I know. Sorry.' Trying to soften his tone, he said, 'It's just . . . I don't work for Yuri. I work for you.'

She crossed her arms, clapping her hands against her shoulders as if suddenly cold. 'Actually, you work for Valentin,' she said, and there was an unspoken message in the pause that followed. *And so do I.*

Liam leaned into the van and reached for a heavy-duty metal toolbox. He was aware of Priya's scent, something light and floral. She was standing just behind him, her hands clasped together. Anxious but not panicked, which was a relief. Maybe she wouldn't turn out to be a total liability.

'Did anyone notice you on the way here?' she asked.

'A guy out front at Nasenko's place.'

'A gardener?'

'No. One of the staff.' Then he remembered. 'What was that noise you made?'

'Oh, I lost my balance. Sorry.'

'Yeah.' Liam gave a brusque nod. Maybe not a *total* liability . . .

He opened the box and the top tier concertinaed out. He removed a set of drill bits and examined the weaponry concealed beneath them. Half a dozen semi-automatic pistols, complete with silencers, and a selection of knives.

He stopped mid-delve. At this point he knew nothing about the threat he was facing. Was a gun a tad excessive? Was a knife too messy?

'Ah, fuck it.' The remnants of his Irish accent were strongest when he cursed: sounded more like *feck it*. He left the toolbox and shut the van doors. Gave Priya an encouraging glance. 'Come on.'

The boundary wall was about five feet high, painted a brilliant white, its curving design mirroring that of the house's front elevation. The wide double gates were carved from Iroko hardwood, electrically operated, with an intercom set into the wall beside them.

Liam knew the building had an extensive security system, with a network of movement sensors and high-definition cameras. It was quite feasible that someone would be monitoring their approach, so he made sure to stroll up to the front door, his leisurely manner and pleasant smile reinforcing his entitlement to be there.

Priya followed, studying the large potted palms along the driveway as if half expecting someone to leap out at her.

'Relax,' he said.

'I'm perfectly relaxed, thank you.'

Definitely an attitude there. He found himself dwelling on her mouth again, that tantalising little gap, and had to push the image away.

Later.

The car was a red Renault Mégane Sport, parked close to the house. Liam casually trailed his hand along the bonnet as he passed it. Still warm.

The front door was made from heavy oak, flanked by narrow windows of opaque decorative glass. There was a security camera mounted above the door, and a covert one embedded at eye level in the door itself.

'Go with me,' said Liam, and knocked firmly.

'What are you planning to say?'

'Depends who answers.'

He heard movement inside. The door was opened quickly, without any caution, by a young man in pinstriped trousers and a puce-coloured shirt. He was about thirty, with dark hair and big brown eyes. A good-looking guy, and didn't he just know it.

But his glib smile died as he registered their presence. His gaze was drawn to Priya, then reluctantly back to Liam, and in his narrowing eyes Liam spotted an unmissable trace of guilt. With that, a number of things became clear.

'We're here for the viewing,' Liam said, taking a step forward.

'What?'

'We arranged it with the agents, Taplin Ward.'

'You must be mistaken. I'm from Taplin Ward, and I don't recall—'

'They told us you'd meet us at the house.'

'But they don't know I'm—'

Thank you, Liam thought, and he punched the man in the throat.

Seven

Joe followed Cassie across the driveway, her flip-flops slapping against her heels with a sound like insistent wet kisses. She branched towards the playroom, where the electronic *thwock* of a virtual tennis ball was accompanied by a cry of victory. Jaden was a demon on the Wii, regularly defeating Joe not just at tennis but at bowling and even boxing.

Joe continued on to the kitchen. It was divided into two distinct spaces. The rear section was about twenty feet square, as sterile as an operating theatre with its white ceramic floors, Poggenpohl units and Corian worktops. A step led up to the front half, where a breakfast table and a couple of easy chairs looked out over the terraced gardens and the grand sweep of the bay.

While he'd been working out front, a sleek motor yacht had appeared and was sitting at anchor just inside the deep-water channel. On the bridge, a crew member in white raised a pair of binoculars and seemed to focus in their direction.

Yuri Deszniak paid it no attention. He was sitting at the table, a pair of mobile phones set before him like cutlery. In one fist he clutched a glass of cognac, and with the other he lifted a cigar to his mouth and took a long, appreciative suck. The maid, Maria Vargas, had just delivered a pot of coffee. In place of thanks, Yuri flapped an impatient hand towards the wall of glass. He required ventilation.

Sniffing disdainfully, Maria turned away. She was a short, squarish woman in her fifties, wearing a plain grey dress and a white apron. Still oblivious of Joe's presence, Yuri watched her stretch up on tiptoe to open one of the high windows.

'You have a big ass, woman. Did I tell you that before?'

Maria made a small gesture, acknowledging that she had heard but didn't necessarily agree. She knew not to take Yuri too seriously, but nevertheless she still feared him.

'I ask myself, is there a man alive who would fuck you, eh?'

Joe snorted. 'That's rich, coming from an ugly bastard like you.'

Yuri spun round, glowering as he saw who was speaking. Maria scurried past, briefly making eye contact with Joe. She was smiling.

'Another thing,' said Joe. 'Next time you want to speak to me, come and get me yourself. Cassie's not here to run errands for you. She's your boss's wife.'

Yuri's bark of laughter told Joe exactly what he was thinking. The marriage was a mistake, easily rectified.

'I answer to Valentin. Nobody else. Not her,' he growled, stabbing a finger at Joe, 'and not you.'

'That's crap.' Joe felt his heart beating faster again. *So much for self control.* 'It's time you started showing her a bit more respect.'

Yuri looked amused. 'Or . . . ?'

Joe held his gaze. He was aware of Maria retreating to the depths of the kitchen.

'Or face the consequences,' he said.

'You would fight me?'

Angela's advice came back to him. *Accept that it's part of who you are.*

'You bet I would,' said Joe. 'I'd kick your arse right into next week, and I'd enjoy every minute of it.'

With the element of surprise, a punch in the throat can be just as effective as any weapon. The estate agent keeled over and landed heavily, his head thumping against the solid oak floor. His eyes shut and for a few long seconds he didn't move.

Maybe he's dead, thought Liam, surprised by how calm he felt. He and Priya entered the house and closed the door behind them. He listened for signs of inhabitation, but the building felt empty.

The estate agent's eyes opened and his body started thrashing, his hands clawing at his throat. He let out a long, strangled noise.

'He's suffocating,' Priya said. 'He can't breathe.'

'He can breathe. He's just forgotten how, because he's panicking.'

Liam gave the man a kick in his lower back. The estate agent twisted away. His frantic gurgling subsided and he took a couple of big gulping breaths, like a baby after a tantrum.

'I suppose he looks like an estate agent,' Priya said. 'That shirt is *appalling.*'

'It was an educated guess. But I think he's AWOL.' Liam crouched down, tugging the man's arm to get his attention. 'What are you doing here?'

The man coughed first, then said, 'None of your business. Who the hell are you, anyway?'

Liam grabbed him by his hair and slammed his head on the floor. The impact reverberated around the cavernous hall. Liam's hand came away sticky with hair gel. The man groaned and shifted a few inches, leaving a smear of blood on the floor.

'I have to get back. I'm due in a meeting at six.'

'Six o'clock on a Friday? I don't think so.'

A shameless flicker of acknowledgement from the estate agent. His was a career where exaggeration came as naturally as smiling: getting caught out was merely an occupational hazard.

'In a bar,' he conceded. 'We all get together every Friday.'

'Not today, you won't,' Liam said. 'You still haven't explained what you're doing here.'

The estate agent swallowed. 'I'm meeting someone.'

'Who?'

'A woman.'

Liam glanced at Priya, indicating the house. 'I suppose you can't blame him. A place like this standing empty and he has the keys. It's got to beat the back seat of his car.'

'My car!' The man groped inside his pocket, brought out a set of keys. 'Take the Mégane. I promise I won't tell anyone.'

Liam feigned interest in the proposal. 'Company car, is it?'

'Well . . . yeah, but—'

'You know, I'm stunned by your generosity. Offering me a car you don't own, while you shag someone in a house you don't own.' He laughed. 'What about the woman? I bet she's not yours, either.'

The estate agent stared at him, uncertain how to reply.

'Of course she's not,' Liam answered for him. 'You worthless piece of shit. I don't want the car.'

The man went to put his keys back in his pocket, but Liam snatched them from his hand. He turned to Priya.

'But we do need to get it in the garage before his lady friend arrives. Bring the van in as well.'

'What if someone sees me . . .'

'I've got to watch Mr Slick here.'

'Please,' the estate agent blurted. 'Tell me what you want.'

'Shut up.'

'If it's something in the house, just let me go. I swear I won't say a word.'

'I told you to *shut up!*' Liam shouted.

Priya waited for him to face her, and said, 'I can deal with him.'

Liam was doubtful. He'd argued against her late inclusion in the team, and he still wasn't sure exactly what she was doing here. All he knew was that she'd been some kind of science prodigy who'd gone off the rails and ended up in rehab, where a former client of Liam's had trawled her up. Not difficult to see what had attracted his interest, but it hardly qualified her to guard a frightened and desperate hostage.

'I don't know if that's wise,' he said.

'Better than someone spotting me and wondering what I'm doing in a builder's van,' Priya said. 'Go on. I can handle it.'

But Liam had spotted a glimmer of hope in the estate agent's eyes. He kicked him in the side, hard enough to crack some ribs. The man screamed and rolled away. His hand fluttered above the injury: too painful to touch. Tears dribbled down his cheeks.

'Try anything', Liam said, 'and I'll take a penalty kick with your skull. Understand?'

He got only a whimper in response. Priya looked on, her arms folded. She wore a grim expression, as though she disapproved of his methods.

You'll see a lot worse than this before we're done, he thought.

There was a tense silence in the kitchen. Then Yuri turned away. He lifted the coffee pot and poured quickly, slopping some on the table.

'If you would fight me for her, maybe you want to fuck her?' He nodded towards the ceiling. 'Maybe I tell Valentin how you feel?'

Joe didn't rise to the bait. He and Yuri had formed a mutual enmity from the beginning. It might have deterred Joe from taking the job, if not for the fact that Yuri was rarely on the island. He was Valentin's personal bodyguard, and Nasenko spent at least two weeks of every month attending to his various business interests around the world. The rest of the time was divided between the Reach and his apartment in Belgravia.

Yuri was in his mid-forties, a short burly man with thick black hair and dark eyes. His features were large and unprepossessing, and his skin had the look and texture of old dough. One side of his neck was disfigured with scar tissue where someone had once thrown battery acid over him. Legend had it that he had ignored the burns until he'd disarmed his attackers and killed them both with his bare hands.

The Ukrainian said nothing as he spooned three sugars into his coffee. Finally he picked up his cigar from the side plate he was using as an ashtray. He inhaled, then jabbed the cigar at Joe.

'Clean up and get ready. You take Cassie to Brighton in thirty minutes.'

'I thought we were leaving at six.'

'Not any more. There is something to collect at Merrion's.'

Joe glanced at his watch. 'We'll be cutting it fine. What time do they close?'

'Don't worry about that. Just do it. And say nothing to her.' Yuri bared his teeth, but it couldn't have been called a smile. 'Valentin has arranged a surprise.'

'Okay. What's the real reason for going early?'

Yuri glared at him. 'His visitor arrives soon. He wants no distractions.'

'Must be an important meeting.' When Yuri showed no sign of responding, Joe indicated the yacht, sitting squarely in their field of vision. 'Is that anything to do with it?'

'This is not your concern.'

Joe kept his voice level. 'If Valentin wants to change the plan, I'd expect him to tell me in person. How do I know I'm not just running some silly errand for you?'

'He is busy. He tells me, and now I tell you. And for Valentin, you are here to fetch, to carry, to be good little worker and keep your *fucking* mouth shut.'

Joe clenched his fists. A glint in Yuri's eye suggested he would relish a fight, and yet he didn't seem overly disappointed when Joe forced himself to relax.

'We're going to have a talk about this tomorrow,' said Joe quietly. 'Get a few things straight.'

Yuri threw back his head and laughed. 'Tomorrow? Very good. See how I tremble with fear!' He motioned towards the door. 'Now go. Go before you make me angry.'

Reluctantly, Joe turned away. He knew he shouldn't let Yuri rile him, nor should he keep trying to fight Cassie's battles for her. If Valentin chose to keep her in the dark, it was her responsibility either to have it out with him or to put up with it.

Crossing the kitchen, he earned another long-suffering smile from Maria. He walked along the hall and descended the stairs to the staff quarters, aware that the prospect of a night away had just become a lot more inviting.

Eight

Liam knew from the floor plans that the garage could be accessed via the house. He hurried through a kitchen so enormous that it was probably larger than some of the flats he'd rented over the years. Then into the adjoining utility room, where he discovered the door into the garage was locked. He looked round for a key but couldn't find one.

He was about to kick the door in when he remembered the estate agent's keys. He pulled them from his pocket, saw that several were on a keyring of their own, along with a plastic tag marked *DREAM-SCAPE*. The second one he tried slipped easily into the lock.

The garage was stifling, the air as thick as soup. Although it was large enough for four or five cars, the interior was clad in timber; there was no natural light and not much ventilation. It was like stepping into a sauna.

At least Liam didn't have to grope for a light switch. The system operated on movement sensors, and a bank of fluorescent tubes fired up as he crossed the threshold. The ceiling was built low to accommodate a strengthened floor for the games room overhead, the centrepiece of which was a full-sized snooker table.

Years since I played snooker, he thought, grinning slyly as he reflected on some of the other things you could do on a snooker table.

That brought him back to the estate agent, and the man's secret assignation. This woman he was screwing could turn up at any moment. Two extra hostages before they'd even got set up. Not exactly the best of starts.

'Well, bollocks to that,' Liam said, his voice resonating in the large empty space. At least he had the experience to know that things like this always happened. There was even a motto for it, for Christ's sake: *Expect the unexpected*. What mattered was how you dealt with it.

Reaching the big double doors, he paused, thinking he'd heard a noise back in the house. A muffled cry, maybe?

He waited a second, wondering how Priya would react if the man made a grab for her. Whether she could fight him off.

But there was no time to go and check. The last thing Liam wanted was the estate agent's lover rolling up just as he got into the Renault.

So hurry . . .

Valentin Nasenko had a permanent staff of more than twenty people: personal assistants, maids and housekeepers, gardeners and bodyguards. Some were based on site at Valentin's various homes around the world, while others travelled with the man himself. At Terror's Reach there were usually two or three live-in staff, including Joe.

Their quarters were in the basement: four bedrooms which opened onto a communal open-plan living area and kitchenette. Joe's room was about ten feet by eight, decorated in neutral colours, with a single built-in wardrobe and an ensuite shower room. The only window was a narrow skylight that ran along the side of the house and poured a little daylight into each of the rooms.

It was an arrangement similar, in Joe's opinion, to a prison cell. Certainly Yuri seemed to think so. He took any opportunity to help himself to one of the guest bedrooms on the second floor, rather than languish down here.

The room could be locked, but since it seemed likely that Valentin had access to master keys, Joe kept his personal possessions in a metal strongbox stashed beneath a spare blanket in the bottom of his wardrobe. As well as nearly ten thousand pounds in cash and a couple of cheap pay-as-you-go mobile phones, the box contained credit cards, passports and birth certificates in two different names, including the one by which his current employers knew him: Joe Carter. There were also half a dozen photos, growing increasingly dog-eared but still without question the most valuable items in the box.

After taking a cool shower and dressing in jeans and a short-sleeved shirt, Joe packed a small rucksack with toiletries and a change of clothes. He debated for a second, then added his Leatherman multi-tool to the rucksack and put one of the mobile phones in his pocket.

Before closing the box, he allowed himself a few moments to look at the photos. He'd considered framing a couple and keeping them on his bedside table, but the same cautious instinct advised against it.

He knew the other staff viewed him as an oddity because of his reluctance to reveal anything about himself. It wasn't always pleasant, deceiving people on matters both trivial and profound, but he'd long since learned to live with it. He didn't have any choice.

And on that bum note, he locked the box and put it back in the wardrobe. Picked up the rucksack and left the room, his heart beating faster at the thought of making the call – and the question he would be compelled to ask.

Like almost everything else in Dreamscape, the garage doors incorporated a fancy gimmick. Operating on an electric motor, they were constructed from what looked like rigid vertical slats of hardwood. But instead of sweeping outwards, tiny hinges on each slat allowed the gates to bend and retract into a housing concealed within the curved side walls. It was an impressive sight as the gates shuffled apart and seemingly disappeared, but Liam was in no mood to admire it.

As soon as the gap was wide enough he ran to the Renault, started it up and drove into the garage. Then he hurried over to the van, casually checking the road in both directions. No one in sight.

He was glad of that, but it also freaked him out. Five houses all on their own on a little island. No pubs, no restaurants, not even a corner shop. If you suddenly needed a packet of cigarettes or a crate of beer, you were looking at an hour's round trip to the nearest town.

Of course, most of the people who *did* live here had servants to run errands like that. But it still wasn't for Liam. No, he'd take their money and get himself a place somewhere busy and vibrant and anonymous. New York, or perhaps Madrid. He'd once been on an amazing stag weekend in Madrid.

He reversed past the gates, pulled onto the driveway and into the garage. Stood and watched the doors rattling together, and when they were shut he gave a nod of satisfaction. Everything back on track.

He opened up the van and took out a couple of plastic restraints from one of the kitbags. There was a lot more stuff to unload, but most of it could wait until the other teams were here: a job for the knuckle draggers.

A neat little Louis Vuitton case caught his eye. God only knew what Priya had brought with her. A change of clothes and some toiletries, fair enough, but somehow she'd managed to fill up a whole case.

Maybe there was some nice lingerie, he thought. So far she'd presented herself as quite the prim little maiden but, as he knew from experience, that kind of woman sometimes turned out to be a tigress in the bedroom.

Liam caught himself whistling as he retraced his steps through the house. He was feeling lucky, thinking about Priya and lingerie. Thinking about christening the snooker table. It wasn't till he reached the kitchen that he detected a subtle change in the air. Something had gone badly wrong.

He recognised the smell immediately: hot, metallic, foul. The stench of a slaughterhouse. A second later he reached the hallway and saw the large spreading pool of fresh blood.

Nine

For a moment, Liam considered aborting the whole operation. It was one thing to expect the unexpected. Quite another to foresee a problem on this scale.

He watched the blood creep across the floor and settle, hot and viscous, darkening the grooves between the sumptuous oak floorboards. He'd never get it all out, he realised. No matter how rigorously he cleaned up, traces of it would remain, soaking deep into the floor. And blood meant DNA. It meant evidence that could put him in prison for the rest of his life.

Almost as quickly, Liam understood that the job had to continue. There were too many elements already in play. And far, far too much at stake.

Tearing his gaze from the blood, he focused on its source. The estate agent lay on his back, arms thrown out at his sides, one leg straight, the other slightly crooked. If you lifted him upright it would look like a dancer's pose.

His throat had been slashed just below the Adam's apple, but Liam guessed it was one of the stab wounds to the chest that had killed him.

'What happened?'

He looked at Priya. She was sitting at the foot of the stairs, her elbows resting on her knees, her lower arms dangling free as if she wanted nothing more to do with them. Her hands were covered in blood, and there was a spatter line on her jeans, crossing both legs just below the knees. Her head was tipped forward, her hair a graceful curtain across her face.

There was no response, so he said it again. 'What happened? Did he try to attack you?'

Priya raised her head, parting the curtain of hair. 'He said he felt sick. Asked if he could go to the toilet. I said no.' Her voice was even, but sounded a little tight. She was very still, he noticed. Not trembling.

'He started to get up, said he just needed to turn over, but then he lunged at me. He grabbed my ankle, tried to pull me down.'

Liam sighed. This was precisely why he'd proposed that she move the cars.

'I couldn't let him overpower me. Not with so much at risk. I just . . . I had to defend myself.' She gestured towards the weapon at her feet. It was a military-style boot knife with a double-edged blade.

'Where did that come from?'

'I always carry it.' She met Liam's eye. 'For protection.'

He nodded, filing the information away. 'Wouldn't a single cut have subdued him?'

'He kept coming at me . . .' She shrugged. 'I had to stop him. Let's face it, he was a dead man from the moment he opened the front door.'

Liam grunted, neither agreeing nor disagreeing. He couldn't rid himself of the feeling that her explanation was a bit too slick. He was about to say so when a burst of dance music startled them both. It was coming from the estate agent's body.

His phone.

When Joe went back upstairs the house was vibrating with the undercurrent of panic that accompanies the preparation for any kind of journey with young children. In the kitchen, Cassie was packing milk and bottles and bibs for Sofia. Joe heard the fridge door open, followed by a crash. Cassie swore, and Maria offered soothing words as she came to the rescue.

Yuri appeared, dumped a couple of overnight bags in the lobby and stalked away, muttering into the phone clamped to his ear. Joe caught the words: 'Ten minutes, okay?'

Passing through the kitchen, where Maria was mopping up a spillage, Joe used the internal door into the garage, which had the look and feel of a school gymnasium. At Christmas Valentin had been briefly gripped by the notion that Jaden should grow up to be a professional basketball player, the better to earn his keep, and so he'd had hoops and a synthetic floor installed. Not surprisingly for a six-year-old, Jaden's enthusiasm for the sport had quickly waned, and after a few weeks the garage had reverted to its former use.

Vehicle keys were stored in a steel box mounted on the garage wall. Valentin's beloved Porsche 911 was away for a service, which left two other cars: a brand new Mitsubishi Shogun and a 7 series BMW. Joe opted for the Shogun, knowing Cassie preferred it to the BMW.

As the big double doors swung open, the glare from the sun was dazzling. Joe rolled the Shogun onto the driveway, got out and opened the boot. Cassie was already at the front door, holding Sofia in one arm. She was flustered.

'I can't find her other sunhat.'

'It's on the back seat.'

Cassie managed to smile and look annoyed with herself at the same time. She reached for the baby's buggy, propped against the wall. Joe beat her to it.

'You take care of the kids. I'll load the car.'

She nodded. Frowned again as she realised that her son was still absent. 'Come on, Jaden! We've got to hurry.'

There was a muffled shout from the toilet along the hall. Cassie wasn't amused.

'They obviously want me out of the way,' she grumbled. 'All this sudden rush, before his precious visitor arrives.'

Joe was searching for something constructive to say, without mentioning the errand at the jeweller's, when the toilet flushed and Jaden came bowling along the hall. Ignoring his mother, he ploughed into Joe, grabbing his legs and roaring like a lion. It was a game they often played, but this time it took Joe by surprise, causing him to stumble.

'You got me!' he said, setting the buggy down and sweeping Jaden high into the air. The boy squealed with laughter and swiped at Joe's face, narrowly missing his nose. Jaden loved physical play, the rougher the better, and Joe was the only member of the household willing to indulge him.

For Cassie it was just another source of tension, emphasising as it did all that was missing from the relationship between Jaden and his stepfather. Mindful of her discomfort, Joe lowered the boy to the ground and pointed out through the door.

'Time to go,' he said.

Liam moved first, circling round the body to avoid the pool of blood.

'Leave it,' Priya said.

'Can't. It's probably his girlfriend.'

'So?'

'We don't know where she's calling from.'

Crouching down, he slipped his hand into the agent's pocket and retrieved the phone. Priya was climbing the stairs towards the big picture window that flooded the hall with light. She looked out.

'She's parked on the road.' Then, more urgently: 'Coming this way.'

Liam felt a rush of giddy confidence. He *loved* this, he realised. Loved the danger. Loved winging it.

'You answer,' he said.

Priya gaped at him. She trotted down the stairs as Liam made to throw the phone. Cupping her hands like a cricketer, she caught it deftly and retreated to the back of the hall. 'What do I say?'

'Pretend he's cheating on her.'

Still unsure, she slid the fascia up and answered, her voice suddenly deeper and slightly breathless. 'Yes?'

Liam took in the confused silence at the other end. Delighted, he hurried over to Priya. She started to pull away, obviously fearing the caller might pick up on his presence. Then it clicked: that was part of the deception.

She said: 'He, ah, he can't speak to you right now.' She moved the phone a couple of inches from her cheek, far enough for Liam to hear the other side of the conversation.

'Who are you, then?' a shrill voice demanded. 'Do you work with him?'

'Not *work*, no.'

Another troubled pause. Liam moved closer and Priya stood her ground, allowing him into her personal space. They maintained eye contact, Liam smiling, Priya's expression giving nothing away. But he could sense her enjoyment of the charade, just as he sensed her physicality; was aware of her thudding heart only inches from his and the subtle intoxicating scent that rose from her skin.

There was a groan, like static in the tiny speaker, as the penny dropped.

'Oh, I don't believe this . . . the two-timing bastard.'

Priya didn't respond, but made sure the woman could hear her breathing. She could probably hear Liam breathing as well.

'I came all this way . . .' the woman muttered to herself. Then, after a big decisive sigh: 'D'you know, you're bloody welcome to him, love. He's a wanker, and you can tell him that from me.'

The call ended, accompanied by a half-hearted slap on the front door. Priya closed the phone, crept past the estate agent's body and back up to the window.

'She's getting in her car. Not a happy bunny.'

Liam, delighted, said: 'She doesn't know how lucky she is.'

Ten

Oliver Felton saw the woman arrive. He watched her walk up to the house, a mobile phone at her ear. He watched her grow increasingly frustrated, then return to her car and drive away. He watched and he was intrigued.

Because he knew who she was, and he knew the house wasn't empty.

Oliver had a voyeur's instinct. He'd known for several weeks that someone was using Dreamscape for secret liaisons with a cheap-looking blonde. He worked out that it was an estate agent from the firm his father had engaged, yet again, to try to offload the monstrosity on someone.

He'd seen the couple sneaking in and out, and more than once he'd watched them having sex in one of the bedrooms. He knew their routine, and Friday afternoon was a favourite time.

But what he'd witnessed today made very little sense. A car, which he recognised as the philanderer's, driving into the garage. A moment later another man, a man he'd never seen before and didn't like the look of at all, trotted out and got into a builder's van parked on the road. He drove the van into the garage and shut the doors behind him.

And now the cheap blonde had called, found no one in, and departed angrily. It was perplexing, but Oliver didn't mind that. There were far worse things to be than perplexed.

With any number of possible explanations, he naturally latched on to the most salacious. Perhaps the estate agent was bisexual: two-timing the woman with another man. Or perhaps he'd invited the woman as well, intending on a threesome, and then decided the woman was superfluous.

But moving the cars into the garage? That seemed like excessive caution. Normally the estate agent was content to leave his car on the driveway, doubtless aware that his client spent most weekends in the south of France. On the one occasion that Robert Felton had noticed the car, he'd accepted Oliver's story that the agent was just checking the place over.

The last thing Oliver wanted was his father putting a stop to these assignations. He enjoyed them too much.

Joe picked up the overnight bags and followed Cassie outside. Jaden was already at the Shogun, wrestling the back door open. While Joe stashed the bags in the boot, Cassie manoeuvred the baby into the child seat. Sofia immediately began to scream and thrash about. Joe hovered at Cassie's shoulder, pulling silly faces, but even this normally reliable distraction technique had little effect.

'She's shattered, that's the problem,' Cassie said. 'She knows the journey will put her to sleep.'

Joe was returning for the buggy when Valentin Nasenko appeared in the doorway. He seemed to recoil at the sight of Cassie's tussle with Sofia and hesitated, pretending to let his vision adjust to the bright sunshine.

Valentin was fifty-four, an unfortunate mix of flabby and thin: bony limbs and a football-sized paunch. His face was long and narrow, with bags under his eyes and a loose turkey neck, but his nose was thick and fleshy. His hair was grey, combed back in a high widow's peak, and his eyes were a filmy pale blue. Despite the heat, he was wearing tailored trousers and a striped purple shirt. A nest of wiry silver hairs protruded from the open neck.

He looked like a minor civil servant, or perhaps a head teacher at a failing school. Joe still found it hard to reconcile such a mild appearance with the knowledge that this grey, anonymous man had tumbled through the Soviet Union's chaotic transition to a market economy and emerged with interests worth hundreds of millions.

Only when Sofia was subdued did Valentin approach the car. Cassie looked up and saw him, and Joe caught a flash of panic on her face. Then, with a nervous smile, she opened her arms and received a quick, clumsy embrace from her husband.

Joe turned away. Gary McWhirter was walking towards him, holding the baby's buggy. Valentin's adviser was in his late forties, a slender South African with wispy reddish-blond hair and a handsome wind-burned face, marred by slightly bulbous eyes.

'Forgot this?'

'I was coming back for it,' Joe said, taking the buggy.

McWhirter yawned expansively and stretched, throwing his arms out wide. There were sweat stains on his shirt.

'Days like this, I envy you. Where is it you're staying tonight? The Blue Anchor?'

Joe nodded. The Anchor was a boutique hotel on Brighton's seafront in which Valentin had a substantial financial interest.

'Perfect summer's evening, you'll be out on the terrace, knocking back Cokes without a care in the world.' He smirked. 'Eyeing up Cassie's friends, too, you lucky bastard.'

'Beats working,' said Joe, electing to play along.

'You bet it does. I tell you, man, you ought to be paying me commission. Must be the cushiest job you've ever had.'

Joe didn't respond. He carried the buggy over to the Shogun. Valentin was speaking in a low voice, forcing Cassie to lean close, her face earnest and dutiful. She looked like a child being addressed by a parent. Joe rebuked himself every time he made the analogy, but sometimes it couldn't be avoided.

After saying his farewell, Valentin leaned into the back of the car and kissed Sofia, who promptly started wailing again. As Cassie scurried round to the front passenger seat, Valentin slammed the rear door shut without so much as a word or a glance for Jaden.

He turned to Joe. 'Take care of them.'

'I will.'

Valentin gazed at the Shogun, nodding absently to himself. 'Make sure Cassie enjoys tonight. She deserves it.'

Today Oliver Felton had been late coming to his post. His sister had called again, for the third time that afternoon. This after a barrage of emails and texts, until finally he'd relented and picked up the phone.

'What are you doing?' she'd demanded.

'Preparing to be lectured by you.'

'Hilarious. I mean, why are you skulking down there on your own? You're supposed to be at Ginny's.'

'I didn't go.'

His sister groaned. 'Dad spent ages setting that up.'

'Best reason to stay away.'

'Christ, Ol. Don't tell me you haven't got the hots for that girl, because I know you have. You can't walk straight when you see her.'

'I've never denied that. But she thinks I'm a freak.'

'And this was the perfect opportunity to correct that impression. You *agreed*, Oliver. I heard you promising Dad. Honestly, I despair of you when you act like this.'

A peevish silence followed. Oliver could picture her expression in every detail. With just a year's difference in their ages their mannerisms were virtually identical, except that Rachel had a habit of pushing her bottom lip out to emphasise her displeasure. Allegedly this was the look that made so many men want to sleep with her, but all it inspired in Oliver was an urge to slap her until she bled.

When his apology failed to materialise, Rachel pressed on. 'You know what Dad'll say? Turning your back on something you want, just because he wants it for you as well—'

'"Cutting off your nose to spite your face",' Oliver intoned in a passable imitation of his father's reedy drawl. 'Well, so what? I'll chop my whole fucking head off before I let him control my destiny. He seems to think marriages are just another form of strategic alliance. That's partly why Mum was eliminated, remember? Once she'd served her purpose.'

'Oliver, don't start. I won't speak to you about Mummy.'

'You can tell him that I have no intention of moving out, and the more it irritates him, the longer I'll stay. And if I don't outlive the old Satanist then I want to be buried in the garden, with a fucking great headstone.' He laughed. 'Better still, build me a monument of jagged shrapnel, dripping with blood. Dad's great gift to the world. *Here lies Oliver Felton, laid to rest on a bed of bullets.*'

From upstate New York, Rachel let out a sigh that might have crossed the Atlantic under its own power. She started to say something, thought better of it mid-way through the word 'regret', and ended the call.

Replacing the phone in its cradle, Oliver was surprised to see the handset flecked with spittle. Perhaps he had argued his case rather too vehemently.

Afterwards, in need of a pleasant distraction, he'd made his way to a landing between two of the guest suites. A hidden switch opened a hatch in the ceiling, concealed by a decorative coving, and a lightweight aluminium ladder slid down, powered by an almost silent electric motor.

This led up to a tiny room, about six feet square, slotted into a peculiar corner of the arched faux-Gothic roof. His father, who had designed both this house and its neighbour, Dreamscape, had wanted lots of unusual nooks and crannies. As a result the library had a bookcase that opened to a secret music room, and the gymnasium could be reached via a fireman's pole from the floor above.

The eyrie, quickly forgotten, became Oliver's hideaway. All it contained were a couple of beanbags and a fine Swarovski telescope, mounted on a tripod and stationed at the small window. The room was on the north-east corner of the house, on the landward side, and the shape of the roof obscured all but a sliver of sea. But the elevation gave him an interesting vantage point from which to observe Dreamscape, and a little of the house beyond it.

To his father and his sister, the room was his observatory, and it was true that for a time he had developed an interest in astronomy. The box of Kleenex he kept up here told a slightly different story, but Oliver didn't much care what they thought. He never had.

Now he mulled over the developments at Dreamscape. As far as he was aware, his father hadn't commissioned any building or maintenance work. So why would the van need to go into the garage?

'Unloading something?' he murmured to himself.

Plausible. But why close the doors?

'Unloading something . . . fragile? Private?' The philanderer must have some sort of scam going, and Oliver wanted to know what it was.

Of course, there was one easy way to find out. Dreamscape still belonged to his father, after all. There was a set of keys downstairs. He could simply go next door and let himself in.

Potentially thrilling, and not a little dangerous. But would it be as much fun as watching, he wondered. So often in life the real pleasure was to be found in anticipation, in allowing the marvellous fertility of his imagination to be unleashed, free from the constraints of grim reality.

For now, Oliver decided, it was better to wait.

And watch.

Joe climbed into the driver's seat, searching for the phrase that summed up his predicament. *Between a rock and a hard place* probably said it best.

He started the engine. Glanced in the rear-view mirror and saw Valentin and McWhirter retreat inside the house.

'What did he say?' Cassie asked.

'Nothing much.'

'He must have said something.'

'Just told me to look after you.'

Cassie didn't push it, but there was a strained quality to the silence that followed. Joe eased the Shogun through the open gates and turned onto the road. There was no one in sight in either direction. With just a single row of houses along the shore, the opposite side of the road was bordered by Smugglers' Copse: several acres of boggy woodland, intersected by a network of overgrown paths. Protected from development by a covenant, these woods formed a barrier between the residential area and the training camp.

It was half a mile or so to the bridge, and Joe kept his speed low. Checking his mirror again, he saw Sofia's head beginning to droop, her eyes heavy. Cassie was staring out of her window, perhaps to avoid conversation.

Just before the bridgehead they passed the entrance to the Ministry of Defence land: a set of high double gates, plastered with stern warning signs. Joe checked to his right out of habit, but he hadn't seen any activity at the camp for months.

Next up, on the left, was the big dilapidated shed that had once housed the chain ferry. The bridge was built alongside the route that the ferry had taken. Barely wide enough for two cars, the bridge was about a hundred and fifty feet long and elevated above the causeway by fifteen feet.

Today, unusually, Joe had to pull in and wait for an oncoming car. It was a black Cadillac limousine, straddling the road as it crossed the bridge. The driver wore a dark suit and sunglasses. He seemed to be staring straight ahead, as though no one else on the road mattered a damn.

It was only when the car drew alongside that Joe caught a glimpse of the single passenger in the back. His impression was of a large, bulky figure, a man in his late fifties or early sixties. Completely bald, with strong, square features and a brooding gaze.

Their eyes met for only a fraction of a second, but Joe felt a jolt of recognition. His reaction was mirrored in the other man's face, and then the Cadillac swept past.

Joe drove onto the bridge, trying to place where he might have seen him before. He glanced to his left, intending to ask if Cassie had got a clear look at him, and saw there was a vehicle tucked in front of the ferry shed. A plain white Citroën van, no livery. The driver's window was open, a man's arm protruding from it, holding a cigarette.

Must be here to do maintenance work, Joe thought, although twenty past four on a Friday seemed an odd time for it.

But it was the identity of the Cadillac's passenger that was uppermost in his mind. He waited until they were across the bridge, then looked at Cassie again.

'I take it that was your husband's visitor?'

'I suppose so.'

'Do you know who he is?'

'Not a clue.'

Joe smiled. He couldn't tell if she was resentful of him, or of Valentin, or just that the line of enquiry bored her.

'What about that enormous boat sitting off the island?'

'Oh, I heard them talking about that. Valentin chartered it. He was moaning because the minimum term is a week and he only needs it for today.'

'What's wrong with his own yacht?'

'Not impressive enough.'

'For this meeting?'

She nodded. 'He's thinking of replacing his one with something bigger. I saw him looking at brochures the other day.'

Joe pondered for a moment, then risked another impertinent question. 'That's a brave move in the current climate, isn't it?'

'It's crazy, if you ask me. But it's up to Valentin. He knows whether or not he can afford it.'

*　　*　　*

The van driver watched the Shogun until it was out of sight. He took a final drag on his cigarette and tossed the butt towards the water. It fell short, landing on the wet mud at the foot of the slipway. He turned to his colleague, who was hunched over, writing on a notepad balanced on his knee.

'Got that?' the driver said.

'Incoming, a Cadillac limo, two male occupants. Outgoing, Mitsubishi Shogun. One male, one female, two kiddies.'

'That was the Russki's lot.'

'Ukrainian,' the passenger corrected. 'Nasenko's from the Ukraine.'

The driver shrugged. 'You're confusing me with someone who gives a fuck.'

Eleven

Priya wanted to leave the estate agent's body where it was, but Liam vetoed the suggestion.

'Someone else might turn up. We can't open the front door while he's lying there.'

Reluctantly she agreed, and helped him unload some of the lighter equipment from the van: the kitbags containing their clothes, masks and gloves. For wrapping up valuables they'd brought rolls of bubble wrap, heavy-duty garbage bags and packing tape, plus paper towels and bleach to erase any trace of their presence.

Not that he'd envisaged a job on this scale, Liam thought.

Donning latex gloves, they placed the body on a bed of garbage bags, then wrapped it and bound it with tape. Liam scouted the downstairs rooms and found an office that would suffice for temporary storage.

Mopping up the congealed blood was a much tougher proposition. Priya had found a bucket in the garage, which she filled with hot water and bleach. Taking a stack of paper towels each, they knelt on opposite sides of the slick and set to work.

Within seconds they were both gagging. The rich metallic odour of the blood was bad enough. Mixed with the acrid tang of bleach and the thick stench of bodily waste, it was almost overpowering. Liam fetched a couple of ski masks and handed one to Priya.

'Try this,' he said. 'It might help.'

Priya nodded. Her posture was unnaturally straight as she tried to keep her head as far as possible from the mess on the floor. She worked with slow, thrifty movements, often with her eyes averted. Not shirking from the task, as he first assumed; but definitely unhappy about something.

Liam endured the mask for less than five minutes, then pulled it off and hurled it over his shoulder. Too hot.

Shortly afterwards Priya did the same. For the first time today there was a sheen of sweat on her face. A few strands of hair had escaped her ponytail and glued themselves to her cheek. Glaring at the floor, she began to scrub harder, grunting angrily, and that was when Liam understood.

It wasn't distaste at the idea of cleaning up blood, but at the idea of *cleaning*.

'Lousy job, eh?' he said.

Priya rinsed her paper towels in the bucket. She didn't speak until Liam had turned away.

'My mother was always cleaning. She probably still is. On her knees, scrubbing floors. Demeaning herself in the service of others. I swore I'd never do that.'

The bitterness in her voice cut short Liam's intended quip. Presumably her mother had never had to mop up the blood of a man she'd just killed?

Then, as he pictured the scene again, he realised what had been bothering him. The blood spatter across her jeans was too low. It meant the estate agent must have been on the floor when Priya slashed his throat.

That called into question how much resistance the man had put up. Or even whether he had resisted at all.

Once on the mainland, Joe followed the road north through several miles of wetlands. To his left he could make out the reed beds and the glitter of water beyond. To his right was a bumpy landscape of bracken and gorse and ancient coppice woods. There were several parking areas with picnic tables, nature trails and bird-watching hides, but hardly anyone was around today. Too hot, maybe.

Sofia quickly fell asleep, while Jaden occupied himself by playing on his Nintendo DS. The baby tended to sleep more soundly with background music, so Cassie had chosen the *Mamma Mia!* sound-track. It was a running joke that the songs had been imprinted in Sofia's DNA, given how often her mother watched the movie. Joe had once found her smiling through tears as she gazed at the giant plasma screen in the living room.

'Can you imagine being as happy as that?' she'd said, almost to herself.

Joe had watched the dancing, joyful women for a moment. Rather than imagine, he believed he knew exactly how it felt to be that happy, though increasingly he feared his recollection was becoming contaminated by nostalgia. Nostalgia and raw longing.

But he hadn't told Cassie that. He'd said: 'It's just a movie. A feel-good movie.'

'Even so, there must be people somewhere who have everything they could possibly want.'

'I guess there are,' he'd agreed. 'But I bet most of them don't know it until it's too late.'

Cassie had nodded sadly. 'That's what I thought.'

Now, as she and Jaden quietly sang along to *Our Last Summer*, Joe reached the A27 and joined the eastbound dual carriageway. It was four-thirty. Even with a clear run it would take a minor miracle to reach the centre of Brighton within an hour.

He considered Cassie's allegation that Valentin wanted her out of the way, and he went on puzzling over the identity of the bald American in the Cadillac. That Valentin would go to the expense of chartering a yacht suggested it was an important meeting. It was unusual enough for Valentin to conduct business on the Reach, so he must—

His train of thought juddered to a halt. *The bald American.* How did Joe know he was American . . . ?

The obvious explanation was that Joe had been present at some prior meeting between Valentin and the other man. If so, he couldn't recall the occasion. And yet he retained a persuasive image of the man speaking. He could recreate the dry Southern drawl in his head, and a particular phrase that had made him smile: *Got ourselves another clusterfuck* . . .

He felt certain the memory was genuine, and that it predated his period of employment with Valentin. That meant the American was probably someone from his old life. The life he had fled.

It took the best part of twenty minutes to clean up the blood thoroughly enough to leave no obvious trace. In places the bleach had lifted the protective coating from the hardwood floor, leaving odd patches where the wood was noticeably lighter. Liam wasn't unduly worried. In the long run it shouldn't matter too much.

While Priya went upstairs to shower and change, Liam took his netbook from the kitbag and carried it through to the kitchen. He powered it up, found himself a glass and drank a pint of water before sitting down at the island breakfast bar.

The tiny laptop contained the fruits of their extensive research, including floor plans for all the homes on the island and detailed profiles of the residents. Studying these documents had become almost a ritual to Liam, but now the reassurance they offered had been compromised. If they hadn't picked up on the estate agent using Dreamscape as a love nest, was it possible that other important details had been missed?

Liam instantly stamped on that question. There was no room for doubt at this stage of the operation.

He ran through the targets again. Five homes, hugging the coast on the south-western corner of the island. The house at the most southerly point, furthest from the mainland, was a chalet bungalow belonging to Donald and Angela Weaver.

Donald was a retired civil servant, while Angela had been a university lecturer and now did some kind of voluntary work. Their only son, Joe, had died in a car accident in 2007, aged twenty-eight. The Weavers weren't particularly high-net-worth individuals: it was their location that made them important. They were too close to the action to be left alone.

The house next to the Weavers belonged to Robert Felton, the real financial heavyweight on Terror's Reach. After a period in the army that included a secondment to the Ministry of Defence, Robert had joined his father's munitions company in the mid-1990s, bringing to it the vigour and ruthlessness of youth, not to mention any number of important connections. Within a few years profits had risen tenfold, and the Feltons sold their controlling interest to an American conglomerate – just as concerns were being raised about their deals to supply landmines, grenades and assault rifles to various dubious regimes in Africa and the Middle East.

While Felton senior retired to play golf and count his money, Robert concentrated on other areas of the business, most notably winning a string of lucrative contracts for security and reconstruction in post-invasion Iraq. He invested some of the proceeds in an underperforming chain of sports shops and again worked his magic, selling it on to a private-equity company for three times what he'd paid.

With a personal fortune rumoured at well over a billion pounds, Felton had designed and overseen the construction of the house at Terror's Reach, a monstrous Gothic pile with eight bedrooms, a squash court and – crucially – a walk-in safe.

A long-time widower, Felton had acquired the image of an unabashed thrill-seeker and playboy of the old school. This weekend he was at his apartment in Monaco, where he could best indulge his passion for girls and gambling, safe from the disapproving scrutiny of his two children. Although they were in their early twenties, neither Rachel nor Oliver Felton had yet shown much desire to make their own way in the world. Rachel was currently taking a photography course in New York, while Oliver was spending the weekend with friends of his father in Oxfordshire.

The third house was Dreamscape, the base for their operation, also owned and designed by Robert Felton. Built on a scale that dwarfed every other property on the island, its completion had coincided with the first signs of a downturn in the property market. For a time it had been rented by an ageing rock star, seeking refuge while he recovered from an addiction to prescription painkillers. Since his departure the house had remained furnished but unoccupied, while Felton sought a buyer to take it off his hands.

Next to Dreamscape was a more conventional faux-Georgian mansion, owned by a high-profile Premiership striker whose ex-model wife, Trina, had boosted their fortunes by putting her name to a range of swimwear, a fitness regime and three volumes of autobiography. With the footballer on loan to an Italian club, the whole family had decamped to Rome, leaving Trina's father, a retired builder named Terry Fox, to house-sit in their absence.

The last of the five homes belonged to Valentin Nasenko. Another modernist design, it had been the most original and imposing construction on the island until Dreamscape had trumped it. To Liam it looked like an electric sandwich-toaster, its open jaws facing the sea. While nowhere near the top tier of oligarchs, Valentin was nonetheless said to be worth several hundred million.

Officially the robbery was expected to net around three million pounds. That was what the knuckle draggers had been told. The true figure was likely to be a lot higher – how much higher, Liam tried not to speculate, but he reckoned his share alone should see him through to old age in comfort.

All in all, it marked a spectacular journey for a working-class kid from Donegal. In his teens Liam had been excluded from school and was continually in trouble with the police for vandalism and minor thefts. He'd fled to England at the age of fifteen, stayed for a couple of years with an aunt and uncle in Southport, then straightened himself out and sweet-talked himself onto a college course.

At nineteen he moved to London and got a lowly administrative job with the investment arm of a large merchant bank. He soon discovered he had a gift more precious than any number of letters after his name. He had charm. He could make people like him. He could take them where they didn't really want to go, whether it was a business deal or a side bet or a fast and brutal fuck at the end of a boozy night.

Some of it was down to good old Irish blarney, of course, but Liam was careful not to overdo that aspect. Just as vital was his instinct for assessing merit and good judgement in others. Soon he was moving up the hierarchy, generating lots of profit but seeing too much of it go to other people. He decided to alter the equation in his own favour and – perhaps inevitably – he over-reached, falling into a trap laid for him by the firm's compliance officers.

He was offered a choice: hand back what you've stolen and leave quietly, or take your chances with the police. Sensing that his bosses were keen to avoid bad publicity, let alone the regulatory attention that would accompany any criminal investigation, Liam managed to negotiate a partial repayment.

Even so, he was virtually broke when he walked out. And with recession looming, his chances of further employment in the financial services industry were non-existent. He had to sell his Audi A5 and his apartment in Canary Wharf, and ditch his high-maintenance girlfriend.

He was renting a one-bedroom flat in Forest Gate when he received a mysterious approach on behalf of a trusted former client, sounding him out about a new and very challenging role. A role, he was promised, that would utilise all his considerable talents.

Twelve

The traffic slowed to a crawl as they reached the outskirts of Chichester. The A27 snaked around the southern perimeter, crossing a series of busy feeder roads running in and out of the city. After clearing the intersection with the A286, which led to a pair of coastal villages known as the Witterings, the Shogun came to a complete stop.

There was a footbridge just ahead: a little gang of schoolgirls using it to cross the road. They were maybe thirteen, fourteen years old, on the impatient cusp of adulthood. You could see that from the jewellery and the make-up, and the way their uniforms had been tucked and rolled and unbuttoned in the name of fashion.

Joe sighed. Looked away. But Cassie had spotted them too.

'Do they remind you of your girls?'

Joe shrugged. The truth was that he didn't know. Amy would be almost ten now, and Hannah was eight. A few years away from these adolescent tricks, or perhaps not. Everyone seemed to agree that kids grew up faster nowadays. Perhaps they had already changed beyond recognition.

No. He had to cling to the belief that he would always know his own daughters. To think otherwise was an invitation to give up hope.

He felt Cassie's gaze still upon him.

'How long since you last saw them?'

'Come on, Cass.' He had only reluctantly told her about them, after succumbing to weeks of attrition. Cassie maintained that she'd known at once, just from seeing how he was with Jaden and Sofia. A natural father, she'd called him, unintentionally twisting the knife.

'I know you miss them,' she said. 'How long has it been?'

'Nearly three years.'

'Oh God. I think I'd rather die than go without—' She winced. Patted his arm. 'I'm sorry. I didn't mean . . .'

'It's okay.'

The traffic in front started to move. Joe put the car in gear, wishing he could stamp on the accelerator and roar away.

'It must be their choice. Their mother's choice, anyway.'

'Why do you say that?'

'Because I don't believe you'd want to shut them out of your life. You couldn't be that heartless. Not like a certain person we know.' Cassie glanced over her shoulder, hoping Jaden wouldn't pick up on the reference to his own absent father. 'And I'm sure they'd want to keep in touch if they could. Most little girls worship their dads.' There was a wobble in her voice that seemed to take her by surprise.

'Maybe it's no one's choice,' Joe said. 'Maybe it's just circumstances.'

'What kind of circumstances could be that bad?'

'You don't want to know.' He said it gently, but with enough feeling to end the conversation right there.

And, for a time, it did. But it was a pensive silence, in which he could almost sense the gears whirring in Cassie's head. He imagined her phrasing and rejecting all kinds of questions. He wished there was a way he could explain, but even Angela Weaver hadn't been given the full story. If he ever told Cassie, it would have to be on the day he ceased working for her. The day he moved on.

The traffic in their lane slowed and stopped. Cassie cleared her throat and said, very carefully: 'When me and Dean split up, it was horrible. Really messy. I hope, if I ever got in that situation again, I'd be able to handle it better. The children have to come first, don't they?'

Joe nodded, but said nothing. Spotting a gap in the outside lane, he checked the mirror and darted into the space. Between focusing on the traffic and his own miserable predicament, several more minutes passed before he grasped exactly what Cassie had been telling him.

At the age of nine, Oliver Felton had sacked an entire workforce.

His father had still been new to the business at that stage, eager to escape the influence of his own father and make his mark. He'd begun by shutting down a factory in Sunderland that made shell casings. After acquiring a rival firm in Spain, all that remained was to inform the British employees – nearly two hundred of them – that their services were no longer required.

Without notifying the other directors or the on-site personnel staff, Robert Felton had arrived at the factory one morning with a briefcase full of brown envelopes and with his young son in tow. In a separate car came three large, sinister-looking men, whose purpose didn't become clear to Oliver until later.

His father had addressed the workers from a metal gantry overlooking the factory floor, introducing himself while Oliver stood a pace behind him, instinctively petrified, clutching the heavy briefcase beneath his chin. He could still remember every word his father said.

'This is my boy, Oliver. He's nine years old. As you may know, I've taken over the reins of this company from my father, and one day Oliver may well take the reins from me. What's already clear is that if I sent him down there right now to work on the production line, he'd do a better job than the rest of you put together. Because you're lazy, and greedy, and useless. Even my boy can see that.'

He gestured, motioning him forward, but Oliver was frozen. Already there were jeers from the crowd below. Robert Felton seemed not to hear them. He grabbed Oliver by the shoulders and thrust him to the front of the gantry.

'That's why we're shutting this place down. My little boy doesn't want a bunch of bolshie layabouts poisoning his future legacy. He's got your redundancy notices right here in this briefcase. Assuming it's not beyond your capabilities, I want you to line up in alphabetical order. He's going to give you your cards, and you're going to thank him, nice and politely.'

The three heavies had prevented an outright rebellion, but for weeks afterwards Oliver still burned from the memory of the loathing those men and women had directed at him as they'd filed past, humiliated and seething with rage, snatching their envelopes from his trembling hand. One of the men – a foreman with thirty years' service – had thanked him and then spat in his face. Later Oliver heard the man's screams from the car park. The thugs had broken both his arms, his father admitted on the way home, pretending to sound as though he disapproved.

Now, as he studied the neighbouring house through his telescope, Oliver felt no qualms about his actions, nor indeed about the personality his father had helped to mould. At school he had been lonely and frightened and subjected to merciless abuse. If voyeurism had become his preferred method of social interaction, it was because it afforded him both distance and a measure of control. At any point he could safely retreat.

But there would be no retreating today.

Today he had hit the jackpot.

He'd been keeping an eye on the house, but hadn't seen anyone else come or go. Then he scanned across the windows and hit on the classic voyeur's dream: a beautiful woman, fresh from the bath or shower, walking naked across the bedroom. She was a young Asian woman with unblemished light brown skin and superb muscle tone. If he had to quibble, it was that her breasts were slightly too big for his liking.

Oliver drank in the contours of her body as she towelled herself dry. She was so close that he could see the pores of her skin, still glistening with steam. Close enough to smell, it seemed, and surely close enough to touch. Unconsciously his free hand drifted towards the window to do just that.

Slowly, lovingly, he moved the scope up over her breasts and her neck. Better even than the sight of her was the knowledge that she was utterly unaware of his existence. He had long suspected that it was this – the secret, stolen intimacy – that offered the greatest thrill.

But just as he gloried in the idea of gazing deep into her eyes, she was gone. She darted out of view so rapidly that it startled him. Oliver turned the scope away and dropped to the floor, uncertain and afraid and excited all at once.

Had she seen him?

Thirteen

Dreamscape's bedroom suites were every bit as luxurious as Priya had anticipated. Although the house was unoccupied, great care had been taken to furnish it. That meant a huge octagonal bed with a leather trim, and a TV that rose out of the footboard cabinet. In the bathroom there were Egyptian cotton towels and a selection of Harrods toiletries, although Priya had brought her own.

Before showering, she stuffed everything she was wearing in one of the garbage bags. Rinsed the knife under the tap, then placed it on a shelf inside the shower cubicle. Her professional relationship with Liam was less than forty-eight hours old: far too early to make a full judgement. Her policy, born of hard experience, was to trust nobody.

Priya had run away from home at the age of fourteen, after cracking under the strain of her parents' relentlessly high expectations. But living rough in London had provided challenges of a very different sort. The first time a man groped her in the street she'd naively wondered if it would be impolite to push him away.

She was raped once, within the first three months, and afterwards vowed never to be caught out again. From then on she always carried at least one weapon, usually a knife. Wherever she was, she made sure there were backups and escape routes to hand.

Her new-found caution quickly paid off. A six-foot-tall, eighteen-stone taxi driver followed her back to her rented bedsit and jumped on her as she let herself in. He threw her on the sofa, drooling as he described what he intended to do with her. Priya let him get started, made him think she was terrified and compliant, then reached for the claw hammer that she kept hidden down the back of the sofa.

She hit him hard enough to crack his skull. It wasn't fatal, but it left him with permanent brain damage. A far more satisfying result, in her view.

She wasn't sure yet if Liam would be any different. He lusted after her; that much she knew. She was somewhat encouraged when he made no move to follow her upstairs, or sidle into the bedroom while she was in the shower. Perhaps he possessed a little more self-control than most of them, but she wouldn't bet on it. By now she had a good instinct for these things.

That was partly why she'd killed the estate agent. To demonstrate her capabilities right from the start.

In Liam's absence the man had quickly grown cocky. He'd taunted Priya, told her he was going to get up and walk out and she couldn't do a thing to stop him. She'd intended to stab him just once, purely to subdue him. But the red mist had descended, the way it sometimes did, and the next thing she knew he was lying dead in a pool of blood, and even once the rage subsided there was no remorse, no regret. He had brought it on himself.

Drying off, she decided she could safely drop the towel and stand naked. The room was warm and quite stuffy. She was debating whether to risk opening a window when she felt the unmistakable crawling sensation of a ravenous gaze. Goose bumps rose on her skin and she knew she was being watched. Not just watched, but *devoured*.

She ducked out of sight, pulling the towel up and wrapping it tightly around herself. Then, cautiously, she moved back to the window and looked out.

The neighbouring property was at least forty or fifty feet away, another big three-storey pile. There were several windows on the side, a couple of them with frosted glass for privacy. All the windows were blank. Dark. No one there.

Then she glanced up at the roof and noticed an odd little dormer, almost concealed by the turret on the north-east corner of the house. The dormer window was as blank as the others, and yet it went on demanding her attention.

Priya stared at it and finally worked out what was wrong. She could just make out a fat black tube, tilted at an angle to the frame, ending in a glinting crescent of glass.

A telescope.

Liam looked up as Priya hurried into the kitchen. She'd changed into a pair of grey tailored trousers and a black top, but she had bare feet and her hair was damp and tousled. She looked shaken.

'I think someone's watching us.'

'What?'

'Next door. The Feltons.'

'Are you sure?'

'Come and see.'

Liam followed her back across the hall, his mind working on the problem.

'It can't be Robert,' he said. 'He's in France, and the daughter's definitely in the States. Unless there's a house-sitter, or some kind of security staff we don't know about.'

Priya said nothing until they entered the bedroom. There was a wet towel on the floor, and various items of clothing were strewn over the bed. No sign of the knife she'd used to kill the estate agent. Liam wondered where she'd put it.

'Look.' Priya moved to one side of the window, while he went to the other side. She directed his gaze to a tiny dormer on the house opposite. 'It's a telescope.'

'And you saw someone looking through it?'

'Not directly. But I could feel it.' There was an edge to her voice that told him something else.

She'd been caught naked.

Liam sighed. 'I bet it's Oliver Felton.'

'He's meant to be away this weekend.'

'Yeah, and he's also meant to be a sandwich short of a picnic. So maybe he didn't go anywhere. Maybe he's holed up on his own over there.'

'What if he reports us?'

'He's not likely to broadcast the fact that he's a pervert.'

'He doesn't have to. He might still call his father and tell him there's someone next door.'

'Then what do you suggest?' Liam asked.

'Let me go and speak to him.'

'And say what?'

A quick smile crossed Priya's face. 'I'm sure I can think of something.'

Liam pondered. This was another departure from the plan, but it also felt like a tactical move on her part, a subtle challenge to his authority. He was tempted to refuse, just to see how she reacted.

On the other hand, her proposal did have its merits. He drew out the silence, watching as she shifted her weight onto her other hip, preparing to hear out his objections.

'Okay,' he said. 'Do it.'

She was coming to him.

Oliver knew it from the moment the woman stepped outside. He didn't even need the telescope; he could see her perfectly well from the window. He was pressed against the wall, contorting himself so as to peer out at an angle which he hoped made him invisible to anyone at Dreamscape.

A pretty pointless endeavour, really, because she already knew he was there. He imagined her fury and revulsion. He imagined her voice breaking as she described the sense of violation to the men in the house with her.

He watched the woman walk across the driveway and turn in his direction. She didn't look particularly angry. He caught himself wondering which one of the men she was screwing: the rough-looking man or the estate agent. Maybe it was both of them.

Odd, then, that neither had come storming next door on her behalf, ready to defend her honour with his fists.

Something not right about this, Oliver thought. Of course, he shouldn't forget that his father owned the house they were in. That might influence their reaction.

It struck him that Robert Felton was possibly involved in some way. Perhaps he'd arranged a party, or lent the house out to friends for the weekend. It would be characteristic of him not to inform his son, especially as Oliver was supposed to be in Oxford by now.

No. He preferred the first explanation. These people were friends of the estate agent, using the place without permission. As such, they were wary about attracting attention. They could hardly object to his telescope if they had no right to be cavorting in the house in the first place.

Then, as the woman strolled out of sight below the window, Oliver made an important correction. The woman *hadn't* been cavorting with anyone.

She'd been alone in the bedroom.

He laughed: a brash, exuberant rattle of noise. Hurried over to the hatch and climbed down the ladder, enjoying the stirring in his groin as he pursued a far more enticing hypothesis to its logical conclusion.

She might not have mentioned the telescope to the two men. She might be coming next door of her own volition. In which case, the possibilities were endless, and delightful, and dangerous.

'She's coming,' Oliver whispered. His voice sounded thick and clogged with saliva. 'She wants me.'

Fourteen

The Felton house had the same entry system as Dreamscape. The call station was set into a plate of brushed stainless steel, mounted on the high perimeter wall. There was a small grille for the microphone and speaker, and just above that, the tiny round lens of a camera.

Priya pressed the call button and waited, feeling uncomfortably exposed. The sun was lower in the sky, but still ferociously hot. The air was sluggish and heavy; not even the gentlest of sea breezes to offer respite. The scent of cow parsley filled her nostrils, so rich and sweet it made her slightly nauseous.

She shouldn't have come. This was a bad idea.

She pressed the button again, and felt a crawling sensation as the hairs on her neck rose. A flush of heat spread across her breastbone and up into her face. She was being watched, by the same hungry gaze as before.

She looked around, scanning the road in both directions. There was no one in sight. No cars or voices or music. Just some muted chirping from the woods behind her, as though the heat had drained the birds of their will to sing.

She backed away from the wall. Shielded her eyes from the sun as she examined the upper floors of the house. At the same time, the crawling sensation receded.

It must be the camera. He was inside, watching her on a monitor.

Priya sighed. She didn't relish telling Liam that she'd failed to make contact. His opinion of her was low enough already. And if her coming out here spooked the boy into calling his father, then the whole operation would be in jeopardy.

She took a slow breath. Making sure she appeared composed and in control, she stepped back to the intercom. She pressed the button and held it in while she spoke into the grille.

'Hello? Are you there?' She had no idea if he could hear her, but by now she had nothing to lose.

'Is that Oliver? Please let me know if you're listening.'

She released the button and waited. Her skin was still crawling, but she fought away her disgust and looked directly at the lens, borrowing a sweet, demure smile from the conscientious young scholar she'd once been.

No response. He wasn't willing to reveal himself. But he was there; she had no doubt of that.

Turning away, she decided it wasn't an entirely wasted effort. More a case of laying the groundwork for what was to follow.

Oliver heard the intercom buzz as he sprinted along the corridor. There was a spare handset at the top of the main stairs, but he ignored it. The one on the ground floor had a bigger screen.

As he reached it, the buzzer sounded for the second time. He snatched up the handset, activating the camera set into the outside wall – and there she was, right in front of him. Cool, calm, beautiful. Huge dark eyes. Lips so full and soft that he could barely imagine how they might feel as they engulfed him.

She frowned at the camera, then backed away. Oliver almost cried out. He didn't wànt her to give up this easily. He wanted her to stay where he could see her.

Most of all, he wanted to let her in. He wanted that very badly. His finger remained on the button; every nerve, every fibre screaming at him to do it. Let her in.

Have some fun.

Then she strode forward, filling the screen once again. She moved so close it produced a kind of fisheye effect, exaggerating the size of her features. Mirroring her, Oliver knelt and put his face against the monitor. When she smiled, he smiled back.

He watched her mouth opening and closing. She was talking to him. But to hear her, he would have to press the button and open a connection, and if he did that she would know.

His finger tightened on the button. He felt it give, very slightly, under the pressure. His heart was beating wildly, pounding away as though it was already out of control.

But he knew he wasn't going to open the gates. He had to let her go.

Oliver opened his mouth, stuck out his tongue and tenderly, in one smooth motion, licked the screen all the way from the bottom to the top. Licked her from the base of her neck to the crown of her head.

The screen had a dusty, electrical flavour: not unpleasant. As she turned away, he groaned. He could feel the adrenalin pumping uselessly in his system and knew he had to find an outlet. Had to vent it somehow.

But he had done the right thing. He couldn't quite trust himself to be alone with her. He was . . . unpredictable. It had taken real courage, real maturity to recognise that fact. And for doing so, he deserved a treat.

Buzzing with good vibes, he leapt to his feet and went in search of fire.

Liam paced the lobby, unconsciously avoiding the telltale patch of lighter wood. On one level the estate agent's death didn't trouble him at all. Human casualties had been factored into the plan from the beginning. But now, with Priya gone and nothing to do but wait, he felt a niggle of concern.

He was doubtful about her mission, doubtful enough to wonder if it was merely an excuse. Perhaps she'd had second thoughts and done a runner, or even gone next door to call the police. He saw how plausibly she could put him in the frame for the estate agent's murder.

The buzzing of his phone was a welcome distraction. He answered, listened for a few seconds, then nodded. At least some things were going to plan.

'We'll take over the surveillance from here,' Liam said. 'Tell Turner to hold steady. And I want the roadblock ready to go when I give the word.'

As he put the phone away there was a knock on the door. Two quiet raps; the prearranged signal. Priya was back.

He opened the door and she stepped past him, wafting in hot, dry air infused with her perfume.

'He wouldn't answer,' she said. 'But he's in there.'

'Shit.'

'He won't tell anyone.'

'How do you know he won't?'

'I just know.'

Liam snorted. 'Don't give me any bollocks about women's intuition.'

Priya said nothing. Just looked at him and blinked slowly, managing to convey both amusement and contempt. For a moment Liam was inclined to grab her by the arm, throw her across the room and get a few things straight about who was in charge here.

Then he thought about the boot knife, and the fact that he couldn't afford to spend every other second looking over his shoulder.

He took a deep breath. Gestured towards the stairs.

'The American's here. They'll be heading out soon.'

Robert Felton wouldn't permit matches in the house, but Oliver had a box of two hundred hidden at the bottom of the vanity unit in his bathroom. He kept them to demonstrate to himself that his craving was under control. Like any recovering addict, he took pride in his ability to resist temptation.

But this was a special occasion. He had earned the right to succumb.

He could have done it outside, but there was precious little thrill to be had from that. Outside, it was just another bonfire.

He chose the kitchen floor. It was some kind of Italian slate. Hideously expensive, so it ought to be fire-resistant. Whether it would crack at high temperatures, he had no idea. If it did, he'd just say he had dropped something heavy on it.

The pyre he constructed was meagre, but symbolic. One of his favourite porno mags – to represent his desire for the woman, successfully restrained. Half a bottle of brandy – to represent another common vice, though not really one of his. And, lastly, the jacket of one of his father's favourite handmade suits.

Oliver tore a few pages from the magazine, crumpling hairless genitals and vacant pouts into surreal erotic waste. He splashed brandy over the jacket. Lit the first of the matches, held it beneath his nose and inhaled, dreamily, until it guttered and died.

He opened his eyes. Took a breath and considered for a moment. Did he have to do this? *Should* he do this?

Silly question.

He lit another match. Ignited the brandy.

Fifteen

The traffic around Brighton was just as congested as Joe had thought it would be. By the time they found an empty bay, in the car park beneath the Churchill Square shopping centre, it was five thirty-five. Too late.

Jaden yawned and announced that he was hungry. Sofia was still asleep. Cassie carefully lifted her out of the car and into the buggy.

'So where are we going?' she said.

'It's supposed to be a surprise.'

She gave him a look, one eyebrow arched. 'Come on, Joe. I'm not a big fan of surprises.'

He shrugged. 'There's something to collect at Merrion and Son. But we're probably too late.'

'I doubt it, knowing Valentin.'

Her cryptic comment made no sense until they reached the shop, nestled within one of the quaint narrow thoroughfares known as The Lanes. This was the oldest part of Brighton, once a tiny fishing village called Brighthelmstone, now crammed with designer boutiques, trendy restaurants and about a thousand jewellery shops. Despite its modest frontage, Merrion and Son was one of the most expensive.

There was a CLOSED sign on the door. Joe tried it anyway: locked. He peered through the glass at the dimly lit interior. Spotting movement inside, he knocked. A moment later a face swam into view. They heard a key in the lock.

The door opened and Merrion Junior greeted them. He was a plump, glossy man in his forties, more car dealer than a jeweller: sharp suit, hair perfectly waxed and parted, and the neatest fingernails Joe had ever seen on a man.

He ushered them inside and locked the door behind them. Embarrassed, Cassie apologised for their lateness.

'Oh, we're always here for a while after locking up. It's really not an issue, Mrs Nasenko.'

Anything for a client as wealthy as Valentin. Joe watched the jeweller scurry behind the counter, unlock a drawer and produce a small velvet case. Cassie was concentrating on Jaden, who was busy planting sticky finger marks on the glass-fronted cabinets.

'I'll keep an eye on him,' Joe said. He beckoned Jaden towards a display of watches. 'Let's see if you can tell the time.'

With obvious reluctance, Cassie approached the counter. Merrion Junior had opened the case and removed something from inside. He held it out to Cassie, who made no move to accept it.

'Nice,' she said, her voice flat.

The jeweller coughed politely. 'Made to Mr Nasenko's exact specification, it's a platinum eternity ring with sapphires, diamonds and the most exquisite centrepiece. A Paraiba tourmaline.' Breathless with excitement, he gushed, 'Isn't it fabulous?'

Cassie said nothing. Joe glanced round and saw the jeweller struggling to hide his dismay.

'I believe Mr Nasenko intended it to be a surprise. I imagine you're somewhat . . . overwhelmed.'

Cassie nodded, finally taking the ring from him.

'How much did it cost?'

'I, uh, I don't think it would be appropriate to divulge . . .' He exchanged a panicked look with Joe. 'Our instructions were—'

'I know. You can't tell me.' She sounded so forlorn, it was as though she'd suffered a bereavement rather than received a present that, in Joe's inexpert judgement, had to have cost around ten thousand pounds.

By now Merrion Junior also appeared to be on the verge of tears. 'Would you like to wear it?' he said.

Cassie shook her head. 'No. Leave it in the box, please.'

When they were outside Cassie acknowledged Joe's anxious look.

'I'm a spoilt little bitch, right?'

'I don't think that,' he said. 'But Merrion Junior certainly will.'

A beat of silence, then laughter.

Cassie said, 'Do you think he'd have waited there all night for us?'

'Possibly. Valentin's an important customer.'

'He must be, the way they suck up to him.' She grew thoughtful. 'I wonder what else he's been buying lately.'

'He can afford it, can't he?'

'That's not what I'm worried about. Not this time.' She indicated that she didn't want Jaden to hear, so Joe took his hand as they walked through the Lanes, while Cassie pushed Sofia in the buggy. They looked for all the world like a perfect family unit, Joe thought.

'It seems like a lovely gift, but it's not,' said Cassie. 'For a start, a gift is something you give to someone. In person. You don't just send them along to collect it.'

'True. I guess Valentin isn't the romantic type.'

'And think about it. An eternity ring. What does "eternity" mean?' Catching Joe's frown, she said, 'It's all right, I'm not that thick. It means *for ever*. That's the message Valentin wants me to get. He's going to own me for ever.'

She picked up her pace, moving a couple of steps ahead of him. Joe might have caught up, asked why Valentin would need to send such a message, but the answer was already there if he cared to look for it.

When he'd taken the job with the Nasenkos he'd never imagined the extent to which he would become bound up in their problems.

He'd reached the point now where he took active steps to avoid knowing more than was necessary. It went against his nature, because he'd spent years in a world where the tiniest missed detail could prove fatal. He'd immersed himself in lives far more chaotic and painful than these without incurring any emotional damage.

Perhaps that was the trouble, Joe thought. This was so much harder, because he actually *cared* about Cassie and her children.

They were wandering back towards the car park when Joe spotted a phone box and remembered the call he'd intended to make. He had his mobile with him, but decided a public phone would be better. Save him having to ditch his mobile afterwards.

'I need to ring someone. Are you okay to wait here a second?'

Cassie regarded him as though he must be joking. 'Borrow my mobile.'

'No. It's fine.' Leaving her perplexed, Joe stepped into the booth. He dialled the number from memory and waited, listening to the burr of the phone and the thudding of his heart.

A familiar but wary voice said: 'Hello?'

'Hi, Maz. Can you talk?'

'Course I can. How are you, Joe?'

'Surviving. You?'

'Same as ever. No point asking *where* you are?'

''Fraid not. Better for you that way.'

'So what's the occasion? Planning a return to civilisation?'

'They wouldn't have me. No, I need a small favour. Can you check an index number for me?'

'I'm off duty, mate. Just about to light up the barbecue. Pop in if you want,' Maz added cheerily.

'Wish I could. Don't suppose there's anyone you could ask?'

A quiet chuckle. 'I'm already dialling the landline. What do you intend to do with the information?'

'Nothing. I promise.'

'Okay. Go on, then.'

Joe recited the number, then heard a clunk as Maz switched phones. He nodded at Cassie through the glass, knowing he'd face an interrogation for this.

Maz came back on, a wry humour in his voice. 'No record. Either you misread it, or they're false plates. Your instincts obviously haven't deserted you.'

'Just a hunch, really.'

'Are you going to tell the local plod about this mysterious vehicle?'

'Not sure if it'll help. But I'll think about it.'

Maz tutted. 'Whatever you do, be careful, yeah?'

'Thanks. Say hello to Jill and the kids.' Then a pause, which both of them were expecting. This time Joe didn't need to ask the question.

'No word from Helen, I'm afraid,' said Maz.

'You are still trying to trace her?'

'I do what I can. But if someone's determined not to be found, then generally they stay that way. You know that better than anyone.'

'Yeah,' said Joe sadly. 'I suppose I do.'

Sixteen

They activated the transmitter ahead of time. For ten minutes there was nothing to hear: just a buzz of silence that had a vaguely rhythmic component to it. In fact the sound quality was excellent, but that didn't become apparent until a seagull squawked and nearly blasted their heads off.

Hastily adjusting the volume, they caught a rueful joke about bird-shit and, soon after, the clinking of bottles and glasses being set down on a table. Another voice said: 'Here they are.'

Two more minutes of silence, then a series of bumps and shuffles and the murmur of conversation, coming closer. The first clear sentence was priceless. It was spoken in a low voice, by a man with a South African accent. McWhirter.

'You've swept the ship for bugs?'

The reply was from another familiar voice: the bodyguard, Yuri.

'Of course. It was the first thing I did.' He sounded resentful that his competence had been called into question.

'All right. Don't bite my head off,' McWhirter said. 'Now, I suggest you make yourself scarce. We'll shout if we need you.'

They heard the vibration on the deck as Yuri stomped away. They also heard the single word he muttered in his native tongue when he judged he was out of McWhirter's earshot.

'*Ppizzda.*'

Seventeen

Joe, Cassie and the children headed slowly up Duke Street amongst a tangled flow of pedestrians: shoppers, tourists, workers on their way home, and an increasing number of revellers kicking off their weekend celebrations. It took less than a minute for Cassie's curiosity to get the better of her.

'Was everything all right?'

'Yes, thanks.'

'Friend or family?'

'Old friend. Just touching base.'

She waited, watching him closely until she grasped that she would get nothing more.

Suddenly full of good cheer, as though moods were sweaters you could change with the weather, she said: 'I've got good news and bad.'

'Go on.'

'The good news is that I'm feeling better. But the bad news . . .'

'You want to go clothes shopping?'

'You got it.' She gave him a playful slap on the shoulder. 'And not the snobby designer places, either. I want to look in some normal shops.'

'Fine. But you know what we have to get past first?'

'What?'

Joe indicated Jaden, then mouthed: 'The model shop.' Cassie's shoulders sagged in mock horror. There was a branch of Modelzone up ahead, on the corner of West Street.

'Oh, well. If I'm going to drag you both round Debenhams, I suppose a few minutes staring at toy cars won't hurt.'

'Cars!' Jaden yelled. He yanked on Joe's hand. 'I wanna look at cars!'

A *few minutes if we're lucky*, Joe thought.

But as it was, they were waylaid by something far worse.

It was a hen party. Advancing up West Street in a slow, clumsy swarm. A dozen women, ranging in age from late teens to sixty or so. All shapes and sizes. All dressed in skimpy black satin dresses that flattered some of them considerably more than others. Already drunk, but in good spirits, laughing and joking and calling out to anyone foolish enough to point or stare in their direction.

Joe saw them as he crossed West Street at the pedestrian traffic lights. Jaden was pulling ahead, desperate to see what treats Modelzone had to offer. As they drew up in front of the shop window, Joe hoped that by standing behind Cassie he could shield her from view. She was leaning over the buggy, speaking to Sofia, and didn't seem to have noticed the hen party at all.

But they had noticed her.

The first indication came when the noise level dropped. Joe risked a look round, thinking they'd crossed the road, but they were about twenty feet away and closing in. Clustered together, nudging and conversing in low voices. A couple of them were already eyeing him up.

Leading the pack was a thickset woman in her twenties, with tattoos on both arms and a pair of plastic devil horns propped in her hair. She veered across the pavement and came to a halt in front of Joe, who was still trying to keep Cassie out of sight.

'That's Cassie Briggs, innit?' she said, and Joe heard a gasp as Cassie broke off whatever she was saying to Sofia.

The rest of the hen party fanned out around them. They peered at the baby in her buggy, and at her mother standing frozen behind it, gripping the handles with white knuckles.

'Oh my God! It *is* her.'

'You still singing, then? Haven't heard anything from you for years.'

Cassie made eye contact, smiling bravely. 'No. I don't really—'

'She had a kid, didn't she?' One of them gestured towards Jaden, who remained far more interested in a display of model sports cars. 'With the bloke from *Hollyoaks*. Dean somebody.'

'Oh, him? God, he shags everything that moves . . .' The girl faltered as she remembered who she was talking to, then dismissed her embarrassment and giggled instead.

'You're probably right,' Cassie said. Her voice sounded amiable enough, but there were bright red spots on her cheeks: a blaze of fury and shame.

'Did you see him in the jungle?' another asked her.

Cassie shook her head.

'You can't blame her,' someone else said. 'She ain't gonna watch him on telly when he's dumped her.'

'I thought she dumped him? That's what it said in *Heat*.'

'I wouldn't mind seeing my ex having to eat a load of maggots,' an older woman chipped in.

'He coped with your cooking, didn't he?'

Wild laughter, which Cassie politely shared. Joe felt someone bump against him: Jaden, sliding along the window, his nose pressed to the glass.

The ringleader took a step closer, examining Joe's face from inches away. Her breath could have stripped paint.

'Are you her new feller?'

As Joe shook his head, one of them said, 'Nah. She married some old Russian bloke. Seriously loaded.'

'So who's this, then?' The woman leered at him. 'Got a name, gorgeous?'

Joe said nothing. There was an edge of threat in the woman's voice, a hint that the mood could turn ugly at any moment. He wondered how he would protect Cassie from a dozen drunken women, and decided he couldn't. He had to get her away from them.

As if they could read his mind, one of them declared: 'I bet he's her bodyguard.'

To squeals of delight, another said: 'Come on, show us your muscles.'

Joe smiled. Shook his head. He caught movement in his periphery and saw Jaden slipping round the corner to examine the other window display. Someone pinched him on the arm.

'Have a feel of this, girls.'

'Hey, we haven't booked a stripper, have we, Shell?'

'What're you doing tonight?' The ringleader tried to slip her hand around his waist, but Joe sidestepped her.

He said, 'Enjoy your evening, ladies.' Then turned away, ushering Cassie to move with him. She gave a start.

'I can't see Jaden.'

'He's gone round to the other window.'

One of the women blocked Cassie's path. 'Come for a drink with us if you want?'

'No, I can't. I'm sorry.' Cassie angled the buggy and found a way through, calling Jaden's name.

They turned into Cranbourne Street, a short pedestrian thoroughfare that led up to Churchill Square. A handful of the women followed, while others were drifting away. One of them complained: 'S'pose she's too good for the likes of us.'

Jaden was gazing longingly at a big remote-control jeep, his hand cupped over his mouth. At his mother's approach he turned away, a guilty look in his eyes. Cassie grabbed his arm and he tried to shake her off, whining in protest.

'Stop it, Jaden. We're going.'

An angry rumbling went through the hen party as the distance between them and Joe's group increased. Some of the comments were loud enough to attract attention from other passers-by, who started looking to see who they were talking about.

'She was a shit singer, anyway.'

'I ain't surprised Dean left her. He can do a lot better.'

'You see that awful boob job?'

'Yeah. No way those tits were real.'

Cassie hurried up the hill, head down, shoulders hunched, pushing the buggy with one hand and practically dragging Jaden with the other. Joe followed close behind, hoping she hadn't heard their comments but fearing that she had, and painfully aware there wasn't a thing he could do or say to make it better.

Eighteen

There were three voices to monitor, each one nice and distinct. It was like one of those 'Three men in a pub' jokes: a Ukrainian, an American and a South African.

The engine noise increased once the yacht was in motion, but the conversation remained perfectly audible. Not that there was much of it, to begin with. Even the small talk was cagey and stilted. Friendly but not warm. Respectful but not entirely sincere.

The American, Mike Travers, said: 'So what's with the name? *Terror's Reach*. Sounds like some kind of horror movie.'

It was left to the South African, McWhirter, to provide a history of the Reach, which he did with all the well-practised glibness of a professional tour guide. It was clear the American had lost interest well before McWhirter reached the part about the oyster smack that had given the island its name.

'So it's nothing to do with what you guys get up to? I'm disappointed.' A throaty chuckle. 'Tell me about the real estate. Some of these homes look like they belong in the Hollywood hills. That one in the middle . . .'

'Dreamscape.'

Another chuckle. 'That's what caused all the trouble? Well, it's sure fucking hard to miss. I can see why it got you so shook up.'

Nasenko: 'No one on the island was happy with it. The media chose to put my name to the objections.'

'You did fight the build?'

'That is all past now. We have moved on.'

'Glad to hear it.'

'So you have not been here before?'

'No. Never got invited till today.'

'But you have a long association with Mr Felton?'

'Bobby and I go back years, but we don't spend time in each other's backyards. He's a man who values his privacy. So do I.'

'You still work with him, though?'

'Not so much nowadays. I'm semi-retired, as my wife keeps reminding me – usually when I'm calling her from some conference room or hotel suite on the other side of the world. But you know how it is.'

'Not easy to let go.'

'Nope. There are exciting times right now. A lot of opportunities out there. I guess that's why we're having this meeting, only I'm kinda surprised you called me.'

'Why's that?'

'Because you know all about my connection to your neighbour over there. And I know that you and he don't exactly get along. So why me?'

A few seconds of silence before Nasenko replied.

'Our proposal is not just to work with you,' he said, 'but also with Robert Felton.'

Nineteen

They took refuge in Churchill Square. It was nearly six o'clock, and although the indoor mall didn't shut for another hour the number of shoppers was rapidly dwindling. It was a relief to be inside, away from the heat and the noise and the crowds. Having just experienced a taste of Brighton's raucous night life, Joe was anxious to avoid any similar encounters.

He followed dutifully as Cassie browsed for a while in Next. After selecting a couple of dresses for Sofia, she called Jaden over to get his opinion on a pair of shorts. His reply came out in a muffled voice, and Cassie frowned.

'Open your mouth.'

Jaden tried to turn away, but she knelt down and held him still. 'What are you eating?'

Reluctantly, he opened his mouth. The remnants of a boiled sweet sat on his tongue.

'Where did that come from?'

He shrugged looking as blankly insolent as any teenager.

'Tell me, Jaden. Where did you get it?'

'A lady gave it to me.'

Cassie exchanged a glance with Joe, who was just as mystified. 'When was this?' he said.

'When I was looking at the cars.'

Joe thought back. He didn't recall seeing anyone approach the boy. Had one of the hen party offered it to him, perhaps feeling guilty about their behaviour?

'That's very naughty,' said Cassie.

'She gave it to me.'

'And you should have told me.'

Jaden broke away from his mother's grasp. Cassie looked at Joe again. He could see she was on the brink of tears.

'Go easy on him,' he said.

Cassie sighed, then nodded wearily. After paying for Sofia's clothes they moved on to Debenhams, the flagship department store at the rear of the mall. Took the lift to the lower ground floor and wandered through the various sections of women's fashion. Here and there Cassie paused to examine an outfit or check a price tag, but Joe could tell that her heart wasn't really in it. There was a distant look in her eyes, as though inside she was still cornered by the hen party, forced to hear their taunts over and over again.

She stopped by a rail of evening dresses. Picked up a pink chiffon baby-doll dress and stared at it for a long time.

'Shall we go?' he said.

Cassie jerked back to the present. 'Bored?'

'I'm fine. I thought you might want to get to the hotel, relax for a while.'

'Relax? All I ever do is *relax*. My whole life is one long holiday, isn't it?'

As she spoke she lifted the dress and held it against her body, almost without realising what she was doing. Then she glanced down, pulled the fabric tight over her chest and gave a bitter laugh.

'I used to love wearing things like this. Now I just feel self-conscious.'

Out of politeness, Joe averted his eyes. Cassie waited until her gaze drew him back.

'I heard what they said. And it's true. My boobs *are* ridiculous. I hate them.'

Joe was trapped. He couldn't tell if she was seeking flattery or the truth. She'd had the operation at Easter, and while he was used to it now, his first impression had been of a girl who'd slipped a couple of apples into her mother's bra.

Feeling shabby for ducking the question, he said, 'You have a great figure. They're just jealous.'

'If only they knew, eh?' She put the dress back on the rail. Picked up another and studied it. Seeking a distraction, Joe guessed, while she opened her heart to him.

'It was Valentin's idea. I did it for him, because I worried that I wasn't living up to what he expected from me.' She rubbed her nose, then sniffed. 'Still, the big question is why I ever married him in the first place.'

'Cassie, it's none of my business. I don't want to intrude on—'

'You're not intruding. You live with us, for God's sake. You must wonder about it.'

'I know you're going through a bad patch, but I assume you were happy at first?'

'I can't really remember any more. I married him because I was young and naive. He was charming, and rich, and he was in love with me – or so I thought. Turned out he just wanted a pretty accessory, someone who'd look good on his arm and wouldn't answer him back or have a mind of her own.' Cassie laughed, opened her hands in a question. 'How could it go wrong?'

He was about to say, 'It's not all bad,' and remind her that the relationship had produced Sofia, when she turned sharply, then looked back at him.

'Where's Jaden?'

This time there was no false alarm, no model cars to absorb the boy's attention. He was gone.

Joe's first duty was to keep Cassie from panicking. 'Don't worry,' he said. 'You just told him off. He's probably hidden somewhere, to give you a scare.'

'To punish me?' Cassie said, stunned by the thought.

'He won't see it like that.' Joe pointed towards the aisle that led deeper into the store. 'You look along there. I'll check the other way.'

He turned and ran. His priority was to reach the exit and the escalators in the centre of the shop. Then he could work his way back, searching each section more thoroughly.

He tried to calculate how long it was since he'd last registered Jaden's presence. Twenty seconds. Thirty, maybe. The boy wouldn't get far in that time.

Doesn't matter, he thought. It's not your job to get sidetracked, listening to Cassie's woes about her marriage.

Your job is to watch them, and you failed.

And then a sound drew his attention. A brief, familiar squeal of pain. Coming from the large open exit to the mall.

Joe ran past the escalators, giving them a cursory glance, and then spotted Jaden. He was being led out of the store by a peculiar-looking woman wearing trainers and a bulky plastic raincoat. She had big, unruly blonde hair that didn't sit right on her head: a wig.

She was pulling on Jaden's hand and he was twisting away from her, trying to break free. When he saw Joe he shouted, causing the woman to hesitate. She was wearing dark glasses, and the collar of her raincoat was turned up. A bizarre sight in the middle of a heatwave, but it meant she'd be virtually impossible to identify from CCTV images.

As soon as she recognised Joe, the woman abruptly released Jaden. The momentum sent him flying. He lost his balance and fell heavily on his front. As he landed, several small objects slipped from his hand and went skidding across the floor.

Sweets.

The woman was already sprinting away. With Jaden wailing at his feet, Joe knew he couldn't go after her. He scooped the boy up, offered a few soothing words, but his mind was working frantically. The sweets hinted at something organised: a concerted attempt to lure Jaden away. First at Modelzone, and now here.

But why? And why give up so easily? With a little more care the woman could have kept Jaden quiet, and gained vital seconds to abduct him.

There was only one obvious explanation. Jaden wasn't their target at all.

He was a decoy.

Drawn by Jaden's cries, a shop assistant was hurrying forward. Joe made a quick, positive assessment. She was a middle-aged woman. Probably a mother herself, judging by the concern on her face.

'I need you to watch him for me,' he said, thrusting Jaden into her arms. 'It's a family emergency. I'll be back in one minute.'

He sprinted towards the section where he'd left Cassie, realising the store was all but empty. A perfect opportunity to strike.

Cassie was just about where he expected to find her. She hadn't gone far. The sight that greeted him wasn't totally unexpected either.

Two men had moved in on her. One tall, one short, but both in good shape. They wore jeans and T-shirts and baseball caps. The tall one had attacked Cassie from behind, pinning her arms at her side and clamping a hand over her mouth. She couldn't scream but she was making a low-pitched keening noise. She was writhing and kicking, desperately trying to fight her way free.

The other man, the short one, was crouched over the buggy, fumbling with the clasp that held the wailing, terrified Sofia in place. They'd obviously counted on the diversion to give them enough time. In normal circumstances Joe could have been expected to stay with Jaden, comforting him, perhaps talking to the store's security staff, not returning to Cassie for at least a minute or two. Long enough for them to overpower her and make off with their real target.

As he ran towards them the short one sensed his approach and half rose, as if unsure how to react. His movement brought him within Cassie's range, and she lashed out with her foot and caught him in the groin. He staggered backwards, but still managed to shout a warning.

In turning to gauge the threat, the tall man must have relaxed his grip on Cassie. She struggled free and hurled herself at his partner, letting out a screech of rage as she clubbed at his head, pushing him away from Sofia. The tall man forgot her and moved into a defensive stance, ready to deal with Joe.

Closing the distance to less than ten feet, Joe skidded to a halt. Without the element of surprise, there was no advantage in launching an attack at speed. More likely that his momentum would be used against him, especially if these men knew what they were doing.

There was a shout from behind him. Joe couldn't risk reacting to it, but the tall man must have assumed he would. He lunged forward, swinging a punch with his right hand. Joe dodged it with ease, but didn't fully anticipate the follow-up: a lightning fast blow to the stomach.

The impact caused him to double over, but as he did he drove himself forward, butting the man on the chin. He followed up with a couple of sharp chops to the man's upper arm, wanting to take the sting out of any further punches.

Another shout, loud and urgent. Joe was aware of the tall man backing away, blood leaking from a split lip, his sunglasses dangling from one ear. He shot an uncertain glance at his partner. Cassie was snarling and fighting like a demon, until a blow to the face sent her sprawling into a rack of dresses.

Both men turned and fled towards the back of the store, just as two of the centre's security team appeared.

'What happened?' one of them asked.

'Tried to mug us,' Joe said. It was the most logical answer, and it sent the security men off in pursuit, which suited him fine.

After a few paces, the one who'd spoken thought to break his stride and call back: 'Wait there.'

Joe nodded, but he had no intention of complying. He helped Cassie to her feet, brushed some hair from her face and examined her carefully. She had the beginnings of a nasty bruise on her cheek.

'Are you okay?'

'Where's Jaden?'

'He's all right. But we have to get out of here.'

As he said it, Cassie's face softened with relief. The shop assistant was approaching, Jaden running ahead of her. He threw his arms around his mother.

'What's going on?' the assistant asked.

'Wish I knew,' said Joe. He spotted an exit sign at the far end of the store. 'Can we reach the car park from there?'

The assistant nodded, looking worried. 'Yes, but shouldn't you—?'

'We're all right. Thanks again.'

He made sure Sofia was still strapped in. The poor girl was sobbing, but unharmed. Joe grabbed the buggy and set off, Cassie and Jaden sticking close to his side. If Cassie was troubled about his decision not to wait for the police, she showed no sign of it.

Probably just wanted to get the hell out of here, he thought. His own concern was that the woman had first approached Jaden outside the model shop, so this represented their second attempt. And if they were willing to try twice, there was no good reason to believe they wouldn't try a third time.

Twenty

The American chuckled quietly, without much humour.

'You have Bobby Felton living, what, a hundred yards along the street? And yet you drag me all the way over here from the States.'

'Our thinking', said McWhirter with a silky charm, 'was that Mr Felton wouldn't be quite so receptive to a direct approach. Not at this stage.'

'Huh. So I'm an emissary, is that it? The go-between.'

'More than that,' Nasenko assured him. 'Believe me, this will be of great benefit to you.'

'Doing what, exactly?'

'We have a number of, ah, opportunities to exploit in Central Asia,' said McWhirter. 'Specifically the republic of Kajitestan.'

'Oil and natural gas. And certain mineral rights. The new president is a man I've known for many years.'

'Yeah, I heard you got good connections over there.'

'But we need other connections, too. In America, and in Britain. We need to know how their administrations will react to our plans. And we need to be sure we have a market in these countries.'

'That's where me and Bobby come in?'

McWhirter: 'We know Mr Felton has close relationships with a variety of key individuals, not just in the present government, but, more importantly, with their likely successors.'

Nasenko added, 'The next general election in Britain must be held by June 2010. A new government would be very good news for Felton, I think?'

Another pause. Then Travers barked: 'That all you want from him?'

'I don't understand . . .'

'Any venture worth pursuing, usually it needs some kind of start-up capital. Especially when it involves one of those shit-ass Central Asian republics. You need security, equipment, manpower. You need to pay a lot of bribes. It all costs, and from what I've heard, you're not exactly "cash-rich" at the moment.'

The silence felt charged with tension. McWhirter cleared his throat, a sound that eloquently communicated his desire to be anywhere but in this meeting. His boss's response was a lot more forthright.

'These are just rumours, spread by my enemies.'

'You're saying you haven't taken a big hit lately?'

'I repeat, it is just lies. I have all the money I need for this project.'

'But if you or Mr Felton want to put up a stake,' McWhirter added, 'I'm sure there won't be any objections.'

'We do not come begging for money.' Nasenko spoke harshly over his adviser. 'The purpose of this meeting is to offer an olive branch. We need Felton's connections. He will also benefit from mine. That is the nature of business, is it not? To put bad feelings aside and work together for maximum profit.'

'Well, it sounds fair enough to me. Can't say what Bobby's gonna think of it.' There was shuffling, a heavy exhalation. 'Will you guys point me in the direction of the john? I need to take a leak.'

Incidental noises, the thump and clang of footsteps, then a distant door closing. Instantly the remaining voices became low and conspiratorial.

'I don't like it, Valentin. When you propose a deal like this you should do it from a position of strength.'

'And we are. This is a greedy man we have here. You saw his eyes light up when I talked about Kajitestan. If the rewards are right, he will help us.'

'Do you think he can bring Felton on board?'

'I am sure of it. Another very greedy man.'

'But what about finance? We *are* going to need Felton's capital.' A heartfelt sigh from McWhirter. 'I don't mind telling you, Valentin, I'm out of my comfort zone.'

'You worry too much.'

'You pay me to worry, remember?'

'Well, now I am paying you to *stop* worrying for a change.' Nasenko chuckled, then put on some kind of accent that he must have imagined was American. 'This time, *go with the flow.*'

Twenty-One

At the western end of the store there was a small lobby with two lifts and a door to the stairs. The car park beneath the centre had three levels. The Shogun was on the lowest. Joe instinctively preferred to take the stairs, despite a warning sign on the door that these were for emergency use only. But he recognised that, with Sofia in a buggy, the lift was a better option. It was certainly no slower or more exposed than carrying two children down three flights of steps.

No one else got in with them, and when the doors closed Cassie dropped to her knees and tried to console Sofia while simultaneously hugging Jaden. Sounding remarkably composed, she made light of what had happened, explaining that it had all been a silly mistake. A kind of game.

'It's all finished now,' she said. 'No one's going to scare you like that any more.'

Joe listened, fuming quietly. But he knew this wasn't the time to reproach himself for his failures. That would have to come later, when he'd got them to safety.

He was also busy reviewing what had happened, trying to extract as much information as possible from the limited data available. The first thing to determine was precisely when the would-be kidnappers had begun stalking them.

If the woman was the same one who'd given Jaden a sweet outside

Modelzone, it meant they had been followed from West Street, at least, and probably earlier. The Lanes had been crowded with tourists: not an ideal environment in which to carry out an abduction. Prior to that, the car park itself would have been the perfect place to mount an attack.

Mindful of this, Joe was first out of the lifts and made sure it was safe before beckoning Cassie to follow. The car park was virtually deserted. Lots of vacant spaces and only a handful of vehicles on the move, none of them suspicious.

That was good news, in some ways. Bad news in others. For the kidnappers to have ignored such an ideal location suggested they didn't know where Joe had parked. That, in turn, meant they hadn't followed the Shogun into Brighton. They must have acquired their target somewhere else.

This was clearly no ad hoc operation. Using Jaden as a decoy showed evidence of detailed planning. The kidnappers must have required – and possessed – knowledge of Cassie's whereabouts. But the decision to go shopping in Churchill Square had been entirely spontaneous, as had the window-gazing outside Modelzone. There was only one destination that had been prearranged.

Merrion and Son.

By sheer good fortune Joe had found a space close to the pay station, which meant he was able to feed the machine and still watch over Cassie as she helped the children into the car. While he waited for the machine to print the exit ticket, he considered who had known they were visiting the jeweller's this afternoon.

Valentin Nasenko, of course. McWhirter and Yuri, and maybe even Maria. Then the jeweller himself, Merrion Junior, and his old man. Perhaps some other staff, although there couldn't be many, given the size of the shop.

Not good. These all seemed like fair assumptions, and what they told him was very ominous.

He grabbed the ticket and ran to the car. Cassie had elected to sit in the back, with the children either side of her. That way she could maintain physical contact with them and still communicate with Joe when necessary. Not that she showed much sign of wanting to do that.

He got in, started the engine and followed the signs towards the exit. He brooded on Cassie's behaviour. She'd been scared, but also very brave. Joe felt huge admiration for the way she had fought the two men.

But since then, she'd barely said a word. She wasn't calling 999. She wasn't ordering him to drive to the nearest police station. He could see that she might be reluctant to discuss it in front of the children, but he would have expected a more forceful reaction than this.

When the barrier came up, Joe drove out and cast a quick look in each direction. They were in a short access road that ran behind Brighton's conference centre and the Grand Hotel. There were junctions at each end that would lead him down to the seafront, but the one to the left, into West Street, was controlled by traffic lights.

He went right. Straightened up, accelerated, then made a smooth left into Cannon Place without having to stop. It was a short run down to the next junction, where the lights were on red. He checked the mirror: no one behind him. He took the right-hand lane and waited for the question that never came.

The Blue Anchor hotel was in the opposite direction.

Joe gave some thought to whether the hotel, part-owned by Valentin, would have been a better location for the kidnappers to strike. He decided not. It was small and well staffed, and usually at full capacity. Cassie was due to meet up with half a dozen friends, most of them from the stage school she'd attended in her teens. All staying the night, on Valentin's tab. There would scarcely be a moment when Cassie and the children weren't surrounded by people.

That first point lingered in Joe's mind. *The Blue Anchor was Nasenko territory.*

When the lights turned green he pulled across the A259 into the westbound carriageway and immediately joined a line of slow-moving traffic. To his left, the rotting hulk of the West Pier crouched in the water like a gigantic rusting birdcage. The sea around it was a gentle milky blue. Crowds of people on the beach: swimming, sunbathing, drinking. The perfect way to kick off a weekend.

Joe checked the mirror again. Saw Cassie staring at her lap, a furious concentration on her face. She felt his gaze and her head snapped up.

'What?'

'You haven't asked where we're going.'

'I don't care. As long as we get away from here.'

'I'm not sure if it's wise to go to the hotel.'

'Fine. I can ring the others, make up some excuse.'

'I only meant it's not a good idea right now. We can probably go back later.'

Cassie looked thrown by his suggestion. 'I'm not sure.'

'Any reason to think it's not safe at the Blue Anchor?'

'No.' But she said it much too quickly.

Before he could comment the distant blast of a horn drew his attention. He looked in the wing mirror and saw a big silver Mercedes SUV cutting into the outside lane to overtake a bus. The car behind it wasn't happy, and neither was Joe.

'Hold on tight,' he said.

The A259 ran east to west along the seafront, two lanes in each direction. There were junctions and pedestrian crossings perhaps every hundred yards, all controlled by traffic lights. Get the lights in your favour and you might glide effortlessly along to Hove and eventually out of the city, reflecting on what a delightful experience the Sussex coast offered to motorists. More likely you'd endure a long, slow journey punctuated by frequent stop-starts and all kinds of frustrating bottlenecks.

Which was how it was now. The city's geography narrowed Joe's options for escape, and the sheer density of the traffic limited them still further. But he would have to try. He'd screwed up enough already today.

Behind him, about ten cars back, the Mercedes changed lanes again, tailgating the car in front until it got the message and indicated to move over. The queue ahead began to stretch, each successive vehicle taking an age to get up to speed. Joe was already in the outside lane and saw no point in switching, even if doing so appeared to offer a minor advantage. For one thing, there were no junctions on the left. To get off this road at all he would have to turn right. But where?

Joe searched his memory. He'd brought Cassie to Brighton on six or seven occasions, and years ago he had worked here for a short time, so he knew the city reasonably well. The next major junction was Preston Street, which led up to Western Road. Before that, there was a turning that would enable him to feed through to Preston Street a little sooner. But traffic on Western Road itself was usually even slower than the seafront: lots of buses, lots of pedestrians.

He got up to thirty miles an hour, sailed through the lights, then watched his mirror, praying the Mercedes would get caught. It nearly did. At the last moment it swerved around a compliant motorist and went through on red, putting an end to any uncertainty Joe may have had about its purpose.

He heard a gasp from Cassie. She'd twisted in her seat and was looking out through the rear window.

'Is that who I think it is?'

'Afraid so.'

The Mercedes leapfrogged a couple more cars. At this rate it would be on their tail by the time they got to the junction at Grand Avenue, where they would be sitting ducks. He had to get off the main road before then.

The Hove lawns were coming up on the left. Lots of people about, walking dogs, playing football, lounging on the grass. On the right, the hotels and restaurants had given way to elegant Regency terraces, their facades the colour of butter in the warm evening sun.

Approaching Brunswick Square, Joe prepared to make a sudden right turn. Then the doubts set in. He had a feeling it was closed off at the top: no way through to Western Road.

He checked the mirror. The Mercedes was still gaining ground, just four or five cars behind them. He could see the vague shapes of two men in the front.

Up ahead, a set of pedestrian traffic lights was turning to red. At the same time, a gap appeared in the oncoming traffic. Joe wrenched the wheel to the right and cut across the main road, into Brunswick Terrace. This was a two-lane slip road, running parallel to the coast road and divided from it by a narrow pavement. With the main road so busy, a few other people were using it as a rat run, and the speed at which Joe was driving earned him some angry looks.

From Brunswick Terrace he turned right into Lansdowne Place. As he did, he glimpsed the Mercedes crossing the A259 in pursuit, bumping over the pavement into the slip road.

Shit.

Lansdowne Road ascended as it ran north. It was a clear route up to Western Road, but offered no concealment. In terrain like this Joe knew he couldn't realistically outrace his pursuers. He had to lose them.

He took the first left into a side road, Alice Street. It was about a hundred yards long, with parked cars on the right and double yellow lines on the left. He flashed past garages and a pub car park, but was forced to brake hard at the junction and wait for a passing truck.

In his mirror he saw the Mercedes almost overshoot the entrance to Alice Street. It stopped, backed up, came after them. Joe turned right into Holland Road and raced up the hill. By now he'd abandoned any pretence at civil driving, and the children had picked up on it. Both were crying softly, with Cassie doing her best to soothe them.

More traffic lights at the top. Joe prayed they would stay on green, and they did. He shot through the junction, crossed Western Road and continued north on Holland Road. He passed a boarded-up Indian restaurant and a Gothic stone church, and even though the lights at the next junction were on red he managed a grin.

'There's a police station up ahead.'

He expected to hear jubilation from the back seat, or at least a sigh of relief. Instead he got a brief, suppressed wail of panic.

'No,' said Cassie. She was looking over her shoulder again. 'They're caught at the last lights. We can get away.'

'You don't want to report this?'

'I can't, Joe. I just can't.'

Twenty-Two

The American returned and sat down heavily. They heard the creak and groan of his chair: possibly canvas on a steel frame. Not quite strong enough for a large man.

He was offered another drink, but declined. 'I'd like to get a few things straight, including remuneration. I'll warn you now, gentlemen, I don't come cheap.'

'But you will do it?'

'I'll talk to him, see if I can set up a meeting. But not till the first instalment is paid. Ten thousand dollars.'

'You want ten grand for making one phone call?' said McWhirter.

'Not negotiable. I'll draw up a fee schedule, then it's up to you. Take it or leave it.'

'Ten thousand is acceptable,' Nasenko told him. 'We can have that transferred to your account on Monday.'

'Sounds good. Bobby's in France this weekend. I'll talk to him when he gets back, see if we can set up something later next week.'

'You have spoken to him recently?'

'I touched base briefly.'

'So he already knows we are meeting?'

'No. I wanted to see what you had to say before I mentioned it. But he did suggest we have lunch while I'm over here.'

'Excellent.' Nasenko couldn't disguise the satisfaction in his voice.

'Hey. All I'm gonna do is pass on what you're telling me. I can't guarantee he'll go for it.'

'Of course not. But I am an optimist.'

'Good for you. But you'd better know that Bobby Felton likes to do his homework. He's gonna want every little detail before he signs up to anything.'

'We can provide that.'

'Right now? To me?'

McWhirter started to speak but something cut him off. A look or gesture from Nasenko, perhaps.

'To show our goodwill we can outline the basic proposal. You have time, while we enjoy the sights of the harbour?'

'Sure.' Travers didn't sound overly impressed – either with Nasenko's alleged generosity or the quality of the views. 'I want enough to convince me that you're on the level. Nothing personal, but I'm far too old to get screwed by anyone.'

'You don't trust me?' said Nasenko.

'Maybe. Maybe not. What's more important, if I'm acting as go-between here, is that I don't endanger Bobby's trust in *me*.' Travers gave another humourless chuckle. 'You remember those stories about the Nazi occupation? How if the resistance ambushed a single German, they'd retaliate by rounding up the locals and wiping out ten or twenty at random? Well, that's kinda how Felton operates.'

Nasenko was bristling as he interrupted. 'It is not necessary to—'

'I sure hope not, but I'm telling you anyway. There are no bound-aries with that guy. No proportionality. He just doesn't understand the concept. If you're loyal to him, and he knows it, there's no better man to work with. But cross him and you've signed your own death warrant.'

Nasenko chose to laugh, making light of the warning.

'Robert Felton is a formidable operator, I don't dispute that. But I am no amateur myself. And you should know that I work on exactly the same basis.'

Twenty-Three

The tone of Cassie's voice left Joe in no doubt of her sincerity. She clearly believed there was a good reason not to involve the police, and that would have to do.

Behind him, the lights changed. The Mercedes accelerated towards him. The lights ahead remained on red. There was no traffic in front of him, and nothing coming through the junction.

Joe put his foot down and blew through the red light. Took a tight left into Lansdowne Road, past an ugly municipal building: the law courts. Went right, then left again, short hops of fifty or sixty yards that he hoped would be enough to throw their pursuers off the scent.

They were in Eaton Road, a pleasant tree-lined street with a mix of suburban homes and small blocks of flats in a grimy pale yellow brick. He passed the cricket ground, recalling an enjoyable Sunday he'd spent watching a game and an even more enjoyable Sunday evening spent in the pub next door.

Another right took him into Wilbury Road, a wide street with parking at each kerb and two lanes of additional parking spaces in the centre of the road. Joe was halfway along the street when a battered old Datsun pulled away from the kerb, coughing clouds of exhaust.

Joe hit the brakes, slowing to a crawl. He checked the mirror: still clear behind them. The Datsun showed no sign of gaining speed. And there were empty spaces in the centre of the road.

Cassie gasped as he cut through a narrow gap between a couple of parked cars, accelerated for fifty or sixty yards on the wrong side of the road, then veered back across to the correct lane. The elderly driver of the Datsun, now safely behind him, seemed oblivious. But coming up fast behind the Datsun was the silver Mercedes.

Worse still, Joe could see the westbound traffic was backed up across the junction at the top of Wilbury Road. That was the route he'd intended to take, and he wasn't sure of an alternative. He knew the railway line was around here somewhere, and that usually meant a lot of treacherous cul-de-sacs.

Reaching the junction, he stared hard at the driver blocking his way. The driver got the message and edged forward, leaving Joe just enough room to squeeze through. There was a road straight ahead, and judging by its elevation it looked as though it went up over the train tracks.

Fingers crossed, he thought, and powered across the road, north into Wilbury Villas. As the Shogun accelerated over the rise he knew the Mercedes wasn't more than a few seconds behind them. Crucially, though, for those few seconds it would be out of sight. Joe had to make that time count.

The next junction gave him three options. Wilbury Crescent to the left or right, or continue straight ahead along Wilbury Villas. Two things made the decision for him.

The first was a sign, proclaiming that Wilbury Villas was a T-junction. In other words, a no through road. A dead end.

The second was a big red removal lorry, double parked, maybe fifty feet away.

Joe went straight ahead.

'It's a dead end,' Cassie shouted.

'I know.'

He hit the accelerator and the Shogun jumped forward. He swung it past the lorry, cut in sharply and skidded to a halt. Looked back at

Cassie, who was still clinging to her seat belt with both hands. Beside her, Jaden let out a laugh, more exhilarated than afraid.

Joe leaned over so he could see the passenger-side wing mirror. It showed him a sliver of Wilbury Crescent. He imagined the Mercedes roaring over the railway line and slowing on the approach to the junction. Pausing as the men inside realised that they'd lost sight of their target. A moment or two to debate their options.

Go left . . .

He counted: five seconds. Nothing. He felt a tightening in his chest at the thought of the Mercedes suddenly rolling up alongside them. If it did, they were done for. No question about that.

Ten seconds. Fifteen. Were they arguing amongst themselves over which way to turn?

Then a flash of silver in the wing mirror, which echoed inside him as a kind of bright, metallic jubilation. It had worked.

They'd gone left.

Joe took a slow, calming breath. 'Everyone all right back there?'

Cassie nodded. 'Just about.'

'Good.'

He studied the road ahead. It was capped off by a wide pavement, with a sturdy metal fence to prevent traffic getting through. Beyond that was a reasonably fast east-west route: the Old Shoreham Road.

He released the handbrake and moved forward. Heard an exclamation from the back seat.

'Aren't we turning round?'

He shook his head. 'If we turn round the only real option is to go the same way they did. I want to check another possibility.'

As Joe got closer to the end of the street he found exactly what he hoped for. The fence was an obvious deterrent, plainly visible from the bottom of the hill. But it didn't run the full length of the pavement. On the left-hand side there was a wide gap between the fence and the last house in the street: easily enough room to get through.

Cassie snorted, as though she couldn't believe Joe's luck. She said nothing as he bumped the Shogun up the kerb and crossed the pavement. They were on the edge of a major junction. Now all he had to do was wait for the lights to change and join the flow of traffic along the Old Shoreham Road.

'Where does that go?' Cassie asked. She leaned forward, pointing to where another road ascended to the north.

'Out of town,' he said, seeing that she'd hit on a much better route. Far less risk of inadvertently coming upon the Mercedes if they continued north rather than west for a bit longer.

Joe timed his manoeuvre well, crossing into the northbound lane as the lights turned green. They raced up the hill to another set of lights, then left into Dyke Road.

After a minute, Cassie said, 'I know where we are now. Valentin has friends who live along here.'

'Makes sense. This is Millionaires' Row,' Joe said as they passed a succession of vulgar mansions. Another mile or so and they reached a major roundabout and joined the A27, heading west. Traffic was busy, but Joe quickly moved into the outside lane and was able to do a steady seventy miles an hour.

As they left the city behind the silence grew increasingly morose. Joe thought it was just his imagination until Cassie issued a series of big, heavy sighs. Finally he grasped that this was an invitation for him to speak his mind.

On the approach to the Shoreham flyover the road widened to three lanes. A light aircraft buzzed overhead, wobbling in a crosswind as it descended towards the airport. Across the valley, the Gothic-revival architecture of Lancing College chapel resembled a Disney creation, a petite fairy-tale castle nestled in the Downs.

Joe moved left into the slip road for the Shoreham interchange. From the back seat came another heartfelt sigh.

'I take it you don't want to loop round and go to the hotel?'

'No.' A distinct emphasis in Cassie's voice. He glanced over his shoulder and saw her nodding towards Jaden. The boy was gazing out of the window with a dreamy, almost comatose expression. He looked exhausted.

Joe said: 'What about home?'

'Not sure about that, either.'

'Okay. I get the feeling you may know more than I do about what just happened?'

'Maybe,' she said. 'I hope not.'

'Let's put it this way. You suspect there might be a Ukrainian involvement?'

Nothing from Cassie for a long moment. Then she said, 'Can we stop, just for a minute?'

Joe found a place to pull in at the bottom of the slip road, bumping onto a patch of grass directly beneath the flyover. They could hear the thunderous roar of the traffic overhead.

Cassie leaned across and opened the door, prompting a cry of alarm from Jaden. She hugged him tight, kissing him gently on the forehead.

'I'm just going to sit in the front and talk to Joe.'

'I'm hungry,' he said.

'Okay. I can fix that.'

She fetched a bag from the boot and produced beakers of juice and a packet of plain biscuits. Once the children were pacified, she got into the front seat.

'We'd better keep driving,' Joe said. 'If they're looking for us anywhere, it'll be on the A27. I want to take the back roads.'

'Fine.'

She said nothing else until they had negotiated the roundabout and were heading roughly north-west on the A283, a single-carriageway route that tended to be less frenetic than the A27. She put some music on, adjusting the sound levels so it was louder in the back, ensuring their conversation wouldn't be overheard.

'I don't know what Valentin's playing at, but something's going on. The relationship's been weird ever since Sofia was born. It's like I don't exist as anything other than her mother.'

Joe saw she was blushing and looked away. Not easy to talk about your sex life, even in coded language.

'A few months ago he got really secretive. A couple of times I discovered he'd been lying about where he was. And he began paying more attention to things like his hairstyle, his clothes.'

'You think he's having an affair?'

'More than that. I think he's fallen in love.' Cassie's voice went a little unsteady. 'After we got married, he started dropping hints about having some fun on the side. With high-class escorts, mainly. He acted as though it was perfectly normal, like he was expecting me to say, "Yeah, fine, go right ahead".'

'But you didn't?'

'No. I went mental. Then he claimed he was just joking, but I don't think he was. That's when I should have got out, really. I was naive. Stupid. And I'd just fallen pregnant.'

She shivered. Joe waited while she collected herself.

'This time it's different. Not just casual sex, but something more important. And knowing Valentin, he'll want the best of both worlds. A wife at his house in Sussex, ready to give him kids whenever he wants them. And a full-time mistress in London.'

'I see now why you thought the eternity ring was inappropriate.'

'It freaked me out. And the timing . . . It can't be a coincidence.'

'What do you mean?'

Almost whispering, she said, 'I've been thinking about leaving him.'

'You've discussed it with Valentin?'

'I wouldn't dare. The one time I tried explaining how unhappy I was, he basically told me not to be so stupid. But I was on the phone to my mum one day and I just lost it. She's really supportive, but she also persuaded me to give it another try, as if it's all going to blow over.'

'Parents are like that, I suppose,' Joe said. 'But you don't think it will?'

'Not any more. But I told her what I think Valentin is up to, and I also discussed how I'd arrange things if and when I go. Pretty much from that moment he's been ice cold towards me.'

Silence for a second or two. Joe wished he could throw doubt on what she was saying, but he couldn't. It was all too plausible.

'He's listening in on your calls?'

Cassie nodded. 'He's paranoid about industrial espionage, and I bet he's spied on people himself in the past. Why shouldn't he also spy on me?'

'If he knows what you're considering, wouldn't he just confront you?'

'Perhaps he thinks there's more to come. The minute he admits to eavesdropping, he loses some of his power over me.' She hesitated, and took an anxious look over her shoulder. 'Anyway, it isn't me running away that bothers him. It's who I'd take with me.'

'Sofia.'

'Yes. She's the main reason he won't allow me to leave. He knows I'd never go without her, and in his view she belongs to him. Therefore I do, too.'

Joe said nothing. He concentrated on driving. The traffic was light, the road clear and fast-moving. They were making pretty good time – wherever it was they were going.

Then Cassie said: 'There's something else. A week or two ago I overheard him talking to Yuri. I don't know what they were discussing, but Yuri asked, "Do you want to kill them?" and Valentin said, "Not if we can find a better way."'

'What?'

'That was all I heard. *Not if we can find a better way.* Then they realised I was there and clammed up.'

'You've no idea at all what it was about?'

'No. I wondered if I'd misheard, but I don't think so. When he saw me, Yuri gave me this look . . . Like all he wants is ten minutes alone in a room with me, you know?' She shivered again, and rubbed her arms. 'Sometimes I worry that one day Valentin will let him.'

'Not if I have anything to do with it,' said Joe. Despite his misgivings, he decided it was his duty to be straight with her. 'Look, I hate having to tell you this, but I don't think they were trying to kidnap Jaden.'

'What?'

He described his perspective on the abduction. His impression that Jaden was merely a decoy. 'I think they wanted Sofia. Or maybe you and Sofia.'

Cassie began to weep, quietly, in a way that didn't invite him to offer comfort. She took a tissue from her bag and blew her nose.

'The last few weeks, I've been trying to convince myself I've misjudged him. Clinging to the idea that at heart Valentin's a good man, not a monster. But it's a lie. Only a monster could stoop to something like this.'

'Cass, we don't know for sure that he's behind it.'

'I think he is.'

'Okay. But what was he going to do afterwards? If he wanted to spirit her away he could easily do it from home.'

'Yeah, but this way he can deny knowledge. He gets to hold her somewhere while he negotiates with me. It's like that saying goes . . .'

'Possession is nine-tenths of the law.' Joe sighed. 'I'm still not completely sure. I'd like to talk to him.'

'I don't want to go home,' Cassie blurted. 'I can't go back there tonight.'

'I know. That's not where we're going.'

Twenty-Four

The top floor of Dreamscape was dominated by a vast room that ran nearly the full length of the house. A huge open-plan living space, furnished to entice prospective buyers with a selection of funky sofas and rugs. A wall of subtly tinted glass gave a stunning view of the bay, the still waters gleaming beneath the sun's slow descent. As a vantage point for their current surveillance, it couldn't be better.

Liam and Priya had watched a motor launch collect four men from the jetty and transfer them to the majestic-looking yacht moored on the edge of the deep-water channel. Then the yacht had set off on a cruise around the harbour, and it still hadn't returned. For Liam it meant another frustrating wait, mitigated only by the arrival of the second team.

A brief call notified him of their approach. Leaving Priya to watch for the yacht, he hurried downstairs, into the garage. He opened the doors so they could drive straight in. He had to assume Oliver Felton was still spying on them. It was making him feel increasingly vulnerable, and that in turn made him angry. The Felton kid was going to pay for that.

A Ford Explorer drove in, pulling up alongside the Transit. Liam hit the button to shut the doors. He took a deep breath. Told himself he was perfectly calm. It was all good. Everything under control.

First out of the Explorer was Jim Turner. A career criminal in his early fifties, Turner was a tall, heavyset man with chiselled features and silver-grey hair. In recent years he'd turned semi-legitimate, setting up a security company that had been doing well for itself until the recession hit. Prior to that he'd earned notoriety in the underworld as a 'taxman', a villain who specialised in targeting other villains. Even Liam had to admit it took a special kind of nerve, not to mention a psychotic temper, to earn a living by torturing and robbing drug dealers.

So far their working relationship had been tense, to say the least. Turner had made it clear he regarded Liam as little more than a white-collar sneak thief who should never have been entrusted with the lead role. Liam saw Turner as an outmoded thug who lacked the brains or finesse to take part in such an ambitious raid. Safe to say they wouldn't be exchanging Christmas cards in future.

Turner shook his head in wonderment as the garage doors rolled back into place. 'Fucking clever, eh?'

Liam nodded. 'I suppose.'

'I want doors like that, and a pad like this.' Turner's gaze alighted on the Renault Mégane, parked beyond Liam's Transit. 'Whose motor?'

'An estate agent. He was here on the quiet, to meet a woman. We managed to get rid of her. He wasn't so lucky.'

Turner's eyebrows went up. 'You're not saying you topped him?'

'Priya did.'

'You're shitting me? Dark horse in more ways than one.' He chuckled, looking round. 'So where is our little Paki babe?'

'She's upstairs. And don't call her that.'

'What's it matter? She can't hear me.'

'It's unprofessional,' Liam said. 'For the next few hours we have to work together. Better if we can all get along.'

'Oh, I dunno,' said Turner, swaying close and glowering at Liam. 'Nothing like a bit of creative tension to keep you on your toes.'

The other members of the team were climbing out of the Explorer and examining their surroundings. The driver, Manderson, was a dumb but loyal associate of Turner's. He was about forty, a scrawny, dishevelled man with long greasy hair, bad skin and missing teeth. Tattoos covered his arms from shoulder to wrist: he'd applied some of them himself, and it showed. If he had been a dog, Liam thought, he would have been put down at birth.

From the back seat came Eldon, a short, slender man with absolutely no physical presence. Softly spoken, with a pale face and thinning blond hair, he was the sort of man you could lose in an empty room. But he knew a lot about art and antiques, and he had the contacts to offload high-end goods with no questions asked. It would be his job to determine what was worth taking.

The last of the four to emerge, Allotti, was also the most presentable. He was in his early thirties, brown-haired and wiry, with a slow, sardonic manner. He had a background in electronics, specifically in the field of communications. His role was to secure and monitor the island's phone network for the duration of the mission.

Liam indicated the Transit. 'All your stuff's in there. Get it unloaded and set up inside.'

Allotti nodded unhappily. Sniggering at his displeasure, Turner and Manderson started wandering towards the inside door, Eldon lagging just behind. But Liam stopped them.

'You three can unload the gas.'

When Liam rejoined Priya in the sunroom she was at the window, a pair of binoculars in one hand. She didn't look round until he was within touching distance.

'Turner's here,' he said.

'Okay.'

He stood alongside her and looked out over the bay. The yacht was back in sight, slowly heading towards them.

'Took their time, didn't they?' he muttered.

'It doesn't matter.' In the same gentle tone, she added, 'You're very impatient, aren't you?'

Liam made a dismissive noise, but it was true. He was itching to get started. The tension was becoming unbearable, especially knowing the Felton kid could blow the whole operation with a single phone call. And every minute the barriers were in place they risked having someone come along and try to use the bridge.

Should have delayed that, maybe . . .

'I've told them to bring the gas up,' he said. 'We'll stash the body in here, too.'

Priya nodded. She handed him the binoculars, stepped away from him and stretched, extravagantly, like a cat. 'I'm going to get changed.'

Resisting the temptation to watch her leave the room, Liam lifted the binoculars and studied the yacht instead. Valentin Nasenko and his associates were standing out on the deck, talking and pointing in the direction of Terror's Reach. Their body language spoke of a more convivial atmosphere than before. The meeting had gone well.

'Congratulations, gentlemen,' Liam said to himself. 'Here comes round two.'

Liam heard Manderson and Eldon trudging up the stairs long before they materialised, each holding one end of a large propane cylinder. They set it down carefully on the floor, cursing from the effort.

'Fucking hell . . .'

'How many of them?' said Eldon.

'We want six up here. Plus the body,' Liam said.

'Done that,' came a voice from the hall. Turner strolled in, as nonchalant as a man can be with a corpse bundled over his shoulder. He dropped it, unceremoniously, like he was delivering a sack of coal.

Manderson said, 'You're not even out of fucking breath.'

Turner jerked his thumb behind him. 'You dipshits. There's a lift, just back along the corridor.'

The two men gaped at him, and then at Liam, as though it was his fault.

'He's right. You all saw the floor plans.'

Manderson looked on the verge of rebellion but settled for another growled expletive. He stomped out, followed by a more chastened Eldon.

'Not chosen for his brains,' Liam said.

Turner pulled a face. 'He does what he's told. That's good enough.' He surveyed the room, hardly seeming to notice the spectacular views. Then he nudged the estate agent's body with his foot.

'So what's the story?'

'I told you. He tried to get away.'

'And the Pak— the Indian bird stuck him?'

Liam nodded, anticipating Turner's next question: *Where were you?*

'The guy had some tart on her way to see him. I had to get both vehicles in the garage before she turned up. Priya couldn't do it because someone might have seen her in the van.'

'Still a bit of a fuck-up, isn't it?'

Liam held the other man's gaze throughout a long, challenging silence.

'I know you don't like it that I'm in charge,' he said. 'But that's the way it is. Are you gonna risk everything because you can't deal with it?'

'I can deal with it. My worry is whether *you* can deal with it.'

'I wouldn't be standing here if I wasn't up to the job.'

Turner merely raised his eyebrows, as if that didn't necessarily follow. 'So what now . . . *boss?*'

'We get changed.' Liam gestured towards the yacht. 'Once they're back on dry land, we're good to go.'

Leaving Turner to keep watch, Liam trotted down to the first floor. Priya was in the bedroom she'd used earlier, but the door was shut. The kitbag and the toolbox full of weapons had been placed outside in the hall, a none-too-subtle indication that Liam wasn't welcome to join her.

He carried them into the room opposite. It was a guest bedroom, with a tiny en suite shower room and a minimum of furnishings: just a small double bed and a chest of drawers.

Liam upended the kitbag on the bed. Their uniforms consisted of black boiler suits, black ski masks and gloves and a utility belt that would carry a torch, a Motorola two-way radio and a supply of plasticuffs, along with a choice of weapons.

Turner came in as he was finishing up. 'They just docked.'

'Good.'

Turner picked up a mask and rubbed the material between his fingers. 'This'll itch like crazy. It's still bloody eighty degrees out there.'

'Can't be helped. We don't want the hostages seeing our faces.'

Turner gave a snort. He opened the toolbox and inspected the contents with a connoisseur's eye.

'I reckon it's bullshit, calling them hostages. The kind of firepower we've brought along, there'll be a lot more bodies before this is over.'

Liam shrugged. In the face of such belligerence there wasn't really much he could say.

'Something else,' Turner said, jabbing his finger at Liam. 'I'll be watching my back, just in case some bright spark thinks it's worth slimming down the team when the job's done.'

'Sounds like paranoia to me,' Liam said.

Turner began to speak, but there was a knock on the door and Priya came in. She'd changed into a virtually identical boiler suit, though somehow hers managed to look a whole lot sleeker than theirs. Turner blew a sarcastic whistle, then pointed at the mask in her hand.

'You won't need that, darling. They'll never see you coming, will they?'

Liam winced, but Priya only smiled.

'Actually, you're right,' she said sweetly. 'That's something you may want to think about.'

It took Turner a second to make sense of Priya's threat. Then he chuckled, unperturbed, and watched as she made her selection from the small arsenal of weapons.

'I hear you've already chalked up a kill?'

'What of it?'

'Just curious, that's all. I've been wondering what you were good for.'

'Well, I'm not here to make the tea,' she said. 'Or flatter your ego.' She slipped a Walther P99 into one of the deep pockets of her boiler suit and clipped a sheathed hunting knife to her belt.

''Course you're not, darling.' Turner grinned wolfishly. 'Though I reckon I know what the boss sees in you. A lot of *potential*.'

'That's enough,' Liam said. 'See if the others have finished unloading. If they haven't, tell them to shift their arses.'

He waited until he heard Turner's footsteps on the stairs, then cautioned Priya. 'Don't underestimate him. Just because he's ignorant, it doesn't mean he's not a devious bastard.'

She nodded coolly. 'I know perfectly well what kind of people I'm working with.'

Whether that was a sly dig at him, Liam couldn't tell. Maybe he'd find out later, he thought.

'I'm pairing you with Eldon,' he said. 'I was going to suggest you took the Weavers—'

'I should do Felton,' Priya cut in. 'I've already made contact.'

'You said he didn't answer the door.'

Priya gave him an enigmatic smile. 'I've made contact, believe me. I know I can get inside.'

'All right.' That had actually been his plan all along, but Liam hoped she'd give him credit for taking her ideas on board. 'We'll hit the Weavers, Felton and Terry Fox simultaneously. Then I want one person from each team to join me before we do Nasenko. A lot of people in that house.'

'Okay.'

'I'll take Eldon from your team. I need you to stay with Oliver Felton.' He saw her fuming, and added, 'He could be very important to us. You know that.'

He unclipped the Motorola from his belt, found the channel for the men at the bridge and pressed the talk button.

A gruff voice answered. 'Pendry.'

'Anything there?'

'Quiet as the grave.'

'Good. Ten minutes, and then we move in. Phones will be out by then, so radios only from now on.'

'Gotcha. Let me know when you need me.'

Twenty-Five

It was almost seven o'clock when they reached Midhurst and turned south on the A286. At Joe's suggestion, Cassie had called several hotels and guest houses in Chichester before finding a bed-and-breakfast place that had a room available at short notice.

She'd also spoken to her friends back in Brighton and explained that Sofia had succumbed to a sickness bug. She urged them to party the night away in her absence, and agreed to meet up again very soon.

'But not at the Blue Anchor,' she murmured to herself after ending the call.

Another twenty minutes and they were on the outskirts of Chichester. There was food in the car for Sofia, but Jaden and Cassie were both starving. So was Joe, he realised. He made a detour to the McDonald's on the ring road and bought some takeaway meals.

The B&B was in the centre of town, a couple of minutes from the cathedral. Joe parked in a small courtyard and helped carry the bags inside. The proprietor was a sturdy blonde woman in her mid-thirties. She fussed over the children and seemed perfectly willing to accept Joe's assertion that they were Mr and Mrs Carter and family. If she found the smell of French fries wafting through her lobby distasteful, she politely refrained from saying so.

The room was basic but clean. A good size, with an old-fashioned dresser in addition to two beds: a double and a single. The proprietor had said she would fetch a travel cot for Sofia. There was also a modest TV, a hairdryer and a tray with the usual tea- and coffee-making paraphernalia.

To Joe it represented an improvement on his current living quarters, and sheer luxury compared to some of the places he'd lived in recent years. It was only when he pictured it through Cassie's eyes that he saw what a step down it must be for her. He watched her examine the room, unsure of her reaction.

'All right?'

She nodded vehemently. 'Yes, it's cosy. Safe.'

Jaden shoved a handful of fries into his mouth and gawked at the blank TV screen. He peered behind it, mystified.

'Why's it in a box?'

It took Joe a second to comprehend the question. 'That's how televisions used to look. Before plasma and LCDs.'

He thought Cassie would smile at that, but instead she seemed shocked – perhaps contemplating a life away from Valentin, and the scale of the readjustment that would be required of her children.

After devouring a couple of burgers, Joe used the en suite bathroom to freshen up. When he came out, Jaden was sitting on the bed, watching *The Simpsons*. The TV might be in a box, but at least it had Sky One.

Cassie was feeding Sofia her milk. She didn't notice Joe surreptitiously plucking his Leatherman pocket knife from the rucksack, but a look of panic crossed her face when he picked up the car keys.

'Where are you going?'

'Like you said, we need to find out who was involved.'

'Can't you phone?'

Joe shook his head. 'I want to see his face when I confront him.'

'But it may be dangerous.'

'I can look after myself.'

Cassie nodded. A moment's hesitation, and then she plunged in.

'You've never really said what you did before you went travelling.'

Quid pro quo, he realised, given what she'd revealed to him in the car.

'I was a police officer.'

'I thought so. What kind?'

'CID. Undercover, for the last few years.'

'So what happened? Why did you leave?'

Joe paused, recalling his earlier promise to himself. That the day he told her the truth would be the last day in her employment. Was he going to keep to that promise?

He sighed, and said, 'An undercover op went badly wrong. My identity was compromised, and the gang I'd infiltrated tried to kill me. I managed to get away, but only just. Some of the gang died in the process. As a result there was a price on my head. As far as I know, there still is.'

Cassie gasped. 'That's why you went abroad? One of those witness-relocation programmes?'

'I was offered that, but I made my own arrangements, because it was probably another cop who blew my cover in the first place.'

'So what about your wife and daughters?'

'They had to start over too, with new identities. Helen was furious, quite understandably. She felt I'd put their lives in danger. And she was right.'

'That's why you don't see them?'

He laughed softly. 'It's a bit more complicated than that.'

'Then what?'

'Look, let's sort this out first, then perhaps we'll sit down and discuss it.'

Cassie nodded, with an expression that said she knew she'd been fobbed off. But she didn't push it. Tears shone in her eyes, and she looked away from him.

'I'm really sorry.'

At the door, Joe stopped and said: 'You'll be perfectly safe here, but as a precaution, don't make any phone calls.'

'Not even from my mobile?'

'Especially not that. In fact, I'd switch it off if I were you. It sounds paranoid, but like we said earlier, a certain person might have access to all kinds of technology. If I need to call I'll ring the landline and ask for you.'

'Mrs Carter,' she said, forcing a smile.

'That's it. I'll be back as soon as I can.'

Joe slipped out, shut the door behind him and hurried along the corridor, past the reception area and out through the lobby. An idea struck him as he reached the Shogun. He produced his mobile, deliberated for a moment, then selected one of the preset numbers.

Yuri answered at once. 'Yes?'

'This is Joe. I thought I'd call in.'

'You are at Blue Anchor?'

'Not yet. One of Cassie's friends wanted to meet her separately and have a chat. Some kind of trouble with her husband.'

'Cassie?' said Yuri, confused.

'No. The friend.' Joe gave a grim smile. 'Cassie's delighted with the eternity ring, by the way. She thought it was a very nice touch.'

Yuri made a dismissive noise: not interested.

Joe pushed it. 'Always good to have surprises, isn't it?'

'Where are you now?'

'I told you. Cassie's with one of her friends.'

'In Brighton?'

'No. Timbuktu.' Joe pretended to laugh. 'Of course we're in Brighton. Where else would we be?'

A puzzled silence. Then: 'So when do you go to hotel?'

'Soon, I guess. I'll let you know if there are any changes to the itinerary.' Joe paused a beat. 'How did Valentin's meeting go?'

'It is not finished. We are busy. Call when you get to Blue Anchor.'

Yuri disconnected. Joe stared at the display for a few seconds, reviewing the conversation. Inconclusive, he decided. Nothing that proved Valentin's involvement in the attempted abduction, but nothing that ruled it out either. Yuri definitely seemed a little too interested in Joe's whereabouts.

It was a short journey to Terror's Reach, through an idyllic slice of the English countryside. Once Joe turned off the A259 he was immersed in a world that had barely changed in decades. A world of narrow country lanes, hedgerows bursting with wild flowers and a patchwork of fields where cereal crops grew in vivid greens and golds.

He passed a couple of villages and then he was on the final stretch of road, travelling through the nature reserve with dark copses and heathland all around him. The only destination ahead was the Reach, and the road was deserted. It never ceased to astonish him that a country as small as Britain could have places that felt so lonely, so remote, even when they were just a few miles from a major population centre.

He crested a gentle rise and the island came into view, about a mile and a half away. Immediately Joe saw something that didn't look right. An obstacle on the bridge. He reduced his speed to give himself more thinking time.

It was a vehicle, he realised, partially blocking the road. Something else in front of it. A sign, and a row of barriers.

The bridge was shut.

He made an instant decision. There was a parking area coming up on the left. He turned into it and parked the Shogun behind an avenue of oak trees, where it couldn't be seen from the road.

Now he recalled the Citroën van he'd spotted earlier, next to the ferry shed. Here to do maintenance work, he'd assumed, and maybe that was what it was. But it was odd that they should close the bridge without notifying the residents in advance.

And then there was the other van, the Transit. The driver with the gunslinger's moustache. The strange noise from the back of the vehicle that had aroused Joe's suspicion. According to Maz's colleague, the Transit's registration plates were false.

Lastly, the belligerent fisherman with what might have been a prison tattoo on his neck. The Honda motorbike had been parked at the wrong angle for Joe to see the registration mark, but he wondered now if that too would have come back as false. Three dubious incursions on a single day. Coincidence?

It could be, but he'd learned to be wary of coincidences.

He went the rest of the way on foot. For a mile or so he was able to stay within the nature reserve, threading through a coppice wood of hazel, ash and oak. Closer to the shore, the trees thinned out and finally stopped. The terrain grew flat and marshy. The only concealment was offered by a scattering of gorse and hawthorn bushes.

He managed to work his way to within fifty yards of the bridge. Close enough to see the row of interlocking barriers, and to read a folding yellow sign that said: BRIDGE CLOSED FOR EMERGENCY REPAIRS. It all looked professional enough. So did the two men standing on the bridge, at first glance.

They wore jeans and boots and high-visibility jackets. They weren't engaged in any kind of repair work, emergency or otherwise, although that in itself didn't mark them out as bogus. But after studying them for a minute Joe was convinced they weren't council workers or private contractors. They had the tense, watchful manner of guards, engaged in a crucial but essentially mundane task. Lots of nervous energy and no way to express it.

One strolled across the bridge, while the other wandered down towards the barrier. Their lack of urgency reassured Joe that he hadn't been spotted. Just an occasional routine patrol back and forth, probably to relieve the tedium. But one thing was clear: there was no way past them.

As the man nearest the barrier came closer, Joe realised there was something familiar about him. A couple of seconds later he got a clear look at his face. The change of clothes and the lack of a baseball cap had thrown him, but now he could see who it was.

The fisherman.

✵   ✵   ✵

Joe retreated in search of a better vantage point. The nature reserve was protected from the sea by a ridge of higher ground, from which a broad shingle beach sloped down to the shore. Using the ridge for cover, he ran, almost crouching at times, until he was perhaps half a mile further east. Then he crawled up the bank and took another look at the island.

The bridge was still visible from here, and so were the guards. Beyond that, he could see a sliver of the island's road, heading south. Within ten yards it was obscured by trees and bushes, and then by the high perimeter fence of the old training camp.

Joe studied the bridge for a minute, weighing up his options. Then he slipped out of sight and lay on his back, staring up at the sky. It was a beautiful evening. The air was warm and fragrant, the sun a plump red ball as it sank towards the horizon. Clouds of midges swarmed above the stones. There was no sound except for the cry of birds and the gentle slurp of the sea.

He considered what he knew, what he suspected, and what he might do about it. It appeared that the island had been sealed off, quite deliberately, at a time of day when the residents were unlikely to be coming or going, and passing traffic was practically non-existent. In addition to the men guarding the bridge, he suspected the involvement of the man he'd seen earlier, driving the white Transit with false plates.

Then there was the abduction attempt in Brighton, which might or might not have any relevance to what was happening here. Another coincidence? Feasibly. Another reason to be cautious? Definitely.

The easiest response would be to return to his car, drive back to Chichester and notify the police. Report some suspicious behaviour on the island and leave them to sort it out.

But Joe couldn't see that achieving much. They were just as likely to greet his call with scepticism, particularly if he phoned it in anonymously. If they gave it any credence at all, the investigation would no doubt consist of a single uniformed patrol, two officers at most, driving out to the island with no real expectation of danger. A recipe for tragedy, if something serious was going on over there.

Of course, Joe could tell them who he was. As a former detective sergeant his word might carry slightly more weight. That was, until they made the inevitable inquiries and learned more about his career history.

Putting his head above the parapet now would have all sorts of consequences, none of them positive.

Whichever way he looked at it, Joe was on his own.

Twenty-Six

They assembled in Dreamscape's grand hall: Liam, Priya, Turner, Eldon and Manderson. Allotti had unloaded and activated the mobile-phone jammer, a four-hundred-watt unit capable of blocking signals within a half-mile radius. Then he took the Explorer and drove to the landline junction box, which was situated on the roadside just north of the Nasenko house.

Standing on the stairs, Liam ran through the details one more time.

'In this phase, we concentrate on securing each property. That means accounting for everyone. You make a quick but careful search of the house and grounds. Collect up any mobile phones to give to Allotti. Priya and Turner stay to guard their respective prisoners, while Eldon and Manderson join me to take Nasenko. Okay?'

There were nods, grunts. An exaggerated yawn from Turner.

'Remember, no unnecessary force. Just what it takes to subdue them.' Liam waited out the inevitable sarcasm. 'And at this stage, you remove *nothing*. Not cash, not jewellery: nothing. You leave the place exactly as you find it until Eldon completes an inventory. Anyone caught helping themselves . . .' He looked at each of them in turn. 'The penalty will be severe. Understood?'

Liam's radio vibrated against his hip. The sign he had been waiting for.

He checked his watch. It was two minutes to eight.

'Okay. Phones are out. Let's do it.'

Joe edged back up to the lip of the ridge and crawled along until he found a shallow groove in the path. He slipped off his trainers and tied the laces together, then looped them round his neck. His knife, keys and coins would survive the journey, but he wasn't so sure about his mobile phone. As a precaution he removed the battery and put it in a different pocket.

On the bridge the two men were walking towards each other. They converged on the far side of the van and were hidden from view. That was Joe's cue to move.

He descended the shingle bank, conscious of the noise of the stones crunching underfoot and the low sun throwing out long shadows. He made it to the shore within seconds and slipped into the water, not even pausing to see if he'd been spotted.

The sea was cold enough to make him gasp. Once soaked, his shirt and jeans began to drag against him. He wondered if he should have ditched them, even if it would take some explaining when he got across.

He focused on a point on the island's eastern flank, perhaps three quarters of a mile away. For about half that distance he would be plainly visible from the bridge. By employing a gentle breast stroke he hoped to minimise the disturbance to the surface of the water.

He swam, knowing that he had little choice but to do this. Besides the need to confront Valentin, besides his concerns for the island's residents, there was another reason why Joe couldn't just turn away from Terror's Reach.

Almost everything he possessed was on that island. His passports, his credit cards and cash, and most precious of all, the photographs of his daughters. Those pictures were all he had left; the only remaining link to his past life. No matter what was going on here, or what might happen in the future, he had to get them back.

*   *   *

The fire had been a disappointment. Oliver was sadly out of practice. The porn magazine just blackened and shrivelled to nothing. His father's jacket melted in places, but otherwise refused to burn. And the brandy fumes made him want to retch.

Probably for the best, though. The abortive blaze was fizzling out when Oliver realised he should have shut off the smoke alarm. The house was equipped with an elaborate fire detection system, but when he typed in the code to deactivate it, a message flashed up on the display: INCORRECT.

Oliver swore softly. His father must have changed the code, no doubt a reaction to Rachel's extended stay in New York. It confirmed a long-held suspicion that his sister was employed to keep an eye on him. He wasn't trusted to live here alone.

Bored, he'd roamed the house for a while. He even considered whether he ought to phone for a car and go to Oxford after all. He'd be a few hours late, and would have to dream up a convincing reason for retracting his earlier excuse, but it wasn't impossible.

Except that, on reflection, it seemed like too much effort. Easier to stay where he was. Easier to stay and watch.

For sustenance, Oliver took a bottle of Coke and a bag of tortilla chips up to the attic room. After cautiously checking the view, he decided he could risk another stint on the telescope. He studied what he could see of Dreamscape's grounds, then concentrated on the upper windows, but saw nothing of interest.

He drank some Coke, grazed on the tortilla chips, and waited. The idea of sneaking next door retained a nagging appeal, like an itch when you're too tired to move.

Maybe later. After dark.

And then, in an act of wondrous fate, she appeared right in front of him. Back at the same window as before, where she knew without question that he could see her.

It was a masterful performance. She was teasing, seductive, brilliantly entertaining. She would drift languorously in and out of view, disrobing slowly, item by item. Sometimes she turned her back on him, as when she tackled the clasp of her bra, bending and leaning as it dropped away and a glimpse of heavy breast swayed into sight.

And it was all for Oliver's benefit.

The tension was maddening, and glorious. She wanted him. There was no other explanation.

Or was there?

The idea was like a shard of ice driven through his skull. That this could be an elaborate prank: something you'd encounter on a cheap reality TV show. If so, it could only be his father who had masterminded it.

Oliver let out a sob and flung himself to the floor. Hastily re-arranging his clothes, he curled into a tight ball and peeked out at a world turned alien and hostile. He stared for long minutes at the ceiling, seeking out the dark traitorous eye of a camera.

Eventually the panic receded. He climbed to his feet and conducted a fingertip search of the room. He found nothing. He used the tele-scope to inspect Dreamscape's side elevation. That too was free of hidden cameras.

Not a practical joke, then.

The relief was extraordinary, and it was celebrated with a burst of sound. The intercom.

He stumbled down the stairs, as jerky on his feet as a newborn foal. Elation fought with a desperate lingering fear. It could still be a hoax. It could still be some cruel game of his father's.

But when he looked at the monitor, a cry escaped him. A cry of sheer unadulterated joy.

It was the woman. She had come back to him.

This time he couldn't ignore her. The question of self-denial never entered his head.

He pressed the button to open the gates.

At first Joe kept his head low, his eyeline barely above the surface of the water. The priority was to avoid being noticed by the men on the bridge; navigating a precise route could wait till he was closer to the island.

After a minute he looked towards the Reach to get his bearings. It wasn't there.

He experienced a moment of pure bewilderment. Instinctively he kicked his legs, pushing his head further out of the water. Instead of being straight ahead, the island was a couple of hundred yards to his right. He'd drifted way off course in a matter of seconds.

Not drifted. He was being carried by the currents. Normally he swam from the island's southern shore, so he'd forgotten about the treacherous current that ran through the narrow channel between the mainland and the northern tip of the island.

A gentle breaststroke was no longer an option. To have any chance of getting through the channel he would have to swim a fast, powerful crawl, increasing the risk that the men guarding the bridge would spot him.

Joe had been a good swimmer since childhood, and had always preferred the sea to swimming pools. Now he had to rely on his strength and technique to make it across. With every kick of his legs, every sweep of his arms, he could feel the current working against him, dragging him away from the island. He was moving sideways almost as quickly as he moved forward. Only by swimming at full strength, with no let-up, could he hope to make it across.

Joe shut out all sensation and focused purely on the reasons he was doing this. For Cassie. For Angela Weaver. For his daughters.

Twenty-Seven

The gate opened. On the monitor, Oliver watched the beautiful Asian woman move past the camera. She was wearing some kind of utilitarian black outfit; not particularly revealing. Perhaps she'd had to dress demurely to avoid arousing the suspicions of the men in the house with her.

Oliver swallowed, his mouth as dry as sawdust. He moved towards the front door, knowing he could still change his mind.

But his hand seemed to act independently of his brain, deftly unlocking the door. There was no going back now. The important thing was that he should keep control of his feelings, as well as his actions. He made a vow: *No inappropriate behaviour.*

By the time he opened the door the woman had crossed the driveway with startling haste. In the flesh, she was a magnificent sight, even clad in what looked like workmen's overalls. Curious, he thought. A fetish of some kind?

'Hello,' she said. Her voice was deeper than he expected, with a certain husky promise. 'You're Oliver, aren't you? Oliver Felton?'

He nodded. He couldn't speak.

She held out her hand. 'My name's Priya. It's a thrill to meet you.'

Oliver swallowed again. The word *thrill* rattled around his head like a ball bearing in a pinball machine.

'You too,' he managed. He reached out and took the woman's hand, aware that his own was damp and trembling. The moment of contact would reveal just how grossly unsophisticated he was. He imagined her pulling free and turning away, revolted by his touch.

But she didn't. She held him in a firm grip and stepped closer, looking deep into his eyes. The scent of her body made his head swim. Her lips came together and formed what he felt sure were the beginnings of a kiss.

Their first kiss. Soft and tender, or hard and hungry. Either way, it would be a spectacular milestone. The first woman he hadn't bought outright.

But Priya didn't kiss him.

She punched him in the stomach.

Angela Weaver almost missed the sound of the doorbell. Brel was loping around the back garden, barking at the gulls as they swooped low over the house: a game she would swear both parties played for the sheer pleasure of it.

Besides, callers were few and far between on the Reach. Those who did come here usually announced their arrival well in advance, often phoning for directions in a mild panic as they negotiated the narrow winding road through the nature reserve. Surely an island with such fabulous homes couldn't be so far from anywhere?

There was another explanation for the lack of visitors, of course. She knew all too well that neither she nor Donald made for enthralling company these days. No one in their right mind wanted to risk the possible contagion of the House of Sorrow and Fury.

It wasn't until the cheerful trilling of the bell died out that Angela properly responded to the sound. She had just finished washing up from dinner – they had a dishwasher but rarely accumulated enough dirty crockery to justify using it – when Donald called from the living room.

'Who on earth can that be?'

You could always answer it and find out, she thought, an uncharitable response that later she would regret.

She dried her hands on a tea towel and hurried to the front door. Through the frosted-glass panel she could see the outline of a man's head and upper body.

As she opened the door she heard movement in the next room: that would be Donald making himself decent. He was a martyr to trapped wind, and after a meal had an irritating tendency to sit with his trousers undone, massaging his lower abdomen.

Angela opened the door and gave a start. What she saw defied logic. For a moment it seemed as though the man had remained a silhouette rather than becoming three-dimensional. Then she identified a pair of narrow, rheumy eyes and understood he was wearing a full face mask.

There was a cry from the living room: Donald must have gone to the window. He was shouting at her to shut the door, but even while she struggled to process the message another masked figure darted into view, pushing past her and into the house.

Angela turned, making an ineffectual bid to stop him. She heard a scrabbling on the tiled kitchen floor as Brel raced towards them. He reached the hall, snarling with a ferocity that made him unrecognisable. Before he could attack, the man lifted his arm, revealing an ugly black pistol with a silencer. He fired twice, and Angela's beloved Labrador collapsed with an audible and very human-sounding groan.

For a full second no one moved. No one spoke.

Then Donald was in the doorway, his face bloodless and contorted with shock. The gunman shifted, training the weapon on him. Donald glanced at it, tried to say something, but all that emerged was a cry of incoherent rage. Angela saw a madness light up his eyes, a madness fuelled by two years of bitter, unrelenting grief at the death of their son.

The gunman growled a warning, but Donald didn't hear it. Didn't hear it or didn't care. He threw himself forward and swung a fist at the man. Angela screamed, but the other intruder grabbed her by the throat, pinning her to the spot.

'Stupid fucker . . .' The gunman batted away Donald's first blow, but he kept coming, baring his teeth, swinging his fists like a drunken barroom brawler. He wasn't going to back down, no matter what sort of threats they made. He was way beyond reason, way beyond self-preservation.

The gunman fired at point-blank range. One bullet, straight into Donald's heart. The furious light in his eyes still blazed as his legs gave way and he collapsed, his brain not yet comprehending that it was over. All the pain and loss and sorrow, finally ended.

Priya worked out with an almost religious fervour. Boxing was a major part of her fitness regime. She was proud of the power she could impart, and the extent to which it took her opponents by surprise.

Oliver Felton didn't stand a chance. A stranger to exercise, he was tall and lanky, with a mop of curly brown hair and pale blotchy skin. He probably weighed a little more than Priya, but had a fraction of her muscle tone.

She watched the lust on his face fade and die like an overpriced firework. When the punch landed he staggered back and fell, crying out as the impact jarred his coccyx. He was wearing expensive but unfashionable jeans and a long-sleeved cotton shirt, buttoned tightly at the wrists and throat. She realised why when she felt the air conditioning working at full blast, cold enough to make her flinch.

Priya glanced round. Eldon was through the gate and sprinting across the drive. He had his ski mask on, and he was holding a Glock pistol at his side. That made her nervous. Eldon was about as much a shooter as Oliver was a fighter.

He reached the front door and slowed, panting noisily through the mask. Earlier he'd queried why she wasn't using hers.

'No point,' she'd said. 'We have history.'

Now he took in Oliver Felton, sitting dumbstruck and almost tearful on the floor, and regarded her with admiration.

'Wow. I thought we'd have to get past all sorts of alarms and stuff.'

'No. Just him.' She looked to Oliver for confirmation. 'Anyone else here?'

Oliver frowned a moment, as though he had to translate what she was saying. He shook his head.

'Good.' Priya kicked the front door shut. Pulled a pair of latex gloves from her pocket and put them on. Horrified, Oliver scrambled away from her, his feet slipping and squeaking on the marble floor. His prominent Adam's apple worked frantically, bobbing up and down above his collar.

At last he got the words out. 'What are you . . . what is this?'

'What do you think it is?'

'I don't know. A robbery?' Even as he said it, he seemed to relax a little. 'You've come to steal from my father?'

Priya nodded. 'Not just him. The whole island.'

Oliver stared at her for what seemed a long time, as if translating again. Then he shook his head, disbelieving. Finally he grinned. When he spoke, his voice bore the same note of admiration as Eldon's.

'What a fantastic idea.'

The gunman dragged Donald into the living room. His accomplice took Angela at knifepoint, forcing her to lie down on the floor next to her husband's body. When she tried to look at him the man slapped her face.

'Please,' she cried. 'Please don't do this.'

She heard a snigger from the gunman, as though he took an active pleasure from her distress. The other man bound her hands behind her back, using some sort of plastic cuffs. His flesh gave off the hot, meaty stench of ingrained body odour. Her skin crawled every time he touched her.

'See if he's alive,' she implored them. 'Don't let him bleed to death.'

'Shut up.'

'Please,' Angela said again. 'We have hardly anything worth stealing, but take it all. Just let me see my husband. Let me help him, if I can.'

The gunman shook her head. 'Will you get the message? He's dead as a dodo.'

'Why did you shoot him?' she asked.

'The stupid fucker came at me,' the gunman said. 'I had no choice.'

No choice. The fallback of every Nazi, every Stalinist, every craven bureaucrat. Angela could scarcely contain her disgust. She fell silent. Rested her cheek on the carpet and felt a tear squeeze from her eye.

By tying her up and keeping their faces hidden, she understood that they didn't necessarily intend to kill her. But it gave her little comfort. At that moment she would have welcomed death. She had nothing left to live for.

Nothing, except perhaps for the first tiny spark of a desire for revenge.

Liam stood outside Dreamscape, the ski mask in his pocket. He tipped his head back and shut his eyes, savouring the warmth of the setting sun. The brilliant orange glow through his eyelids seemed like the colour of success, the colour of victory.

A gentle breeze had sprung up, stirring the thick air, flavouring it with the faint tang of salt water. The distant cry of gulls took him back to the summers of his childhood. Grim holiday camps on the north-west coast: soggy chips, dreary skies and an aching, pulverising boredom.

After tonight he would never know boredom again. He would anticipate its onset and spend his way out of it.

Priya and Eldon had gone next door a couple of minutes ago. Liam wondered how Priya intended to play it with Oliver Felton. He regretted not being able to watch her in action.

At the sound of an engine he opened his eyes. Allotti was in the Ford Explorer. Liam directed him to park outside the footballer's residence, tight up to the boundary wall. The wall was of brick construction, about seven feet high, topped with some kind of decorative tile. No deterrent to a serious intruder. The real security had been provided by live-in bodyguards, but they'd accompanied the footballer and his family to Rome. Only the father-in-law living there now.

There was an intercom, but Liam decided not to use that. With no plausible reason to bluff his way in, he felt a different approach was called for.

He put on the mask and drew his gun. A 9 mm Glock 17, with a silencer. He racked the slide to make sure there was a round in the chamber, then tucked it back into his belt.

He clambered onto the bonnet of the Explorer and up onto the wall. Allotti climbed up alongside him. They paused for a second and examined the house. A couple of first-floor windows were open, but there was no one in sight.

They dropped down onto a small area of lawn that ran alongside the driveway. Followed a concrete path to the front door, where Liam stopped and listened. He could hear music playing inside. Some kind of opera.

He led Allotti to the corner of the house, made sure it was clear, then crept along the path towards the rear. Allotti's breathing, muffled by the mask, sounded like a poor impersonation of Darth Vader.

Liam peered round the corner. A stone terrace ran the full width of the property. In the centre there was a round aluminium table with two chairs. Terry Fox was sitting in one and had his feet propped up on the other. He was angled away from them, reading a magazine and sipping a glass of red wine.

He was wearing blue swimming shorts and leather sandals. For a man in his early sixties he looked in good shape. The muscles in his arms and legs were still well-defined, and he had only a slight paunch. His skin was the colour of mahogany, with a nest of white hairs on his chest.

The music was louder here. The singer was possibly one of those fat fellas from the World Cup concert, all those years ago. Opera had never been Liam's thing, but now it came in useful, covering the sound of their approach.

Liam walked towards the table, with Allotti just behind him. It took a few seconds before Fox registered their presence. First he looked up from the magazine and stared straight ahead, across the bay. Then, slowly, he turned his head in their direction. He had close-cropped silver hair and the strong, rugged features of an ageing movie star.

His eyes went from the guns to the masks, then back to the guns. His hand jerked, slopping the wine in the glass. A couple of drips landed on his chest and he glanced down, studying the wine as though it might be the cause of this hallucination.

Then he lifted the glass to his mouth and drained it in one quick gulp. Smacked his lips together and declared: 'Well, bugger me.'

'No, thanks,' said Liam. 'Your daughter, maybe.' He moved closer, saw the magazine was one of those glossy, celebrity-fixated rags. 'Is that how you find out what she's up to?'

Fox snorted. 'Funny.' Then: 'She is in this one, as it happens. She's got a new puppy. And a new tattoo.'

He put the glass down, tossed the magazine aside and sat back. Laced his fingers together and rested them on his stomach, a picture of mature composure.

'So what now?' he asked. 'Stand and deliver?'

Liam nodded. 'Something like that.'

Twenty-Eight

The swim was a battle, but at no time did Joe ever consider that it was one he might lose. Partly it was experience, partly his training, and partly just the way he was wired. If giving up had been in his nature he'd have done it years ago, the day his wife and daughters were placed out of his reach.

Eventually the pull of the current weakened and he began to make better progress, slicing through the water with clean, fast strokes. The island's eastern coast was rocky and inhospitable, but Joe managed to weave his way through without getting cut to pieces, and finally he came ashore on one of the intermittent stretches of shingle beach.

He crawled out of the water and collapsed. After resting for a couple of minutes, he checked himself over. His jeans were torn and he'd picked up a few scratches, but they weren't serious. He took a look at his phone. He had nothing to dry it with, and decided not to risk putting the battery back in yet.

Ahead of him, the beach rose steeply for about fifty feet, then gave way to clumps of brambles and blackthorn, growing along the side of the high chain-link fence that enclosed the old training camp. To reach the far side of the island, Joe would have to circle round the coast and head inland somewhere close to the road.

He put his trainers on and laced them up. They squelched with every step but still allowed him to move a lot faster across the beach.

He set off at a run, not yet dwelling too much on what might lie ahead. Better to have an open mind and face each challenge as it arose. After what had already happened today, he didn't think there was much more that could surprise him.

He was wrong.

Terry Fox seemed more resigned than afraid. There was a polo shirt draped over the chair. Before submitting meekly to the handcuffs, he asked if he could put it on. Liam felt irritated that the old guy wasn't begging for mercy, but he wouldn't let it spoil the moment. Better that everyone should surrender so easily.

Leaving Allotti to deal with Fox, Liam made his way through the house, barely glancing at what was on offer. As he'd suspected, the footballer and his wife had never really left their roots behind. There was very little art on display, and what they had was mostly tat. Every single picture on the wall was a portrait of themselves.

Liam found the control panel which opened the main gates and let himself out through the front door. He tore off the mask and wiped sweat from his face. He'd be glad when this stage was complete and he didn't have to wear the bloody thing any more.

Eldon was waiting for him by the Ford Explorer. He sounded hyper as he described how Priya had waltzed past Oliver Felton.

'It was like he was expecting her,' he said. 'I dunno who he thought she was. I swear he had a hard-on.'

Liam nodded vaguely, as though this didn't interest him much. Then Manderson lumbered into view, and just from the grim satisfaction on his face Liam had an instant premonition: *the Weavers were dead.*

'Had to snuff one of 'em,' Manderson said.

'Who? Why?'

'The geezer. Silly fucker went apeshit on us. Threw himself at Turner. He had to put him down.' Manderson mimed a gun with two gloved fingers and made an explosive sound, as though words alone couldn't convey the message.

Liam sighed. 'The next target is a lot more important. No casualties unless it's absolutely unavoidable. You clear on that?'

Both men nodded, though Manderson's savage grin didn't inspire confidence. One of the many stories about Manderson was that he'd once beheaded a man with an axe. Looking at him now, Liam could believe it.

Once again they masked up, drew their weapons and set off on foot. They rounded the bend in the road and Nasenko's house came into view.

They were less than ten feet from the edge of the property when a man in a plain grey suit wandered out through the gates, cupping his hand around a cigarette as he lit up. He glanced in their direction, saw three masked men carrying guns, and reacted faster than they did.

He didn't freeze or do a double take, and he didn't run back into the house. He took off along the road, heading towards the bridge. Maybe thought his chances were better out in the open. He'd probably forgotten how isolated it was here.

Manderson dropped into a shooting stance, but Liam grabbed his arm. He didn't want gunfire out in the street; not when they hadn't yet taken Nasenko.

'Go after him,' he told Manderson. At the same time he unclipped his radio and called Pendry.

'The American's driver is coming your way on foot, with Manderson on his tail. Make sure he doesn't get away.'

It took Joe several minutes to round the curve onto the north-east coast of the island. From here the mainland was in clear view. Joe could see the point on the ridge opposite where he had formed his plan to swim across. In the soft evening light the narrow strip of water in between looked deceptively benign.

The foliage along the top of the beach grew thickly enough to conceal him, but after another hundred yards it began to thin out. Eventually he reached the last of the bushes and made the unfortunate discovery that he didn't know the island as well as he'd thought.

He was trapped. Caught in a corridor between the sea to his right and the MoD land to his left. The north-west corner of the training camp extended to within a few yards of the road. The only way Joe could move was directly ahead, across a patch of open ground. The bridge lay beyond it, about fifty feet away. The fisherman from earlier in the day was on the bridge, lounging against the Citroën van. The other guard was pacing up and down the approach road.

Joe reviewed his options. The light was fading, but it wasn't dark enough for him to sneak past. In any case, the ground underfoot was a mixture of soil, sand and pebbles. If he tried to move quickly they would hear him. If he moved slowly he would be seen.

That left two choices. One was to breach the fence and go across the training camp. The other was to take the direct route. Rush the two men and overpower them.

A big decision. Before Joe could make it, the man pacing the road reached for something in his pocket. A two-way radio. He listened, then made a brief reply. From this distance, Joe could see that he was in his forties, plump and sandy-haired.

Replacing the radio, he shouted, 'Gough' and gestured at the fisherman, who picked up on the note of urgency and propelled himself away from the van. The older one relayed a message, then both men drew ski masks and pistols from within their fluorescent jackets.

Joe froze, wondering if he'd been spotted, perhaps by a hidden accomplice. Had there been another guard, posted somewhere along the route he'd just come?

He prepared for the worst – not afraid; just angry with himself. Angry at the prospect of failure.

But the guards showed no awareness of his presence. Both put on their masks and took up positions behind the van. They were facing inland, as though expecting a threat from the interior of the island. Joe had no idea what was happening, but it put paid to any thoughts of a direct assault. Pitching the short blade of his pocket knife against two handguns would be suicidal.

That left just one option, for which his multi-tool was far better suited. He shifted up to the fence, lay flat and used the wire cutter to create a flap large enough to crawl through. It took him a couple of minutes. He was confident the guards couldn't see or hear him, but that didn't stop him glancing round every few seconds.

He wriggled through the gap, his wet clothes slithering across the grass and weeds. He'd just got clear of the fence when one of the men shouted: 'Hey!'

Liam watched Manderson set off in pursuit of the American's driver. There was no question of waiting for him to return. He and Eldon would have to take Nasenko on their own.

The routine was the same as with Terry Fox. They hurried across the drive, keeping a sharp eye on the front of the house. Crept along the path at the side and reached the back door. Liam checked his gun, took a breath and opened the door.

He stepped into a boot room. Saw wet-weather gear and fishing rods and a pile of inflatable beach toys. There was a toilet or shower room to his right, and the kitchen lay straight ahead.

Liam entered the kitchen. It was empty apart from the maid, a thick set Hispanic woman. She was cleaning a marble worktop, putting real effort into it. When she saw him she dropped the cloth, slapping her hands over the counter as if groping for a weapon. Liam was impressed. In this house even the maid fancied herself as a warrior. He pointed the gun at her face and shook his head: *Don't be silly.*

Eldon cuffed her hands behind her back, then Liam took a step closer, prodding the gun into her ample belly.

'Where are they?'

The maid's eyes flashed. 'Yuri will kill you.'

Liam shoved the gun in harder, and she groaned. Her whole body was trembling with fear and rage.

'Where?'

Another moment of defiance, then she flicked her head upwards. 'Office,' she said. 'Up the stairs, turn left.'

Once inside the training camp, the ground fell away into a large natural depression. This, combined with the thick vegetation that grew along the western perimeter fence, meant that very little of the camp was visible from the road.

The shout was still echoing through the air when Joe sprinted down the bank and back up towards the bushes on the adjacent corner. A distant part of his mind prepared for the sudden punch of a bullet, followed by oblivion.

But it didn't happen. As he got closer to the fence on the western side he could hear movement from the road beyond. Thudding footsteps and a harsh, desperate panting. Someone running fast towards the bridge.

The older guard shouted again, real venom in his voice. The rhythm of the footsteps altered. Joe found a patch of bracken and carefully parted the fronds, easing himself amongst them until he could see through the fence.

The runner was directly in front of him, about thirty feet from the bridge. Joe recognised the grey suit of the Cadillac driver. His face was pale and glistening with sweat. He stumbled to a halt and almost collapsed. The older guard hurried towards him while the fisherman remained at the bridge, holding his pistol in a two-handed grip.

'On your knees,' the guard commanded.

The driver obeyed like a man who was only just in control of his own body, dropping to the ground with a thump that made Joe wince. Then another masked gunman ran into view. This one wore a black boiler suit, with a utility belt that held a two-way radio and half a dozen plasticuffs.

He stopped behind the driver, aiming his gun at the back of the man's head. He was obviously out of breath, and his gun hand was unsteady. If he fired now, it would be a messy execution.

But the guard shook his head. 'Not here. Take him back, let Liam decide what to do with him.'

The gunman muttered something, shoved his gun in his belt and took out one of the plastic restraints. He cuffed the driver's hands and pulled him to his feet. The older guard conferred briefly with the fisherman, Gough. Then he rejoined the gunman and they escorted their prisoner away.

Gough returned to his original position on the bridge, next to the van. He took off his mask but kept his gun at the ready. The incident with the driver had obviously made an impression. He looked a lot more alert than before.

Joe found himself replaying this afternoon's incident on the beach, wondering if there was some clue he had missed. He realised that Gough must have been reconnoitring the island. He'd probably had the gun on him, even then. If Joe had escalated the row about litter, both he and Jaden might have ended up dead.

Joe was conscious of the loathing he felt for the man who'd run Angela Weaver off her bike. Reluctantly he concluded that there was no way he could sneak up on the bridge. Any thoughts of retribution would have to wait.

He turned away, descended the grassy slope and followed a route parallel to the road. This corner of the camp was open ground, dotted with bushes and the occasional small pond. It was a good running surface, the grass springy and soft, although he had to watch out for molehills and rabbit burrows. The last thing he needed right now was a broken ankle.

While he ran, he analysed what he'd seen so far. The guns and two-way radios showed this was a serious, well-organised operation. The masks and the cuffs implied that the gang were intent on taking prisoners, rather than killing indiscriminately. That meant the island's residents could still be alive, in which case Joe's objectives were clear. He had to find them, and help them escape.

He also had no illusions about his own predicament. If he was caught, there was a fair chance they would kill him.

Angela Weaver had advised him to come to terms with his anger. Learn to live with it, she'd said, whether dormant or awake. She'd even suggested it might be there for a purpose.

Well, she got that right, he thought.

And now it was very much awake.

Twenty-Nine

The sound of voices swam into range as Liam and Eldon climbed the stairs. They'd tied the maid's ankles and gagged her with a cloth, then shut her in the boot room as an extra precaution.

The kitchen aside, the house was a lot more traditional than Dreamscape: thickly carpeted, with dense wallpaper and dark wood. It might have been built to endure harsh Ukrainian winters; on the balmy English coast it felt gloomy and stifling. The faint aroma of cigar smoke added to the impression of a fusty old gentlemen's club.

They reached a wide landing. The first door to the left was closed. They heard the American speaking, then a burst of laughter from McWhirter. Liam nodded to Eldon: *Are you ready?*

Instead of affirmation, Eldon's eyes betrayed panic. 'Four against two,' he whispered.

'It's okay,' Liam said. And it really was. He wasn't faking how calm he felt.

He turned the handle and threw the door open. He was first into the room, and for a second he wondered if Eldon would let him down, just turn and run. Then he felt movement at his side, saw the shock on the faces of the room's occupants, and he knew it was going to be all right.

Valentin Nasenko was seated behind a desk so imposing that his laptop looked the size of a playing card. The American visitor, Travers, was seated opposite, staring over his shoulder at Liam.

The lackeys, McWhirter and Yuri, were standing at either side of the room. McWhirter looked like he was going to pass out. He grabbed the edge of an antique roll-top bureau for support.

Yuri wore a tiny, bitter smile. His hand reached slowly towards his pocket, but stopped when Liam turned the gun on him. 'Uh-uh.'

'Who are you?' Valentin demanded. He half rose from his seat, waving his arms as though shooing away cattle.

'Sit down,' Liam ordered. 'Hands flat on the table. The rest of you, face down on the floor, hands behind your backs.'

For a second, nothing happened. No one spoke. No one moved.

Liam fired the Glock, aiming for the wall a couple of feet above Nasenko's head. The bullet struck a small framed watercolour of a Ukrainian landscape. The shell casing rattled across the floor and came to rest at McWhirter's feet.

Valentin blinked rapidly. He sat down and placed his hands on the desk.

The American sniffed, as though he didn't think much of English hospitality. He looked from Yuri to McWhirter.

'We better do as he says, gentlemen.'

Priya consulted her watch again. It was only a few minutes since Eldon had gone to join Liam and already time was dragging.

But there was a plan to adhere to, and she had to accept that. She knew it was prudent to keep the prisoners in their own homes until the whole island was secure. She just hadn't foreseen that she'd be the one left to babysit.

Of course, the Felton house was supposed to have been empty. It wasn't really Liam's fault that their reconnaissance had been inadequate. He'd argued that surveillance risked more than it gained, and Gough's little confrontation on the beach had proved him right.

'You're eager to get on with it?'

Oliver's voice made Priya jump. She glanced at him but said nothing. The silence resumed, intensified by the whirr of the air conditioning.

They were sitting in the principal living room on the ground floor, a massive space with a minimalist decor of marble, steel and leather. There were no soft fabrics and virtually no colour. The overall effect was bleak and impersonal. She couldn't imagine anyone truly relaxing in here.

Oliver Felton continued to watch her. His confidence had been growing from the moment he'd realised they weren't going to kill him on the spot. He seemed entranced, not just by her, but by the situation.

She remembered what Liam had said: *a sandwich short of a picnic.* Not a phrase she'd heard before, but its meaning was clear enough.

And it certainly seemed appropriate. Her impression was that Oliver had a whole range of issues. He was a voyeur. Socially inadequate, withdrawn, perhaps slightly autistic. He also displayed various tics and gestures that she'd seen before in people with obsessive-compulsive disorders.

In short, he was a mess.

After a minute or two he tried again. 'You're waiting for a signal of some kind. Confirmation that the other residents have capitulated?'

It was phrased as a question. Priya couldn't help but shrug in response.

Oliver smiled. He was sitting very precisely in the centre of a black leather sofa, his long thin legs pressed together. His arms were also together, partly because of the restraints on his wrists. His hands, one cupping the other in a fist, rested on his knees. It was a posture that invited him to curl into a ball, but he seemed to be resisting that urge, holding his head abnormally high.

'The Weavers will be easy enough,' he said, 'though Donald has a fierce temper on him, especially since his son ended up as roadkill. You know about that?'

Priya nodded.

'I bet Terry Fox was a tough nut in his younger days, but that was a long time ago. His bitch of a daughter will be fuming that she missed out on the excitement. Think of all the photo spreads. *My Robbery Hostage Hell!*' Oliver giggled, then grew thoughtful. 'If there's anyone you have to worry about, it's Valentin Nasenko. No one hates being robbed more than another thief.'

'Nasenko's a thief?'

Oliver frowned, as though he expected better of her. 'Of course he is. Growing up under a communist regime, it wasn't hard work and entrepreneurial spirit that made him rich. He was just in the right place at the right time. By accident or good fortune he was able to plunder state assets and get away with it.'

He paused for breath, licking his lips. 'And good luck to him. Most of us would do it if we had the chance. But be aware – just because Nasenko stole and bribed and extorted his way to a fortune, it doesn't mean he won't be *livid* when someone does the same to him. It's a curious moral universe these men inhabit.'

Priya nodded, as though she took his ravings seriously. *'These men?'*

'Oh, I fully include my father amongst their number. I mean, he came from family money, took their wealth and grew it spectacularly. But it's tainted with blood, every last penny.'

He must have seen that she didn't understand, and he laughed. 'My God, you're either very naive or you haven't done your research. The family fortune was built on arms dealing. They call it the "defence industry", as if that fools anyone. I mean, when you're in the factory, watching a rocket launcher being lovingly packed in a crate, you don't stand there picturing how wonderful it'll look on someone's mantelpiece. Do you?'

He sucked in the excess saliva bubbling at the corners of his mouth. Priya looked away.

'Of course you don't. What you're picturing is how effectively that weapon will obliterate a peaceful little village suspected of harbouring terrorists.'

Priya nodded. Her radio buzzed, but with Oliver in full flow she ignored it. She sensed he was building up to something.

'If you're in the arms trade, your product is death. Maybe the drones on the production line can delude themselves that they don't contribute to the suffering in the world, but the men at the top know exactly what they're doing. Some struggle, then learn to live with it. Some never have a problem in the first place.' He smiled. 'My father falls into the latter category, and that's why you're welcome to his money.'

She stared at him, wondering if she'd misheard. Her radio buzzed again. She had to answer, or Liam would think the worst.

Angry at the interruption, Oliver began to rock back and forth, pressing his arms down hard on his thighs, digging his elbows into his groin.

On the radio, Liam told her: 'Terror's Reach is ours. We're moving the non-essentials to Dreamscape.'

'And mine?'

'Keep him there. I want to talk to him.'

Priya put the radio down. Oliver was rocking faster, the forward motion nearly tipping him on to the floor. His eyes gleamed with an unnatural fervour.

'You look disappointed,' he said.

'Not really.'

'You're jealous of someone. They're not giving you the respect you deserve.'

'What you said about your father's money. You mean that?'

'Of course I do.' Oliver stopped rocking, but his elbows remained wedged into his abdomen, concealing – or perhaps assisting – his arousal. 'I'll open the safe for you, if you want.'

After half a mile or so, Joe knew he had gone as far as he could while staying parallel to the road. From here the training camp veered left, while the road towards the residential part of the island turned to the right, with the woods in between.

As he crossed the uneven ground a cluster of buildings came into view. They looked oddly familiar: a terrace of half a dozen modest dwellings that might have been plucked from a council estate in 1970s Belfast or Armagh, complete with a sectarian mural on the gable-end wall. There was even a small playground, with a roundabout and a set of swings. Within the confines of a military establishment, it looked eerie and out of place.

Just beyond the playground a picnic table rested on a weed-strewn patch of grass. There was a man sitting at the table. He wore a blue jacket and a bright red scarf. The sight of him made Joe's stomach lurch – until he realised he was looking at a dummy. A mannequin, presumably used during training exercises, now frozen in time and place, redundant.

Feeling foolish, Joe turned away from the houses and approached the boundary fence. There were thick bushes on both sides that would give him cover as he cut his way through the wire. From here he calculated that he was only a couple of hundred yards from Valentin Nasenko's property.

He took out his multi-tool and knelt down. And immediately sensed someone watching him. He spun, looking first at the picnic table, half-convinced that the dummy in the red scarf would have gone. But it hadn't moved.

Then he noticed he was overlooked by the last house in the terrace. There was a figure behind the curtains in the upstairs window. Another mannequin.

Get a grip, Joe told himself. He turned back and started work on the fence.

Liam stayed close to the door, from where he could cover the prisoners while Eldon applied the cuffs and patted each man down for weapons and phones. They found a gun on Yuri, a Sig 9 mm automatic pistol. More surprising was that the American had an illegal folding knife in his jacket.

'Didn't trust your hosts?' Liam asked.

Travers smiled ruefully, but said nothing. Of the four men it was McWhirter who looked most afraid. He was visibly upset, casting desperate glances at Valentin and then at Yuri, as if he felt sure that one or both had it within them to produce a miracle solution.

Once they were all secure, Liam made Yuri, Travers and McWhirter sit in a line against the wall. With their hands tied behind their backs they had no way of rising quickly to their feet. He left Nasenko at his desk, his hands cuffed from the front.

Liam sent Eldon to search the house for more phones or weapons, then radioed an update to the other teams. He pulled up the chair vacated by Travers and sat down, swinging a foot up on to the table. He waited a moment, relishing the knowledge that he had the un-divided attention of everyone in the room.

'I hope we all understand what's going on here,' Liam said. 'Keep it civilised, and no one has to come to harm.'

'You won't get away with this,' McWhirter said, his voice an octave too high.

'We will hunt you down,' Yuri added.

But it was Valentin who remained cool and businesslike. 'What do you want?'

'It's nice and simple,' Liam said. 'You open up your vault. We empty it. We leave. You claim on your insurance. Nobody loses.'

'Nice and simple,' Valentin echoed. 'You think I can allow this to happen?'

Still facing Nasenko, Liam held his arm out at his side, aiming loosely at the three other prisoners. In his peripheral vision he saw McWhirter squirming, Travers and Yuri sitting stock-still, glaring at Liam.

Eldon came back in, holding another handgun and several more phones. He picked up on the tension and loitered uneasily by the door.

'You have no choice,' Liam said.

Valentin spoke softly. 'Leave now, and I will treat this as a mistake. A foolish misjudgement. But go through with it, and I promise you will never get to enjoy what you took from me.'

Liam sighed. He steadied his arm, checked his aim with an almost lazy glance at the three men against the wall, and then fired without warning. One shot. It hit McWhirter in the chest and killed him instantly. His head flopped onto Travers's shoulder. The American shifted sideways in disgust.

'Jesus Christ,' he said. To Valentin: 'Open the damn vault, will you?'

Valentin regarded Yuri, who scowled for a moment, then nodded.

'Very well,' said Valentin heavily.

As Liam stood up there was a commotion from the hall. Manderson and Pendry hauled the American's driver into the room. His face was covered in blood.

'He got a bit mouthy on the way back,' Manderson said.

'All right,' said Liam. 'Take them along to Dreamscape. Everyone except Nasenko.' He gestured to Eldon. 'You'd better get the maid.'

'You okay here on your own?'

Liam nodded. He felt shaky and light-headed from the adrenalin rush, but he was disguising it well.

He watched as the prisoners were led from the room. Apart from a few muttered obscenities from Yuri, no one said anything. McWhirter's body was left slumped against the wall. There was very little blood visible. He looked as though he'd passed out after a heavy drinking session.

Patiently Liam waited through the tramping of feet on the stairs, and a distant thump as Eldon fetched the maid from the boot room. Finally the house was silent. Empty but for the two of them.

Liam turned back to Valentin Nasenko. The Ukrainian hadn't moved. He was gazing intently at his desk, and he didn't react when Liam tore off his mask and slowly drew the knife from his belt.

'Ready to open the vault?' Liam said.

'Yes.'

Valentin rose to his feet. He thrust out his hands. Liam came around the desk and cut him free. For a moment the two men shared a sad, awkward smile, like strangers at a funeral.

Then they embraced, and clapped each other on the back.

Thirty

The true force of her grief didn't hit Angela Weaver until she had been marched along the road to Dreamscape, led through the house and deposited in the garage. Sitting on the dusty concrete floor, her hands bound painfully behind her back, it finally struck home that this was not a dream, not a hallucination or a practical joke.

Donald was dead, and now she too might die.

Tears leaked from her eyes, almost grudgingly. The air in the garage was stuffy and nauseating, but her body felt as though it had been plunged in ice. She began shivering, and then vomited without warning.

The guard snarled at the mess. 'You're gonna stink now, you silly bitch.'

Another prisoner was escorted in and thrown down beside her. Angela recognised him as the father of the footballer's wife. *Terry someone*, she thought, and felt ashamed. There had never been much community spirit on the Reach, and for that she and Donald bore as much responsibility as anyone else.

Once he'd taken in his surroundings, he shifted so he could see Angela better. His eyes narrowed with concern.

'Are you all right?'

She nodded, then saw the absurdity of reaching for platitudes in a situation like this.

'Actually, no. They murdered my husband.'

'Jesus. I'm sorry.' He regarded her for a moment in sombre silence. 'I'm Terry Fox. Trina's dad.'

Angela introduced herself. They watched as her guard strode back into the house, leaving them alone with the man who had brought Fox. His manner seemed less threatening than his colleague's. Certainly Terry didn't seem intimidated by him.

'Hey! Get this woman cleaned up. You can't leave her like this.'

'Shut up,' the guard said. He was leaning against the bonnet of a Renault Mégane, inspecting a number of mobile phones. Angela remembered that the Mégane belonged to the estate agent. She hardly dared contemplate what must have happened to him.

'Look, I don't care if you're going to rob us,' Terry said, 'but you can bloody well treat this lady with a bit of respect.'

He kept up the protest until finally the guard relented and fetched a wad of paper towels and a glass of water. He knelt down at her side and hesitated.

'Let her do it herself,' Terry said.

To Angela's astonishment, the guard proceeded to cut her restraints. He drew his gun and kept a close eye on her while she mopped her blouse and rinsed her mouth with water. Afterwards Terry tried to persuade him to leave her hands free, but the guard wasn't having it.

'Cuff her in front, at least. She's no threat to you.'

Once again the guard complied, but he didn't just tie her wrists. He bound her ankles as well. Then he did the same to Terry, before returning to his collection of mobile phones.

'Thank you,' said Angela.

Terry nodded. 'Thank me later, when we get out of here.'

Angela was taken aback. Until now it hadn't occurred to her that she might have any kind of future beyond tonight.

Her pessimism seemed justified when three more of the gang trooped through the house and into the garage. They had four prisoners with them. She recognised Valentin Nasenko's maid and bodyguard, but not the other two men. Her heart jumped as she wondered what had happened to the family – and most of all, to Joe.

She didn't particularly care for Valentin himself. He had always struck her as a mean-spirited man, given to petulant tantrums. By contrast his young wife seemed friendly and sweet-natured, if rather shy, and her children were adorable. Angela prayed that no harm had come to them.

And then there was Joe. She knew he possessed the skills to put up a fierce resistance to these men, but he was hopelessly outnumbered. She had to consider the very real possibility that he too was dead.

Joe stayed close to the trees until he was level with the southern flank of Nasenko's property. Then he dashed across the road to the cover of the boundary wall. He crept towards the gates and almost immediately heard voices. Someone coming out of the house.

There was no time to reach the trees. He ran back to the corner and ducked down behind the wall. Heard what sounded like several people walking across the drive and onto the road. If they turned towards the bridge they'd spot him instantly.

He waited, heart pounding, but the footsteps receded. After a few seconds he risked a look. He counted seven figures, moving briskly towards the other homes on the Reach. Four prisoners and three guards. One was the older man from the bridge, still in his high-visibility jacket. The other two were in the same black uniforms. The four prisoners were Maria, Yuri, the American he'd seen in the Cadillac, and his driver.

Joe watched them disappear round the bend in the road. The Cadillac driver must have evaded the initial attack on the house. They'd chased him to the bridge and brought him back here. Now he and the other prisoners were being taken . . . where? Some kind of central command point?

Dreamscape, he guessed, since that was the only empty property on the island. Then he realised he had posed the wrong question. There was another, more critical issue.

Why had they made a detour into Nasenko's house?

Oliver felt he was making excellent progress with Priya. Even the handcuffs worked to his advantage, preventing him from overstepping the mark.

Priya. He liked that name. Probably an alias, but it suited her all the same. From the moment he'd offered to open the safe, she had become much warmer towards him. He hadn't yet worked up courage to broach the other side of the bargain. *If I open the safe, what will you do for me in return . . . ?*

In the meantime he was grateful for the opportunity to vent his feelings about his father, something he was rarely able to do. His sister had stopped listening years ago, and he had no real friends.

But Priya was clearly fascinated. She gazed deep into his eyes, deep enough to see all his frustration and pain.

'You truly hate him, don't you?'

'I despise him,' Oliver said, and his voice caught as he added: 'He killed my mother.'

Priya frowned, exhibiting some of the doubt that usually greeted this statement. However, she didn't dismiss it or laugh it off the way so many others had.

'She came from a very influential family. Her uncle was Cabinet Secretary, and she had other relatives in the Foreign Office, the military, the judiciary. That was the main reason he married her. With Dad, it's connections that matter, not emotions.'

He paused. It always upset him to recount this story, but he was exaggerating the effects a little, hoping that Priya might reach out and touch him. Even just her gloved fingers resting on his shoulder . . .

He shivered. 'My mother was a moral person. She restrained him. He couldn't lead the life he wanted while she was around, and she wouldn't countenance a divorce. So he arranged an accident, at our place in Scotland. She was driving home one night, skidded and lost control.'

Another pause. His eyes were moist, but Priya didn't move an inch.

'Couldn't it have been a genuine accident?'

'No. They found alcohol in her bloodstream. Way over the limit. But my mother never touched a drop when she was driving. Never. Dad used to tease her for being so uptight about it. That's how I know it was murder.'

He sent her a pleading glance, just as another member of the gang swaggered into the room and destroyed all his hard work.

Oliver felt a flare of anger. The man had a mask on, but he wasn't the one who'd been with Priya earlier. He was taller, stronger, exuding a gruff masculine authority that Oliver found oppressive.

Priya didn't look particularly glad to see him, either. She stood up, leaning forward as she studied what little she could see of his face through his eyeholes.

'Turner? Shouldn't you be with the Weavers?'

'The husband's dead. I took the old woman to Dreamscape. Thought I'd check things out here.' He gestured at Oliver. 'Is this streak of piss any use to us?'

Oliver stiffened. 'I told Priya that I'm prepared to cooperate—'

'Oh, how spiffingly good of you!' Turner grabbed Oliver by the hair and pulled him to his feet. Oliver shrieked, and the thug slapped him hard across the face.

'Shut the fuck up, and show me the safe.'

Priya wasn't pleased. 'We should wait for Liam.'

'Sod Liam. I wanna see what's in there.'

Thirty-One

Valentin opened a drawer in his desk and produced a silver hip flask. He removed the cap and took a swig. Offered it to Liam, who was about to say no, then changed his mind. He deserved a drink.

It wasn't vodka, but whisky. It burned a trail down his throat and swelled his confidence still further. After Liam gave it back, Valentin had another sip and wiped his mouth with the side of his hand.

'Did we convince him?' Valentin asked.

'Travers? Definitely.' Liam stared at McWhirter's body. The knowledge that he'd taken a life didn't seem to weigh heavily on him at all. If anything, he was surprised at how easy it had been.

'He served me well,' Valentin said, with a note of regret. 'But he was losing faith in me. For McWhirter, certain things were black or white. He would never have agreed to something like this.'

'A wise move, then.'

Valentin gave him a measured look, then snapped back to the business at hand. 'Do we have other casualties?'

'A couple. Donald Weaver. And there was a problem earlier at Dreamscape.' Liam described what had happened with the estate agent. Valentin's reaction was stronger than he'd expected.

'Priya killed him? Was she hurt?'

'No. She's fine.'

'Where is she now?'

'At Felton's. We got a surprise there, too. It turns out Oliver Felton didn't go to Oxford.'

'You mean he's *here?*'

'Don't worry. We're not going to harm him.'

Liam saw the Ukrainian relax slightly as he thought it through. 'No. This could be very useful.' Valentin looked at his watch. 'Come on. We must not be away too long.'

Liam followed the older man down two flights of stairs. The vault was in the basement, between the servants' quarters and a lap pool. It was a bespoke design, shipped over and installed by a specialist firm in California. Liam watched Valentin tap in the code and open the door.

The interior was approximately ten feet square, and contained a fairly sparse collection of artwork and antiques. Valentin was a keen and knowledgeable investor, specialising in nineteenth-century Russian landscapes as well as contemporary Ukrainian paintings and sculpture. But the highest value pieces had been moved to alternative storage, where they would remain until Valentin had concluded an insurance claim for his entire collection – a nice little side scam that Liam had suggested, and for which he was receiving a separate bonus: twenty per cent of the proceeds.

They left the vault open and returned to the ground floor. Valentin held out his hands for Liam to fit another set of plastic cuffs.

'The other prisoners are at Dreamscape?' he asked.

'In the garage. It won't be very pleasant.'

Valentin shrugged. 'Yuri and I must be treated the same as everyone else. And Travers must see that we are.'

They were almost at the front door when Valentin nudged him. Thinking there was some kind of ambush, Liam reached for his gun.

'Your mask.'

Liam let out a nervous laugh. He pulled the mask from his belt and put it on, aware that Valentin wasn't smiling at all. This was nearly a major fuck-up, and they both knew it.

*   *   *

When he judged it safe to move, Joe advanced as far as the gates of the Nasenko property and paused again. The front door was standing open, the hallway beyond in shadow. He had to assume that Valentin and McWhirter were still inside, and probably not alone.

He waited another minute, then decided to risk moving forward in stages. If he could get into the house, maybe he'd find a way to overcome whoever was holding them.

Joe crept over to the pallet of paving blocks and crouched down. Waited thirty seconds and was about to move when he heard a noise from inside. It sounded like a laugh. He looked round and glimpsed a man approaching the doorway, adjusting his ski mask. Valentin Nasenko was alongside him, his hands bound at the wrists.

The two men hurried away, taking the same route as the first group of prisoners. Valentin was talking quietly, but Joe couldn't make out the words. Although Nasenko had a fearsome temper when aroused, on this occasion he seemed to be successfully holding it in check. Perhaps trying to negotiate with his captor.

A brave attempt, but Joe couldn't see it succeeding. Not when the gang held all the cards.

He watched the house for another minute, then made his decision. McWhirter was still unaccounted for, and Joe wanted to know why.

He emerged from hiding and ran up to the front door. Hearing nothing inside, he stepped over the threshold.

As Oliver led the way upstairs, he experienced a crisis of confidence. Was cooperation the right course of action? It wasn't a question of moral qualms so much as pure self-preservation. They may simply kill him once he'd outlived his usefulness.

It wouldn't be Priya who pulled the trigger, he thought. At least, he hoped not. But this man Turner was an out-and-out gangster. He'd do it without the slightest hesitation.

Oliver rarely went near his father's bedroom. The whole suite had recently been refurbished, at a cost of some eighty thousand pounds.

Oliver couldn't see anything that justified such extravagance. The interior designer must have laughed all the way to her bank.

He opened the fake panel that covered the safe door, and remembered his earlier discovery that the code for the fire-protection system had been re-set. If his father had changed this combination as well, a bullet in the brain might be only seconds away.

Oliver's hand trembled as he reached out. *81-23-66.* Just three numbers, but the process wasn't quite that straightforward. He had to turn the dial three times to the left, stopping at 81 on the fourth turn. Not so easy to do with shaky hands.

He was conscious of Turner at his shoulder, snorting like a hungry raptor. Priya had hung back a little. Twice she'd said they should be waiting for someone called Liam. The ringleader, presumably.

Oliver turned the dial to the right, going twice round, stopping at 23 on the third time. There was a shuffling behind him: Turner, growing impatient. Oliver felt cold metal pressing against the back of his neck.

'Don't get any ideas,' Turner said. 'We know there's a silent alarm.'

'I won't set it off.'

'You'd better not. No one would get here in time to save you.'

Oliver swallowed. He could feel sweat prickling on his brow. He turned the dial one full circuit to the left, then again, stopping on 66. Then right, back to zero and just beyond, until he met resistance. The dial wouldn't turn any further.

The moment of truth.

He gripped the door handle and turned. There was a heavy metallic *thunk* as the lock disengaged and the bolts drew back. Oliver shut his eyes. The relief was like a flood of warm water.

He pulled the door open and stood aside.

Thirty-Two

It wasn't until eight-thirty that both children were finally sleeping soundly. Only then did Cassie allow herself to reflect upon the day's terrible events, and what seemed like the utter hopelessness of her position.

She ran a bath and soaked in it for twenty minutes, leaving the door open so she could see the children. She listened to the gentle rhythm of their breathing and wondered how she'd be feeling now if the abduction had succeeded. Just trying to imagine it was like being speared in the heart.

And yet that was the kind of loss Joe had to endure every day: his daughters growing up without him. To Cassie, it was an unbearable tragedy. She'd been raised in a noisy, vibrant household with three older siblings and parents who were still devoted to one another after forty years together. Family was everything to her.

But after today her life would never be quite the same. The hairline cracks in her marriage had split wide open, smashing the relationship to pieces. She and Valentin were finished as a couple.

After the bath, Cassie dried off and dressed again. She saw no point in going to bed. The prospect of sleep seemed impossible while there was so much uncertainty.

Instead she sat on the double bed, next to Jaden, and tried to watch TV. Every thirty seconds or so her gaze drifted to the phone, or to her watch. Joe had said she mustn't use her mobile, but how long was she supposed to wait?

The fears wormed their way into her mind. What if he didn't call? Would she just sit here, hour after hour, growing ever more hysterical?

He'd already been gone nearly ninety minutes. Even if Valentin was still in his meeting, he must have spoken to Joe by now. So why hadn't she heard something?

She stared at her mobile phone. It felt wrong to ignore Joe's advice. He'd been an undercover policeman, after all. He knew what he was talking about.

But one quick call. Could it really hurt?

Yes, it could. Cassie shifted position, trapping her hands under her thighs. No more looking at her watch.

It's just like dieting, she thought. Forget how much you want it, and be strong.

Liam took Valentin to Dreamscape, collecting the Ford Explorer from outside Terry Fox's place on the way past. Valentin joined the other prisoners, now seven of them in total, seated in a circle on the garage floor.

Liam noted that, as well as Valentin, Angela Weaver was also cuffed with her hands in front. The others had their hands behind their backs, which was far less comfortable. Liam wondered if he should alter it so they were all the same, then decided it wasn't that important.

Allotti had collected up the mobile phones and taken them into a small office on the ground floor. Pendry and Manderson were standing the other side of the cars, where they'd removed their masks to smoke and talk in conspiratorial whispers. That left only Eldon to keep watch on the prisoners.

'Where's Turner?' said Liam.

'He went next door,' said Eldon. 'The Feltons.'

Liam frowned. Apart from himself and Priya, Turner was the only member of the team who knew that Valentin was in on the robbery. The others believed he was merely another victim, and it was vital to keep it that way.

But Liam had his doubts as to whether Turner could be trusted with such an important secret. Like Priya, Turner was one of Valentin's recruits, and didn't inspire much confidence. Privately Liam had resolved to eliminate him if he came close to compromising the operation.

Now he sighed, and checked his watch. Nine-fifteen.

'I'm going over there myself,' he told Eldon. 'When Turner comes back, you and Pendry can get to work. Take the Citroën and start with the Weavers, okay?'

Eldon nodded. Liam scowled at Manderson and Pendry; they felt his gaze but brazenly continued smoking and chatting. As he turned away, Liam made eye contact with Valentin. The Ukrainian gave an almost imperceptible bow of his head.

Good luck.

On the way out Liam detoured to the office. Allotti was splayed in a chair, chuckling to himself as he scrolled through the menu on someone's phone. He saw Liam and scrambled to sit upright.

'What is it?'

'McWhirter. Nudie pictures of some hooker. Much too young for him.'

Liam grunted. 'You turned the jammer off yet?'

'No. I can do, if you want.'

The plan had been to restore the mobile phone network once the island was secure, allowing incoming calls to be intercepted rather than blocked. Allotti's job was to monitor texts and phone messages, and either respond to them himself or get the prisoners to reply, to maintain an illusion of normality.

'We'll risk leaving it on a bit longer,' Liam said. 'You can monitor anything coming in on the landlines, though?'

'Oh, yeah.' Allotti gestured enthusiastically at a small receiver and telephone handset on the desk. 'We're piggybacking from the junction box, with wireless transmission to here. I'm using a similar frequency to the two-way radios, so the jammer won't affect it. It's a sweet set-up. I don't even have to get out of my seat,' he declared happily.

Liam nodded. Allotti was a clever bastard, but a lazy one.

Then his radio buzzed, and he forgot all about Allotti and the phones.

It was Priya. Her voice sounded tight and unfamiliar, almost vibrating with tension.

'There's a problem.'

The mystery of McWhirter's whereabouts didn't take long to solve. Joe found the South African's body in Valentin's study. He felt for a pulse, but knew it was useless. McWhirter's eyes were open, waxy and sightless. Nothing that could be done for him.

Scanning the room, Joe noticed Valentin's hip flask sitting on the desk next to his laptop. A few drops of whisky had run down the side and pooled on the glossy walnut surface of the desk. The image troubled him somehow, but he couldn't say why.

And there was no time to dwell on it. He left the office and swiftly checked the rest of the house: partly to make sure he was alone, but also to search for a weapon. He paid particular attention to the guest bedroom appropriated by Yuri, hoping there would be a gun stashed somewhere, but found nothing.

In Cassie's room he made an unwelcome discovery. A Cartier watch and a set of diamond earrings lay in full view on her dressing table. It was inconceivable that such items would be excluded from the robbery, which meant the gang might come back at any moment.

Joe drank some water in the kitchen, then opened the cutlery drawer and selected a six-inch boning knife. Not very effective against a gun, but useful for close-quarter combat.

His last call was the basement. As he reached the communal living area he saw the vault door standing open. He looked inside, and frowned. He'd last been in here about a fortnight ago, when he'd accompanied Valentin's insurance assessor, who was producing an updated inventory. On that occasion the room had been bursting with treasure.

Around half of it remained, sitting undisturbed, but the other half was missing. Had it already been removed?

Joe puzzled over it for a second or two, but reached no conclusion, other than a vague sense that this was something more complex than a simple raid. More complex – and therefore more dangerous.

Outside, the light was rapidly fading. With most of the houses in darkness, and no street lighting, the twilight had a more emphatic quality than it did in towns and cities. Already the woods across the road looked impenetrable and slightly sinister, like something from a ghost story. Soon they would need flashlights to see their way from place to place, Liam thought.

But at least it was cooler now, too. Liam tilted his head to catch a gentle breeze coming in off the sea. The mask was driving him mad, but he couldn't dispense with it until Oliver Felton had joined the other prisoners at Dreamscape.

And that wouldn't happen until Oliver had served his purpose.

In the minute or so that it took Liam to walk next door, he tried to push Priya's gloomy message aside, half fearing that she'd gone and stabbed the boy to death. He didn't want anything to detract from the anticipation he felt right at this moment – for Robert Felton was the reason they had come to Terror's Reach.

The plan had been hatched by Valentin Nasenko, after his fortune had taken a pounding in the banking crisis of 2008. He and Felton had been enemies for years, for all kinds of reasons that were frankly of no interest to Liam. He'd quickly learned to tune out whenever Valentin began ranting about all the lucrative deals which Felton had supposedly denied him, thanks to his network of political cronies around the world.

What interested Liam was that Nasenko wanted revenge, and he needed money. Stealing from Felton satisfied both objectives. The catch was that it had to be done in a way that avoided any suspicion falling on Valentin.

It was Liam who had provided the solution, which had three main elements. Firstly, target all the homes on the island to make it appear that Felton was just one of several victims. Next, find a way to ensure that Travers – a trusted associate of Felton's – was present to witness and later corroborate Valentin's ordeal at the hands of the gang.

The last touch, which really added the seal of authenticity, was the cold-blooded murder of Valentin's loyal adviser, Gary McWhirter. Even Felton was unlikely to think his rival capable of such a ruthless gambit.

Valentin himself had dreamed up an additional component. He planned an overture to Robert Felton, via Travers, regarding a business deal in some godforsaken Central Asian republic. This was a quite genuine proposal, albeit one that Felton would normally reject out of hand. After all, he had no incentive to do business with Nasenko.

Except that, as a result of tonight's activity, Valentin's offer would be made from a position of strength, having helped himself to a large slice of his neighbour's fortune.

Reaching the open front door, Liam gave a short, gleeful laugh. It was a hell of a fortune. A hell of a slice.

He found Turner in the living room, sucking on a cigarette and pacing up and down like an expectant father in an old movie. When he saw Liam he dropped the cigarette and ground the butt into the floor. He looked worried and upset and aggrieved all at once. There was no sign of Priya or Oliver Felton.

'Where are they?' Liam asked.

'Upstairs.'

'So what's the problem?'

Turner just glowered, shouldering his way past Liam.

'What?' Liam asked again. His hand drifted towards the gun in his belt.

'See for yourself,' Turner said without looking back. He marched across the hall and started up the stairs.

'Mask,' Liam said, hurrying after him.

'Fucking thing,' Turner said. But he put it on.

The master-bedroom suite occupied about a quarter of the first floor. It was a ridiculously large space, with dressing rooms, twin bathrooms and even a sitting area with sofas and a coffee table. Oliver Felton was perched on a sofa, rigid as a dummy in a shop window, staring blankly at the far wall. Priya was standing over him, absently biting her lower lip. She hardly reacted when Liam and Turner walked in.

One of the walls was clad in light-oak panelling. Robert Felton's safe was set into the wall, concealed by a section of fake panelling, which had been swung aside. The safe door was open. Operated by a dial combination lock, it was made of heavy reinforced steel with three-way boltwork and anti-drilling plates: exactly as their research had suggested.

The interior space was about six feet high, three feet wide and two feet deep. There were five shelves, but four of them were bare. A handful of trinkets lay gathering dust on the top shelf, and there was an old foolscap box file on the floor.

And that was it. Nothing else.

The safe was empty.

Thirty-Three

Joe was relieved to find his own room still intact. He locked the door behind him and dragged his bed across it for greater protection. Then he stripped off and allowed himself thirty seconds in the shower. He dried and got dressed in clean jeans, black T-shirt and trainers. Pocketed his multi-tool and keys and the boning knife, and then remembered his mobile phone.

He took out his strongbox from the wardrobe. There was another phone in there, and he could swap the SIM card. Although he'd told Cassie not to call, he didn't like the idea of her being unable to contact him if she really needed to. That meant he had to keep hold of the number she had for him.

But he was also aware of the time ticking away. He couldn't afford to get caught down here. Besides, he ought to find a better hiding place for his own possessions, to prevent his IDs from falling into the wrong hands.

Joe moved the bed away from the door and tucked the strongbox under his arm. He crept upstairs, listening hard for any movement in the house.

Back in the hall, he paused. There was a landline extension on the wall. He thought about McWhirter, lying dead in the study. He thought about the prisoners, marched off to an unknown fate. Shouldn't he call the police while he had the chance?

Still he hesitated. The junction box was just along the road from here. He felt sure they would have cut the line, or disabled the phones in some way.

He looked at the receiver for a long second, then snatched it up. Expecting nothing, he felt his heart stutter as he recognised a dialling tone.

Maybe they thought cutting the lines was too great a risk. If someone called the island and couldn't get through, they might report a fault.

As he pressed 9, a voice in his head warned him:

The police won't believe you.

He pressed it again.

They haven't cut the lines, but they must be—

A blast of feedback made him jump. He nearly dropped the receiver.

The line went dead. Someone had cut him off.

'Shit,' Joe whispered. He'd just made a really big mistake.

Liam stared at the safe in disbelief.

'What the hell is this?'

'You tell me,' Turner growled. 'There's meant to be a fucking fortune in there, not this old crap. Makes me wonder if it isn't some kind of stitch-up.'

Liam was so stunned, it took a few seconds for the accusation to permeate. When it did, his own temper flared.

'When did you open this?'

'Don't be so fucking—' Turner started, but Priya spoke over him.

'I radioed you straight away.' She glanced at Oliver Felton, who looked like a rabbit caught in headlights. He nodded.

Liam said, 'My orders were to wait until I got here.'

'Like that matters now,' Turner shouted.

Once again, Priya intervened. 'Be quiet. Fighting amongst ourselves won't achieve anything.'

Turner glared at her, but Liam knew she was right. He leaned inside the safe, dumped the cheap jewellery on the floor and rattled the shelves to see if any were loose. He was hoping for a hidden compartment or a door to another storage area, but there was nothing.

He knelt down and picked up the box file. 'Have you looked inside this?'

'Didn't seem any point,' Priya said.

Liam opened the file. There was a stack of paper crammed inside, held down by a lock spring. Dozens of documents of varying size and age. He lifted the lock spring and skimmed a few: deeds of sale, interest statements, shareholder accounts. Nothing that screamed high value, or any value at all. And certainly not what they'd come for.

He sighed. Gave Oliver a long, critical appraisal. Priya said, 'He swears he didn't know.'

'Do you believe him?'

'Yes. Otherwise he wouldn't have opened the safe so readily.'

In unison, their radios buzzed. The emergency frequency.

Turner got to his first. He identified himself and held out the handset so they could all hear.

It was Allotti. 'Someone just tried to make a phone call.'

Liam grabbed Turner's handset. 'What?'

'At Nasenko's place, just now. Pendry's gone to take a look.' Allotti's short laugh emerged as a burst of static. 'I didn't imagine it. Someone tried to dial out.'

Stupid, stupid, stupid.

Joe put the phone back and took a quick look round, trying to work out if he'd left any trace of his presence. Hopefully the steam from the shower would dissipate before they searched his room. But they might notice his old clothes, still wet from the sea.

Nothing he could do about it now. Just get out of here.

Leaving the front door open at the same angle he'd found it, he stepped outside and hurried across the drive. He had the strongbox under one arm and held the boning knife in his right hand.

The street was clear, but from the direction of Dreamscape Joe heard the roar of an engine. Headlights swept the bend as he raced across the road and plunged into the trees. Within fifteen or twenty feet he was in almost total darkness. Branches tore at his face as he blundered his way deep into the undergrowth. He tripped on a root and nearly lost his balance, dropping the strongbox as he fought to stay upright.

The box hit the dry earth with a thud. Joe turned and looked back along the route he'd just taken. The road and houses were already out of sight. He couldn't see a thing.

He heard the engine noise settle to a steady purr. A door opened and slammed shut. Then nothing more.

Feeling carefully around him, Joe knelt down and brushed the ground clear of leaves and twigs. From his pocket he took out the SIM card from the phone he'd had earlier. Then he opened the box and located the other phone. By now his eyes were adjusting to the dark, and he could see the phone clearly enough to remove the rear cover and change the SIM card.

Once that was done he shielded the phone with his body before pressing the power button. The phone was set to vibrate, but even the single low-pitched hum it emitted on start-up seemed dangerously loud.

Joe took a quick look at the display and was disappointed on two counts. The battery icon was down to a single bar, and the signal strength indicator showed no signal available.

He knew that the island had its own mobile-phone mast. Either they had disabled it, or they were jamming the signal.

Liam told Priya to stay and guard Oliver Felton while he and Turner went next door. Priya started to protest, but Liam wasn't in the mood.

'Don't argue. Just do it.'

She turned away as if he'd slapped her. Turner made it worse by chuckling. Liam picked up the box file and waved Turner towards the door.

At Dreamscape, Allotti met them in the hall. He spread his hands and said, 'I dunno what's going on. It doesn't add up . . .'

Liam shrugged. 'But you blocked the call?'

'Yeah. I had to fry the line to do it. And the jammer's still on, so mobiles won't work. Pendry's at the house, and Manderson's checking along the road.'

'Good. You'd better go and patrol the waterfront. Have you warned Gough at the bridge?'

'I will do.' Allotti drew his gun and left the house.

As they walked through the kitchen, Turner said, 'Who do you reckon it is?'

'Just Allotti's over-active imagination. I hope.' Liam paused before they entered the garage. He came to a decision, and drew Turner close.

'I want you to get Valentin and Yuri, and take them into the lounge.'

'But I thought—'

'Now,' said Liam quietly, and strode into the garage. Eldon was watching the prisoners on his own. He seemed agitated as he hurried towards them.

'Shouldn't I be starting on the inventory?'

'Soon. In the meantime you can sort through this.' Liam handed the box file to Eldon, who stared at it with dismay in his eyes.

'What am I looking for?'

'I haven't got a clue. Surprise me.'

There was a commotion from the prisoners as Valentin and Yuri were led away at gunpoint. Liam deliberately kept his back to them. Right now he didn't want to make eye contact with anyone, Travers in particular.

Even so, he could feel the hatred they directed towards him. It made his neck tingle. Made him want to spin round and open fire, wipe them all out and bring an end to the total fucking calamity this operation had become.

✳   ✳   ✳

Joe put the phone back in his pocket and closed the strongbox. He decided this was as good a hiding place for it as anywhere. To make sure he'd be able to find it again he crawled back towards the road and noted his position in relation to the Nasenko house.

There was now a Ford Explorer parked on the driveway. He pictured the gang, searching the house. If they found his wet clothes they'd want to know who he was. That would mean interrogating Valentin.

With the phone system disabled, Joe's immediate concern was to gather as much information as he could. Find out where the prisoners were being held, and how many people he was up against, then review his objectives once again. Perhaps there was still a chance he'd be able to rescue them himself, but by squandering the advantage of surprise he'd just made the task a lot more onerous.

And now that he knew they were looking for him, he couldn't risk taking the road. Instead he set off through the trees. Although there was a path of sorts, it was narrow and hard to follow in the darkness. Occasionally he spotted the faint glimmer of water in time to avoid it; at other times his feet sank into boggy mud and he had to step back and find a different way through.

In any case, he had to move slowly, for the other problem was noise. The ground was covered with dry leaves and hard, brittle twigs. Each snap seemed to resound like a gunshot in the still, silent evening.

After what seemed like an age he reached a junction with another path that led back out to the road. He crept along it and saw he was almost directly level with Dreamscape's front gates. It was too exposed to emerge here. Better to move on and find another route at a more oblique angle to the property.

He was moving away when something set off his internal alarm. Something he'd registered subliminally, his body responding before his mind could catch up.

He stopped. Tried to throw out his senses like a net, scooping up every tiny scrap of data. He was certain that he hadn't set off a trap of any kind. And he hadn't seen or heard anything to give rise to the warning. So what was it?

Thirty-Four

Liam waited for a minute or two, then made his way to the living room. Once inside, he tore off his mask. Turner had already removed his. Yuri and Valentin were sitting like patients in a doctor's waiting room, faces passive, hands still bound.

Valentin's anger ignited the moment Liam shut the door behind him. 'Why do you drag us in here?'

'Allotti thinks someone tried to use the phone. At your house.'

Valentin frowned. 'One of the team?'

'Apparently not. Any idea who it could be?'

'No.' Valentin still looked more angry than worried. 'You've accounted for everyone?'

Liam nodded. 'I'm hoping it's just a mistake. But I've got men out there looking.'

'Not enough,' said Yuri. To Valentin, he added, 'The team was too light. We needed more people.'

Valentin ignored him. 'You cannot spend too long making the search. You must start loading the vans.'

Turner gave a loud, sarcastic snort. Both Valentin and Yuri caught the unspoken message and looked at him for an explanation.

'The safe's empty,' Liam said.

Valentin's head swivelled back towards Liam. 'The . . . ?'

'Felton's safe. The big combination safe sitting right there in his

190

bedroom, just where it was meant to be. His boy opened it up for us without a murmur. We didn't have to drill it or blow the door off. The only downside – there wasn't a fucking thing in it.'

Valentin stared at Liam through a long, incredulous silence, then bowed his head as if yielding to a crushing weight. He raised his hands towards his face, realised they were cuffed and let them flop back onto his lap.

Yuri stood up. 'Let me go and I will help to search.'

'What do we tell the rest of the team?' Liam asked.

'Say I was inside man all along.' Yuri nodded towards Valentin. 'Say I betrayed him.'

Liam glanced at Turner, who said, 'An extra body would help, at least till we know what's going on.'

While he considered it, Liam had another question. 'Supposing this phone call really happened. Why your house?'

'First place on the island, coming from bridge.'

'But who could it be?'

Yuri shrugged. 'That's what we have to find out.'

Liam addressed Valentin. 'Are you okay with this?'

The Ukrainian barely seemed to hear him. He gave a distracted nod. 'Yes. If we must.'

Liam motioned to Turner, who took out a knife and cut Yuri free. Yuri rubbed the life back into his wrists, then held out his hand.

'I need a weapon.'

Turner scowled, but gave him the knife. He unclipped his radio and passed on the message that Yuri would be joining the search.

'He's with us, you got that? So don't go topping him by mistake.'

Valentin didn't even look up when Yuri left the room. He was like a man in a trance. There was a tremor in his hands as they rested on his bony knees, and a tremor in his throat when he found his voice.

'It's there somewhere,' he said. 'It has to be there.'

'What if it's not?'

'It is there, I tell you!' Valentin growled, leaping to his feet with a ferocity that made Liam take a step back. 'It is in that house, and we have to find it. Take the boy and make him tell you. Cut him to pieces if you have to.'

'Oliver doesn't know,' Liam said. 'He wouldn't have opened the safe if he'd known it was—'

'*He knows*,' Valentin insisted. 'Now go and make him admit it.'

Joe waited, his eyes straining to distinguish something out of place, his ears alert to the tiniest sound. He got nothing back.

And yet . . .

If someone had heard him moving and knew he was here, they too would be frozen, hardly daring to breathe. They too would be desperate not to give away any hint of their presence.

But maybe there was something they couldn't help but give away. Something beyond their control.

Joe's nostrils twitched. Earlier he'd been struck by the rich aromas of evening, as the plants and trees released their scent into the accumulated heat of the day. Now those aromas were overlaid by a much harsher smell, meaty and sour.

Body odour.

Joe lifted his foot and took one cautious step. Then another. He turned his head while slowly inhaling, testing the air. The smell was slightly stronger behind him and to his right.

The path back to the road.

He moved carefully, knowing he'd been found, knowing too that he couldn't run. He had to fight instead.

The smell intensified as he crept along the path, a keynote of fresh sweat riding the stale odour beneath. In the grades of darkness at the copse's edge, an ominous shadow took shape and form.

The man was lying in wait for him on the edge of the path. Joe assumed he had a gun, but perhaps the lack of light or the trees deterred him from using it. Instead he was half crouching, holding a fallen branch above his right shoulder like a baseball bat, poised for the swing.

Two feet from the end of the path Joe stopped. But not for long. He steadied himself, then took another step, deliberately pressing his weight down. Twigs crunched underfoot with a sound like small bones breaking.

Right on cue the man attacked, swinging the branch with both hands. If it had caught Joe unawares it would have just about taken his head off. But he was already ducking, moving sideways and forwards, throwing out his right arm and catching the attacker by the neck, using his own momentum against him.

The man's eyes widened with shock, a white gleam in the darkness. He couldn't believe he'd been outwitted, but he had no time to react. He was tumbling forward, propelled by his own body weight. His neck slammed against Joe's arm, his head jerking back. Joe darted behind him, wrapped his left arm over his assailant's masked face and wrenched his head round. There was a sickening crunch as the man's neck snapped, and his body went slack.

Joe went on clinging to the man's head until he was sure it was safe to loosen his grip. Then he lowered the body to the ground and let out a breath. He'd had extensive training in self-defence, and over the years he'd had to call on those skills a fair few times. He had also taken a life before, but not like this. Not with his bare hands.

Everything was changed now. He'd engaged the enemy, and there would be any number of consequences. But in truth he felt little remorse. He'd seen McWhirter's body. He knew what the gang were capable of.

He grabbed the man's feet and dragged him into the woods. A noisy manoeuvre, but a necessary one. It hadn't escaped Joe's notice that the man was roughly the same size as him, about an inch or two shorter and a few pounds heavier.

Once he was well back from the road, Joe tore off the man's mask and undid his utility belt. As well as the two-way radio, he found a handgun and some cuffs.

He started to unbutton the boiler suit. The man was wearing shorts and a T-shirt underneath, but the suit itself had still absorbed his smell. Joe swallowed back his revulsion. This was too good an opportunity to miss, especially now the gang were actively looking for him.

It was perfect camouflage, and might just keep him alive.

Oliver was disconsolate. He knew he had blown his chances.

Priya was keeping an eye on him, but she managed to do it without looking directly at him. Oliver burned with shame and desire. If he'd had a gun, or a knife, or even just his box of matches, he would have ended it all right now.

'I'm going to die here tonight.'

'What?'

Priya's reaction made him start. He hadn't intended to say it aloud.

He said it again, this time savouring the truth of the words as they were spoken. 'I'm going to die here tonight.'

She shrugged, perhaps interpreting it as a question rather than a statement.

'Maybe,' she said. Then: 'You don't seem all that bothered.'

He shook his head. Slowly he lifted his cuffed hands and stretched them towards her, causing the sleeves of his shirt to drop. Then he twisted his arms outward to display the thin white scars that ran for several inches from the base of each palm.

'Vertical, not horizontal,' he said. 'That's how you do it properly. Anything else is just a cry for help.'

Priya nodded, and seemed to be studying him from a fresh perspective. 'So why—?'

'My sister found me.' Oliver looked her in the eyes. 'I wish she hadn't.'

Thirty-Five

Liam stayed in the hall while Turner took Valentin back to the garage. If the other prisoners queried Yuri's absence, Valentin was to say that he'd been taken away somewhere, and that was all he knew. To make it convincing he had to sound both angry and fearful. Given the news about Felton's safe, that shouldn't be too difficult to fake.

Leaving Dreamscape, Liam was expecting Turner to take the piss, having just witnessed his dressing-down. But although he was clearly brooding on it, the other man said nothing.

Out on the road, Liam stopped abruptly. 'Did you hear that?'

'What?'

'Over there.' Liam stared at the trees, his hand resting lightly on his gun.

They waited a few seconds, then Turner shook his head.

'You're just getting jumpy. We've got four men searching. If someone's out there, they'll find him.'

'Yeah. All right.'

Liam hurried on, Turner scrambling to catch up. As they approached Felton's front door, Turner said, 'Feels like this is going to shit.'

'We're fine,' Liam said. But he knew exactly what Turner meant.

Priya and Oliver were still in the master bedroom, Oliver sitting exactly where they had left him. Priya looked weary and distracted, as though she'd been trying to convince herself that none of this was happening. She was standing at the window, watching the dark sea fade into the coming night.

'Any progress?' said Liam.

'He's adamant that he didn't know.'

Turner clicked his tongue. 'How about if we cut his dick off, and then ask him?'

Oliver gave them a sickly smile. Even as his body remained immobile, there was a restlessness in his eyes that wasn't quite normal.

'You never saw your dad clearing it out?' Liam asked. 'You didn't hear him mention it at all?'

'No. I don't pay any attention to what my father does.'

A glance at Priya, who nodded: Oliver was telling the truth.

Liam sighed. He had a feeling that threats of violence wouldn't work. The sick little bastard would probably get a thrill out of it.

'Look,' he said. 'We know the safe is a decoy.'

'It's not,' said Oliver, but there was a flash of something in his face. Uncertainty.

'We *will* cut it off,' Turner warned him. 'Stuff it down your throat.'

'And we'll do it in front of Priya,' Liam added. If they had any leverage at all, it was that Oliver seemed to have an adolescent crush on her. 'There's another safe, isn't there?'

'No, there isn't—' Oliver began, and then stopped. His gaze lost focus and his lips came together in an expression of pure agony. Whatever he was seeing in his head, it wasn't pleasant.

Liam thought back to this afternoon, when Priya had first noticed Oliver spying on her. The weird little attic room.

'Your dad's got a thing about hiding places, hasn't he?'

Oliver nodded slowly, like a naughty child boxed in and unable to lie.

'So what is it? What do you need to tell me?'

'There's . . . There's a panic room.'

Turner clapped his hands. 'Thank fuck for that.'

'Where is it, Oliver?' Liam asked.

'I want to help you. I really do.'

'I know. Just tell me where it is.'

Oliver was still nodding, big fat tears rolling down his cheeks.

'I can show you,' he said. 'But it won't be enough.'

Joe put on the boiler suit over his own clothes. It wasn't a perfect fit but it would do. At least he was acclimatising to the smell.

He fastened the utility belt, slipped his knife into it and transferred his phone and Leatherman multi-tool to the suit's outer pockets. The dead man was wearing latex gloves, but Joe decided to dispense with those. He picked up the two-way radio and switched it off. He didn't want it burping at him when he was within earshot of the house.

Pulling on the mask, he took one more look at the body, the pale flesh ghostly in the darkness. Joe felt guilt nudging at his heart, but wouldn't let it in. The lives of many innocent people still hung in the balance.

When he reached the edge of the copse, he paused. There was just sufficient light to check the gun in more detail. It was a Glock 17. Joe knew that particular model was regarded as a very reliable firearm, but if he had to use this one he first wanted to make sure that it worked properly.

From the position of the trigger he could tell there was a round in the chamber. He removed the magazine, which held seventeen 9 mm cartridges, and racked the slide to eject the chambered round. He dry-fired the gun to test the mechanism, then picked up the spilled cartridge and reloaded it in the magazine. Lastly he slotted the full magazine back into the grip and racked the slide again. Now there was a round in the chamber, ready to fire.

Across the road several of Dreamscape's windows were lit up. The front door was standing open, beckoning him. He left the cover of the trees and walked into view, fighting the urge to keep low and hurry. Now that he was in disguise, he had to stand tall. Act like he belonged.

It felt odd for a second or two. Then something in his mind clicked and he was instantly back in the job. Back at doing what he did best: becoming someone else. Mixing with the bad guys in order to beat them.

And he didn't much like admitting it to himself, but it felt good.

'Sneaky bastard,' Turner said. He had it about right, Liam thought.

The panic room was part of the master-bedroom suite. A logical place for it, given that the worst case scenario for most people was to have armed robbers bursting in during the middle of the night. Better still, anyone who searched the bedroom would find the safe first, and probably wouldn't explore any further.

Still snuffling like a baby, Oliver led them into one of the dressing rooms. There were floor-to-ceiling wardrobes on three walls. Liam opened one at random and found dozens of bespoke suits in a variety of colours and styles, ranging from flamboyant to deeply conservative: maybe two hundred grand's worth of exquisite tailoring.

Oliver gestured towards the wardrobe opposite the door. There was a full-length mirror on it, which showed the four of them crowding into the tiny room, bumping shoulders. Oliver fumbled with the handle, then turned back to them.

'You need to untie me.'

Turner cut the restraints and Oliver opened the door. The wardrobe was empty but for a high rail that held a couple of overcoats and a vintage leather biker's jacket. Watching as he leaned inside, Turner drawled: 'Where are we going? Fucking Narnia?'

Oliver swept the coats aside and pressed a hidden switch on the wall. The rear panel slid away on castors, revealing a solid steel door set into a steel frame. It looked even heavier and more forbidding than the door to the safe.

Liam pushed past Oliver so he could see more clearly. Instead of a combination dial there was a small black screen and a keypad. Liam whistled softly, then said: 'Go on.'

Oliver looked at him, stricken. 'I can't open it.'

'Bullshit,' said Turner.

'You just opened the safe. Now open this, and save yourself a lot of pain.'

'Look, I don't care how much you threaten me. I can't open it. If I could, I would.' He made an appeal to Priya. 'You have to believe me.'

'You mean you don't know the combination?' she asked.

'Even if I did, it wouldn't help,' said Oliver. 'It's a two-stage lock.'

'So?' said Turner.

Liam was staring at the small blank screen on the door, and he saw what Oliver meant.

'Biometric.'

'That's right,' said Oliver. 'Without the correct fingerprint, the keypad won't even operate.'

Liam exchanged a look with Turner, both of them perhaps recalling Valentin's orders. *Take the boy and make him tell you. Cut him to pieces if you have to.*

'But this is a panic room,' Priya said. 'You must have access to it.'

'We used to,' Oliver said. He swallowed heavily. 'Rachel and I. When it had the same kind of door as the safe we both knew how to get in. But Dad had some work done a couple of months ago. When it was complete, I came in one day and found he'd had a new door fitted.'

'And he moved everything from the safe into here?'

'I don't know.'

'You bloody live here, don't you?' Liam yelled. 'A filthy little pervert, spying on people all day. How come you don't know?'

Oliver shrank back from him, but there was nowhere to go. He bumped his head against the wardrobe door and screwed up his face at the pain.

'Dad said the work was going to be messy. He told me to spend the week in Scotland. We have a place on Loch Lomond.'

'So this room could be empty?' Turner said.

'Maybe. Dad said something about getting the door programmed for us, but he never got round to it.' Oliver sniffed. 'Our safety has never been his primary concern.'

'Yeah, save it for Jerry Springer.' Liam turned away, kicking one of the wardrobe doors in frustration. It put a satisfying split in the timber, but it wasn't nearly enough to assuage his fury.

The other three watched him as if this were completely normal behaviour. It was left to Turner to summarise their position.

'We're up shit creek, aren't we?'

Thirty-Six

Cassie lasted out until ten o'clock. Then her discipline failed her. This was much harder than dieting.

She couldn't comprehend why Joe hadn't been in touch. Had Valentin forbidden it for some reason? Through fear and anxiety she worked herself finally into an indignant rage. Her children's future was at stake here. How dare they discuss it without her.

Finding it much easier to act now she was angry rather than scared, Cassie snatched up the mobile phone, turned it on and scrolled through the address book. She remembered Joe's advice. Don't make any calls, especially not from a mobile.

She wavered, then put the phone down. There was a landline extension on the bedside table. She lifted the receiver and quickly punched in Joe's number, her heart pounding so loudly it made her feel faint.

But his phone went straight to voicemail. It must be switched off. Why?

Her fury now blunted by despair, she left a brief, incoherent message. *Joe, it's Cassie. It feels like you've been gone for ages. What's happening over there? Can you call me when you get this, and let me know how it's going? Sorry, Joe. I just want to hear that you're okay . . .*

Infused with self-loathing, she shuddered and put the phone down.

*   *   *

Joe stepped boldly over the threshold into Dreamscape's grand hall. Half a dozen rooms led off it, all the doors shut. He listened at a couple and heard nothing, then continued on to the kitchen.

That, too, was empty, but there was an adjoining utility room. As he approached it, he felt a vague claustrophobia. Sweat poured from his face, causing the mask to prickle and sting.

The utility room boasted an internal door to the garage. The door was open and the air from the garage was hot and putrid. Joe moved to the corner of the room and found an angle that let him see about half the garage. The first thing he noticed was the Ford Transit that had driven past him a few hours ago. Then he saw the prisoners.

They were arranged roughly in a circle. Joe spotted Angela Weaver, but not her husband. Terry Fox was there, and the bald American. He couldn't see Valentin, or Yuri, or the American's driver, but he guessed they were in there somewhere.

There was only one guard in sight. He was standing just beyond the prisoners, watching them closely. There was a box file at his feet, which he tapped a couple of times as though to remind himself not to forget it. He was holding a gun at his side, but his movements had a nervous quality to them, as if he were unaccustomed to this level of responsibility.

If Joe strode in there now, he reckoned it would take two or three seconds for the guard to realise he was an impostor. That might be enough time to overpower him without any weapons being fired, but it wasn't a sure bet. And if it came to a shoot-out the prisoners would be squarely in the firing line.

Reluctantly Joe decided the risk was too great. He backed away, consoling himself with the knowledge that he'd achieved his first two objectives. He had located the island's residents, and verified that they were still alive. Now he had to find a way to raise the alarm.

Liam couldn't accept that the panic room was a lost cause. He grabbed the clothes rail with both hands and pulled until it snapped in half. Tossed the broken pieces on the floor and stepped into the wardrobe.

'Show me how it works.'

Warily, Oliver moved alongside him and pressed his thumb on the screen. A message flashed up in the display: NOT REGISTERED. Liam made him try every finger. Then he made him bend down and stare into the screen, just in case the sensor worked on iris recognition.

'I told you,' Oliver said. 'It's only been programmed for my father.'

Liam fumed silently. Suddenly claustrophobic, he pushed past Oliver and stalked back into the bedroom. Turner followed him out.

'We're fucked.'

'We can't be. We've got to find a way in.'

Turner shrugged. 'Let's have a look round.'

They conducted a methodical search of the upper floor, Turner slapping the walls and mumbling to himself as he estimated the dimensions of each room. Then Priya took Oliver back to the sofa in the master bedroom, enabling Liam and Turner to check the dressing room more thoroughly. They emptied out the other wardrobes, tossing the clothes into a heap, and broke through the rear panels to examine the walls behind. Finally Turner straightened up and outlined his conclusions.

'I'd say it's about eight by ten foot. The door may be new, but the panic room itself is an integral part of the house. Built into load-bearing walls. Concrete and steel, and nigh on fucking impenetrable.'

'What about blowing the door?'

'Pendry's good, but he ain't that good. You'd bring the whole frigging house down with it.' Turner stared thoughtfully at the door. 'This doesn't even have a manufacturer's logo. If we knew who made it we could at least do some research. Find the weaknesses.'

Liam groaned. 'There must be a way to reprogram the scanner. Get it to recognise a different fingerprint.'

'Can't get at it. Set into a tamper-resistant shell, same as the ones the banks use for their ATMs. Anyway, we need the fingerprint *and* the code. One without the other is useless.'

'So there's no way in?'

'Afraid not. You'd better go and tell the boss.' Turner gave him a grim look: still no gloating. 'I'll back you up.'

Liam scowled. He didn't need the reminder that Valentin would be waiting for a progress report.

'Can you take Oliver next door?' he said. 'I want to have a think about this.'

Now he knew that the prisoners were grouped in one place, Joe conducted a brisk search of the other downstairs rooms. The third door led to an office, furnished with a modern glass desk and a sleek leather chair. There was a big aluminium box on the desk. It was about the size of an overnight case, with three fat antennas poking from the top.

He recognised what it was at once. A phone jammer, and a high powered one at that. It was a larger version of the one that Valentin kept at his London office. The Ukrainian employed a battery of counter-espionage equipment to alleviate his fears that his enemies were constantly seeking ways to destroy him.

Joe wanted to disable it permanently, but smashing the box would make too much noise. Instead he pulled out the mains plug and used his knife to sever the cable. Then he unscrewed the antennas and put them in his pocket.

He opened the door and casually walked out of the room. As he did, he heard footsteps on the driveway, approaching the house. Joe turned and ran lightly up the stairs. There was no half-landing, so he wasn't out of sight until he reached the top.

He glanced round and saw two figures moving across the hall. One of the gang was escorting a tall, thin young man in jeans and a long white shirt. Oliver Felton. Neither of them appeared to have seen Joe.

Lucky, he told himself. Now that he was up here he decided to survey the rest of the house. If it came to it, the police entry team would welcome as much information as he could give them.

The bedrooms yielded nothing of interest, though a couple had kitbags and spare clothing lying around. This was where the gang had got changed.

Then he took the stairs to the top floor. He'd heard this was Dreamscape's key feature, though evidently not quite spectacular enough to persuade anyone to part with six and a half million pounds. The floor was dominated by an enormous room that ran almost the full length of the house. A massive open-plan living space and a wall of glass that gave stunning views of the bay. But Joe hardly gave it a thought.

His attention was focused on the centre of the room. The gang had obviously been up here as well – and what they had brought with them filled him with horror.

Thirty-Seven

Although she hadn't been born until 1946 Angela was doing her best to invoke the spirit of the Blitz. That meant plenty of eye contact, lots of encouraging smiles and, whenever possible, whispered messages of support for her fellow captives.

So far she'd had mixed success. Terry Fox clearly approved, and had adopted much the same approach himself. So had Valentin's maid, Maria, who had stopped weeping and even managed a watery smile or two. But Valentin himself remained surly and uncommunicative, staring into the middle distance as if he were alone in the room.

The men with him were little better. The American, Travers, was constantly muttering to himself: either prayers, curses, or both. His driver, who'd introduced himself as Pete Milton, looked shell-shocked and petrified, his breathing ragged as a result of a broken nose. The guard had refused to help him stem the flow of blood, and it was only now beginning to clot.

If there was one consolation, it was that Valentin's dreadful body-guard, Yuri, was notable by his absence. While Angela didn't actively hope they would shoot him, she realised that she wouldn't exactly grieve if they did.

It was an appalling admission to make, even to herself, and sobering to consider how rapidly she'd fallen prey to such bloodthirsty sentiments.

Is this what we all revert to, she wondered, once the veneer of civilisation is stripped away?

A foot nudged against hers, and she looked up to find Terry Fox watching her solemnly. 'You're doing a grand job,' he said. 'Your husband would be proud of you.'

Before Angela could summon a reply, another of the guards brought Oliver Felton into the garage. He looked unharmed, but his expression of distracted sorrow was hardly uncharacteristic of him. He was a strange young man; by some accounts, really quite disturbed. In all their years as neighbours Angela had barely exchanged a dozen words with him.

The prisoners were made to shuffle along the floor to make room. Oliver sat down between Maria and Travers, directly opposite Terry and Angela. Like Valentin, he didn't acknowledge any of them; just dipped his head and stared fiercely at the ground.

Angela sighed. Here was a young man who'd had every advantage in life and yet resolutely refused to make anything of himself. She couldn't forget that when her own son had died, she'd found herself shamefully wondering why God or fate couldn't have spared him and taken Oliver Felton instead.

Another of the gang came in. Like the others he was masked, but the way he moved betrayed a sense of urgency, even alarm. Angela pretended to take no notice, but strained to hear as he addressed the guard who had accompanied Oliver.

'Where's Manderson? He's not answering his radio.'

'Isn't he at Nasenko's?'

'No. There's no sign of him.' The man lowered his voice, said something else, then turned and hurried out.

A *problem?* Angela wondered. Then she thought: *Good.*

Joe stared at the large red cylinders. There were six of them, each weighing forty-seven kilogrammes and filled with propane, suitable for ordinary domestic heating. It was highly combustible. Joe had seen the effects of a propane explosion once before, when a terrace of council houses had been demolished during a violent feud between rival drug gangs.

As far as he could recall, the quantity of gas on that occasion had been less than was present here. Not only that, but Terror's Reach had no mains gas supply. Instead, it had to be delivered by lorry and stored in bulk tanks, most of which were above ground. An explosion that detonated those stores might level every home on the island.

The obvious conclusion was that the gang intended to use that destruction to cover their tracks. But it seemed an excessive solution. A lot of extra planning and effort, given that they'd need a timer, a detonator and possibly some kind of conventional explosive to ignite the propane. Joe's instinct told him there must be another reason for it, but he had no idea what.

His immediate concern was for the prisoners downstairs. He couldn't assume that they were going to be spared.

He completed his search of the room, but found no sign of a timer or detonator. For safety's sake they would probably be kept elsewhere, most likely in the garage.

There was one other grim discovery, however. A body, wrapped in black garbage bags. Joe knelt down and cut away a flap of plastic. The dead eyes and waxen flesh hindered identification for a moment, but then he had it. The estate agent who'd driven past this afternoon.

Joe stood up, feeling a fresh surge of anger. The poor guy hadn't done anything except be in the wrong place at the wrong time.

He returned to the landing and took the stairs to the first floor. Reaching the second flight of stairs, he met one of the gang on his way up. It was the older of the bridge guards, his sandy-coloured hair now slicked down with sweat. He looked up and frowned, perhaps wondering why his colleague should have chosen to keep his mask on away from the prisoners.

'Manderson?' he said. Plenty of doubt in his voice.

Joe grunted an acknowledgement while casually swivelling round and heading towards the master bedroom at the back of the house.

'Where the hell are you—?' the man exclaimed. 'Hey! You're not Manderson.'

Joe didn't bother to speak. He didn't even look back.

He ran.

'I'm sick of this house.'

Liam looked up. Priya had made no comment when Turner led Oliver away. If she wondered why Liam wanted her to remain here with him, this might be the closest she'd get to saying so.

They were still in the dressing room, standing just a foot or so apart amidst the heaps of fine clothing swept from the wardrobes. He could feel the gentle puff of air when she exhaled.

Priya had her hands on her hips and looked ready for a confrontation. Liam thought he might welcome that.

'Yeah, well,' he said. 'I don't much like it either.'

'We're already behind schedule.' Her brow furrowed. 'Do you honestly believe there's someone out there?'

'I can't really see it.'

'Then you should call it off. Better to concentrate on what we came for.'

Liam waved towards the panic room. '*That's* what we came for. And we can't get to it.'

'So let's talk to Valentin, and come up with a contingency plan.'

'If you can think of a way to get in, I'd love to hear it.'

Priya absorbed his sarcasm with a sweet smile. 'I do know a way, thank you very much.'

'Go on, then.' He edged closer to her, and was encouraged when she didn't step back.

She won't admit it, but she wants me.

'If Robert Felton is the only person who can open it,' she said, 'then we must get Robert Felton to come here.'

Liam thought it was a stupid idea, but it was worth humouring her for the time being.

'Through Oliver?'

She nodded. 'We call Robert. Threaten to torture his little boy if he doesn't cooperate.'

'Felton's in the south of France.'

'So? He has a private plane. And we can wait all night if we have to.'

'But the longer we wait, the more chance of getting caught.'

Priya's smirk implied that his objection was cowardly rather than practical. It produced in Liam a not unpleasant pulsing at his temples: a familiar queasy excitement that usually signalled danger.

He said, 'We know that Felton doesn't rate Oliver much. He may not give a damn what we do to him.'

'In my opinion that's a chance we have to take. If you disagree, you'd better inform Valentin that it can't be done. Tell him we've failed.'

She smiled again, as though she was doing him a favour, laying it all out nice and simple so that even a moron like him could see it. And the way she said 'We've failed', in the kind of mocking tone that actually meant 'You've failed'. He felt the pulsing grow stronger, louder, unstoppable, and then—

Liam was on her before he knew what he was doing. He knocked her to the ground and fell on her, ripping the boiler suit open, tactically aware of the weapons she was carrying, a gun and at least one knife, reassuring himself that he just needed to keep her pinned tight so she couldn't reach them.

Priya hissed and spat at him, trying to form words even as he put his head down and kissed her, pressing so hard against her lips that she couldn't open her mouth to bite him. He ground his erection against her thigh, wanting her to know exactly what this was about, as if she didn't already, and even when he saw her eyes blazing with fury he was undeterred, maddened by frustration and a brutal determination that if he couldn't unlock the treasures of the panic room, he'd settle for unlocking whatever treasure she had to give. He would take it by force and afterwards convince himself that she had wanted it as much as he did.

But he got greedy. He tried to paw at her breasts, and that meant releasing one of her arms. She immediately raked his face, pressing hard enough to split her gloves and draw blood from his forehead. He reared up, and she bared her teeth at him.

'I won't make this easy for you,' she snarled. 'You'd better be prepared to kill me.'

Liam grabbed the stray arm and forced it down. He was now on all fours, each one of his limbs trapping one of hers. They were both panting, gasping for breath. He could feel blood trickling down his face.

Stalemate.

'If you do this,' Priya said, 'you'll never get out of here alive.'

Liam already knew it was over, but he said nothing. Just looked at her and let it sink in what a fucking idiot he was.

'Oh, Christ.' He let go and rolled over, collapsing on his back right beside her. In that moment he was unprotected, and he knew she could quite easily carry out her threat. He didn't care. If they couldn't get into the panic room he was a dead man anyway.

The bedroom door blasted open as Joe slid back the glass doors that led out to the balcony. From there it was about a six-foot drop to the flat roof below. Joe vaulted the balcony and felt something whistle past his head. A bullet, he realised, fired from a silenced gun.

He landed heavily on the roof and was instantly up and running for the edge. There was no time to pause or look back. Not even time to consider using the gun he'd taken from Manderson. His pursuer would be on the balcony in a second or two. If Joe was still on the roof he would be an easy target.

The next drop was a lot further: ten or twelve feet. The safest method would have been to lower himself down, but that wasn't an option. Instead he leapt out, clearing the path that ran in front of the building, and landed on grass, using the fall-and-roll technique he'd learned from a couple of parachute jumps he'd done many years ago. *Too long ago,* he thought, as it caused a jolting pain through his ankles and shins.

As he got up he spotted the gunman on the balcony, peering down at the garden. Joe's leap had triggered a security light, but he'd managed to roll into a patch of shadow. The harsh halogen beam worked in his favour, intensifying the contrast between light and dark.

But he couldn't stay here for long. The gunman was already calling in reinforcements as he turned and went back inside.

Joe dashed across the garden. Fortunately it was mostly turf and paved terraces, without too many obstacles. There was a low wall at the end, which led on to the communal deck. Joe slowed as he approached it, conscious that there might be more men out here.

He climbed over the wall, looking carefully in both directions. He decided he couldn't risk turning left towards the beach. The danger was that he'd get caught in the relatively narrow gap between the deck and the road, with no other escape route.

Instead he headed towards Valentin's. If he could get onto the property he was sure he could find a decent hiding place while he made the vital phone call. After all, he reasoned, he only needed a minute or two.

It was a challenge to run on the deck without making a lot of noise. He was moving as fast as he dared, trying to stay light on his feet, at the same time keeping alert for any sound or movement around him. As a result he almost tripped over the obstacle in his path: a formless black shape stretched across the deck.

Joe came to a stop just in time and instinctively dropped to his knees. He brought his gun up, his finger already tight on the trigger.

Half fearing that a bullet might come winging at him out of

the blackness, he cast a quick look at the obstacle itself. He ended up staring at it for a long time, trying to make sense of what he had found.

A body.

Thirty-Eight

It was another member of the gang. Same black boiler suit, same utility belt with the mask still tucked into it. No sign of his radio or gun. He was lying on his side in a pool of blood. Joe could hear the steady dripping as it seeped between the wooden planks and dropped into the water.

He leaned over and saw a glistening shadow in the folds of the man's neck. A deep slash had opened his throat. It was essentially the same wound that the estate agent had sustained, except this one was deeper: a cleaner, more ruthless strike. The work of a professional.

Joe examined the man's hands. Like his accomplices, he was wearing thin latex gloves. There was no evidence of any defence injuries. Must have been a surprise attack, probably from behind, and incredibly swift. Either that or he'd been attacked by someone he knew. Someone he trusted.

Out of habit, Joe lifted one of the wrists, rolled the glove up and felt for a pulse. A voice in his head urged him to keep moving. He couldn't begin to comprehend what was going on, and right now he shouldn't even try.

But then he detected a pulse, weak and thready. Perhaps in response to Joe's touch, the man's eyes opened briefly, but it was a dull, unseeing gaze. He was beyond help, and yet Joe couldn't bring himself to let go of the man's hand during his dying moments.

That decision cost him dearly. As he felt the pulse fading beneath his finger, the timber behind him groaned. Joe started to rise, but strong arms clamped down on his shoulders. He saw the flash of a blade, and then there was a knife pressing at his neck. The same knife, he felt sure, that had just cut the throat of the man lying before him.

Priya could have taken her revenge, but she didn't move. They both lay in silence for a long time. Then Liam pushed his fingers through his hair and sighed. He risked a quick glance at her.

'Jesus, that was stupid of me. I'm sorry.'

'And I'm disappointed,' said Priya. 'I thought you might be different from most men, but you're not. Because you're attractive, you find it impossible to believe that a woman might not want you. Well, the fact is that I *don't* want you.'

He nodded, neither of them looking at each other as they spoke.

'Are you with someone?' he asked.

'That's irrelevant.' After a moment, Priya added quietly: 'Yes, I am.'

Liam said nothing. He sensed the admission had cost her in some way, but he didn't know why.

He got up on his elbows, then twisted and rose to his knees. Facing her, he offered his hand to help her up. Priya ignored him, turned in the opposite direction and climbed to her feet. She kept her back to him while she zipped up her boiler suit and put on a fresh pair of gloves.

Ruefully, he said, 'Guess I'd better watch out for a knife in my ribs.'

'I have better things to think about,' she said. 'And so do you.'

She kicked aside Felton's suits to find her radio, which had been lost in the mêlée. It buzzed as she picked it up. So did Liam's.

It was Turner, breathing hard. Talking on the run.

'The intruder was at Dreamscape. We're after him now.' He paused, and they heard his urgent footsteps. 'Thing is . . . he's wearing Manderson's gear.'

✳   ✳   ✳

Joe was trapped. The knife was digging into his skin, just below his Adam's apple. He felt a tickling sensation as a few drops of blood bubbled up on his neck. A little more pressure and his skin would split like an over-baked potato.

He wouldn't have been so careless in his former life, he thought. Focusing on the dying man at the expense of his surroundings had been a clumsy mistake.

His assailant leaned closer, crouching over him to keep him on his knees. Joe became aware of a revolting blend of smells: booze and sweat and nicotine. It was a cocktail he'd encountered before.

A familiar voice growled: 'Not such a tough guy now, eh?'

Joe felt shock, then relief. 'Yuri?'

'Drop the gun.'

Confused, Joe did as he was told. The Ukrainian kicked it away, then used his free hand to pat him down. He missed Joe's boning knife, but he did find the Leatherman and his mobile phone. As he pocketed them there was a noise from further along the deck.

'Yuri, it's me. Let me go.'

A deep rumbling chuckle from Yuri. 'I know who it is. Tell me why you came here.'

Clattering footsteps vibrated through the timbers, flashlights spearing the darkness just yards away. Yuri had squandered their chance to escape. *Why would he do that?*

Only one answer made sense. A robbery on this scale stood a far greater chance of success if there was a man on the inside.

'You're a traitor,' Joe said. Then he looked at the dead guard lying in front of him. 'But why did you—?'

He wasn't allowed to complete the question. Yuri clubbed his fist against Joe's skull, sending him sprawling to the deck. As Joe lay there, dazed and helpless, two men ran up to them. Neither wore their masks, although in the dark it was hard to make out their faces. One was the bridge guard who'd challenged Joe back at the house. The other was about a decade older, perhaps early fifties, with grey hair and a face as hard as Sussex flint. The way they nodded at Yuri confirmed Joe's suspicion.

'I caught him,' Yuri declared. 'But not before . . .' He gestured at the dead man.

'Manderson?' the bridge guard said. He peered at the body, then gave a start. 'Fucking hell, it's Allotti.'

Joe said, 'That wasn't me, it was Yuri.'

'Yeah, and I taught Elvis to sing,' the older man said.

'Look at the knife he's holding,' Joe said. 'The same one he used on your man.'

Yuri sneered at the accusation. He bent down and retrieved the boning knife from Joe's belt. Held it out for them to see.

'He has knife too.'

Joe didn't respond. He'd underestimated the extent of Yuri's sly intelligence. The Ukrainian had left the boning knife there on purpose.

'How come he knows you?' the older man asked Yuri. 'Who is he?'

'This is Joe Carter,' said Yuri. 'He works for Valentin.'

The bridge guard directed his flashlight at Joe's face, studying him carefully. 'Hold on. We counted him out earlier. He had the wife and kids with him.' He sounded defensive, as if preparing to deflect criticism.

'Well, it looks like he came back,' the older man said. To Joe: 'Where's Manderson? And don't give us any bullshit. You're wearing his fucking clothes.'

Joe knew it would be hopeless to lie. 'He's in the trees opposite Dreamscape.'

'Dead?'

Joe nodded. The older man stared at him for a second, his eyes cold and blank. Then he lashed out with a surprising agility, punching Joe in the chest. At the last moment Joe read the blow and was able to ride with it, but still he felt a searing pain in his ribs. A little higher, a little harder, and it might have stopped his heart.

Thirty-Nine

Liam and Priya ran next door, too preoccupied even to speak. Liam had no doubt that the tension between them would resurface, but for now it had been rendered virtually immaterial.

In Dreamscape's kitchen they stopped to put on their masks. Liam was grateful that his would conceal the scratch on his forehead, but he was aware that Priya's boiler suit looked crumpled. The zip had been damaged and wouldn't go all the way to the top. Someone was bound to comment on it before long.

'Wait here,' he told her. 'I'll check on the prisoners.'

He found Eldon pacing the garage, his gun drawn. As Liam walked in he spun round, nervously raising the weapon.

'Easy,' said Liam. He pointed at the box file on the floor. 'You find anything?'

'I've not had a chance to look at it yet. I'm here on my own, aren't I?'

'All right. We'll get you some backup.'

Liam returned to the kitchen. Priya was standing by a set of glass doors that led out to the garden. He joined her and saw the flashlights approaching.

Turner was first inside, pulling on his mask as he stepped into the light. Pendry and Yuri followed, bringing the prisoner with them. Liam recognised him at once: it was the man he'd seen this afternoon.

Cassie Nasenko's bodyguard. His hands were cuffed behind his back, but his strength and defiance were almost palpable.

Liam cursed. Of all the possible intruders, why did it have to be someone who worked for Valentin?

Turner had even more bad news. 'He killed two of our lads. Manderson and Allotti.'

'Allotti as well?' Liam glared at Joe, who shook his head but said nothing.

'Cut his throat, down on the deck.' Turner produced three metal rods from his pocket and showed them to Liam. 'And he's knackered the phone jammer.'

'He made no call,' Yuri added quickly. 'I stopped him in time.'

'But not in time to save Allotti.' Liam turned to Pendry. 'Put him with the others. And bring Nasenko out here. I want to see if he knew about this.'

'He had nothing to do with it,' Joe called out as he was led away.

Liam waited till both Joe and Pendry were out of earshot, then glared at Yuri.

'This could blow everything apart. He'll tell Travers that you're working with us.'

Yuri seemed unconcerned. 'All that matters is that he does not suspect Valentin.'

Liam reflected for a moment, before conceding the point. 'I guess it could help to convince Travers. One bodyguard betrays Valentin, while the other risks his life to come here and save him . . .'

Yuri nodded. 'Best that I stay away from them. You want me to help patrol?'

'No. We need to get things back on track. Start clearing Valentin's place. I'll send Pendry along with the van.'

Yuri went out the way he'd come in. Turner looked from Liam to Priya, zeroing in on the damage to her clothing.

'What happened to you?'

'Accident.'

'You look like you got mauled by a dog.'

Priya started to answer, but Liam broke in.

'Come on. We'll speak to Valentin in the lounge.'

Joe was hauled into the garage and put with the other prisoners. He ended up taking Valentin's place, sitting between Maria and Angela Weaver. Both women greeted his appearance with delight, which promptly gave way to sorrow when it sank in that he was now every bit as helpless as they were.

Valentin's reaction was very different. He gaped at Joe and made a choking noise in his throat. For a second Joe thought the Ukrainian was having a heart attack. The guard had to hold him steady.

Regaining the ability to speak, he said, 'Where's my daughter?'

'She's safe,' said Joe. 'No thanks to you.'

Valentin's expression darkened. He wasn't used to his employees addressing him in such a tone. But he also looked anxious and bewildered. Joe wondered what kind of punishment awaited him. As Joe's employer, the gang could very well hold Valentin responsible for what Joe had done.

While brooding on that, and on the many unpleasant forms that their retaliation might take, it was an image from earlier that kept nagging at him. Valentin emerging from his home with one of the gang. Probably the man who'd just spoken to Joe in the kitchen: a subtle Irish accent and a conspicuous air of authority. Was that 'Liam', the name he'd overheard at the bridge?

Angela Weaver leaned towards Joe, brushing her arm against his in a gesture of affection.

'Try not to worry. They took him out once before, but brought him back a few minutes later.'

Joe nodded. Perceptive as ever, Angela had read his mind.

'But not your colleague Yuri,' she added in a low voice. 'He's been gone a while.'

'That's because he's working with them. It was Yuri who caught me.'

Angela gasped, and a rumbling of anger and disgust spread around the group. Joe realised he could have been slightly more diplomatic.

But then she said: 'I can't say I'm surprised, actually. He's a despicable man.'

'I wouldn't disagree with that.'

'They murdered your other colleague, Mr McWhirter.' Angela paused. 'And my husband.'

Joe turned towards her, aghast. 'I'm very sorry.'

And he was. He'd failed these people. He had been their best hope of survival and he'd blown it.

Maria caught his eye and gave him a comforting smile. He returned it in kind, but felt like a fraud for doing so.

The bald American had been watching him closely the whole time. He had the cunning look of a man who always has his eye out for the main chance, filing away every interaction for future profit.

Of all the prisoners, only Oliver Felton seemed detached from the situation. He was leaning back, staring intently at the ceiling as if there was another world playing out up there.

In a way, there was. Joe assumed that none of them knew about the propane, and he certainly didn't intend to enlighten them.

What he'd seen already convinced him that the operation was in disarray. Just how badly it had gone wrong, even the gang themselves didn't appreciate. They all believed that Joe had killed the man on the deck: Allotti. But he hadn't.

Right now that worried him more than anything. If things got any messier, the temptation to make a clean break would become irresistible. And there was no better way to sterilise Terror's Reach than blowing the place apart.

Once again they convened in the living room: Liam, Valentin and Turner. This time Priya was with them. She ignored the sofas and stood with her back against the far wall, where she could keep an eye on them all.

She pulled off her mask and shook her head, causing her hair to shimmy and cascade over her shoulders. Liam looked away, but not before Turner had caught him watching her. At the same time Turner spotted the scratches on Liam's face, and gave a little snigger.

When Valentin entered the room, Priya was the first person he saw. He faltered, as though he'd forgotten that the team included a woman. He looked old and confused, a shadow of the powerful figure who had put this operation together. Liam found himself wondering how on earth he'd come to invest so much confidence in the man.

Priya seemed equally shocked by Valentin's appearance. She took a step forward, but he shook his head and collapsed onto the nearest sofa. His malevolent gaze scoured the room and came to rest on Liam. 'What is going on?'

'We have the same question.' The use of the plural was deliberate. Given the bad news he was about to deliver, Liam thought it a judicious moment to introduce the notion of collective responsibility. 'What the hell is this Joe Carter guy doing here?'

'I don't know. I arranged for him to be in Brighton.'

'With your wife and children?'

'My wife and *daughter*,' Valentin corrected him. 'And the boy.'

There was a soft, contemptuous snort from Priya. The tension in the room ratcheted up a notch.

'So where are they, then?' Turner asked.

'I was not given a chance to find out,' said Valentin. 'This is a mistake, to keep bringing me in here. Travers will suspect something.'

'Not necessarily,' said Liam. 'At least Joe's presence helps us there. Travers will think he came running back to save his boss.'

'But Joe knew nothing of this. Why did he come here?'

Liam thought of Gough, getting jittery about Joe's presence on the beach. Then, later, Priya bumping against the side of the van and Joe watching as they drove past. He decided not to mention either incident.

'What matters is that he's here. He sabotaged the phone jammer and he killed two of our men.'

'*What?*'

'Manderson and Allotti,' Turner chipped in. 'He cut Allotti's throat. We haven't found Manderson yet.'

Valentin looked horrified. 'You must handle him very carefully. We cannot afford any more of these . . . *disasters.*'

The comment seemed to be directed wholly at Liam. He bristled, but Priya spoke before he could defend himself.

'I don't agree that Joe's presence is a benefit. I think we should kill him.'

'Fucking right,' said Turner. 'Payback for Manderson and Allotti, if nothing else.'

Valentin pondered for a moment, then said, 'Very well. But question him first. Do it in the garage.'

'You want us to hurt him?'

'Of course. Make it painful, so the others take note.'

'In that case you should appeal to us to spare him,' Priya said. 'Nothing too theatrical, though.'

Liam expected Valentin to be insulted, but instead he nodded vigorously.

'Yes. I will plead for his life. Good.' He smiled. The discussion seemed to have revived him, but Liam knew the bombshell that was coming. He felt a flutter of anxiety in his stomach.

'Now,' said Valentin. 'The Felton boy – did he give you the information? There's another safe, I am sure of it.'

Liam swallowed hard.

'It's not quite that simple.'

Forty

The reason for Joe's introspection might have been lost on some of his fellow prisoners. It wasn't lost on Angela.

'There's no point dwelling on it, you know.'

'What?'

'Reproaching yourself, after you risked so much. Valentin told me you'd gone to Brighton with Cassie and the little ones. You came back to help us, didn't you?'

Joe nodded. 'I should have made a better job of it.'

'I'm sure you did your best. But how did you know what was happening?'

'I didn't, at first.' He described the first niggling concern after he'd seen the builders' van, then the later barricade at the bridge and the sight of the Cadillac driver being chased by armed men.

'That fisherman from this afternoon is part of it, too,' he told her. 'I saw him at the bridge.'

'Our litter lout? I had wondered if he was. He looked like a hoodlum.' She tutted. 'No matter. The past can't be undone. We must focus on what lies ahead.'

Joe couldn't help grinning. Angela might have been gearing up for a campaign against an environmental outrage or an unpopular government policy, not facing a gang of heavily armed criminals from a position of utter weakness.

But she was absolutely right.

They continued to talk in low voices. By pooling their knowledge they managed to put names to most of the gang. The dead men were Manderson and Allotti. The Irishman who seemed to be in charge was indeed called Liam. His second-in-command was Turner, the man who'd punched Joe in the chest.

Oliver Felton was initially reluctant to contribute. He'd been held next door on his own for some time, but steadfastly refused to discuss what had happened. Finally he revealed that the woman whom Joe had seen in the kitchen was called Priya, and she too enjoyed a senior status.

The man guarding them was named Eldon. According to Angela he seemed timid and out of his depth. Hearing that, Joe wished he'd stormed the garage when he'd had the chance. Now Eldon had been joined by the bridge guard who'd helped capture Joe. His name was Pendry.

So nine people in total, including Yuri and the fisherman, Gough. Two dead, leaving six men and one woman. Not great odds, Joe thought.

Throughout the discussion the American had remained quiet. Now he weighed in. 'This is a two-bit operation. And they're a bunch of lousy amateurs.' He spoke loudly enough for the guards to hear.

'Doesn't feel like that from where I'm sitting,' Terry Fox muttered.

The American ignored him, fixing his gaze on Joe. 'You agree with me?'

'Maybe.' Joe didn't care for the American's tone, implying as it did that they might share a common outlook.

'They just got lucky,' the American assured them. 'And this guy Liam? He may be running the show on the ground, but there'll be a whole other layer above him. At least one man, and probably several, don't you think?'

Again the question was directed at Joe. He shrugged. 'It's feasible.'

The American nodded with satisfaction. 'Since we're putting names to faces, I'm Mike Travers.'

'Joe Carter.'

Travers smiled. The twinkle in his eye said he knew it was an alias.

'I hear you work for Valentin?'

'That's right.'

'Been there long?'

'A while.'

'Always done security work?'

'In a manner of speaking.'

Travers nodded, as if this kind of verbal chess merely confirmed his theory.

'I passed you on the bridge, didn't I?'

'That's right.'

'And he came back,' Angela cut in, aggrieved at what she interpreted as hostile questioning. 'He didn't have to, but he came back to help us.'

Travers looked amused. 'You'll pardon me for saying so, Angela, but it hasn't helped us a whole lot yet.'

Angela made a huffing noise, but was stilled from further comment by Terry Fox. In the silence that followed, Joe was left wondering if anyone else had picked up on the American's subtle but unmissable emphasis on the word 'yet'.

Liam's explanation came out in a rush, bombarding Valentin with facts in the hope that the cumulative effect would be to wear the Ukrainian down.

There wasn't another safe, as such. It was a panic room. An integral part of the building. The loot was almost certainly inside, but a new door had been fitted. Biometric security. Oliver Felton had demonstrated beyond doubt that he could not open it up. The room was impregnable . . . as Turner would confirm.

At that point Liam's heart skipped a beat, until Turner nodded. 'We could maybe blow the whole house apart. Other than that, not a cat in hell's chance.'

Valentin's mouth tightened. His face flushed. Liam thought he was going to explode, but when he spoke he surprised them all by talking quietly. They had to strain to hear him.

'First you come to me and tell me the safe is empty.' He put on a high-pitched sing-song voice: '"It is all over, Valentin. We are finished." But I say: "No. It is a decoy. There is another safe." So you go away and what do you find? It is a decoy! There is a panic room. This is where Felton has put his money. So that is good news, yes? If I had not told you this, would the panic room have been found? No. And yet still you come back here and tell me: "Oh, Valentin, it is impossible. There is no way to get inside."'

Valentin slowly shook his head, as if marvelling at the chasm between his wisdom and their incompetence.

'So now I say to you: "Do not keep returning to me for every tiny decision. *Open. This. Fucking. Door.*"' He punctuated each of the last four words by thumping his bound hands on the arm of the sofa.

'Pendry is the explosives man, yes?' he asked Turner.

'Yeah, but he'll tell you the same—'

'No. Pendry will *not* tell me the same. Pendry will find a solution.' Valentin gritted his teeth, virtually snarling as he looked at each of them in turn. 'You will not leave this island until we have found a way to get inside that room. And yes, destroy the entire house if that is what it takes. But *don't* come back to me until you have succeeded.'

Liam sighed. He tried to look both stern and conciliatory, all the while thinking: *I didn't sign up for this.* From the way he was glowering Turner seemed to share the sentiment.

But Priya did not. She said: 'I have a better idea.'

Valentin's temper immediately cooled. 'Aha! Someone who can bring me answers not problems for a change. Well?'

'We use Oliver Felton as a hostage and summon his father here. Either he opens the panic room or we dismember his little boy.'

Valentin looked sceptical, which gave Liam a small boost.

'Does Felton care enough about his son?'

'Not ordinarily. But this is an extreme situation. I can't believe he'd let Oliver die.'

It was the first that Turner had heard of the idea, and he looked far from impressed. 'Yeah, and what if he just calls the cops?'

'Felton's a professional. An experienced man. He'll know better than to act so rashly.'

Both Liam and Turner started to add their objections, but Valentin cut them short.

'There are hazards, yes. But I do not think we can reject it without some more thought.'

'And what happens while we wait for Felton to arrive?' Liam said. 'Every minute that we're here increases the risks. We're two men down already, for Christ's sake. There's hardly anyone spare to load up the vans . . .'

'Then some extra time will be of value to us,' said Valentin. 'No one will come here during the night. As long as the phones are monitored, we should be safe until morning.'

He stared at Liam, challenging him to disagree. Liam felt Priya's gaze upon him, solemn and steady and gently derisive. After his botched assault on her, he knew some of his authority had slipped away. How he reacted now could determine whether he lost it completely.

'All right,' he said. 'But first let's find out what brought Joe here. I'll get Pendry and Eldon started on the inventory and then we'll make a decision, okay?'

Adding insult to injury, Valentin glanced at Priya before he replied.

'Very well. But any more mistakes and the decisions will not be yours to make.'

Gough wasn't sure whether to feel pleased or resentful that he'd wound up guarding the bridge. It was boring as hell, but at least it didn't require much effort. Generally that suited him fine.

After abandoning the beach early, he'd feared that he had blown his chances altogether. He probably would have done if he'd admitted to playing chicken with the silly old cow on her bike. Wisely he had said nothing to Liam or Turner.

Still, seeing her take a tumble had been the best part of his day, no question. It made him smile to think about it now.

After some trial and error he'd found a comfortable spot where the bridge joined the island. The kerb was raised just high enough to sit on, and he could rest his back against the railing. The gentle lapping of the water against the old slipway almost had him convinced he was on holiday. He'd kill for a cocktail now, he thought. Something big and fancy, loaded with spirits.

He shut his eyes for a moment, just to help him visualise the drink. He wanted to get the ingredients right, even if he was only making it in his imagination. Maybe a daiquiri. No. Havana Beach. A measure of white rum, two measures of pineapple juice, half a lime and a teaspoon of sugar . . .

He didn't fall asleep. He was quite sure of that. So the noise couldn't have woken him.

Unless he had dozed off, just for a second or two, and there hadn't been a noise at all. Maybe he'd dreamed that.

He sat up, rubbed his eyes and checked the time. It was ten-thirty. Was that right?

Gough looked across the bridge. Without getting up he could see that the road on the mainland was as deserted as ever. It was paler than the empty, mysterious landscape which surrounded it, and seemed to be glowing gently in the starlight.

He wondered about the wildlife. There had to be all kinds of things moving around out there. It was a bloody nature reserve, after all. Foxes, badgers, rabbits. Those little rodent things from that kids' book about the frog. What was that? *Wind in the Willows*. They must have willows here, as well, not that he'd know what they looked like . . .

The next noise was definitely real.

It was a voice. Right behind him.

'Too bad,' it said. The tone was one of mocking disappointment, which for a second made him think that Turner had caught him napping. That would have been bad, but not disastrous.

Then Gough felt the blade against his neck, and he knew it was much, much worse than that.

Forty-One

A few minutes after Pendry took over guard duty, Eldon picked up the box file and retreated to a corner of the garage. Joe watched as he sat down on the floor, crossed his legs and rested the file on his lap. He fidgeted for a moment, then opened it up.

The box was bulging with what appeared to be a mass of old documents. Eldon lifted the metal clip and tried to separate the first sheet of paper. The gloves made it difficult, so he stripped them off. Wiped his hands on his trouser legs and then got to work. He read both sides of the first document, set it down on the floor and picked up the next one.

Joe was making a note that the police might be able to lift Eldon's fingerprints from the paper when there was a low, despairing groan from close by.

It was Oliver Felton. Visibly trembling, he seemed unaware of the noise he was making.

'Oliver?' said Angela, trying to reach towards him. She glanced at Terry Fox. 'Is he having a seizure?'

'I don't think so,' said Terry. He called Oliver's name, sharply enough to catch Pendry's attention. The guard growled at him to shut up.

Oliver looked at Terry, then shook his head from side to side, as though denying some horrible accusation.

'No no no no no nooooo . . .'

Angela tried again. 'Oliver, what's wrong?'

But the young man was unresponsive. Joe heard activity behind him and twisted round. Valentin was being led back in. He looked furious but unharmed. For the first time it struck Joe that the Ukrainian's hands were cuffed from the front, as were Angela's, whereas everyone else was bound from behind. He wondered why that was.

There were three members of the gang with Valentin, all masked and distinguishable only by their shape and posture. He could see that the two men were Liam and Turner, and the third was the woman: Priya.

'What's his fucking problem?' Turner said, pointing at Oliver.

'I dunno,' said Pendry. 'He's a fruitcake, isn't he?'

'He'll get a bullet in the gob if he doesn't button it.'

As he spoke, Turner kicked Oliver in the back. The young man fell forward, crying out with pain. He straightened up, tears spilling down his face, snot bubbling from his nose.

Joe was forced nearer to Angela as Valentin resumed his position amongst the prisoners. Liam and Priya had moved towards the far side of the garage, where they were in quiet conversation with Pendry.

Travers lifted his head, catching Turner's eye before he moved away.

'Hey, I wanna speak to whoever's in charge here.'

Turner studied him for a moment, his eyes narrowed. 'Why?'

'I want the boss man, okay? I've got something for him.'

Turner made a dismissive noise, and ambled casually in Liam's direction as though unwilling to be seen in the role of messenger boy.

Joe looked at Travers. 'You're making a mistake.'

The American met his gaze with a blatant lack of shame. 'No mistake, buddy.'

Terry Fox gasped as he realised what was happening. 'You're not seriously intending to bargain with them?'

'Maybe.'

'That's pathetic,' said Angela. 'If they're the amateurs you claim they are, it'll all fall apart soon enough.'

Travers regarded her with contempt. 'It's the fact they're amateurs that scares me. Professionals would have taken what they wanted and hightailed it out of here by now. These jokers have screwed up – and that means we're much more likely to die. That's why I'm gonna trade my way out of here.'

'Traitor!' Angela said with disgust. 'Anyway, what have you got to give them?'

Immune to her scorn, Travers grinned. He stared at Joe as he answered.

'Oh, I got plenty,' he said. 'Don't you fret about that.'

Liam was explaining the probable layout of the panic room to Pendry when Turner sauntered up.

'The Yank wants a word.'

'What?'

'Says he has something to tell you.'

Liam nodded irritably. 'Bring him over here.'

He told Pendry to take a look at the panic room, then join Yuri at Valentin's place. Pendry climbed into the Transit and started it up, while Priya pressed the button that opened the garage doors. There were gasps of relief from the prisoners as fresh air wafted into the room.

The tall American smiled as Liam approached. He gazed out at the darkness and murmured: 'Freedom.'

Liam said nothing. He resented the American's easy manner, acting like the two of them had just stepped out for a cigarette at a cocktail party.

'You're Liam, right? The big man in charge?'

'Yeah.'

Travers tutted. 'So who's in charge of you?' He made a show of surveying the room. 'Is he here too?'

At that moment Liam was grateful for his mask. He reassured himself that it wasn't anything more than a throwaway comment. If Travers genuinely believed that Valentin was involved, he'd surely have come right out and said so.

'What do you want?'

'Got a proposal for you. Something you need to know.'

'Go on.'

Travers sucked air between his teeth, in the time-honoured manner of a negotiator.

'A few things to get straight first. You see, I don't much care what you fellas are up to. Far as I'm concerned, you're welcome to every last cent on the island. All I want is my car and a route out of here.' He chuckled. 'Hell, you can even keep my driver. I won't breathe a word about what happened because, like I said, I don't give a damn.'

'That part's clear enough. What I don't get is why we should let you go.'

'You're a man of honour, right?' Travers didn't wait for a reply. 'Sure you are. And believe me, you really need to know this. So do we have a deal, yes or no?'

Liam almost had to laugh. *Talk about full of shit.*

He glanced over the American's shoulder and saw Turner give a shrug. *Can't hurt to listen.*

'All right. But you'll have to give it to us first.'

'And trust you to let me go?'

'That's the deal. Take it or leave it.'

He watched Travers weighing it up, uncertainty in his eyes.

'Okay,' he said. 'Now, I saw you took Nasenko out just now. What has he told you about his man over there?'

Travers turned and nodded towards Joe, who was watching them with a determinedly neutral expression.

'Like what?' Liam asked.

'Like his career history. His résumé.'

Liam affected a lack of interest. 'Get to the point, or go back and sit down.'

'The point is that Joe Carter, or whatever he calls himself, isn't just a common or garden bodyguard.' Travers grinned. 'He's a cop. An undercover cop.'

Forty-Two

Joe was too far away to hear, too far away to read anything but body language. But that was enough.

He knew what Travers was going to tell them – because now he remembered where he'd seen the American before. Going back ten years or more, Joe had been attending a meeting at New Scotland Yard. During a break, he and a fellow officer had queued for the coffee machine behind the American, who'd been deep in conversation with a couple of people from what was then known as SO12, or Special Branch. The man had been unfamiliar to them both, but Joe's colleague had deduced who – or what – he was.

CIA.

Reflecting on it, Joe guessed that Travers would have retired from the Agency by now, and had probably transferred his skills and contacts to the more lucrative civilian arena. If so, that would explain his meeting with Valentin earlier today.

Joe felt a calm descend on him. Whatever was about to happen, there was little he could do but wait and see how it played out. But Angela looked sick with fear, as though she too had worked out what leverage Travers might have. Joe tried to reassure her that he wasn't going to panic, and neither should she.

Valentin ought to have been desperate to know what Liam and Travers were talking about, but he appeared remarkably unperturbed.

Perhaps nothing that Travers told them would alter Valentin's own predicament. After all, Yuri had already betrayed him—

Joe shut his eyes. When he did, the image that came to him was a drop of whisky, sliding down a silver hip flask. It had stuck in his mind for a reason, and now he understood what it was.

A toast. They had drunk a toast to their success.

And then he recalled the conversation that Cassie had reported overhearing. Yuri asking, 'Do you want to kill them?' and Valentin's reply: 'Not if we can find a better way.'

When Joe opened his eyes the other prisoners were staring at him, aware that something important had happened. Angela spoke to him, and so did Maria, but Joe's mind was elsewhere.

He looked at Valentin. 'You knew about Yuri.'

Valentin shook his head, but the gesture lacked conviction.

'What are you saying?' Terry Fox demanded.

'This is a set-up,' Joe said, still working it through in his mind. 'A big, elaborate con-trick.'

Then everyone started talking at once: a few seconds of noisy outrage, brought to a halt when Liam marched over. Travers was alongside him, looking smugly pleased.

Liam drew his gun, glanced at Valentin and then turned his attention to Joe.

'Mr Travers here claims you're a cop. Is that right?'

Liam watched Joe carefully. He believed he would be able to spot the lie, if and when it came.

He also felt sure the allegation was true. Joe's composure had bothered him from the start. It was characteristic of a professional of some sort: police, army, special forces. After all, why else would Valentin have employed him?

Joe took a long time to reply. Liam could sense the other prisoners hardly daring to breathe. Turner and Priya stood off to one side, watching and waiting.

'Well?'

Finally Joe nodded. 'I was a police officer, just like he was in the CIA.' He indicated Travers. 'But I'm not a cop any more. Haven't been for years. I work for Valentin.'

It was a neat manoeuvre, Liam thought, passing the onus on to Nasenko. It was also a reminder that the prisoners would expect him to question Joe's employer.

'Did you know this?' he asked.

The Ukrainian shook his head. 'No. We suspected the ID he gave us was false, but there can be many reasons for this.'

Stupid fucker, Liam thought. He came dangerously close to saying it aloud. *Organising a job like this with a bloody ex-cop on your books . . .*

He put it aside for now. Looked from Valentin to Travers, then to Joe. 'You killed two of my men. I'm sure you'd allege it was self-defence, but I doubt if you can prove that.'

Joe started to protest but Liam cut him off.

'That means you've crossed a line, a line no serving policeman would dare to cross. Therefore I conclude that you're not a threat to us.'

Now it was Travers who began to speak. Liam turned and aimed his gun at the American's belly.

'Hey, we had a deal, buddy,' Travers shouted. 'I was trying to help you.'

'Bullshit,' said Liam. 'This was about saving your own skin.'

He fired twice, hitting Travers in the stomach and chest from a distance of less than four feet. Because of the silencer, the noise was unspectacular. A couple of the prisoners had their backs to him and didn't fully comprehend what they'd heard until the American crashed to the floor.

Joe watched Travers fall, his eyes still wide in disbelief that his scheme hadn't paid off. The only consolation was that it was a quick death; perhaps better than Travers deserved. But Joe took no satisfaction from it.

'You didn't need to do that,' he told Liam. 'It just demonstrates how frightened you are.'

The Irishman laughed off the comment. With his acolytes in tow, he returned to the far side of the garage. Joe kept an eye on Valentin, who looked genuinely staggered by Travers's murder.

'It's not going according to plan, is it?'

Valentin sighed. 'Please, Joe. No more crazy talk.'

The weariness was genuine, Joe could see, but the reason for it was false.

'It's not crazy. You and Yuri worked on this together.'

'Is that true?' Terry Fox asked. He looked as though he would tear Valentin to pieces given half a chance.

'It had better not be,' Angela said. 'If I thought you had anything to do with my husband's murder . . .'

Valentin flinched. 'I tell you, no, it is not true. I am here, aren't I? A prisoner, like you.' Joe spotted the tiny, calculating glance at his audience: trying to gauge the effectiveness of his performance. 'Remember that McWhirter is dead, too. My adviser, my friend for many years.'

These last words carried enough weight to create plausible doubt. Angela and Terry fell silent, but Maria caught Joe's eye and shook her head emphatically. Like Joe, she wasn't convinced.

'We were attacked in Brighton,' he told Valentin. 'Two men and a woman, driving an M-class Mercedes. They were trying to abduct Sofia.'

'What?' Valentin looked thunderstruck. 'Is she all right? Is she safe?'

Joe nodded. 'You're saying you didn't arrange for it?'

'Me? Why would I . . . ?'

'To pre-empt a custody battle. Because you and Cassie are on the verge of separating.'

Valentin slowly worked through Joe's accusation. His body seemed to sag, and he looked around hopelessly, as though he no longer cared whether anyone believed him.

'No,' he said at last. 'I swear to you, I know nothing of this.'

*   *   *

Liam was aware of Priya seething quietly as she followed him across the garage. The pressure on him was suddenly overwhelming. At that moment he could have happily slaughtered everyone in the room just for the chance to take off his mask and breathe some fresh air. He felt the walls closing in, the garage no more than a cell, getting smaller, tighter, as his options ran out . . .

And a cell was where he might end up. Liam knew he could never survive that. He'd kill himself rather than face incarceration.

The first time Priya spoke, he missed it and she had to repeat her question.

'I said, do you think that was wise?'

'I don't care. The Yank was pissing me off.'

Priya's eyes narrowed. 'Travers was a vital link in the chain. We need someone Felton trusts, to corroborate what happened.'

'Not any more we don't. Because we're going to get Felton over here, and then he can see for himself.'

Priya sighed. Not the reaction Liam expected.

'What's the matter with you? Calling Felton was your fucking idea.'

'And if for some reason it doesn't happen? By killing Travers you've just destroyed your back-up plan.'

'We don't need a back-up plan.'

Turner, not quite eavesdropping, muttered: 'Could have fooled me.'

'Look, we've had some setbacks,' Liam said, 'and we've dealt with every one of them. Believe me, once you see inside that panic room you'll forget all about this.'

'I bloody well hope so,' said Turner.

'All right,' said Priya, sticking rigidly to business. 'What about Joe?'

'Like I said, I'm not worried about him. When we're done here we'll strap him to a propane canister and it'll be like he never existed.' Liam laughed, but no one else joined in.

'Come on,' he said. 'We'll take Oliver into the lounge to make the call, then you two can help the others. Once we get the vans loaded up we'll feel a lot better.'

They turned back towards the prisoners. Liam noticed Eldon sitting against the wall, the box file from Felton's safe open on his lap. As he watched, Eldon added another sheet to the loose pile of papers on the floor and turned to the next item in the box.

Then he stopped. He looked up and back down again, staring at a small brown envelope. He picked it up, examined both sides, then glanced over as he heard Liam approaching.

'What?' said Liam. 'You found something?'

'I'm not sure,' said Eldon. He sounded confused. 'I think so.'

Forty-Three

This was the moment Oliver had been dreading. The last piece of the puzzle had fallen into place only minutes before, when the guard opened the box file and Oliver remembered . . .

. . . the file materialising in his father's study, four or five days ago. Oliver carried out regular if desultory sweeps of the room. He knew that anything valuable or vaguely scandalous would be kept well out of his grasp, but still it amused him to search from time to time.

But riffling through the box had yielded nothing of interest. A couple of days later, when he'd gone back into the study, there had been an envelope sitting on top of the box. At the time it had left him intrigued, but not particularly excited. It was just one of those things that didn't make much sense.

Until now.

'What is it?' Liam said.

Eldon shrugged. He held the envelope at arm's length, as if he wanted nothing more to do with it.

Liam took it from him. The envelope felt thin: probably no more than a single sheet of paper inside. No stamp or postmark. But it was sealed at the back, and on the front there was a name, handwritten in capital letters.

VALENTIN NASENKO

Liam looked at it for a long time. He wanted to believe it was a bizarre coincidence, or some kind of joke.

'Where did you find it?'

Eldon lifted a thick wad of documents. 'Right at the bottom, tucked between a couple of old share certificates.'

Liam felt Priya at his side. He showed her the envelope. Her arm brushed against his shoulder as she leaned over to look; neither of them reacted to the contact.

She stared at the name on the envelope, then at Liam. She opened her mouth to speak but he shook his head. *Say nothing.*

The letter might have been addressed to Valentin, but there was absolutely no question of giving it to him, or even alerting him to its existence. This understanding passed swiftly between them, confirmed by Priya's nod of approval as Liam hooked his thumb into the flap and ripped the envelope open.

No going back now.

Then someone shouted his name.

Joe was inclined to believe that Valentin knew nothing about the abduction attempt. He was far less confident when it came to Valentin's denials of complicity in the attack on Terror's Reach.

One thing Joe did know: Valentin Nasenko played second fiddle to nobody. If he *was* involved, it was more than likely that he'd masterminded the entire operation. And Robert Felton would be the principal target, for two reasons.

Firstly, once the Nasenkos were discounted, Felton was far and away the wealthiest individual on Terror's Reach. Secondly, and perhaps more crucially, there was a deep personal animosity between the two men.

So far, so logical. But there were still missing pieces of the puzzle – like the abduction, and Allotti's death.

He looked up, aware that Liam had made an abrupt detour towards

Eldon. Joe wondered why the guard was spending so much time looking through old paperwork. What did they hope to find?

Dismissing it, he went back to the twin anomalies: the kidnap attempt and Allotti's murder. This time he made the connection at once. They were linked by one man.

Yuri had been only yards away from Allotti when Joe stumbled upon the body.

Yuri had instructed Joe to take Cassie and the children to the jewellers at a specific time.

'Oh shit,' Joe whispered.

He sat up, craning to get a clear sight of Liam. He was holding an envelope, which he showed to Priya before tearing it open.

'Liam!'

The Irishman glanced at him, irritated, then turned away.

'Listen to me,' said Joe. 'You have a guard at the bridge, right?'

'Shut up!' From Turner, striding towards him.

'You need to speak to him. Right now. Otherwise he'll end up like Allotti.'

'Bollocks,' said Turner. 'You killed Allotti.'

'No. Believe me, you have to call him. Make sure he's still alive.'

Liam could hear what Joe was saying, but the words barely penetrated. He felt strangely apprehensive as he opened the envelope, as though its contents might somehow prove more hazardous than anything they'd encountered so far.

Inside there was a sheet of good-quality A5 paper, folded in half. He unfolded it and held it out for them both to read. One word, written in the same block capitals as on the envelope:

CHECKMATE

Priya reacted first. 'What does he mean by that?'

'No idea. But I don't like it.'

'Do you think it's a . . . I don't know, a draft version or something?'

'Maybe. But the envelope was sealed.'

'So he just hadn't got round to sending it?'

'They live virtually next door to each other,' Liam said. His mouth had gone dry, and he swallowed with difficulty. There was an idea forming in his mind, and it was one he wanted desperately to ignore.

He saw that Turner had moved away from the prisoners and was talking on his radio. He must be taking Joe's warning seriously. Liam would have bawled him out for that, but he had more important things on his mind.

He strode towards the prisoners. When they saw him coming, they shuffled like nervous livestock. They avoided direct eye contact, but watched him with wary sidelong glances.

Oliver Felton was the exception. Head down, gaze fixed on the floor, brow furrowed with concentration; he might have been trying to vanish by sheer willpower.

Liam thrust the paper in front of Oliver's face. 'Explain this.'

Oliver said nothing. With his free hand, Liam took out his gun and jammed the muzzle against Oliver's temple.

'Tell me.'

Oliver looked up at the note, then back at the floor. 'I can't explain it.'

'Do you recognise the handwriting?'

'It's my father's, I think. But I've no idea what it means.'

'Not good enough,' said Liam. 'When your dad cleared out the safe, why did he leave that box of documents?'

'Most of it is worthless,' Oliver said. 'I suppose he didn't think there was any need to move it.'

'So why not throw it away?'

'I don't know.'

'It was left there on purpose, wasn't it? For us to find.'

Silence. Liam tapped the young man's head with the gun. 'Wasn't it?'

'I suppose so.'

Now that Oliver was responding, Liam casually moved the note, holding it in such a way that Valentin would be able to read it. He heard gasps as the other prisoners also digested the message.

'You knew this was here,' said Liam.

'I . . . I saw the envelope,' Oliver admitted in a small voice. 'I didn't understand it, not until . . . all this happened.'

'Sure about that?' Liam's finger tightened on the trigger. Oliver must have felt the tension, the desire within Liam to shoot, but he looked untroubled by it. There was a dreamy expression on his face as he whispered something that Liam didn't catch.

'What?'

'Do it,' said Oliver. 'I want you to do it.'

Joe read the unease in Liam's movements, in his voice. The man was on the brink of panic. If Joe misjudged now, he might very easily push Liam over the edge. But neither could he sit there and let Oliver die the way Travers had done.

'You need to think carefully about this,' Joe said.

'Don't interfere,' said Liam, 'or you'll be next.'

But his trigger finger relaxed, just slightly. The barrel of the gun drifted a couple of inches from Oliver's head.

Checkmate.

Joe had seen the message, as had the others. He suspected Liam had deliberately allowed Valentin to read it. The Ukrainian had given no reaction, even when Liam's questions had also revealed that Felton's safe was empty.

They told Valentin earlier, Joe thought. *That's why he was taken out of the room: for a progress report.*

'You've been played,' he said, but his words were lost as Turner stomped over.

'Nothing from Gough,' he told Liam. 'And I know he was alive after we caught Joe, because I spoke to him.'

'Try him again. He may not have heard you.'

'I tried three times. I've sent Pendry to look for him.' Turner noticed the paper in Liam's hand. 'What's that?'

Liam showed him the letter and the envelope. Turner exploded. 'What the fuck is this about?'

Joe got in first. 'It's Yuri. I thought maybe he'd got greedy, wiping out some of your team so he could make off with a larger share. That's why I tried to warn you. But it's worse than that.'

Liam started to rubbish him, but Turner, who looked like the sort of man who trusted no one, said, 'Hold on. I wanna hear this.'

Joe nodded, then addressed Valentin. 'I think you should have the guts to explain. After all, it's you that got us all into this mess.'

Valentin recoiled at the accusation. 'Wh-what do you . . . ?'

'This is all about Robert Felton, isn't it?' said Joe. 'Your pathetic feud. You wanted revenge, so you planned to rob him. And you pretended to be a victim yourself so Felton wouldn't suspect it was you.'

Angela Weaver cried out, and there was an angry exclamation from Terry Fox. Even Oliver lifted his head to stare at Valentin.

'This is more crazy talk,' Valentin said, forcing sarcasm into his voice. 'Just a way for you to buy your freedom, like Travers tried to do.'

Joe shook his head. 'You're the one who's been lying through his teeth. And you're the one who bears responsibility for what these people have done.'

'What did you mean about Yuri?' Liam demanded.

Joe paused for a moment, making sure he had their full attention. 'He's double-crossed you.'

Forty-Four

The clock moved inexorably towards 11 p.m. while Cassie tried without success to sleep. The room was uncomfortably hot, but because they were on the ground floor she didn't dare open the main window. Instead she'd opened a small trap window, but the air in the room hardly stirred. The night was warm and still, and they were too far inland to benefit from the cooling sea breezes that made sleeping at Terror's Reach so pleasurable.

At the thought of her home a sadness and longing enveloped her. She considered making another phone call, perhaps this time to Valentin himself. She didn't know whether to feel frightened or betrayed that Joe hadn't called back. Surely by now he would have heard her message?

She turned over, facing towards Jaden. He was sleeping under a sheet, snoring softly, his face almost impossibly serene. Cassie lay on top of the covers, wearing only knickers and a thin T-shirt. She curled into a foetal position and fought off another bout of tears.

The knock on the door was nearly too quiet to hear. Her body jerked, the way it did sometimes when she was on the verge of sleep. She waited a few seconds, then dismissed it and shut her eyes again. She must have been dozing off, after all.

Another knock. Cassie flinched. She lifted her head, staring at the door in the murky half-light. She held her breath and listened with all her concentration: heard a creak from the travel cot as Sofia kicked her leg, and an answering snuffle from Jaden; further out, the rumble of traffic on the ring road and the bass thump of a car stereo. But only silence beyond the door.

And then a woman's voice, hushed with concern for the sleeping children: 'Mrs Carter? Are you awake, Mrs Carter?'

The landlady. Cassie swung her legs off the bed and jumped up, reeling as her circulation tried to adjust to the sudden movement. It didn't seem right to waste time getting dressed so she grabbed up the towel she'd used after her bath, wrapped it around her waist and padded across the room.

She started to unlock the door, then caution overcame her. Joe wouldn't want her to open up without knowing it was safe.

'What is it?' she hissed.

'I'm terribly sorry, Mrs Carter. There's an urgent message for you. I didn't want to transfer the call to your room in case it woke the kiddies . . .'

Joe, she thought, fumbling with the lock. *It must be Joe. Thank God.*

Cassie turned the handle and the door opened as if on a spring. It hit a glancing blow to her wrist as she threw herself sideways. She heard a thud as the landlady's body crumpled and was pushed into the room, followed closely by the two men who had tried to abduct Sofia in Brighton.

Joe said: 'You went next door, but Felton's safe was empty. Just that box full of paper, is that right?'

No one responded. They didn't have to. Joe saw the whole picture with a clarity borne of long experience. Bank heists, drug deals, frauds: they all had their own distinctive patterns. But throw together a group of individuals whose principal traits were greed, aggression and stupidity, and the results were miserably predictable.

'You found a note inside the box, which you seem to think is for you.'

'It's addressed to him,' Turner said, looking at Valentin.

'So Felton must have known about this from the start. He set this up to fail.'

'Using Yuri?' Turner said. Of the three, he seemed most willing to get to the truth.

Now the woman, Priya, said, 'You're claiming that Yuri has been working for Robert Felton?'

'Yes.' Joe remembered something. 'I want to know why you turned him loose. When I first saw him, he was being brought here as a prisoner.'

There was an awkward silence before Liam said, 'He offered to help the search, after someone tried to make a phone call. I take it that was you?'

Joe nodded. 'I made a mistake there. But it gave Yuri the perfect opportunity. Once he was free he could get on with following his orders, which came from Robert Felton.'

Priya again: 'Why would Felton do this?'

'Because he wants more than just a laugh. The note's there to illustrate how brilliantly he outsmarted you. It's like a practical joke. It also shows he could have prevented your attack if he'd wanted to. But he didn't. He let it go ahead, and now he's got Yuri picking off your men one by one. Killing them. That means there's a far more serious motive.'

'Revenge,' Valentin whispered, and it sounded as though his spirit leaked out with the word. 'He wants revenge.'

It was true. Liam knew it in his heart. Joe wasn't simply trying to talk his way out of here. He'd supplied a plausible explanation for every discrepancy.

There was a heavy silence. For captors and captives alike, it seemed as though nobody grasped what this meant, or how they should respond.

To Liam, the only sensible option was to cut and run. Whether he could bring himself to do it was debatable, having been promised so much.

Valentin was first to move. He strained to get up, leaning heavily against his maid as he tried to stand. The woman scowled, jabbing him in the side with her elbow.

'What are you doing?' Liam asked.

'Let me go.'

The other prisoners started to protest, throwing insults at the Ukrainian. Valentin did his best to turn a deaf ear to them. Once upright, he thrust out his hands.

'Free me, then get away from here. It is your only hope.' He nodded graciously at the seated prisoners. 'I'll release them, and call the police.'

'You're fucking joking!' Turner growled.

'It won't work,' Joe said.

'I'm a victim here.' With difficulty Valentin stepped back, out of the circle of prisoners. 'There's no evidence to say otherwise.'

'Yuri,' said Joe.

Valentin kept his gaze on Liam. When he spoke, it sounded as though he was reading from a prepared statement. 'I have no idea what Yuri has done, whether he has betrayed me, or you. I am a victim here. Let me go, and I will help the others.'

'Oh no, you're not getting away with this,' Angela Weaver shouted at him. 'You killed my husband.'

Valentin wore a patient frown, as though regretting this outburst from an emotionally unstable woman.

'I killed no one. These . . . strangers killed your husband. As you can all see, I am merely trying to negotiate our freedom, so that no one else has to die.'

Joe laughed. 'Your plan failed, and now you're going to portray yourself as a hero?'

Valentin kept up the pressure on Liam. His eyes flashed a warning that the prisoners didn't catch.

Go. Go while you still can.

It was tempting. Liam could see the fear hiding in the Ukrainian's face. And if Valentin was scared, then Liam knew they should all be scared.

He glanced at Turner and Priya. Both seemed dubious, thinking it through. Liam was doing the same, and he believed there was a glimmer of hope.

It might just work. If they went now there was no reason to assume they'd get caught. The masks and gloves had protected their identities. Of course, Valentin knew who they were, but he couldn't reveal that without incriminating himself. And maybe he really would convince the police that he was a genuine victim. It didn't matter what allegations the other residents hurled at him: without solid proof to back them up, Valentin would be in the clear.

No one else has to die.

Lie low for a few months, then have a serious talk with Valentin about compensation. *Generous* compensation.

It was a very appealing concept, and Liam basked in its glow for all of five seconds.

Then the lights went out.

Forty-Five

The darkness was absolute. Joe felt as though he'd been sucked into oblivion. For maybe half a second he had nothing to go on: no light or sound or movement. No sensory input at all.

But he knew it wouldn't last. This was the calm before the storm.

Right on cue, the next half-second produced a sensory bombardment. The garage's internal door blew open and Joe felt the vibration of urgent but coordinated movement. He heard the stomp of heavy feet and the clatter of weaponry. Beads of red light danced across the garage like fireflies, alighting on the invisible forms around him. Several voices bellowed at once.

'Drop your weapons!'

'Get down now!'

'Everyone on the ground!'

Joe was already reacting. Despite his restraints, he managed to grab hold of Angela's sleeve. He felt her turning, trying to get her legs out from beneath her, but the prisoners were too tightly bunched to move easily. As Joe pushed himself backwards to make room he hit someone's foot: Liam's, perhaps, or Priya's.

A red spot roamed across Angela's head and lingered at the base of her neck, illuminating a swirl of grey hair. Joe threw himself against her.

'Lie flat. Flat as you can.'

He hoped his voice might cut through the shock. He could sense that some of the prisoners were only just beginning to process what was happening; their actions sluggish and uncertain. Behind him, Liam, Priya and Turner seemed equally unresponsive, as if the roving red dots had pinned them to the spot.

Joe knew they were infrared sights, probably from scopes attached to high-powered automatic rifles. Often their primary purpose was intimidation rather than operational necessity. To move with such assurance in a complete blackout their attackers had to be equipped with night-vision goggles.

Another long second passed. The men at the doorway were still shouting orders. Joe heard the scuffles as they fanned out to cover the room. Good solid tactics against an enemy that was blind and stunned, but not entirely helpless.

And, worse still, susceptible to panic.

Joe couldn't tell who fired first. He'd given up trying to see anything and ducked his head, his cheek pressed against the cool concrete. One shot, away to his right, from a handgun with no silencer.

The response was a multiple burst of gunfire. Two automatic weapons, each firing several rounds. Joe glimpsed the muzzle flash from one, saw the gunman moving as he fired. The *clink clink clink* of spent cartridges bouncing on the concrete evoked surreal images of a slot machine paying out. *No winners here tonight,* he thought, as screams and a grunt from close by confirmed that someone had been hit. Along with the crash of falling bodies came a shower of dust and grit and fragments of concrete. The air smelled hot and dense with smoke and blood and fear.

In that very first second, one conclusion had leapt into Joe's mind: a police raid. Now it was replaced by another. This time the image was of a handwritten letter, and a single word.

Checkmate.

Liam understood. At least, that would be his impression afterwards. That he worked out right away what he was facing, but just couldn't respond. It reminded him of those dreams where running feels like wading through syrup. He couldn't force his limbs to obey.

Hopelessly he thought: *If only I could jettison the mask and suit, throw myself amongst the prisoners . . .*

No time. He absorbed the order to get down and from the tone he knew these people weren't messing. Then something hit his foot, and in jerking away his knees unlocked and he started what felt like an agonisingly slow descent. At the same time he heard Turner muttering an angry curse and Liam gauged that he was moving too, but in a very different way.

The gunshot, at such close range, was a shock but not really a surprise. Neither was the answering barrage of fire.

Must be Turner, he thought. As stupid as he was aggressive. Well, tough. Liam didn't give a shit about him.

By then he was on the ground, one leg wedged under someone else's body. He felt the passage of the bullets, close enough to sense their energy, their unremitting potency and purpose. This was Death rushing past, and what Liam knew above anything else was that he was still alive, *he hadn't been hit,* and the hot viscous blood that splattered against his mask was not his own blood but someone else's; someone who deserved whatever they got.

Angela was suffocating. There was a scream trapped in her throat like a chicken bone. She could feel it pressing against her windpipe, the pain sharp and dull at the same time. Her eyes were tightly shut, but her vision was filled with dazzling light, exploding in her brain with a dreadful intensity.

She had always feared the dark. Combined with the frantic activity, the shouts and then the gunfire from just a few feet away instilled an almost primeval terror. It rendered her incapable of thought or movement, unable even to draw a breath.

Someone had been shot. In the midst of the chaos Angela felt a sickening impact, close enough to shake the ground beneath her.

The gunfire left her ears ringing, but as the sound of the blasts echoed and died she was at last able to suck some air into her lungs. The relief was so great that she opened her eyes, but she couldn't see a thing. She shut them again, feeling the sting of tears from the dust and smoke. Someone's head was brushing against hers: a tickle of hair on her forehead.

And Joe was beside her. Thank God. Angela realised now that he had saved her, pulling her below the path of the bullets before she fully appreciated the danger.

With that came a far more profound realisation. For all her earlier vows to the contrary, she found that she was desperate to survive. The yearning was like a hopeless thirst, a dry hollow ache in her throat.

She wanted to live.

On the ground, Liam could hear the ragged breathing of the person lying next to him. Someone else was moaning, and one of the female prisoners was sobbing quietly. Above that noise, the men who'd burst in were still shouting orders. He heard their feet pounding on the concrete, coming closer, and waited for the bullet that would end it all.

But no bullet came. Instead rough hands grabbed his arms. There was a clatter as his gun was snatched from his hand. Dazed and frightened, he didn't resist as they pulled him to his feet. The utility belt dropped from his waist as if it had been cut, but he couldn't tell. Even inches away, his assailants were completely invisible.

His hands were wrenched behind his back, and then a deeper darkness suddenly enveloped him. He heard muffled cries and guessed that others were being subjected to the same process.

Were they being separated: the guilty from the innocent?

Until that moment he'd harboured the erroneous belief – not quite a hope – that the authorities had caught up with them. Now, as he contemplated what might lie in store, Liam found himself fervently wishing that he'd been right.

* * *

Lying completely still, Angela concentrated on ignoring the flurry of movement around her. The panic had abated enough for her to think more clearly, and now her memory dredged up news footage from the 1980s: the Iranian Embassy siege in London, which had ended after a dramatic intervention by the SAS, in full view of the world's media.

Was this the same? Were the good guys coming to the rescue?

Her arms, trapped awkwardly beneath her, began to tingle as the blood drained from them. She shifted a little, not daring to turn over. When no one stopped her, she rose an inch or two from the ground and flexed various muscles in turn, urging her circulation back to life.

As the seconds passed, her hearing returned to normal and she judged that a measure of calm was descending. The men who'd taken charge continued to bark their orders, but the volume had dropped. There were other sounds: dragging and scraping, and the secretive rustle of fabric. Cries and moans, questions or protests quickly muted.

Angela opened her eyes. There remained nothing to see, but she had a sense of the pressure easing, a falling-away that led, quite inexplicably, to a moment of silence.

Maybe this is a dream, she thought. *A terrible dream.*

The bang that followed was so loud that it nearly stopped her heart. She collapsed back on the floor, convinced she'd been shot. While she lay in a clammy panic, mentally probing her body for a wound, the lights came back on.

She gasped, pressing her face against the floor. But she was unharmed. The noise had been the inner door closing.

Tentatively, squinting as her eyes adjusted to the glare, Angela raised her head again, bracing herself for all manner of carnage. Around her, the other prisoners were doing the same: taking stock of the situation, even while it sank in that they were still alive.

Not rescued, but still alive.

What she discovered made her gasp. There was only one fatality evident, and it was the meek, nervous guard by the wall: Eldon.

He lay in a pool of blood, his body shot to pieces. The box file he'd been searching was overturned at his side.

The brutish guard, Turner, was injured. He'd been placed in a sitting position by the wall, his arms behind his back, presumably bound with the same tape that secured his ankles. A wound on his thigh was bleeding heavily. There was a man attending to him, wrapping a bandage around his leg. The man was dressed in black combat gear, with body armour and a helmet. There was no insignia that she could see.

Priya was tied up alongside Turner. Both had their masks removed. Both had been gagged with a strip of tape. They looked scared and baffled by their abrupt reversal of fortune, and Angela thought they had every reason to be.

She shivered. *Meet the new boss, same as the old boss.*

But the greater shock was the number of people missing: spirited out of the garage in a display of horrifying efficiency.

Liam, the gang's leader, had been removed, as had Valentin Nasenko and Oliver Felton.

And worst of all, Joe was gone. They had taken Joe.

Forty-Six

It was a short journey, memorable for all the wrong reasons. Joe was bundled out of the house, his hands still tied behind his back. There was a hood over his face, with a drawstring tight around his neck. The hood's material was thick and rough and impregnated with some sort of chemical that made his head spin. He kept his breathing shallow and slow. Determined not to vomit.

Blind and disorientated, he was forced to walk at a rapid pace. His captors directed him with jabs from their rifles, but they said nothing. If he tripped or faltered he earned a punch in the kidneys. This was all part of the plan: they wanted him terrified, confused, vulnerable.

But Joe felt oddly impassive. They could have killed him already, back in the garage, but they hadn't. Therefore they must have something else in mind, something that entailed keeping him alive for at least a while longer.

And that meant he still had a chance.

Out on the road, Joe didn't hear any engines. He wasn't surprised. He had a feeling they wouldn't be going far.

Sure enough, they walked a short distance, then turned right again. Another driveway underfoot. Joe tried to savour the image of a world beyond the choking claustrophobia of the hood. Balmy night air and a sky thick with stars. The gentle slap of the sea against the deck's wooden pilings.

They led him indoors and ascended a flight of stairs. Someone behind him slipped and cried out. Joe recognised the voice, and another of his suspicions was confirmed.

They hurried along a passageway, then came to a halt. Shuffling and jostling, they were filed through a doorway and thrown to the floor. Joe immediately tried to sit up, but was clubbed on the side of the head.

Then the real beating began. A barrage of kicks that forced him to draw his knees up to his chest and tuck his head down. The blows were fierce, but not lethal. His assailants left his head alone, aiming instead for the muscles and soft tissues of his legs and torso. Like tenderising meat.

The same treatment was being doled out to at least two other people. Joe could hear them gasping and groaning. Like him, they were wriggling and rolling on the floor, trying to evade their attackers, and sometimes they collided. But none of them spoke up. None of them begged for mercy. The plea to desist came from another source altogether, somewhere across the room.

'Can't you make them stop?' Oliver Felton cried.

'Just softening them up for interrogation,' another voice replied.

'It's sadistic.'

'They're only getting what they deserve.'

'You're just as bad as they are.'

'Be quiet, boy.'

Oliver sounded distraught. 'At least go easy on Joe. He wasn't part of this.'

A laugh, cruel and contemptuous. 'Oh, I know exactly what Joe's part was. Crawling over my island like vermin. I've got special plans for him.'

There was another muttered objection, which was silenced with a snarl.

'If you'd gone to bloody Oxford the way you were supposed to . . .
You defied me by staying here without my knowledge. Now you can
live with the consequences.'

Nothing more was said, but Oliver's intervention seemed to have
had some effect. The assault dwindled to a few lacklustre kicks, then
Joe felt hands moving at his neck, loosening the drawstring. The
hood was wrenched off, and Joe found himself staring at Robert
Felton.

They had been brought to a vast bedroom suite, decorated in a
minimalist style. Acres of pale carpet, subdued lighting with a blueish
tint, light wood panelling along one wall. There was a large open
safe set into the panelling. It was empty.

Robert Felton was sitting on the bed, which occupied a circular
platform in the centre of the room. His legs were crossed and one
arm was draped across his knee, a glass of champagne in his hand.
The picture of relaxation.

Joe was lying on the floor between the bed and a sitting area with
a couple of white leather sofas. Oliver Felton was on one of the sofas,
about ten feet away. His hood and restraints had been removed, but
he looked as helpless a captive as the others.

As Joe had guessed, two more men lay on the floor beside him.
Both remained hooded, but he could see that one was Liam and the
other – the one who'd tripped on the stairs – was Valentin.

Their three assailants were almost identical in size and demeanour:
wiry, compact men with watchful expressions. They wore black
uniforms with body-armour vests and combat assault helmets with
microphones and earpieces attached. Night-vision goggles hung from
their necks, and they carried Heckler & Koch MP5 sub-machine guns
with muzzle-flash suppressors.

Had to be ex-special forces, Joe thought. Well-trained, well-
equipped and deadly calm. They made Liam's men look like a bunch
of amateurs.

Not *Liam*'s men, he corrected himself.

Valentin's.

At Felton's command, one of the guards moved towards Liam and began loosening his hood. That was when Joe saw there was another person in the room with them.

Yuri. He was leaning back against the door, staring at Joe with undisguised malice. Joe held his gaze for a moment, then turned away. Liam's hood was removed, along with his ski mask, and Joe saw that he was indeed the driver of the Transit who had passed him this afternoon.

The last to be uncovered was Valentin. He noticed Liam first, and then, with a shudder so subtle that possibly only Joe detected it, he forced himself to face Robert Felton.

For his part, Felton drew out the tension for a while longer. He stood up, nodding gently to himself. He was as tall as Oliver, well over six feet, but much broader. Not quite plump, but certainly well fed: prosperity oozed from every pore. He was dressed in a navy blue suit and a white shirt. He had the kind of thick brown hair that a middle-aged man would take great pride in: immaculately styled, and not a trace of grey. Full, slightly feminine lips, Hollywood teeth and tan, and big blue eyes that sparkled with delight at the misfortune of others.

He raised his glass in a mock toast. "To a productive evening . . .' He took a sip. 'I hear you found my little note?'

The question was directed at Valentin, who didn't respond. It was left to Liam to supply a grudging nod.

'I'm disappointed in you, Valentin. Greed, I can understand. I know you're on your uppers, and this must have seemed like the perfect solution. But blowing Dreamscape to smithereens just because you don't care for my architecture? That's plain vindictive.'

Oliver gaped at his father. 'What do you mean?'

'Hadn't they told you? The sun-room is filled with propane cylinders.'

'We didn't intend to ignite it with the prisoners inside,' Liam said.

Felton chuckled. 'Forgive me if I take your denial with a pinch of salt—'

'It's immaterial what they planned to do,' Joe cut in. 'Call the police and let them deal with this.'

'That won't happen, Joe. And I suggest you keep your mouth shut. You've caused me more than enough trouble already.'

'So they were *your* people in Brighton?'

Before Felton could respond, Liam said, 'You'd better do as he says. He's an undercover cop.'

Felton was momentarily taken aback, but quickly recovered.

'I'm sure he was something of the sort. But judging by his exploits today I doubt very much that he's still a serving police officer.'

He looked to Joe, who knew at once that Felton would see through any attempt to lie. Joe shook his head.

'Sorry, Liam,' Felton said. 'I dare say it was worth a try, from your point of view. But it changes nothing.'

Valentin seemed belatedly to pick up on Joe's reference to Brighton, remembering what he'd heard about the abduction attempt. But if he was grateful to Joe for saving his family there was little sign of it.

He drew himself up, acquiring an imperious demeanour that sought to convey to Felton that no one else in the room counted for anything. Just the two alpha males, talking man to man.

'No police,' Valentin said. 'This is business. We sit down together. We make a deal.'

Felton looked amused, until his attention was drawn to Oliver. He was rocking to and fro on the sofa, his fingers plucking rhythmically at his knees as if plagued by insects.

'Oliver! I think it's best if you go to your room.'

After a second's delay, Oliver's movements ceased and his head jerked up. 'I have every right to hear this.'

'No, you don't. As Valentin says, we have business to discuss. Not all of it will be pleasant, especially for someone with your "delicate" constitution.'

Oliver ignored the taunt. 'You mean you don't want any hostile witnesses.'

With the manner of any long-suffering father, Felton motioned to one of his troops. The man strode over to Oliver, who let out a strange yelp: part laugh, part cry. He studied the sub-machine gun while chewing thoughtfully on his lip.

'What will you do? Have them shoot me?'

His father didn't crack a smile. 'There's something you need to know – and this applies to you all.' Felton waved a languid hand around the room. 'As far as the outside world is concerned, none of this is happening. Unless I decide otherwise, these men aren't here, and nothing they do tonight will be attributed to them.'

'And what about you?' Oliver said as the guard pulled him to his feet. 'Are *you* here?'

'Of course not. There's no official record that I entered the country.' Felton glanced at his watch. 'In fact, at this moment there are several very reliable witnesses who will swear I'm partying the night away at my favourite little bistro in Antibes.'

He looked at each of them as he spoke: Oliver, Joe, Liam, Valentin. The message was unequivocal: *I can do whatever I want.*

At the door, Oliver looked back. 'He's a cold-blooded killer, remember that.' His voice was quietly heartbroken, as if he was already resigned to his fate. 'He murdered his own wife. My mother. He'll wipe out everyone on this island if he has to.'

Joe took careful note of Felton's response. He gave a disappointed sigh, but made no effort to deny his son's accusation. Joe was well aware of Felton's reputation as a tough, uncompromising businessman, but had never dreamt that his ruthlessness might extend to murder.

And yet the way their capture had been orchestrated gave Joe the impression that nothing had been ruled out. Hitting the garage in darkness, ensuring that the prisoners inside had no idea what was happening, meant that Felton's options were wide open. He could commit mass murder, sneak back to France on whatever private plane or yacht had brought him here, and no one would be any the wiser.

Maybe Oliver was right.

Forty-Seven

The interruption caused by Oliver's departure appeared to have made no impact on Valentin's confidence, or on his apparent delusion that he and Felton were operating on equal terms.

'I suggest we go to your office, where we can talk privately.'

'You suggest? Actually, Valentin, I think there's one thing we'd better establish right now. You have no status here. None at all.' Felton tapped his chest. 'This is *my* agenda, and you're going to follow it. I've been waiting a long time for this moment. I intend to enjoy it.'

The put-down was delivered with such scorn that Joe feared Valentin's temper would erupt, and get him killed. But Liam eased the tension with a question of his own.

'How long, exactly?'

'Yuri approached me within a few days of the plan's conception. I knew about this even before you did.'

Liam nodded, as if he'd thought as much. 'I guess you offered him a better deal?'

'It could hardly be worse, could it? I knew the hit Valentin had taken in the credit crunch, and Yuri knew it too. All he had to do was pose a simple question. Why run the risk of something going wrong when he could jump ship and guarantee himself a fat profit? Very wisely, he chose the latter course and began feeding me every little detail of your grandiose dream.'

Another hateful glare from Yuri as he saw that he had Joe's attention. Felton picked up on it and nodded sharply at Yuri, as if in reply to some unspoken query.

'Soon,' he murmured. 'Now, moving on.'

He gulped the last of his champagne, handed the glass to one of his men, and took something from his pocket: a small electronic gadget of some kind.

'Let's review the outcome of your meeting, shall we? See if we can make some progress?'

With a sickly smile, Felton pressed a button on the device and the voice of a ghost filled the room.

Oliver couldn't walk straight. He kept stumbling and bumping into the walls as he was escorted along the corridor, while the guard's disdain burned like acid on his skin.

He probably thought Oliver was drunk, but it wasn't alcohol that had destabilised him. It was shock. Shock, fury, bitterness, humiliation: a cocktail of emotions more potent than any drug on earth.

His home, Terror's Reach, represented no more than an elaborate trap, designed to lure Valentin and Priya and Liam into a position where his father had absolute control over them. Those who'd lost their lives in the process were merely collateral damage.

Oliver assessed his own situation. Did his father truly care that he hadn't gone to Oxford as planned? As he thought about it, he began to suspect that his father had known he was here. His sister was bound to have reported back after their conversation this afternoon.

By then, of course, Valentin had already launched his ill-fated scheme. It would have been far less satisfying for his father to have brought everything to a halt at that stage. He pictured Dad receiving the news that his troublesome offspring was refusing to budge from the family home. The resultant decision must have taken all of a nanosecond: proceed as planned.

'Fuck him,' said Oliver.

The guard didn't respond; just gave him the sort of searching look that meant: *not right in the head.* Oliver laughed.

He stopped outside his bedroom door, where the guard conjured up a key. Oliver kept the door locked at all times, and only he knew the whereabouts of the spare key.

He patted his pockets. Realised they had frisked him thoroughly in the garage and found the key. So maybe they didn't know about the spare. That was promising . . .

'You're locking me in?' he asked, faking incredulity.

'I am. I'm sure it'll not be for long.' The guard had a soft Scottish accent. He opened the door and stood back, ushering Oliver inside like a rather brusque hotel proprietor.

'You know my father's a psychopath, don't you?' Oliver said.

'Aye,' said the guard. 'What's your point?'

The voice on the recorder was McWhirter's. He sounded worried. Turned out he had every right to be, Joe thought.

I don't like it, Valentin. When you propose a deal like this you should do it from a position of strength.

Felton hit the pause button and tutted. 'Wise words, Valentin. Your man deserved better than he got.'

Next came Valentin himself, quiet and assured: *And we are. This is a greedy man we have here.*

The setting was clearly nautical. Joe could hear the background hum of a powerful engine and the distant cry of gulls. In the end, Valentin's obsession with eavesdropping had proved futile. The bug had been planted by Yuri – the very man he employed to sweep for them.

The conversation moved on. McWhirter, yet to be mollified, asked: *Do you think he can bring Felton on board?*

Valentin: *I am sure of it. Another very greedy man.*

Felton paused again.

'I'm a greedy man? Well, yes, I can't deny that. I won't go all Gordon

Gekko on you, but I'm sure there's a consensus in this room as to the benefits of market capitalism. Even amongst its more recent adherents,' he added, with a cheerful nod at the two Ukrainians.

He resumed the tape. They heard McWhirter say: *But what about finance? We are going to need Felton's capital.*

Then a big sigh of frustration from the South African. Joe appreciated it better than most. He'd also been in situations where Valentin had refused to heed his professional advice.

'Now there's the rub,' said Felton, looking pleased enough to burst. 'Poor Mr McWhirter couldn't reconcile your blithe confidence with the reality as he knew it. Whereas you assumed you'd have the capital you needed to come in as an equal partner because you were going to help yourself to what's in there.'

He jabbed viciously in the direction of an en suite dressing room. Valentin and Liam seemed to know what he was talking about. Joe realised there must be another safe in there: one they'd been unable to breach.

Felton's face was reddening, his voice growing slow and deliberate, as though he were tiptoeing through a whole minefield of fury.

'You wanted what was mine. That's a common enough instinct, I suppose. You were poor, relatively speaking, and I was rich. But you of all people should have known better, Valentin. That's not the way it works. Not in business, nor in life.'

Felton eyed them all closely, making sure every word hit home.

'In the real world it's the rich who steal from the poor. The strong take from the weak. That's a much safer bet. Try it the other way round and it ends in tears. McWhirter's the proof of that. So is my friend Travers.'

He turned and strode towards the dressing room. Perhaps he gave a signal to his men, or perhaps this manoeuvre had been prearranged, for the guards immediately roused the three prisoners, herding them in Felton's wake.

Joe caught Liam muttering to Valentin: 'Rubbing our fucking noses in it . . .'

Felton tutted again as he inspected the dressing room. Dozens of suits had been discarded on the floor and some of the wardrobes vandalised. Expecting a show of anger, Joe was surprised when Felton faced them, his air of bonhomie apparently restored.

'You'll have to crowd around the doorway, but no further,' he said. 'Step inside this room and my men will shoot. Is that clear?'

The warning was reinforced with the prod of an MP5. All three men had a guard stationed right behind them. Their guns were angled downwards so they could fire without any risk of hitting Felton.

'Good. Now, I know how desperate you were to see inside the panic room, so I'm going to grant your wish.'

Turning away, Felton concentrated on something concealed within the wardrobe. Joe spotted an electronic keypad and what looked like a biometric scanner, set into a steel door. There was a bleep, followed by the clunk of retracting bolts, and the big heavy door rolled open.

Forty-Eight

Oliver was out of luck. They *had* found the second key. He'd kept it taped to the underside of his computer keyboard, which didn't seem terribly ingenious now it was missing.

For a few minutes he slumped on the bed like a grounded teenager and thought seriously about embracing defeat. After all, his father's dispute was with Valentin Nasenko. Providing Oliver kept his mouth shut, there was no reason why he wouldn't be spared.

As for Liam and his gang, they had treated him abominably. Why should Oliver care what happened to them? Let his father annihilate every last one.

But Priya . . . Even though her betrayal was the most painful, he couldn't shake off the feeling that he'd connected with her. Maybe not at first, when she'd tricked her way into the house, but later, when he had displayed the scars on his wrists. He'd seen something in her face: an echo of his own torment.

Or was that completely fanciful? Was he kidding himself?

A spurt of anger propelled him to his feet. It was irrelevant what Priya thought of him. This wasn't about her. It was about himself, and the way he had been treated.

He had to do something. Show them he wasn't weak or impotent.

Perhaps try to break the door down? He examined it, tapped gently on the wood with the pad of a finger. Solid timber. Even if he had

271

the brute strength, which he doubted, the noise would bring the guards running. His father's warning still rang in his mind.

These men aren't here, and nothing they do tonight will be attributed to them.

Oliver searched the room, regretting his lack of interest in sport. A cricket bat would have made a useful weapon. Better still, a knife of some sort.

He laughed out loud at the thought. As a physically inept coward, even wielding a knife he would stand little chance against several highly trained former soldiers armed with sub-machine guns.

In the bathroom Oliver discovered that his matches remained in their hiding place. If he set fire to his bedding, could he sneak past the guards in the ensuing chaos?

No. Too many of them. Anyway, his father might just leave him in here and let him burn to death.

But he shoved them in his pocket all the same, hoping they would provide a talismanic boost to his confidence. There was only one sure way to escape from the room and Oliver knew it. He was just trying to avoid thinking about it.

Because he was a physically inept coward.

But he was still determined to do it.

Felton stepped back from the wardrobe, directing the attention of his audience to the open door with a theatrical sweep of his arm. *Like a cheesy quiz-show host*, Joe thought, complete with a smile of gleeful regret. *Here's what you could have won!*

And what a prize it was. Staring into the vault, Joe knew he would never forget the sight that greeted him. For the others, the effect was even more powerful. Liam gasped when he saw it. Valentin groaned as though he'd been kicked in the stomach.

The room was piled with gold. A huge stack of gold bars, almost unreal in their size and quantity. In the muted light they shone with a dull yellow gleam. They looked at once both magical and yet somehow more ordinary than Joe would have expected. Plain metal bricks that just happened to be worth a king's ransom.

The bottom tier was formed of large 12.5-kilo ingots, arranged in piles of a dozen. There were twenty piles that Joe could see, and possibly more beyond his view. At least two hundred and forty in total. He could scarcely begin to estimate their value.

The top tier was mostly one-kilo: neat rectangular slabs the size of chocolate bars. Too many to count, but there had to be hundreds.

Along each side of the room, Joe could see sealed boxes and what looked like artwork bundled in thick layers of bubble wrap. Some of it may have been priceless, but it seemed almost insignificant in comparison to the gold.

Felton waited in silence, allowing them all to absorb the sight – and in Liam and Valentin's case, to reflect on their failure.

'How much is it worth?' Joe asked.

'Including the art, about a hundred and fifty million.' Felton sounded vaguely dismissive. 'I'd like more, but liquidating assets and moving into gold hasn't been that easy lately. The trouble is, everyone's doing it.'

'Because of the recession?'

'Broadly speaking. I've always kept a healthy percentage of my wealth in precious metals. Another problem is that some of it isn't strictly kosher.'

A hollow laugh from Liam. 'You stole it?'

'Of course not. Just acquired it in somewhat unorthodox circumstances. Usually as payment for services rendered, in parts of the world where it's wise to avoid regulatory interference.'

Joe snorted. 'And tax.'

'Absolutely. Paying tax is for muggles. It's bad enough that I'll lose value on the bars that don't have sound provenance.'

'It's a tough life.'

'It certainly is,' Felton agreed without a trace of irony. He turned his attention to Valentin. 'Perhaps you can enlighten me on one thing. How did you know about the gold?'

Valentin frowned. 'It was my maid.'

Felton appeared relieved. 'That's what Yuri claimed. I wasn't sure whether to believe him.'

'She is friendly with one of the women who cleans for you. This woman overheard a phone call. You were making arrangements to store gold at home. She mentioned it to my maid, and Maria told me.'

'So we owe all this to the gossip of servants?' Felton pretended to be marvelling at the thought, but that theatrical air was back. He was playing with them again. 'I had my reservations, but to be on the safe side I dispensed with the cleaning woman in question.'

'"Dispensed"?' Joe repeated.

'Well, the police will most likely treat it as a domestic burglary gone wrong.' Felton chuckled. 'I thought that would be rather fitting.'

Valentin scowled. 'Enough of these games. If you wish to kill us, do it. If not, tell me what you want.'

Felton raised an admonitory finger. 'My agenda, Valentin.'

'Fuck your agenda.'

Liam told him to cool down. Felton agreed. 'If ever there was an occasion to keep that famous temper in check, this is it.'

He produced the voice recorder and scrolled through its menu. 'Let's have another reminder, shall we?'

He pressed play, and they heard Travers's disdainful growl:

There are no boundaries with that guy. No proportionality. He just doesn't understand the concept. If you're loyal to him, and he knows it, there's no better man to work with. But cross him and you've signed your own death warrant.

In response, Valentin's laugh was high and mocking and slightly false, because even then he must have been aware of the high-wire act he was attempting.

Felton cut off the tape.

'I'm disappointed in you, Valentin. You rejected some very good advice there. So far you've shown yourself to be arrogant, and stupid, and selfish.' He gestured at Joe. 'Earlier today this man saved the lives of your family. Have you expressed your gratitude to him? No. You're so caught up in your bid for survival, I bet you've hardly given it a thought.'

He grinned, and Joe felt a twist of fear in his gut.

'In fact,' Felton added slyly, 'I bet you don't even have a clue where they are right now.'

Forty-Nine

Oliver's bedroom window was large enough to escape from, but it didn't lead anywhere. Just a twenty-foot drop onto a concrete path. He knew the fall wouldn't necessarily kill him, but it might shatter his ankles, and then what would he do? Suffer yet more humiliation when his father's goons discovered him bleeding and broken on the path.

Instead, he opted to climb out of the little window in his bathroom. It was a tight squeeze, even with the window shoved wide open. Made worse because he had to go out backwards, head and shoulders first, facing the room.

He managed it by climbing onto the toilet seat, then turned his back to the window and hoisted himself up onto the cistern. He leaned out, gripping the underside of the window frame as his head protruded into the cool night air.

He stopped for a moment, considering whether he possessed either the aptitude or the will to go any further. He was no one's idea of an athlete. His arms and legs were pitifully weak, and if they gave out on him now it might be the last thing he did. He wouldn't survive landing on his head.

And he didn't like heights: a fact he'd been neatly skirting around until now, when it was impossible to block out any longer. Even though he was trying not to look down, he could sense the void that existed between his body and solid ground.

He took a deep breath and pushed the fear away. He imagined that Priya was in the bathroom with him. *Do this right*, she was saying, *and I'll give you anything you want. Anything you desire . . .*

Oliver wriggled backwards, his thighs digging into the frame. The window was set into one of the dormers that his father had incorporated into the house design, and it meant there was a small rectangle of flat roof directly above the bathroom. Thanks to his long limbs, Oliver was able to reach up and grip the edge of the roof, while his feet were planted on the toilet cistern.

That left him crouching, half in and half out of the house. Now the void beneath him had assumed mythic proportions. He levered himself up, knowing he must present a comical but precarious sight, clinging on for dear life. And the worst was yet to come.

The dormer roof was clad in some kind of smooth dark material – possibly lead. It was slightly raised at the front, presumably to direct rainwater towards the gutter at the rear. Oliver found he could hold it quite comfortably. But could he lever himself up onto the roof?

Only the thought of outflanking his father gave him the impetus to try. Because it wasn't just Priya's admiring gaze that spurred him on. It was picturing the look on his father's face when his goons came to report Oliver missing.

The guards ushered Joe, Liam and Valentin back across the room and forced them to sit on the floor between the sofas. When Felton didn't emerge from the dressing room, Yuri strode over to the doorway and said something.

A moment later Felton stepped into view, nestling one of the large gold ingots on his forearm as though it were a favoured pet. He dropped it on the bed and smiled as it sank deep into the covers.

'What did you mean about Cassie and the children?' Joe asked. ·

Acting as though he hadn't heard, Felton poured himself another glass of champagne.

'Had an idea for a wager. Yuri's chomping at the bit to have some quality time with his erstwhile colleague, so we may as well spice it up a little. It's some sort of private dispute, I take it?'

Felton addressed the question to Valentin, who played it dumb. Joe gathered that Felton was talking about him.

'What did you mean about Cassie?' he asked again.

'My agenda, Joe.' Felton raised the glass to Valentin. 'That one bar will fetch about two hundred and twenty thousand. Interested?'

Valentin looked mystified. 'You are offering me this . . . for what?'

'I just told you,' said Felton, exasperated. 'My man Yuri versus your man Joe.'

'So what is the deal?'

'If Joe wins, you get the gold bar. If Yuri wins, Joe gets to stay alive.' Felton turned to Yuri. 'Unless you'd prefer a fight to the death?'

Yuri shrugged: *Fine with me.*

'Well, let's keep an open mind on that. If Joe dies, maybe I'll take whatever's left in your safe. That seem fair?'

Valentin still looked perplexed. 'And this is it? The whole deal?'

'Lord, no. This is just a side bet, purely for our amusement. Rather like the sort of stunts your pal Liam used to pull in the City. No, the *main* deal we're doing here concerns your mineral rights in Kajitestan.'

'No,' said Valentin. It was a gut response, but Felton took no notice.

'You're going to sign it all over to me. Every last drop of oil, every scrap of copper and zinc. And I want a signed undertaking that you'll provide all the necessary permits, introductions and inducements necessary for the maximum exploitation of those rights.' A beat of silence. 'Oh, and I'm taking your house as well.'

'*What?*'

'I want you off the Reach. This is *my* island now.'

Valentin finally tried to speak, blustering something that sounded like gibberish in English or any other language.

'Don't get so worked up,' Felton cautioned him. 'This is a very generous proposition. You'll still have that nice apartment in London, and that tacky one in Miami where you entertain your whores.

I'm letting you keep all the decent art, the stuff you sneaked into hiding. In fact, you can still go ahead with your fraudulent insurance claim for all I care.'

'And what about the rest of us?' Liam asked.

Felton gave a sombre nod, as if to say he had been coming to that.

'Your role will be to take the rap for what's happened here, and think yourselves lucky. You get to escape with your lives, providing you keep your mouth shut about Valentin's involvement.'

'And if we don't?'

Felton clicked his tongue. 'Even when you're detained at Her Majesty's pleasure, don't for one second think you're beyond my reach.'

'What about the other residents?' said Joe.

'They'll be released unharmed. At the appropriate time, they'll receive a very generous offer to sell up. From now on I intend to control who lives here.' He flapped his hand in Valentin's direction. 'No more foreign undesirables, for a start.'

Valentin spat on the carpet. 'And if I refuse?'

'If you refuse, well . . .' Felton took a slow, measured sip of champagne. 'What do you think might happen, Joe?'

Oliver split a fingernail, clawing at the roof as he hauled himself up. Oddly, the sight of blood gave him a comforting rush. He was engaged in the type of strenuous physical challenge that real men welcomed with gusto. It was a mindset he normally despised: right now he could appreciate the thrill of it.

Kneeling on the tiny rectangle of lead, he breathed slowly and waited for his nerves to settle. It was extraordinarily quiet out here. A brilliant starry night with only a sliver of moon, the sea black and glistening like oil. White flashes in the air revealed themselves as seagulls, gliding through the darkness. For a moment Oliver felt humbled by his lowly place in the universe: as though anything that happened here tonight could possibly matter in the scheme of things.

Eventually he felt secure enough to plan his next move. The main roof rose above him at a pitch of about forty-five degrees. It was clad in grey slate, with contrasting red clay tiles on the ridge. By lying flat, Oliver thought he should be able to crawl the thirty feet or so to the top, then work his way along to the opposite side of the house.

Scared and yet exhilarated, he stood up and pressed himself against the interlocking slates. They felt rough to the touch, still warm from the day's heat. He knew they would bear his weight, but was the angle of elevation shallow enough to prevent him from sliding to his death?

'Guess I'll soon find out,' he murmured.

'Why are you asking me?' said Joe. Even before the words were out, he realised he knew the answer.

'Your boss doesn't seem too bothered about his family's whereabouts, but I take it you are.' Felton grinned. 'That was impressive work, fighting your way free. And some nifty driving, from what I heard.'

'They're safe,' Joe said. But it was a hollow declaration, the words of a man endeavouring to convince himself.

'Sure about that?'

'I won't give them up.'

'You misunderstand, Joe,' said Felton, his voice silky in victory; almost musical. 'You see, you might have foiled the first attempt to snatch them. But the second attempt succeeded.'

Fifty

'You're lying,' said Valentin.

'You don't really believe that,' Felton said. 'I have them all. Cassie, and her boy, and your baby daughter. My ultimate insurance policy against any mishaps tonight. Any over-confidence, any defiance or displays of rebellion, and it all ends badly for the children.'

'Felton's bluffing,' Joe told Valentin. 'I got them to safety. No one knows where they are.'

A cackle from across the room, to which Felton added: 'Not quite true.'

Joe turned and saw Yuri holding a mobile phone between his finger and thumb. Joe's phone. Yuri had taken it when he'd captured Joe down on the deck. But it shouldn't have been of any use to them, unless . . .

'She left message for you,' said Yuri. 'Stupid bitch didn't use her cellphone. She called from landline.'

'A homely little B&B in Chichester, wasn't it?' Felton said. 'I really have to thank you for bringing them so close to home. It took us no time at all to fetch them.'

'So where are they now? Here?'

'Nowhere you'll find them.'

'If any harm comes to them . . .' Joe said, but Felton only laughed.

'You won't be in a position to defend anyone. Besides, as Valentin says, this is business. Once the paperwork's been signed and authenticated by lawyers, they'll be released untouched. A matter of a few days at most – providing I have Valentin's complete cooperation.'

'Prove it,' Valentin said. 'Prove this is not a bluff.'

'Very well.' Felton produced the voice recorder and selected a file.

For a second or two all they heard was a low electronic buzz. Felton noticed Joe desperately listening for background noise that might give a clue to the location of the recording. He shook his head: *You won't do it.*

Then a woman's voice broke the silence. 'Valentin? It's me, Cassie. Please give them what they want.' They heard the tears spill over into her voice. 'Don't let them hurt us. Please, Valentin . . .'

Felton cut the tape. 'I think that's more than sufficient.'

He was Batman. A creature of the night. A dark avenger.

Oliver smiled. He adored *The Dark Knight*, had watched it a hundred times, knew every line and move and nuance. But it was never the Batman whom he wanted to emulate. It was Heath Ledger's Joker that had spoken to him, made a connection deep in his soul. Amoral, adrift and utterly *alive* in every moment of his existence.

That was the lesson Oliver took from the movie. That was the lesson he tried to apply now.

The climb to the ridge of the roof was perilous but exciting. He clambered up and sat astride the red clay tiles. Riding the house like a mighty steed. He giggled at the image, and wondered if he wasn't a little *too* high on adrenalin. Might have to tamp it down a bit.

Shuffling along to the front of the house was easy, but he wasn't looking forward to the descent. Much easier to fall when you were already heading down: the momentum always threatening to take control.

In the end he was able to negotiate it without too much difficulty. There was a valley on the roof's north-east corner, which lessened the gradient. Oliver crept down and eased across to the next dormer.

It was about the same size as the one he'd emerged from, but with a narrow pitched roof. It too had a single window, just large enough to accommodate him.

He stood to one side of it, his toes pointing into the gutter. Gripping the top of the dormer roof tightly with both hands, he braced one foot against the main roof and used his other to kick at the glass.

The impact was horribly loud and hurt his toes, but it failed to break the glass. He should have anticipated this and brought a tool.

He kicked the window again, aiming for the top corner rather than the centre of the glass. He'd read somewhere that it was weaker around the edges than in the middle. The window still didn't break, but it cracked. Almost broke his foot as well.

The third time did it. The glass shattered with a sound that seemed to expand and fill the universe above him. It made Oliver jump so badly that he nearly let go. He clung to the dormer roof, too petrified to move, waiting for the inevitable response: shouts, doors slamming, even gunfire.

But none came.

After a couple of minutes he leaned out and confirmed that the attic room, his beloved sanctuary, was empty. He kicked the remaining shards of glass from the frame, swung his body round and went in feet first. He landed as softly as he could, crunching on the broken glass, and waited again, his heart racing.

Still nothing. Oliver pressed the button to open the hatch. More noise as the ladder began to extend: a low-pitched metallic grinding that seemed to rattle through the house like a dentist's drill.

He made it down the ladder, and there was no ambush; no one came running. He debated whether to put the ladder back up and decided that he must. After pressing the button he hurried away, pushed through the door to the main corridor, and that was when he heard footsteps coming towards him.

He ducked into the nearest room. Crouched behind the door and listened as several people tramped past. Risked a look and glimpsed the tail end of the group – Valentin Nasenko and one of the guards – turning the corner onto the short landing that led towards the games room.

It seemed a peculiar destination, but Oliver had long ago given up trying to fathom the logic of his father's actions. At least they were moving beyond the main stairs, which meant he should be able to get out of the house safely.

But why the games room? What on earth could they want in there?

Fifty-One

Liam watched in sullen silence as the other prisoners were herded from the room. It stung his ego that he wasn't deemed important enough to be taken along for the show. He was left in the custody of a single guard, a thin-faced man with eyes as small and black as rabbit droppings.

He consoled himself with the thought that at least he wasn't being fed to Yuri in the name of sport. Yuri was an ogre, a fact that Liam had conveniently managed to ignore all the time he was *Valentin*'s ogre. Now that Yuri belonged to Felton, he was a very different proposition.

Joe had proved himself pretty resourceful so far today, but Liam couldn't see him putting up much opposition to the Ukrainian. No doubt that was why Felton was so enthusiastic about the wager in the first place. It might be all over in a minute or two.

And then what?

His guess was that Felton would carve out the deal he wanted, and Valentin would meekly go along with it. With his wife and daughter held hostage he really had no choice. Then Felton and his men would melt away into the night, leaving Valentin to summon the police and let nature take its course.

Liam felt a tightening in his throat at the thought of what lay ahead: decades of incarceration, impossible to endure. He noticed the guard smirking at the misery etched on his face, and he found the strength to push the self-pity aside. He nodded towards the dressing room. 'Don't suppose your man left the panic room door open?'

The guard said nothing.

'Only I'm thinking, we grab ourselves a couple of bars each and get the hell out of here. What do you say?'

The guard shook his head. 'What I say is: I'm earning plenty for this. And I'm going nowhere with a fucking Paddy. It was you bastards killed my uncle, on patrol in Armagh.'

Liam almost had to laugh. Just his luck.

His thoughts turned to Priya, and whether she had survived the assault on the garage. He was certain he'd felt Turner go down, and maybe someone else as well. If Priya was alive, it was odd that she hadn't been brought next door. Such an exotic creature would definitely intrigue a ladies' man like Felton. Unless he didn't know that much about her—

The revelation was stunning – a forehead-slapping moment, if his hands hadn't been taped behind his back. Liam felt a turbulent mix of emotions. Anger at himself for not working it out sooner. Disgust that he'd wasted such an opportunity, and made a bloody fool of himself in the process.

She'd told him herself, hadn't she, when he had her pinned on the floor?

If you do this, you'll never get out of here alive.

That already seemed a lifetime ago. When Valentin had ruled the world, with Liam and Priya his faithful lieutenants.

And Priya a lot, lot more besides.

But Felton obviously wasn't aware of her significance. That gave Liam a tiny jolt of pleasure, even though it was far too late for the information to be of any value. Selling her out now would only earn him the same grisly fate as Travers.

She's untouchable, Liam thought. *The lucky cow.*

And then he spotted the problem looming for Nasenko. Valentin would surely have no qualms about accepting Felton's terms when it involved handing Liam over to the police. But could he do the same to Priya?

Her position seemed hopeless, but Priya wouldn't accept that. She was a fighter. All the time she was still alive, she knew she had a chance.

What she had to do was find that chance, and make it count.

She had been placed close to the side wall of the garage, some distance away from the other prisoners. Her mouth was covered with tape, a tight, foul taste against her lips. Her hands were behind her back and her wrists and ankles were bound with the same tape. A moat of blood surrounded her.

Turner was a few feet to her right, slumped against the wall. He was conscious but weak, every breath a wince of pain. He'd been hit in the thigh and had lost a lot of blood. The guard had applied a rudimentary dressing, which seemed to have stemmed the flow, but Priya doubted he would last very long without proper medical attention.

Their other colleague, Eldon, was to her left. He'd been killed in the initial gun battle and his body lay forgotten amidst the papers he'd been searching through. His blood had run along shallow depressions in the concrete floor and pooled with Turner's, only inches from Priya's outstretched feet.

It was a repellent sight, but she had already worked out how it could be used to her advantage.

The air in the garage reeked of violence and death and the acrid tang of digestive juices. One of the prisoners had vomited, and the guard's remit obviously didn't include cleaning up the mess. His only concession to their well-being was to drag Travers's body into the corner.

At first there had been plenty of questions, mainly from Angela Weaver and Terry Fox. They demanded to know what was going on, who was in charge. If Liam's gang were no longer a threat, why couldn't the innocent prisoners be released?

The guard fielded the questions with a stock phrase – 'I can't tell you' – and a diminishing supply of patience. Eventually he took up a position by the inner door, a distance from which he could more easily ignore their interrogation.

Priya made no attempt to communicate with anyone. She knew it was futile. The guard wasn't going to speak to her, and the other prisoners, when they looked at her at all, made no attempt to disguise their loathing. *Hand any of them a gun*, she thought, *and they'll kill me without hesitation.* She had no problem with that. In their position, she would do the same.

Part of her mind remained sufficiently detached to admire the man who'd orchestrated this operation. The planning and execution showed great skill and professionalism. It made Valentin's team – herself included – look like clumsy amateurs by comparison.

If this was the work of Robert Felton, it raised some interesting questions about Oliver's role. Priya believed she'd played him skilfully enough to know if he was concealing information from her. If he'd had any inkling of what was to come he would have betrayed that knowledge in some way.

So it was feasible that Oliver had not been pre-warned, even though Felton must have known his son was still on the island when he'd launched his counter-attack. If only she had heeded Oliver's warnings about his father, she might have seen the danger in time. Instead she was facing, at best, a life behind bars.

Or maybe not.

From this point on it was every man for himself. That was how Valentin would see it, and Liam too. A matter of straightforward common sense.

Priya had no one to rely on but herself.

Fifty-Two

Yuri descended the stairs three at a time, his breath emerging in quick, excited snorts. Eager to get on with it.

Behind him, one of the guards escorted Joe with the slow, respectful pace of an executioner. They followed a wide hallway into the depths of the house, until finally Yuri reached a door and stopped. He turned, waiting for Joe to catch up.

'You remember what you said to me today, in the kitchen? How you would kick my ass?'

'That's right.'

Yuri bared his teeth. 'Well, now we will see.'

'Yep,' said Joe, as though he relished the opportunity. He couldn't afford to show any fear at this stage.

Pushing the door open, Yuri strode into the room like a gladiator entering the arena. Shoulders thrown back, chest puffed out, chin in the air. Another obvious attempt to intimidate him, but Joe was determined that it wouldn't succeed.

The guard took out a knife and cut the tape from Joe's wrists. He stepped back, looking slightly abashed, as if reluctant to be a party to slaughter. When he wished Joe good luck he sounded as though he meant it.

* * *

Joe stepped through the doorway and immediately understood why this room had been chosen. It was a large, airy gymnasium, two storeys high, overlooked by a gallery on the first floor.

The wall to his left was lined with impressive machines: a bike and a rower and a full set of weights, an elliptical trainer and a treadmill the size of a small car. But the centrepiece, undoubtedly, was the full-size squash court.

As the venue for a public battle, it couldn't have been more ideal. A square room, enclosed on all sides, with a glass wall at the rear and a viewing platform above. A ready-made arena, with no furniture to encumber them and nowhere to hide.

Felton was waiting on the gallery above the court. The room behind him contained a pool table and, bizarrely, a fireman's pole that led down to the far side of the squash court.

Valentin was alongside him, a far less enthusiastic spectator. A guard hovered close by, MP5 at the ready. The third guard had stayed with Liam.

Yuri was already inside the court, limbering up, his feet alternately thumping and squeaking on the timber floor. Joe didn't wait to be prompted. Massaging the circulation back into his wrists, he marched up to the glass wall, stepped through the door and shut it behind him. He pointed at the guard in the gallery.

'Is this a fair fight, or will he open fire if I'm winning?'

Felton looked offended. 'There'll be no interference with the result. As for whether it's a fair fight, you'd better ask Yuri . . .'

The Ukrainian chuckled, and said quietly, so that only Joe could hear: 'To the death.'

'Are those your orders?'

Yuri glanced up at Felton and shook his head. 'Fuck orders.'

Felton cleared his throat. 'I'm going to up the stakes. If Joe loses, we'll kill the kid. Jaden – is that his name?'

He looked at Valentin, who barely managed a frown. 'The other terms are the same?'

'Oh, the gold's still up for grabs. Don't worry.' Felton leaned over the balustrade and smiled at Joe. 'I'm guessing you'll fight a bit harder if you have someone else's future at stake. I've seen you out on the beach with the boy, playing the surrogate father.'

'You'd better not hurt him.'

'Well, you'll have to sharpen up, then.'

The message had only just sunk in when Joe felt a heavy impact to the side of his head. He spun away, falling, and heard a grunt of satisfaction from Yuri.

So much for a fair fight.

Joe hit the floor hard and awkwardly on his right-hand side, his knee and elbow taking the brunt of the landing. His vision was distorted by flashes of light, and he felt bile rising in his throat. He sensed Yuri moving in, aiming a kick at his skull, and he knew he'd be dead if it connected. And then Jaden would die, and perhaps Cassie and Sofia along with him.

No. He couldn't let that happen.

He was still too dazed to avoid the kick, but he managed to roll onto his back and twist at the hips, shifting his upper body away from where Yuri expected it to be. But instead of retreating he moved closer, reducing the distance of travel, and threw up both hands to grab Yuri's foot midway through its arc.

It was a partial success. There was too much power in the kick to stop it completely but Joe got enough of a grip to divert its path. Yuri's boot thudded into his shoulder and the Ukrainian wobbled, off balance.

Reading Joe's next move, Yuri leaned forward, intending to stamp down on Joe's arm, but Joe wrenched Yuri's foot sideways, bending the ankle as much as he could. As Yuri's legs splayed out, Joe curled up tight and swung his foot into the air, aiming for his opponent's solar plexus.

He missed his target but landed a kick in Yuri's groin instead. The Ukrainian let out a whoosh of air and staggered backwards. Joe used that space to get to his feet, helped a little by the springiness of the court floor.

He blinked several times, and was relieved to find that he could still focus. He had the start of a pounding headache, and a lot of bruising down his right side, but the adrenalin was pumping now, numbing the pain.

With Joe in a defensive stance, prepared for the next assault, Yuri grew cautious. For a few seconds the two men circled each other, searching for a weakness to exploit. A couple of times Yuri dropped his guard, taunting Joe, but it was a bluff. Yuri wanted him to lunge forward, to commit himself totally, on the basis that he would be no match for Yuri's brute strength. But Joe stood a much better chance on the counter-attack – and they both knew it.

There were jeers from above. 'Get on with it.'

Joe ignored the order, and for another full minute there was no contact. Felton thumped the balustrade in frustration.

'Maybe we'll see how well you fight with your legs shot to pieces.'

The guard trained his MP5 on the court. Joe saw it but reasoned that he had no particular incentive to obey, since he'd already assumed that Felton couldn't be trusted. For Yuri it was different. He couldn't afford to disregard a direct order from his boss.

He barrelled forward, a mass of fury and muscle, charging Joe with all the strength and subtlety of a wild boar. In a larger room Joe could easily have sidestepped him, but within the confines of the court there was far less scope for evasive action. He had about five feet of clear space to his left, and no more than three feet to his right.

He waited until Yuri was about to strike him, feinted left, then dodged to the right. It meant that he crashed into the front wall, but it sent Yuri stumbling the wrong way, his big hands snatching at fresh air.

Before the Ukrainian could turn, Joe laced his fingers together and clubbed Yuri on the back of the head. He put all his strength into it, enough force to have knocked most people cold, but Yuri only juddered a little, like a man being jostled on a busy commuter train. Then he spun with astonishing speed and threw a punch. It sideswiped Joe's chin but still nearly lifted him off his feet. He heard a crack from his jaw; tasted blood in his mouth.

There was another punch coming in, this one to the body. Joe had no choice but to absorb it, letting its force drive him backwards, while at the same time he was able to land a punch of his own: a good right-hander that hit Yuri on the cheek, just below the eye, and raked his nose as the Ukrainian reared away.

Probably the hardest punch he'd ever thrown, Joe thought, judging by the screaming pain in his knuckles. He was pleased to see Yuri falter, blood on his face and confusion in his eyes. *Maybe this isn't going to be as easy as he'd expected . . .*

But Joe was still reeling from the blow to his jaw. He knew there was no way they could go on trading punches for long. A few more like that and his hands would be useless.

Yuri must have come to the same conclusion. With the agility of a man half his age, he launched a flying drop kick that caught Joe completely unprepared. He managed to turn slightly, but that was all. Not enough.

Joe was dimly aware of a whoop of disbelieving laughter from Felton, then Yuri's feet struck his hip and thigh and slammed him against the wall. His head fell forwards and then whiplashed back, and his last conscious thought was: *It's over.*

Fifty-Three

What next? That question had been running ceaselessly through Angela Weaver's mind. It was now nearly forty minutes since the garage had been invaded and she was no closer to an answer.

The man guarding them had stonewalled their pleas for information and help. In Angela's estimation, forty minutes seemed ample time to have located and subdued Liam's band of thieves. Surely by now they should have released the innocent prisoners and summoned the police?

But that hadn't happened, which suggested that the new regime – headed by Robert Felton, if Joe's assumptions were correct – didn't necessarily have their best interests at heart.

As the time wore on Angela found herself becoming increasingly downhearted. Four hours of captivity had left her exhausted, emotionally drained, and at times quite faint. Added to that, she was hot and grimy and very, very thirsty.

While the dehydration helped in some respects, she was terrified that eventually she would lose control of her bladder in front of Terry Fox. It seemed a ludicrous preoccupation, compared with the day's other ordeals, but perhaps that was why it gripped her so fiercely: a distraction from the far greater horrors that lay beyond her influence.

Angela was hardly surprised when Priya started coughing. There was a terrible stench in the garage, and because of the gag Priya was being forced to breathe through her nose. She was sitting next to the bodies of Travers and Eldon, with a huge slick of blood only inches from her feet. Until now, Angela had done her best not to look in that direction. Eldon's corpse was particularly distressing. He had been shot several times in quick succession, and one of the bullets had struck him full in the face.

Whilst Angela couldn't help feeling a tinge of pity for Eldon, she felt no such compassion for Turner, who had sustained a serious leg wound, or for Priya, who had glared at her a couple of times, angry and unrepentant.

But now the Asian woman appeared to be in trouble. After pausing to take some long, wheezing breaths through her nostrils, she erupted with another burst of intense coughing. The noise was muffled by the tape over her mouth but still made Angela wince. It sounded as though Priya's lungs were being shredded.

Angela turned to the guard. 'Shouldn't you see if she's all right?'

Terry Fox muttered, 'We should let her choke.'

Angela shook her head. 'Then we're just as bad as they are.'

As the second bout of coughing subsided, Priya slumped against the wall. Her face was flushed, her chest rising and falling at an unnatural rate. Her mouth worked uselessly, twisting and writhing against the tape. Suddenly her cheeks bulged, and her eyes widened in shock.

'She's been sick,' Angela cried. She made another appeal to the guard, 'At least take off the gag. Otherwise she'll suffocate.'

The man grumbled to himself, but strode across the garage for a closer look. Priya was throwing her head from side to side, making a frantic keening noise in her throat. For a moment her gaze settled on Angela and her expression seemed to soften. Gratitude, or something else?

'Okay, okay.' The guard slowed as he reached the pool of blood. He made a detour to avoid it and took a couple of awkward, mincing steps to bring himself alongside Priya.

She twisted her body towards him, but didn't think to lift her head.

The guard couldn't kneel, because of the blood, so he had to bend over, crouching awkwardly while he reached one hand towards her face.

Then he hesitated. 'Don't try and bite me.'

Priya gave him a meek, reassuring nod. The guard tried to prise away a corner of the tape, his gloved fingers struggling to get it loose. Angela watched, bracing herself for the unpleasant sight of Priya expelling the vomit that filled her mouth. But as the tape finally tore loose there was a blur of movement, and then an outpouring of something very different.

Blood.

Priya had never given up hope. Even when her plan took much longer than she expected. Even when the pain almost made her vomit for real.

She went on, undaunted, twisting and pulling until she had eased her hands apart by half an inch. Not far, but enough to get a better angle for her fingers to pluck at the tape. Her nails had been filed down so she could wear the latex gloves, but as Priya dug them into the tape they started to split, creating sharp edges that she could use to dig further.

It took her twenty minutes of constant surreptitious activity. By the time the tape came apart her wrists were slick with blood. She wiped her hands against the back of her boiler suit, then rested, easing her arms apart a fraction to release some of the tension in her shoulders.

The guard had done her a favour by retreating to the far side of the garage. Every now and then his attention wandered for a moment. Priya waited for her chance, then carefully retrieved the knife that she carried in the back pocket of her suit.

During the assault on the garage the guard had patted her down while simultaneously cutting off her utility belt. With so many weapons on the belt he hadn't given much attention to the body search. The knife he'd missed was a push dagger, a broad three-inch blade on a T-shaped handle. It was designed to be gripped in the fist, with the blade protruding between the second and third fingers.

Once Priya had it ready, it was simple enough to fake a choking fit to lure the guard over. The pool of Eldon's blood meant he couldn't approach her directly: instead he was forced to stoop alongside her, in a posture that hindered the use of his MP5.

He was on her right-hand side, fumbling with the tape. Priya readied herself, looking up at him with big pleading eyes, and as the gag was ripped from her face she swung her left arm round and punched the knife into his inner thigh, aiming for the femoral artery.

A jet of blood told her that she'd hit the target. One of the prisoners screamed. The guard didn't make a sound. He was staring dumb-founded at the spurting blood.

Priya pulled the dagger free and stabbed him again, this time in the groin. He let out a howl and stumbled backwards, desperate to get away. Priya moved with him, clutching his injured leg with her right hand, and as he overbalanced she clambered on top of him, stabbing him in the abdomen. The MP5 hit the floor, and her heart missed a beat as she waited for a burst of accidental gunfire.

Then the moment passed and she was grabbing the tiny micro-phone at his throat. Ripping it free, she hurled it across the garage, pushed herself up and reached for the MP5.

Leaving the guard to bleed out, she shuffled backwards, ignoring the smears of blood over her legs. She used the dagger to cut the tape from her ankles, and then she was on her feet.

She took a couple of deep breaths, studying the mess she'd made with her wrists. There was a lot of skin scraped off, and her finger-nails were broken and bloody, but it was superficial. It generated the kind of pain she welcomed. The kind that told her: *I'm alive.* The kind that told her: *Never give up.*

The guard was dead. Priya smiled. Angela and the other prisoners were staring at her, transfixed. But it wasn't their reaction that inter-ested her.

It was Turner's.

*   *   *

The flash of the blade didn't make sense until the blood started to flow. Then Angela understood many things at once: Priya wasn't choking. She hadn't been sick. Somehow she'd freed herself.

She had a knife and she was attacking the guard with a ferocity unlike anything Angela had ever seen. It was a savage, inhuman assault; in some ways more shocking to witness even than Donald's murder for its sheer brutality.

And she, Angela, had made it possible. An unbearable truth: she had been suckered into helping Priya kill a man.

Angela thought she would pass out. She heard herself groan and felt the room tilt and spin. Then Terry was bumping against her, whispering her name, doing his best to comfort her.

When it was done, Priya got to her feet, panting from the exertion but otherwise unruffled. Her boiler suit was plastered in blood. It was in her hair and on her face, but she seemed not to know or to care.

She glanced at the prisoners, and now Angela deciphered the look she'd seen a few moments ago.

Not gratitude, but contempt.

'You used me.'

Priya snorted, as if to say: *Of course*. Angela drew in a breath to speak again, but Terry hissed: 'Leave it.'

He was right, of course, though it took a while for Angela to accept that. He was only expressing what the other prisoners were thinking: *Don't antagonise her.*

But for now Priya showed no interest in them. Her focus was upon Turner. Angela could only see her face in profile, but it seemed calm, composed.

Turner, on the other hand, was petrified. He stared at Priya as though she was all his nightmares come to life. When she leaned towards him he shrank back and made a high-pitched pleading noise beneath his gag.

Priya tore the tape from his mouth so roughly that everyone winced.

Blood oozed from his lip and into his mouth. He spat it out, and said: 'Jesus! Thanks.'

The gratitude seemed heartfelt, as did his relief, but Angela felt it was misplaced. Priya straightened up, her body language still wary, hostile.

Turner wriggled away from the wall, trying to give Priya access to his bound hands. 'These are killing me. How d'you manage to get free?'

Without responding, Priya lifted the MP5 to chest height and examined it carefully. There was some sort of switch on the side of the gun, and she idly flicked it back and forth a couple of times while Turner made another desperate pitch.

'That was a fucking good move. Always thought you had hidden talents.' A brief snigger, cut short when he registered her blank expression. 'Come on, then. Are you gonna untie me?'

'Why would I do that?'

'Wha—?' Turner looked incredulous. 'Because it's one against Christ knows how many. With two of us, we've got a real chance.'

'So we abandon Liam? And Valentin?'

'They're probably dead anyway.'

'But if they're still alive?'

Turner gave a dismissive shrug, as if he thought it unlikely. 'Why not? Just you and me. We deserve it, after all this shit they put us through.'

Priya tipped her head to one side, as if deep in thought. Then she said, 'I don't think so.'

She hefted the gun into a firing stance. Turner looked from side to side, then back at Priya. He was close to tears. Angela felt Terry nudge her, another warning, but this time it wasn't necessary. She had no intention of getting involved.

Turner changed tack: tried exasperation. 'Think about this, eh? You want to get out of here, don't you? Because I'll tell you something, love, you won't get far on your own, even with that big fucking gun.'

'Really? You must have forgotten what you said to me earlier.'

At first Turner was confused. 'What?' Then he remembered. 'Hey, come on. I didn't mean—'

Priya's finger wrapped around the trigger. She was smiling.

'They'll never see me coming, will they?'

Fifty-Four

Joe heard Valentin shouting his name. For a nanosecond he wondered if he'd dozed off on the couch and Jaden had crept up on him. It would be typical of the boy to leap onto his chest and playfully strangle him.

But the weight on his body was immense. The hands around his neck were thick and meaty and extremely powerful. This was no game.

It was Yuri. Squeezing hard and intent on killing him, while Felton and Valentin watched from the gallery, enjoying a show which was about to climax with Joe's death.

The urge to react was overwhelming. It took every ounce of his self-control not to open his eyes and try to fight Yuri off. But he had to be disciplined. He couldn't afford to squander the one small opportunity the Ukrainian had given him.

For this was the first time he'd had Yuri in such close proximity, with his defences lowered. Yuri believed the fight was as good as won; that Joe would die without ever regaining consciousness.

The pain in Joe's neck made him want to throw up. His head was starting to throb and his lungs were burning from the lack of oxygen. He knew he was in danger of blacking out again. Couldn't wait too long . . .

Another second to run it through his mind, visualise the manoeuvre so it could be performed smoothly and quickly. And then he struck.

He didn't think he'd ever moved so fast in his life. With lightning speed his arms flew up and his hands slapped against Yuri's head. Anchoring his fingers around the Ukrainian's ears, he rammed both thumbs into Yuri's eyes. Joe heard the tiny exhalation of surprise choked off by a much harsher sound: an involuntary scream.

The grip on his own neck was suddenly relieved, but Joe knew this was no time for half measures. He couldn't afford to be tentative, or squeamish, or compassionate. He went on digging his thumbs as deep as they would go, feeling the gelatinous tissues yield beneath them.

With a primal screech, Yuri reared up, swatting blindly at Joe's arms. Joe ignored the blows, allowing himself to be lifted by Yuri until both men were sitting up. Then Joe released his right hand, his thumb emerging from Yuri's eye with a wet sucking noise and a gout of blood.

Joe curled his fingers over and with an upward trajectory he drove the heel of his palm into Yuri's nose. He heard a satisfying crunch of bone and followed through, forcing Yuri's head back while at the same time pulling his own body to one side, enabling him to get out from under the Ukrainian.

They broke apart with another gloopy popping sound as Joe's other thumb came out. Joe caught a clumsy punch to the side of his head and rolled away, quickly jumping to his feet. While he carried out a swift assessment of his own injuries, he watched Yuri backpedalling, still blinded, blood gushing from his eyes and nose.

He had to be in agony, Joe thought. Surely this was enough to put him out of action.

From Felton, there was a bloodthirsty roar of encouragement. 'Go on! Finish him off!'

Whether this was directed at him, or at Yuri, Joe wasn't sure. He spat in disgust at Felton's depravity even as he saw, to his dismay, that Yuri had no intention of conceding. Of course not. A creature like Yuri never accepted defeat.

Felton shouted: 'Fight, you buggers! Fight!'

Yuri nodded. Scraped blood from his eyes and blinked furiously. The skin around his nose was swelling fast, but he seemed to have a little vision in one eye, at least. He wiggled his fingers at Joe, taunting him: *Come and get me.*

And, like a fool, Joe accepted the bait. He took a few cautious steps towards Yuri, hands up in a boxer's stance, thinking he could now settle this with his fists.

Yuri wiped his eye again, while his other hand drifted behind his back for a second. For Yuri it was quite a subtle movement, but Joe spotted the misdirection. He took another step forward, inviting Yuri to reveal whatever surprise he had in store, then dodged sideways, out of reach.

As he did, he heard a click and Yuri swung his hand into view, jabbing at the space that Joe should have occupied. Joe had good reason to be grateful for reading the move in time, because Yuri was holding a knife.

Lurking just outside the gymnasium, Oliver watched the fight with a mixture of fascination and revulsion. There was something extraordinary about seeing two grown men beat the living shit out of each other. It had an integrity, he thought. A kind of primitive nobility that you rarely saw any more.

At least, that was how it seemed until Yuri pulled a knife. A typically underhand move, and one of which his father would no doubt approve. Robert Felton appeared to be delighting in the role of a modern-day Roman emperor. To Oliver it was the final confirmation that his father was beyond redemption.

Now that Yuri was armed, Oliver guessed the fight was heading towards a suitably barbaric conclusion. He was debating whether to stay and watch when he heard a noise from behind him.

He turned, but there was nothing to see. The noise had come from around the corner. It sounded like someone trying to cross the marble hall without being heard.

One of Dad's storm troopers? Maybe, but they had no obvious reason to be stealthy. They ruled the roost.

With some reluctance, Oliver left the fight and went to investigate.

Felton laughed when he saw the knife, but Valentin was incensed.

'You did not say he had a weapon. This is not fair.'

'As it happens, I didn't know he had it. Anyway, what's fair is what I say is fair.' But a moment later he gestured towards the guard standing outside the court. 'Give him a racquet.'

Joe frowned. He was trying to follow the conversation going on overhead, at the same time evading Yuri's clumsy but forceful attempts to stab him. The one eye that was working seemed to be having difficulty focusing, and Joe suspected he had done some serious damage to the Ukrainian. Only a supreme act of will kept Yuri on his feet, hence his desperation to finish Joe off with the knife.

Joe was aware of the guard fetching something but had to turn away as Yuri thrust the knife forward. Once again Joe managed to avoid it, this time by an uncomfortably narrow margin.

He only has to get lucky once, Joe thought. If he catches me with the blade, or even gets a hand on me, then it's all over . . .

Yuri's momentum sent him hurtling into the wall, but he immediately rebounded, slashing the blade through the air like a demented butcher. As Joe backed away, there was a clattering from behind him. Turning quickly, he saw that the guard had thrown a squash racquet onto the court.

'Thought that would even the score,' said Felton.

Joe snorted. 'A gun would be better.'

But after dodging another attack he snatched the racquet up. It was a good, sturdy model. Not only could it be used to deflect the knife but, more importantly, it extended Joe's reach.

He gripped the top of the handle just below the racquet head and held it at arm's length, using the head as a shield. Yuri growled in frustration at this new obstacle, but refused to countenance any other option but attack.

His face was a mask of blood. His breath rattled noisily in his chest. He was unsteady on his feet, and yet he kept on coming. Determined not to be beaten.

As Yuri lunged and overreached, Joe leaned back but kept his feet where they were, planted well apart. He parried with the racquet head, then turned his wrist and smacked the butt of the handle into Yuri's face. It caught him just below the good eye, where his cheek was already swollen and purple.

Yuri roared with pain. His knife hand dropped to his side and Joe danced closer, striking him another half a dozen times in quick succession, aiming for the face and the neck. Yuri started to buckle, but still he wouldn't go down.

Joe swerved to Yuri's right and stamped on the side of Yuri's knee. There was a terrible cracking noise and Yuri's leg gave way and he dropped, hitting the sprung floor with enough force to shake the room.

Joe kicked the knife out of his grasp and watched it skid across the blood-splattered court. Then he looked down at Yuri. At last the Ukrainian had lost the will to fight. It was over.

Fifty-Five

The prisoners pleaded to be released, even after they'd watched Priya kill Turner. In her view, they should think themselves fortunate that she'd spared them from the same fate.

For now, anyway.

As she hurried next door, she pondered Turner's last words. Could Liam and Valentin still be alive? And did it really matter? Maybe she was better off taking his advice and getting out of here. Empty-handed, but free. Wasn't that the best option?

Quite possibly. But she couldn't do it. There were things she had to know first, things that mattered more to her right now than freedom. More than life or death.

From the entrance hall, Priya reconnoitred the main living rooms and found nothing. But she could hear noise off to her left, where she knew Felton's little leisure complex was located: a gymnasium and games room over two floors.

She climbed the stairs, wondering if the main bedroom would be empty. She felt sure that Felton, having thwarted their robbery, would be unable to resist gloating over the contents of the panic room.

On the upper landing she heard more activity coming from the gym. It sounded like a fight in progress. She went the other way, towards the bedroom. The door was shut and she couldn't hear anything, but her intuition told her it was occupied.

She checked the MP5, took a deep breath and opened the door. She made sure the barrel of the gun went in first, pointing downwards. She was counting on the guards to recognise the weapon as belonging to one of their own and relax, just for a second.

The room contained two people, but only one guard. He *did* relax, and it only took a second. Priya fired a short burst and cut him down before he'd even begun to comprehend who she was.

The room's remaining occupant was cringing on the floor. Slowly he looked round and stared at her in amazement.

'How did you—?'

'Sshh.' Priya kicked the door shut behind her and pulled the knife from her pocket.

Joe staggered away from Yuri, then grimly awaited Felton's reaction to the Ukrainian's defeat. Before either of them could speak there was the harsh rattle of gunfire from the other side of the house.

Felton frowned at his men. The one guarding Valentin spoke briefly into his microphone, waited for a reply, then shook his head. 'Nothing.'

'What's he playing at?' Felton murmured to himself. He leaned over the balustrade and addressed the other guard, who was standing just outside the squash court. 'Go and find out what that was about. We can watch Joe from here.'

Joe studied the distance from the squash court to the doorway out of the gym and reluctantly concluded that Felton was right. There was no way he'd outrun an MP5.

Having sent someone to investigate the shooting, Felton's attention returned to the court. So did Valentin's, and for the first time this evening his mood perked up and he managed a smile.

'My man wins,' he declared.

'Not yet he hasn't.' Enjoying the bafflement on Valentin's face, Felton indicated Yuri, still on his back and gasping with pain. 'Not while my man's still breathing.'

*　　*　　*

Oliver followed the intruder at a safe distance, which meant he could hear but not see who it was. The warning voice in his head grew shrill as he climbed the stairs. *You risked your life to escape from this snakepit, and now you're going back in voluntarily . . .*

It was a foolish act. Quite reckless. But he didn't care. If he was caught, so be it.

He heard the bedroom door open, but by the time he reached the hallway the intruder had entered the room. The subsequent gunfire sent Oliver dashing into the bedroom next door to hide. The noise was bound to bring a call for reinforcements.

Sure enough, within seconds he heard footsteps approaching. Only a single set, though. Clearly his father didn't want to be dragged away from the entertainment in the gym.

Pressing his ear to the dividing wall, Oliver strained to hear what was happening next door. No machine gun fire this time, just several distinct clicks, followed by a heavy thud. Then voices, urgent and excited—

'No,' said Oliver. He clamped his hand over his mouth.

A few more seconds and there was movement in the hall again. Oliver hurried to the door, opened it a fraction and saw two figures in black striding purposefully along the corridor. One of them was Liam, newly released, carrying a silenced pistol.

The other one, armed with an MP5, was Priya.

Joe said: 'I won't do it.'

'Then you haven't won,' said Felton. 'If you want to claim victory, you have to finish it.'

Joe glanced down at Yuri. He was a pathetic sight, moaning softly, his one functioning eye flickering like a worn-out TV. He seemed to be drifting in and out of consciousness and probably had no idea that his fate was being discussed in such a callous manner.

'You want me to kill the man who made all this possible for you?'

'He's certainly been useful. But I don't think you could argue that he's anything but a liability in the longer term. Could you?'

Felton looked to Valentin, who spared Yuri a brief, lizard-like contemplation, his tongue flickering over his lips as he meditated on his verdict. Observing him, Joe saw a man whose entire outlook was now governed by one thing and one thing alone: self-preservation.

Then Valentin said: 'You should kill him.'

'No.' Joe turned and strode to the opposite corner of the court. The barrel of the MP5 tracked his movement.

'Sure about that?' Felton asked.

'I won't be party to killing a defenceless man.'

'Very well.'

Joe braced himself as Felton turned and whispered something to the guard, who promptly stepped closer to the balustrade and opened fire.

The shots boomed like thunder around the tight walls of the court. Yuri's body was pummelled by the impacts, the bullets plucking at his shirt. A spray of spent cartridges rained down on them and Joe turned away, shielding his face, wondering if Yuri felt it coming or if it was over too quickly to feel anything; then wondering if he was about to find out for himself.

Fifty-Six

Priya stopped when she heard shooting from the direction of the games room. She hid her face away from Liam, so he wouldn't see what she was thinking.

Am I too late?

Liam stood beside her, waiting for instructions. From the moment Priya had cut him free there had been no question that she was in charge. Even now, with a gun in his hand, she doubted that he had the nerve to challenge her authority.

She wasn't entirely comfortable that he carried a weapon, but it gave her some useful support, at least for the time being. If nothing else she could use him as a decoy.

Admittedly it had been quick thinking on his part to frisk the man she'd killed. And finding a handgun with a silencer meant he'd been able to shoot the second guard without alerting Felton.

But it had been a messy kill. After dragging the first man out of sight beyond the bed, Priya had hidden in the entrance to the dressing room while Liam had resumed his position on the floor, apparently still handcuffed.

The second guard had entered the room, assumed that Liam posed no threat, and turned to search for his colleague. Liam had pulled the gun and fired. The first bullet only winged the man's shoulder, the second missed altogether, and the third got him in the stomach as he dived for cover and would have been fatal if not for his body armour.

The guard hit the floor with enough presence of mind to bring his own weapon up and level it at Liam. Before he could get off a shot, Priya leapt out and stabbed him in the neck.

'How many more?' she'd asked.

Liam had taken longer to recover, his hand trembling as he stared at the body. 'S-sorry, I fucked that up . . .'

'How many?'

'Um, only one more of these fellers, I think. Plus Yuri, and Felton.'

'What are they doing in the gym?'

Liam gave her a garbled explanation about some sort of duel between Joe and Yuri, with Valentin standing to win a gold bar if his man triumphed.

'Not that he's got a hope. But the bloody *gold* in there, Priya.' Liam's face lit up as he realised they now stood a chance of reconstituting the original plan. 'Wait till you see it. Makes all this worthwhile, and then some.'

Before leaving the room Priya had exchanged the magazine in her MP5 for a fresh one taken from one of the dead guards. Wisely, in her opinion, Liam had chosen to stick with the handgun.

Now she considered how best to use the firepower at her disposal. The decision made, she jabbed a finger at the stairs.

'You go down, through the gym. I'll go this way. Whoever gets a clear sight on the guard takes him out, all right?'

For about a minute after Priya's departure there was an uneasy silence in the garage. Nobody moved. Nobody could be sure it was safe.

Then Terry grinned boyishly at Angela. 'Well, I guess we can sit around like lemons and wait for whichever bunch of bastards wants to kill us next. Or we can try to get out of here.'

Angela nodded, and managed to summon a smile of her own. 'My thoughts exactly. First we need to find a knife. Something sharp, at least.'

Because she was the only one who'd been cuffed with her hands in front of her, it made sense for Angela to carry out the search. Terry objected to this, on the basis that whoever did it faced the risk of punishment if Priya should return.

Angela put him right. 'Terry, if that damn woman comes back I suspect we'll all be in big trouble.'

She made straight for the body of the guard that Priya had killed. The restraints on her ankles meant that she had to move in a kind of ungainly shuffling crawl. It was a slow and demanding task, made worse by the sheer quantity of blood on the garage floor. The smell repulsed her, as did the warm, sticky feel of it on her hands.

Then, when she reached the guard's body, she had to search his clothes and feel inside his pockets. It was an appallingly intimate act: a desecration, almost. A couple of times she retched and had to stop and look away, breathing slowly through her mouth until the nausea receded. She had to disassociate herself from the reality of what she was doing, and concentrate on what was at stake.

The first stage of that objective was to find a knife, and she did. A thin-bladed dagger in a leather sheath. She cut her ankles free, stood up and nearly fainted as the blood rushed from her head.

Feeling ridiculous, but cheered on by the encouragement of the other prisoners, Angela tottered back to the group, brandishing the knife like a prize, praying that someone wouldn't march in with a gun at the very moment when escape seemed like something more than an absurd fantasy.

The guard checked that Yuri was dead, then stepped back from the balustrade. Joe experienced a mixture of confusion and relief. He was still alive – but for how long?

Felton barely glanced at the body. He turned to Valentin, briskly moving to the next item on his agenda.

'Congratulations. I must confess, I hadn't expected Joe to perform so well. That could present us with a problem.' He gave a brief, mirthless chuckle. 'Perhaps I'll have to make him an offer he can't refuse.'

'You're welcome to him.'

Felton looked at Joe and tutted, as if to say: *How's that for loyalty?*

'Very well,' he told Valentin. 'We'll fetch your gold just as soon as we conclude the terms of the main deal. What do you say?'

'I have no choice,' said Valentin, with a touch of petulance. 'But I don't see how you can make this work.'

'It's perfectly straightforward. Liam and Priya arranged a robbery. You were an innocent victim, the same as everyone else on this island. I was in the South of France, but thankfully some of my security team were here, guarding the house. They were captured at first, but after several hours they managed to escape. A fierce battle ensued, in which most of the gang were killed.'

'Most?'

'I think we have to spare Liam. Maybe Priya, too, if she's willing to play along.'

'And my family?'

'You'll tell the police they're in Brighton, just as you planned to do. They're no part of this.'

'But you still keep them?'

'Until everything's signed and sealed.'

Valentin nodded, but he looked disgusted. Not surprisingly, Joe thought. Felton had every detail nailed down.

'Very well,' said Valentin at last.

'Excellent.' Felton clapped his hands together. He wore a look of intense satisfaction that lasted only until he caught the guard's eye.

'Has Briggs reported in yet?'

The guard shook his head. Spoke into his mouthpiece and then coughed. A fine mist of blood blew from the side of his neck.

Joe saw his chance and ran for the door at the back of the squash court. He wrenched it open, then froze.

'Nice try,' said Liam. He was standing just inside the gymnasium, holding the silenced pistol that had killed the guard. Up in the gallery, Priya had an MP5 trained on Felton. Her boiler suit was caked in blood: she looked like she'd just crawled out of an abattoir.

It was the first time Joe had seen her without her mask. He was shocked by the contrast between the startling perfection of her face and the cold, jaded look in her eyes.

Liam stood on tiptoe and peered through the glass at the body on the squash court. 'Jesus. I'd have put a grand on Yuri winning that one.'

'I got lucky,' said Joe.

'You sure did,' Liam agreed. 'Until now.'

Fifty-Seven

While Priya cut Valentin free, Joe slowly backed across the squash court. Liam followed, walking up to the glass wall, where he was in full sight of the people on the floor above. That was when Felton spotted him and groaned, as if he'd just been thinking it couldn't get any worse, and then it had.

But there was another side to Felton's character, Joe realised. The reckless gambler. The supremely arrogant businessman, buoyed by years of success and accustomed to flattery and deference on every continent. That side was evident when Felton asked, scornfully, 'What happened to my team?'

'They're dead,' said Priya.

'You're kidding me. Who did it?'

'Who do you think?'

'Good grief.' Felton looked Priya in the eye and jeered. 'A skinny little runt like you?'

It seemed like a deliberate taunt, designed to provoke a reaction. For that reason, perhaps, Priya responded with nothing more than a warning look. It was Valentin who lost his temper, swinging a well-telegraphed punch at the other man's jaw. Felton easily dodged the blow, stuck out his foot and sent Valentin to the floor in a clumsy sprawl.

Liam's spluttered laugh earned a rebuke from Priya. No one spoke while Valentin climbed slowly to his feet, burning with humiliation.

Felton shook his head as if disappointed to face an adversary of such poor quality. 'Oh, Priya,' he said in commiseration, 'I suppose you think this gives you the upper hand?'

To Joe's eye, it seemed there was almost a glint of admiration in Priya's smile. 'Doesn't it?' she asked.

'Not really. I think my proposal is by far the best option.' He pointed at Valentin, as if expecting him to concur. 'You see, unless we play it my way an innocent woman and two young children will die a slow, lingering death.'

Priya was spectacularly unimpressed. 'Maybe. But you're still going to open that room full of gold.'

She was a far better poker player than Valentin, who turned on her. 'You don't get to—'

Priya shushed him, reaching out and patting him gently on the arm. It was an oddly affectionate gesture, and Joe wasn't the only one to take note of it.

For the first time since Priya had walked in, Felton looked taken aback. 'Something you're not telling me?' he asked Valentin.

'We want the gold,' Priya said. 'In return, we'll spare your life.'

'Young lady, you don't understand. Cassie and the children are alone, locked in a room at a location known only to me. No one else is going to find them. Now, I'm prepared to be reasonable and revise our earlier deal. But if you want to see them again you'll have to accept my terms.'

Valentin looked undecided, while Priya suddenly frowned, looking around the room. She turned to Liam.

'Where's Oliver?'

The mention of his name made Oliver jump, and nearly gave him away.

He'd come downstairs and hidden in the hallway just outside the gym. The danger only added to the excitement. He was in his element: spying on others while remaining unobserved.

His view of the gallery was limited, but if he concentrated hard he could hear almost every word. The acoustics of the gym helped: all those hard shiny surfaces reflected the sound of voices.

Now Priya was demanding to know where he was. He felt a stab of pride that she cared enough to ask, followed by a vague resentment that it had taken her until now to register his absence.

It was Liam who supplied the answer. 'He's locked in his bedroom. Daddy didn't want him around while he discussed business.'

'Where's the key?' Priya demanded.

'Probably in the lock,' said Robert Felton. He seemed absurdly confident, given the circumstances.

'Will you fetch him?' Priya asked. Now her tone was strikingly different: warm, feminine, sensual. Intrigued, Oliver crept nearer to the doorway and discovered that she'd been talking to Valentin Nasenko.

Before leaving the room, Valentin leaned close and brushed his lips against her cheek while trailing his hand across her belly and hip. It was a crude display of possession and, judging by Priya's expression, not exactly something she relished. But she didn't fight him off, either.

Oliver felt something vital curl up and die deep inside him.

With Valentin gone, Priya turned back to Robert Felton. 'Now we have an obvious transaction. You give us the gold and the girl, and you and Oliver will be spared.'

'Just the girl?' his father repeated. Oliver barely heard him over the sudden loud buzzing in his brain. 'What about the others?'

'Cassie and the boy? I don't care about them. Neither does Valentin. We only want his daughter. Either you release her, or Oliver dies. And I guarantee I'll hurt him in ways you've never dreamed of, and I'll make you watch.'

The static filling Oliver's head was almost unbearable, like a radio caught between stations, blasting out at full volume. He had to shut his eyes for a moment.

When he opened them, his father was still staring at Priya, his eyes narrowed as if conducting a professional evaluation, trying to assess exactly what manner of creature he was dealing with.

Frankly, Oliver couldn't see why there wasn't instant recognition. If you went on character alone, his father might as well be looking in a mirror.

'Interesting,' said Felton. 'But I'm afraid your threats don't work. You can do what you like with Oliver.'

'Bullshit!' It was Liam who reacted. 'What do you take us for?'

'I assure you, Liam, my son is a source of constant regret. A dysfunctional parasite. A waste of oxygen.' He gave them a complacent smile. 'In all honesty, you'd be doing me a favour.'

'You think you could stand by and watch your own son tortured to death?' Liam again.

'I'm not claiming that I'd take any pleasure in witnessing it, of course not. But I'd get over it. I have a remarkably strong constitution, you see.'

Oliver wanted to scream. He wanted to throw himself into the room and do battle with his father one last time.

But he didn't. Somehow he not only controlled himself, but even summoned the presence of mind to consider whether his father was bluffing. Felton senior could have reasoned that the best way to save Oliver was to profess no concern for his survival.

On the other hand, Robert Felton was also a ruthless sociopath, and every one of his insults bore the ring of truth. In fact, most of them had been said before – to Oliver's face.

A room full of gold versus a dysfunctional parasite? There was really no competition.

Oliver knew he couldn't listen any more. As his gaze fell away he realised he wasn't as well hidden as he'd thought. Valentin's bodyguard, Joe, was standing inside the squash court, staring straight at him.

They made eye contact for a second. Oliver was grateful that Joe's expression never wavered, because Liam would surely have noticed if it had.

But that moment of silent communication was enough. Oliver hurried away, believing he knew what Joe wanted him to do.

Joe couldn't decide what to make of Felton's performance. Priya was bound to assume that Felton was feigning his disdain for Oliver, but Joe wasn't so sure. He knew a little about the tensions between them, mainly from gossip passed on by Angela Weaver. And with so much at stake, it seemed all too plausible that Felton would be willing to sacrifice Oliver for his cause.

But one thing was certain. Regardless of which side prevailed, Joe's fate was sealed. No one would trust him to keep quiet about their deal: therefore he had to be eliminated.

When he glanced at the doorway, trying to gauge if he could take Liam on, he was confronted with the unexpected sight of Oliver Felton. The young man's face was a white mask of shock as he listened to his father's ruthless condemnation.

He'll believe it, Joe thought. *He'll want to believe it, to fuel his paranoia and self-pity.*

But at least Oliver was going to get away. That was one small mercy. And if Priya really had killed Felton's men, maybe the other prisoners at Dreamscape had a chance of freedom as well. With any luck, Oliver would help them escape, and then raise the alarm.

Fifty-Eight

When Angela cut Terry free, the first thing he did was wrap her in a heartfelt embrace. It lasted only a couple of seconds, but its effect was extraordinary: obliterating all the pain and fear in an instant. She could scarcely believe how wonderful it felt. Her instinctive response was to clamp her arms around him and not let go, but Terry was already stepping away.

Of course he was. They had two more people to release. To keep them waiting would be rude and selfish. But she was sorry it had ended so soon.

While he cut the restraints, Terry set out his escape plan. 'We may have to get past guards or a roadblock at the bridge, so I suggest we go to my place first. My Hummer's parked in the garage.'

Angela nodded her agreement, but Maria gave an apologetic smile. 'So sorry. But first I need . . .' She made a face, embarrassed.

Terry frowned. 'What?'

Then the driver, Pete Milton, said, 'Me too. I feel like my bladder's gonna explode.'

'You know that every second we stay in here—'

'We know, Terry,' said Angela. 'But we've been trussed up in here for hours, and frankly I'm also in no fit state to run anywhere until I've visited the loo.'

She started towards the inner door, but Terry stayed where he was. When she turned, he waved her away.

'You go on. I'll meet you in the hall.'

They found two cloakrooms on the ground floor. Angela took one, and Maria the other. Milton didn't discuss what arrangements he'd made, but when Angela came out she found him strolling back from the kitchen, looking a lot more relaxed. He'd also managed to wash off some of the blood around his broken nose.

Terry was waiting for them in the hall, bouncing on his feet like a hyperactive teenager. He too looked much happier, and he showed her why, lifting a handgun into sight.

'Found this on the guard,' he said. 'Loaded and ready to go.'

'You really think you'd use it?'

'Too bloody right I would.'

Making sure the way was clear, Terry led them outside. Angela and Maria followed close behind him, with Milton bringing up the rear. The night was clear and starry, the air cool and sweet after the evil stench of the garage: to breathe it was a heady delight.

They made it across the driveway, but as Terry reached the gates he suddenly flapped his free hand in a downwards motion. He dropped into a crouch, checking over his shoulder to make sure they'd done the same.

'What?' Angela mouthed, but by now she could hear the footsteps. Somebody coming . . .

Priya didn't like the way Felton was looking at her: with a lazy smile and half-closed eyes, an expression that was at once smug, disrespectful, even faintly lecherous. He radiated the type of blithe natural confidence that seemed impervious to threats.

Worst of all, she didn't think he was faking any of it. He really did believe he was immune to failure.

'Lot of mopping up to do,' he observed. 'The poor buggers next door, and those two, of course.' He nodded towards the squash court: Liam and Joe. 'If we do it your way, there can't be any witnesses.'

'You don't have a say in the matter.'

Felton shrugged, then called out to Liam: 'How do you feel about being surplus to requirements? Priya and her lover boy won't want you playing gooseberry.'

'Shut the fuck up,' Liam responded.

Grinning, Felton turned back to Priya. 'The truth hurts,' he said quietly. 'It's the same with you, I'm afraid. You made a poor choice with that wannabe oligarch.' He leaned slightly, peering along the corridor behind her. 'Valentin was never a player. Just look at his wife. He couldn't get a supermodel or a Hollywood star, so he settled for some one-hit wonder from a TV talent show. Believe me, Priya, you can do much, much better than that.'

She smiled. 'You're wasting your breath.'

'Oh, I think you're tempted. Even if Valentin does get his hands on that gold, he'll find a way to squander it somehow. And then where will you be?'

Far away from any of you, Priya thought. *With my own money safe and sound.*

Felton opened his hands palm out: a straight-talking gesture. 'Look, I could pour on a lot of flattery about how smart you are, how beautiful, but I don't need to do that. All I'm suggesting is that you reassess your position. It's not too late.'

'To change sides, you mean?'

He nodded. 'To be a winner.'

His gaze flickered past her, and a touch of caution entered his face. Valentin returned, one hand caressing the small of Priya's back as he came alongside her. He looked about twenty years older than Felton, grey and drab and weary.

One foot in the grave, she thought.

He showed her the key in his hand. 'I can't find him. The door was locked, but the room is empty.'

Felton displayed grudging admiration. 'He's escaped? My God, I didn't think he had it in him.'

'The bathroom window was open,' Valentin went on, 'but it's a long drop. Unless somehow he climbed down?'

Priya was picturing the house, the peculiar little dormers and concealed attic room. She shook her head.

'He went up. Climbed over the roof.'

As she said it, Felton was waiting with a congratulatory smile: one step ahead of them as always. It was the smile of a man who believed he was home and dry, because without Oliver they had no leverage at all. Reason dictated that Priya would have to take his offer seriously. She would see the merit of his argument and climb aboard.

It could be done in an instant, she thought. Valentin was just inches away from her: unarmed, unsuspecting, his attention focused mostly on Felton. Point-blank range.

Easy as a bullet, once the decision was made.

Easy as a bullet.

The footsteps were light but rapid. Angela felt her stomach clench at the thought of yet more violence. She had sensed a subtle change in Terry, now that he was wielding a gun. Not quite a swagger, but definitely a swelling of confidence, as though he would welcome a chance to use it.

For all her misgivings, it was quite understandable. And if their survival depended on his willingness to kill, Angela knew she would not object.

A figure loomed over them as Terry launched himself up, ready to shoot. Angela was the first to recognise Oliver Felton, but it was too dangerous to shout or grab Terry's arm. Instead she rushed past him and threw herself in front of the tall, thin, bewildered boy.

'Oh, Jesus.' Terry whipped the gun away from them, and Angela saw the white spots on his knuckles. 'I nearly . . .'

Angela touched Terry's cheek; she could feel his warmth, and the roughness of his stubble. 'It's all right. Oliver's on our side. Aren't you?'

For a moment Oliver just stared at her, as if she'd spoken in a foreign language.

'So is it your dad over there?' Terry asked, indicating the Felton house. 'Is that who those other men are working for?'

'His storm troopers,' Oliver said, his voice strangely placid.

'Why didn't they release us when they had the chance?' Angela asked.

'He had a deal to make first. With Valentin. It's all he cares about: deals, money, power. My father is a monster. Always has been. Always will be.'

His voice tailed off as he looked beyond them and fixed his gaze on Dreamscape. Angela had the unsettling impression that he'd been talking to himself, and barely knew they were there.

'We need to hurry,' Terry reminded her.

'Yes.' She waved her hand to attract Oliver's attention. 'Come on. Leave them to their in-fighting and let the police take over.'

'He'll only buy his way out. Police, judges, politicians, they all succumb at the right price.'

He smiled, as though he found his own wisdom immensely satisfying, and continued to stare at the huge empty house.

Angela flinched as a hand gripped her shoulder. Terry. 'What he does is up to him. But we're leaving. *Now.*'

He eased her towards the road, but she went sluggishly, still trying to persuade Oliver.

'Please come with us. Don't stay here.'

But it was no good. Oliver's dreamy smile never faltered as she backed away, and finally she allowed herself to turn, hurrying to keep pace with the others, her heart wrenched by a sudden conviction that she would never see him again.

* * *

'Is that how he got out? Did he climb over the roof?' Priya asked. The answer was immaterial, but she needed time to think and this bought her valuable seconds.

'I've no idea,' said Felton. 'Maybe he built a glider and flew away on it.' He lifted his hand and made a fluttering motion with his fingers, all the time his eyes locked on Priya, glinting with the thrill of their illicit communication.

We could fly away . . .

'Where will he go?' Valentin demanded.

'Why would I tell you that, even if I knew? He's soft in the head. Impossible to predict.' Enjoying Valentin's frustration, Felton added, 'You know, do you, that this young lady is quite happy to let your family perish?'

'That's not true,' said Priya.

'I beg your pardon. You want me to spare the daughter, but Cassie and her son can die, paving the way for your own . . . liaison. Will you marry her?' Felton snapped the question at Valentin, who baulked.

'Enough of this. Give me my daughter, and the gold, and we will spare your life.'

Felton ignored him. 'I wish Yuri had told me she was your Achilles heel.'

'Yuri did not know about us,' Valentin said. 'No one knew.'

'She's a hell of a catch, Valentin. In fact, we were just saying, she's really a bit *too* good for you. I can't see it lasting, to be honest.'

For a second Priya thought Valentin was going to snatch the gun from her and shoot Felton on the spot. She knew all about Valentin's short temper; his eagerness to take offence and bear a grudge. She'd told herself that it wouldn't matter once they were together; that his negative qualities would be outweighed by security and wealth.

Besides, Valentin had rescued her, like a knight in a fairy story. If not for him, she'd have sunk into a morass of drug addiction and prostitution.

She owed him. Didn't she?

'One last chance,' Valentin said slowly. 'Tell me where my daughter is, or Priya will shoot. We start with kneecaps. Very painful.'

Felton looked unfazed, and Priya knew why. Valentin couldn't afford to hurt him too badly, in case something went wrong and his daughter was lost for ever.

That was the key moment. The moment when Priya saw with absolute clarity that Felton was right. He *did* hold all the cards. He had the gold, and he had Sofia, and they had nothing comparable; just empty threats and guns that might as well have been toys for all the use they were.

And Valentin was to blame. It was his arrogance and poor judgement that had allowed Yuri to deceive him. His sloppy planning that had allowed his family to be kidnapped.

All signs of the fundamental weakness of character that Robert Felton had described.

And Felton, watching with that wise, crafty, penetrating gaze of his, followed every tiny stage of Priya's realignment, took note of every single calculation and waited for the inevitable conclusion.

When it came, his eyes widened and warmed a little, and Priya thought he was going to ruin it all by offering his congratulations prematurely. But he didn't get the chance. Because that was also the moment his phone rang.

Fifty-Nine

In the context of this night, the everyday trilling of a phone seemed banal and nonsensical. Joe didn't know what it meant, that someone should call, but he was glad of the interruption.

He'd followed the conversation between Felton and Priya and saw how she might be tempted to jump ship. Soon Liam would reach the same conclusion. Felton's taunt about playing gooseberry had struck a nerve: since then Liam had been restlessly shifting his weight from foot to foot, keeping his gun hand up and ready. Not trusting anyone.

And this is how it falls apart.

In the gallery, Priya allowed Felton to ease the phone from his pocket. He looked at the screen and did a double take.

'Oliver?'

As he listened, Felton made eye contact with Priya. He shrugged, then frowned, pressing the phone against his ear as if striving to hear or understand.

Oliver's impulse would be to gloat, Joe thought. He'd phone to tell his father he was safely off the island, and that he'd called the police. Joe prayed that he'd also thought to release the other prisoners.

Then Felton made a stuttering sound, and said, 'Wh-what do you mean? Matches?'

*   *   *

'I kept some,' Oliver told him. 'I've had them for years. Hidden in my bedroom, as a test of will.'

'A test . . . ?' His father seemed incapable of anything but dumb repetition.

'That's right. But I don't need to do that any more. I can face up to what I am.'

'Oliver, I haven't got a clue what you're talking about, as usual. They said you escaped. Where are you?'

'Next door. It may be an ugly house, but the view from up here is incredible. The sea is shining like a vast oil slick—'

'Oliver . . .' Felton gave a sigh that seemed intended for his other audience. 'That's not really the wisest location, is it? But since you're there you could save me a lot of trouble by coming back with a gun and shooting these bastards.'

Oliver moved the phone away from his ear, correctly anticipating the big, ingratiating laugh that followed.

When it faded away to a flat silence, Oliver said, 'I'm not interested in guns. I was pleased to get my phone back, though. They had a room full of them downstairs. And then I wasn't sure if Priya would let you answer it.'

'Priya and I are getting on fine.' More false jollity. 'Talking things over. Like I said, why don't you join us?'

'I'm not riding to anyone's rescue. But I will solve all your problems. Can you hear that?'

He held the phone at arm's length. It took less than three seconds for his father to dump the good-pals routine and snap: 'What?'

'Doesn't matter. It's not loud enough.'

'What isn't?'

'The sound of gas, escaping.' Quite unexpectedly, Oliver discovered tears running down his cheeks. He sniffed, then grimaced. 'I'm inhaling it already, I suppose.'

Now he had his father's attention. His *full and final* attention, Oliver thought, recalling a form of wording his father liked to employ in his business correspondence.

'Oliver, think about this. Think very, very carefully—'

'I have.'

'No, I mean it.' His father's voice was low and husky, like a bad late-night DJ. 'Please, Oliver . . .'

The P-word. He hadn't heard that from Dad in . . . what?

A lifetime.

'It's too late. I've opened a couple of the canisters. Liam's people brought a small quantity of explosive, but I'm not au fait with this sort of detonator. Rather than risk any mistakes, I'm going to make doubly sure by igniting the gas myself. With my trusty box of matches.'

He laughed, perhaps a little too enthusiastically, and once again his father reverted to type.

'No, Oliver. You'll stop this nonsense immediately. Don't be so bloody stupid.'

Stupid. Some epitaph, Oliver thought.

He dropped the phone and picked up the matches.

Joe heard snatches of the conversation, and then only Felton's side of it, but that was enough to figure it out.

Oliver was inside Dreamscape, and he had matches.

After swearing at his son, Felton listened for a moment and then shook his head. He stared at Priya and said, 'The propane.'

She didn't get it at first. Didn't react when Felton retreated across the games room, out of Joe's sight. She watched him go, curiosity giving way to anger as she decided this must be a ruse. She raised the MP5 but Valentin screamed and lunged for the barrel, knowing its power might tear Felton apart, and Priya swatted him away while also nodding that she hadn't forgotten his concern. The gold was at stake, never mind Valentin's daughter.

Priya fumbled with the selector switch, perhaps trying to set it to single fire, so she could wound him, bring him down with a leg shot but keep him alive.

Madness. Joe saw that, and so did Liam, for both men began their dive for cover in what must have been the first millisecond of the explosion. Long before they heard it. Long before they felt anything but the greedy suck of air as every window on the northern side of the house blew out.

Joe hit the floor and rolled, seeking the relative protection of the squash court's side wall. He was facing upwards for just long enough to witness the first devastating impact of the pressure wave: Valentin and Priya, snatched off their feet and hurled across the games room. Then a searing flash of light had him throwing his arms up over his face and pressing his head into the space where the wall met the floor.

He felt the whole house shift, and heard a boom louder than thunder as the sound of the blast caught up. It was accompanied by a deep, rending noise that scared him more profoundly than anything he'd ever heard in his life: it was the sound of stone and timber and brick and glass being torn apart; a sound like the end of the world.

Priya was still conscious when the shock wave picked her up. Her head snapped back and her arms and legs splayed out and the sub-machine gun went flying off in another direction. She tried to keep control of her limbs, tried to reach for Valentin as he too was caught in the blast, and for an instant she thought her hand might have grasped his – she was sure she felt the soft, comforting touch of human flesh for a single fleeting moment – and along with her belated understanding of Oliver's betrayal came the knowledge that this was the very last touch, the very last moment.

Liam was better placed than most to comprehend what was happening. He'd been responsible for acquiring the propane. He was the one who'd researched its effects and made a rough estimate of the quantity needed to destroy Dreamscape. Valentin hadn't been too worried whether any of the other homes were damaged in the explosion: just as long as Felton's extravagant design was obliterated.

So in that sense Liam should have had a good idea of what to expect. But the reality was far worse than anything he'd imagined.

Too much gas, he thought as the world turned to hell around him. They should have kept the canisters on the ground floor so the house would absorb more of the blast.

Got it wrong.

And now they were all going to die.

Sixty

There weren't any guards patrolling the island, and there was no road-block on the bridge, but Liam's man nearly got them killed just the same.

Terry charged into his house, opened the garage doors and rolled out at the wheel of his huge black Hummer. Angela had always regarded it as a ludicrous vehicle: a hideous, planet-killing beast.

'Very small penis,' had been Donald's inevitable wisecrack whenever Terry Fox thundered past in it. Now Angela made a silent vow never to criticise the Hummer again, if only it transported them to safety.

They piled in, Angela still fretting that they'd left Oliver Felton behind, then Terry gunned the engine and she was thrown back in her seat as he accelerated away. She assumed he'd maintain the same furious velocity until they were well clear of the island, but after less than a hundred yards he slammed on the brakes.

By the time she'd recovered her equilibrium Terry had jumped out and was crouched over a dark shape by the side of the road. He turned and motioned at her to join him, and when she did she found that the shape was human, unconscious, and bleeding heavily from wounds to the head and chest.

It was one of the original gang. Pendry, she thought his name was. He was barely alive, and must have fallen foul of Felton's men, or possibly Yuri.

The new, battle-hardened Angela could almost have told Terry to leave him there. Get back in the Hummer and just *go*. Thankfully, the day's experiences hadn't quite brutalised her to that extent.

Even with the four of them working together, lifting the injured man into the Hummer ate up precious seconds. It was hard, hot, messy work. All the time she had to ignore an insistent voice in her head, reeling out horror after horror: that moving him would kill him, or they'd get him to a hospital and he'd die anyway, or he was exaggerating his wounds and might spring up and attack them. Worst of all, that Priya would come after them . . .

But none of these things happened, and they set off again, moving cautiously once the bridge came into sight. There was a Range Rover parked at the side of the road, and Terry watched it closely, holding the gun in his right hand while steering with his left. Thankfully it was unoccupied.

On the bridge itself there was a Citroën van, also empty, and beyond that a line of interlocking plastic barriers. Terry eased past the van and then blasted right through the barriers, muttering something about his paintwork, and then they hit the mainland and at last the island was behind them and they could dare to relax.

Angela let out a long breath, thinking she understood how astronauts must feel when the space shuttle touched down on the runway at the Kennedy Space Center. Now they were only minutes away from civilisation, working phones, normality.

Then Terry glanced at his rear-view mirror and said, 'What the hell . . . ?'

As Angela turned to him, she caught a flash of light in the corner of her eye. The Hummer rocked on its suspension and the rear window shattered. Both Angela and Maria screamed, and all four of them ducked in their seats, assuming they were under attack. The noise of a tremendous explosion drowned out all other sound, and only when it passed could they hear the rattle of debris raining down on the roof.

Terry brought the Hummer to a stop in the middle of the road, applied the handbrake and twisted round to get a proper look. In the passenger seat, Angela did the same, their shoulders pressed together as they stared at the island behind them.

A huge fireball was climbing into the sky above Terror's Reach. It had the shape of an atomic explosion, boiling and swelling like something alive and malevolent, forming an enormous mushroom cloud that blotted out the night sky.

On the back seat, Maria shifted upright and then leaned over to make sure Pendry was still breathing.

'Is he all right?' said Angela.

'I think.' Maria's eyes were red from weeping, and her face twitched as she glanced back at the island. 'What was that?'

'Someone blew the whole place,' Terry said.

'Oliver,' said Angela.

Terry grunted. 'Christ knows how. I mean, there are the LPG tanks, but I don't see how they'd produce an explosion like that.'

'Maybe Liam's gang brought a bomb with them?'

'Or maybe Felton did.' Terry shifted in his seat, facing forwards again. 'We need to get Pendry to a hospital.'

Angela reached for his hand and squeezed it. She couldn't quite control her voice as she said, 'Do you think they're dead?'

Terry sucked air between his teeth. 'Depends if they got any warning, I suppose. But it doesn't look good, does it?'

'No.' Angela turned away and shut her eyes. 'No, it doesn't.'

Sixty-One

Joe wasn't certain whether he blacked out, or if it was simply that the turmoil following the explosion scrambled his senses. But after what might have been seconds or minutes he moved his head slightly and realised he was alive.

After that, his first thought was: *Felton*. And then: *Cassie*.

He was lying under a pile of rubble, his face caked in dust. He tried opening his eyes and felt grit scraping against his eyeballs. Next he flexed his arms and legs and got the desired response. Not paralysed, then. But he might still be trapped.

He felt for obstructions around him before easing first one and then the other arm free of the wood and plaster that lay on top of him. He wiped his eyes and blinked until his tears washed them clean.

With his vision restored, Joe was able to see how lucky he'd been. A large slab of masonry had fallen and ended up propped against the wall about a foot above his head, shielding him from the worst of the debris. If it had landed any differently he would have been crushed or buried alive.

After making sure he wouldn't dislodge it when he moved, he was able to wriggle out from under it and look over the rest of the room. It wasn't a pleasant sight.

*　　*　　*

The gymnasium was hardly recognisable: two of the squash court's walls destroyed, the floor punctured and pitted and strewn with rubble. And there was a lot of blood.

The first body Joe noticed was Valentin's. The blast must have thrown him off the gallery, which had itself partially collapsed, with loose sections of balustrade dangling just inches above the floor of the squash court.

Valentin was sprawled on a pile of bricks and splintered wood, his right leg twisted at an obscene angle. Looking more closely, Joe saw that the limb had been almost torn from his body. His right arm was also severed, and the back of his skull had been caved in.

Joe stared at the body for a moment but found it hard to summon any real regret. Too many innocent people had paid the price of Valentin's stupidity and greed. What sympathy Joe felt was directed towards Cassie and Sofia.

And that sympathy won't be worth a damn if I can't find them, he reminded himself. It looked as if those on the upper floor had borne the brunt of the explosion, and the severity of Valentin's injuries didn't bode well for Priya or Felton.

Now standing, Joe checked himself over. He had a few minor lacerations and a lot of bruises, but no broken bones, no serious cuts or dents. The fight with Yuri had done more damage to him than the blast.

The boiler suit he'd taken from Manderson was tattered and filthy. He tore it off, and was gratified to find the jeans and T-shirt beneath still looked presentable.

He took a couple of steps and then a violent coughing fit had him doubled over. He hacked until his lungs burned, but afterwards he could breathe more easily.

As his convulsions subsided, he heard what appeared to be an echo; then he realised it was the sound of someone else trying to clear their lungs. Joe felt a stab of relief. There was one other survivor, at least.

It was Liam. He was lying about fifteen feet away, close to the mangled ruin of an expensive-looking treadmill.

He was buried more deeply than Joe had been: only his head and shoulders visible in the rubble, his hair grey with dust. There was a plank of splintered wood lying across his back, one end poking towards his neck. As Joe approached, he started to writhe.

'Don't move!'

Liam ignored him: he was either scared of what Joe might do or perhaps deafened by the blast. But he must have felt the wood jabbing his neck, for he suddenly froze.

'Joe?'

'Keep still. You're going to skewer yourself if you're not careful.'

Joe knelt down and carefully lifted the timber, in the process dislodging some of the bricks and plaster that were covering Liam's lower body. The Irishman shrieked.

'Ah fuck, that hurts!'

'Pain's a good sign. It means you've got feeling in your legs.'

'I don't know . . .' Liam must have flexed something, then he gasped. 'My right leg won't move, and the left one hurts like hell.'

Joe examined him as best he could, removing some of the bricks. 'You've got some nasty cuts, but they're not bleeding too heavily. There's no sign of any bones protruding—'

Liam made a retching sound, spat, and said, 'Thanks.'

'—so it's looking positive,' Joe finished, electing not to mention the possibility of internal bleeding. 'I don't have time to dig you out now, and frankly I want you staying put till I can get help.'

Liam groaned. 'And the paramedics'll have fucking cops at their elbows.'

'They will, yeah.'

Joe stood, peered at the field of debris around him, then nudged a lump of concrete aside with his foot and scooped up what he'd spotted: Liam's gun.

As he turned away, Liam twisted his head and shouted, 'Ah, show some mercy. Don't leave me here.'

'Be thankful you're still alive.'

'But I'm in agony.'

'Tough.'

Joe picked his way across the gym while looking the gun over. He unscrewed the silencer and slipped it in his pocket, then removed the magazine and checked the barrel. The weapon didn't seem to be damaged or jammed, but he wanted more than a visual inspection to rely on.

He pointed the gun at the far wall and fired once. Saw the bullet strike within a couple of inches of the spot he was aiming for, and decided that was good enough.

To reach the gallery, Joe climbed up on a pile of masonry and then grabbed a section of the balustrade, testing its strength before hauling himself up. It was a risk, but a quicker option than negotiating his way to the main staircase.

The games room had sustained heavy damage in some places but remarkably little in others. The pool table had overturned, while the flimsier table-tennis table, set further back, remained upright. It looked as though the force of the explosion had blown through the wide doorway on the inner, north-facing wall but had left the wall itself intact. Why?

Sketching the layout in his head gave Joe the answer. The panic room. Its reinforced walls formed the inner core of the building, and had acted as a barrier between the room they were in and Dreamscape. If they'd still been in the bedroom suite, on the far side of the panic room, they'd almost certainly be dead now.

Joe turned to his left, visualising his last glimpse of Felton, retreating from Priya, who'd been standing with her back to the doorway, catching the blast full on from behind. He estimated that both of them would have ended up somewhere close to the south-facing wall.

Priya's body was exactly where Joe thought it would be. She'd been thrown some twenty feet across the room and had struck the edge of a glass-fronted cabinet that contained a selection of pool and snooker cues. She was lying face down, one arm thrown out at the side, her fingers reaching toward the hole in the floor that accommodated the fireman's pole.

Joe crouched down for a closer look. The sight of her long, dark hair, its lustre of life barely diminished, stirred his emotions more powerfully than he would have cared to admit. Gently he lifted her head an inch or two, to allow him to see her face.

What he saw made him flinch. It sparked an unwelcome memory of the night when, as a young PC, he'd had to search a muddy field for the decapitated head of a motorcyclist. On that occasion he'd located it, and then embarrassed himself by vomiting. Here he quelled the nausea by reminding himself who Priya was, and what she had done. At least her death had been mercifully quick.

Now Joe had to prepare for the next discovery to be equally grisly. He tried consoling himself with the thought that there might yet be a clue to Cassie's whereabouts in Felton's pockets, or maybe on his phone.

It took him less than ten seconds to make a circuit of the room. There weren't many places where you could conceal the body of a fully grown man, but Joe searched them all and found no trace of Felton.

Sixty-Two

There were two windows on the south-facing wall. One had shattered; the other hadn't. Joe thought it unlikely that Felton could have been hurled clean through the broken one, but he checked it carefully all the same. There was no blood on the frame or the sill. No body on the lawn at the side of the house. Somehow Felton had vanished.

For a second Joe wondered if he could trust his own memory. Maybe he'd suffered concussion, and had imagined Felton's presence in the first place?

No. Felton had definitely been there, just before the explosion. Backing away from Priya, less afraid of her than of what his son was about to do . . .

Joe turned and stared at the spot where Priya lay, as if this time he might see Felton lying next to her. He'd expected to find both bodies in the same part of the room. So where was he?

Reluctantly he walked back towards Priya's corpse. This time he noticed what he'd missed before. The fireman's pole had a sweaty handprint on it, about two feet off the ground. He pictured Felton slithering through the hole, perhaps falling just as the explosion hit.

Joe peered down at the gymnasium below – and immediately spotted drops of blood on the floor.

*   *   *

340

Tucking the gun into his waistband, Joe used the pole to get down to the gym. He landed heavily and dropped to a crouch, half fearing that Felton would be lying in wait for him.

But there was no one in the gym except Liam. He'd made a lack-lustre effort to free himself and was now lying on his side, still buried, in a position that looked even less comfortable than before.

'Did you see Felton?' Joe demanded.

'What? When?'

'After the explosion. I think I blacked out. I don't know how long for, but Felton must have come past.'

'He's escaped? You're joking!'

Joe's voice hardened. 'Did you see him?'

'Of course not. I was unconscious, too.' Liam shook his head. 'We're lucky he didn't kill us on his way past.'

Joe shrugged. 'He's got better things to do.'

He made his way through to the entrance hall and discovered that half the main staircase had collapsed. The marble floor looked as if an earthquake had hit it, and a couple of small fires smouldered in one of the living rooms. Weighing it up, Joe decided that the risk didn't warrant the time it would take to carry Liam out of the house.

The front door had been blasted off its hinges and lay broken in a corner of the driveway. Most of the perimeter wall had been demolished and there were more fires taking hold in the trees across the road. That could be serious, he knew, given the recent dry weather, but there was nothing he could do about it.

Joe walked briskly, his muscles and joints protesting at the hammering they'd endured. Reaching the road, he looked north, in the direction of the bridge, nursing a desperate hope that he'd spot Felton hobbling along just a short way ahead of him. But there was no one to be seen.

After a few more steps Joe turned to survey the extent of the damage. Despite having prepared himself for the sight, it still came as a shock.

Dreamscape was gone. Although he hadn't lived to see it, Valentin's wish had been granted: the entire house, wiped from the face of the earth, and in its place a burning wasteland. There wasn't even a lot of debris to be seen: Joe guessed that most of it had been blasted into the sea or far across the island.

Of the houses on either side, Felton's had fared better than Terry Fox's, again probably because of the panic room. There was a lot of damage to the outside wall and the north-facing roof, but nothing that couldn't be rebuilt. Terry's place, on the other hand, looked dangerously unstable, the roof drooping like a lazy eye over a missing gable-end wall. It would have to come down, Joe thought.

Assuming he'd set off the explosion by hand, Oliver Felton would have been vaporised in an instant. It was unlikely that any trace of him would ever be found. The same would be true of Angela and the other prisoners, if they'd still been in the garage.

The thought made Joe pause and bow his head in sorrow. He tried to envisage a scenario where Oliver, deranged and suicidal in his final moments, had summoned the humanity to release a group of innocent men and women.

Deep in his heart, Joe couldn't see it.

He started along the road, heading in the only direction that made sense: towards the bridge, and the mainland beyond. He had no plan as such, except to keep moving. If ever he needed a lucky break, it was now.

In a moment of despondency he remembered how Felton had described him: *Crawling over my island like vermin.* The blunt truth was that not only had Felton thoroughly outwitted them all, but the momentum was still going his way.

Unless the man had been badly injured, which now seemed unlikely, he felt sure that Felton's priority would be to reach the place where Cassie and the children were being held. They were his one trump card, if he still imagined some kind of deal was possible; and if not, they were inconvenient witnesses whose silence offered him a chance of freedom.

Joe thought back over the conversation in the bedroom suite. Felton had boasted that his hostages would never be found, but in mocking Joe's efforts to hide them at the B&B in Chichester he'd also said it had taken no time to 'fetch them'.

That suggested they were still close by. Perhaps one of the villages south of the city?

How to narrow it down: that was the problem.

Fretting, Joe kept his eyes on the road. The surface was littered with bricks and tiles and various household items: a kettle sitting upright by the verge; a paperback book with its pages fluttering gently in the night air; a bathrobe curled up like a sleeping cat. Joe looked for signs that a car had driven over the debris, and could find nothing to suggest that one had.

Very little would have survived in Felton's garage, and the single vehicle parked near Dreamscape had been reduced to a twisted, smouldering wheelbase. If Felton was on foot, then Joe had a real chance of catching him.

He increased his pace, trying to dredge up some encouragement, a spark of hope that he could convert into energy. Felton's taunt kept on rolling around in his head, nagging at him for some reason he couldn't grasp.

Crawling over my island like vermin.

When he reached the corner his spirits lifted further as he saw that Valentin's property had sustained only minimal damage. By now he'd got used to the pain in his limbs and he was able to run the rest of the way.

He stopped at the threshold, crept inside and waited, attuning himself to the vibrations of the house. It felt empty. He pressed the light switch in the hall and discovered that the electricity was out. Of course it was.

Groping through the blackness, he made it to the garage and found the keys to Valentin's BMW. He started it up, turned the headlights on, then got out and tussled with the big garage doors. The frame must have warped slightly: one of the doors jammed when it was only half open.

Joe kicked it a few times, achieving nothing but a bruised foot, then gave up and returned to the car. He revved the engine and drove through the gap, ignoring the piercing metallic shriek as the nearside bodywork scraped against the door.

North of Valentin's the road had a lot less wreckage on it, but Joe knew he had to be careful to avoid a puncture. He leaned close to the steering wheel and peered at the road, lit up by the headlights and by the distant glow of the flames. The fire was spreading fast in the wood and might soon engulf the whole island.

'Shit,' he said aloud, and stamped on the brakes.

Joe backed up, his head turned to the side as he tried to spot the gap in the trees. He missed it the first time and reversed too far. He eased forward, stopped and jumped out. Ran towards the trees, looking back to align himself with the house and driveway. Then he plunged into the copse, thick with grey smoke and alive with the crackle of approaching fire.

His strongbox was just where he'd left it. A few more minutes and it would have been a lump of melted junk.

He ran back to the car, threw the box into the rear footwell, then accelerated away, a distant part of his mind contemplating how Terror's Reach would look if destroyed by fire. Again he thought back to Felton, languidly sipping champagne and declaring: 'I want you off the Reach. This is *my* island now.'

The bitter irony was that Oliver might have done his dad a favour, particularly if the fire spread as far as the old training camp. With the buildings destroyed, it could tip the balance in favour of redeveloping the whole site. And if Felton found a way to evade justice, he could end up owning—

Joe's train of thought was jolted by the sight of flashing blue lights on the mainland, still about four or five miles away. He slowed down on the approach to the bridge, flicked the headlights to main beam and swore again.

The Citroën van used by Liam's gang was still parked on the bridge, but the plastic barriers were lying broken in the road. It might have been the explosion, but Joe doubted it. More likely someone had driven through them at high speed.

Felton's men were likely to have stationed a vehicle at the bridge, once Yuri had disposed of the original guard. All Felton would've had to do was get here on foot, then drive away. Even with only a ten-minute start he could be on the A27 by now. Impossible to find.

So what am I doing? Joe asked himself.

Fooling myself. Fooling myself that I'm going to find them. Fooling myself that I was ever a bodyguard worthy of the name.

He saw Felton raising his glass to toast his own success. Couldn't get that smug voice out of his head.

This is my island now.

Crawling over my island like vermin.

Both times he'd referred to Terror's Reach as 'my island'. Why would he say that?

Simple arrogance – or something else?

Sixty-Three

Joe gnawed at the memory, wondering if he was trying to read in it something that wasn't there. *My* island. Could be just a lazy figure of speech, a kind of shorthand prompted by the fact that Felton had been so firmly in control at that point.

Or . . . he had a legitimate reason to claim ownership.

Either way, Joe couldn't take long to decide. The emergency vehicles were obscured by the trees in the nature reserve, but he could track them by the faint pulse of light in the sky. Less than two minutes away, if they were pushing hard.

He repeated both lines out loud and realised what was troubling him.

Not *my island* but *crawling*.

The choice of such a specific word had jarred at the time, but he hadn't been able to consider its significance until now. *Crawling over my island* had hit a nerve, because Joe *had* been crawling, literally, to get in and out of the training camp.

And Felton had seen him.

Joe turned in the driver's seat and looked over his right shoulder. The entrance to the base was less than a hundred feet behind him, mostly hidden by the vegetation that grew alongside the perimeter fence.

He swung the BMW round in a brutal three-point turn and rolled it up to the entrance, dimming his lights as he came to a halt. As he got out he noticed a slight gap where the two gates met, a couple of padlocks hanging loose from the central bar. His heart did a crazy little skip.

Joe eased the gates apart and hurried back to the car. He couldn't afford to be caught here when the emergency services came past: otherwise he'd be spending the rest of the night in a cell.

Leaving the headlights off, he drove forward as fast as he dared while navigating by starlight. The main cluster of buildings was about a quarter of a mile away, over a low ridge. Joe recalled the feeling he'd had that someone was spying on him from an upper window of the terrace, and he shivered. He pictured Felton and his men waiting patiently for Valentin's operation to unravel. Selecting their moment to strike . . .

As Joe pulled in close to the top of the ridge, the first fire appliances hurtled past the camp, sirens blasting through the still night air.

Joe got out of the BMW, made sure the gun he'd taken from Liam felt comfortable, and warily approached the crest of the hill. Shielding his eyes from the glare of the fire to his right, he made out two dabs of light in front of the terrace.

Another few yards and he saw the lights belonged to a Range Rover. Its engine was still running, and the driver's door was open. Joe felt a surge of hope.

As he ran down the gentle incline towards the row of houses, he noticed a weak, roving light in a window at the end of the terrace: a flashlight.

He was less than ten feet from the house when the front door opened and Cassie appeared, her hands tied behind her back, tape over her mouth. Jaden was stumbling alongside her, also bound and gagged. The sight of black tape across the six-year-old's mouth filled Joe with revulsion.

Cassie looked frantic with worry. She glanced behind her, then made a screeching noise in her throat: a single long note, directed at her son. It sounded like she was urging him to run, but either he didn't understand or he was too traumatised to respond.

From the doorway came an angry growl: 'Get in the car. Back seat.'

Felton emerged, Sofia propped under his left arm like an unwanted parcel. She wriggled and let out a tiny, anxious mewling. Joe felt a cold rage building.

Felton was covered in dust and blood, his once immaculate suit in shreds. He had a nasty gash on his forehead and another on his upper arm. He was holding a Maglite in his right hand. When Cassie faltered at the end of the path, he swatted it across her shoulders. She lurched forward and fell to her knees, her scream muffled by the tape.

'Stand up!' Felton shouted, raising the flashlight to strike again.

Joe moved along the side of the Range Rover and stepped into view, bringing the gun up and sighting on Felton's chest. 'Leave her alone.'

Felton saw him and reacted at once, hurling the Maglite at Joe while simultaneously twisting, lifting the baby up in front of his chest. Using Sofia as a shield.

Joe registered what Felton was doing even as he ducked away from the flashlight, which landed harmlessly in the road behind him. He regained his balance and made quick eye contact with Cassie, signalling her to move clear. But she stayed on her knees, Jaden standing helplessly next to her, his shoulders heaving as he sobbed.

Joe looked back at Felton, whose right hand was now free. He reached into his pocket and produced a gun of his own. Placed the muzzle against Sofia's writhing body and said: 'We're leaving here, Joe, and you're not stopping us.'

Sixty-Four

Joe felt sure that someone was going to die here. With so many elements beyond his control, and three innocent people caught between the two guns, he could only pray it would be Felton rather than Cassie or the children.

He hoped it wouldn't be himself, either. But if it was, he probably deserved it.

'Put your gun down,' he told Felton.

'Uh-uh. It's still my agenda, Joe.'

'You won't make it out of here. Can't you hear those sirens?'

'They've got fires to put out. No one's going to notice me.'

'And where will you go? What can you hope to do now?'

'Recover. Regroup. Make a deal.'

'Who with? Valentin's—' He stopped, but Felton gave a thin smile.

'Don't worry: she knows. And believe me, there's always a deal to be made.'

'Not this time.'

'You're forgetting, I was never here. I can be back in France in time for breakfast.'

'And what about your hostages?'

'They're coming with me. With some time to reflect, I'm sure Cassie will recognise the wisdom of my proposal.' Growing bolder, Felton took the gun away from Sofia's body and waved it to emphasise his command. 'Drop your gun and move away from the car.'

'And let you shoot all four of us?' Joe shook his head. He was still aiming at Felton's chest. His double-handed grip remained steady, but he remembered the test shot he'd fired in the gymnasium: a couple of inches out. Even that margin of error would put Sofia in mortal danger.

'I have no reason to kill them,' Felton said, turning his gun on Joe. 'I'll have to kill *you*, of course, but that's the risk you accepted when you took the job. A good bodyguard should be willing to take a bullet for his clients.'

Joe said nothing. The critical moment was approaching. He'd either have to shoot or else accept Felton's terms and surrender his gun.

Felton saw Joe wavering and, as with Priya, assumed that he'd won the argument. Sofia was still wriggling and moaning under his arm. Irritated, he hoisted her up to stop her from slipping free.

But he lifted her too high. As Sofia's head drew level with his chin, her left hand swatted against his face and snagged on Felton's mouth, her fingers dragging his lower lip down. She'd done the same thing to Joe many times, and he knew it could be surprisingly painful, especially if you weren't expecting it.

Felton grunted, twisting his head away from her, but Sofia clung on. He couldn't lower his left arm without the risk of dropping her – which would clear the way for Joe to shoot him – and his right hand was pointing his gun at Joe.

For half a second Felton was lost to indecision, his face contorted as he tried to break the baby's grip. His gun hand fell to his side, and as Sofia finally released him Cassie saw her chance and sprung up, propelling herself towards Felton.

She had difficulty balancing because her arms were tied behind her back. As a result, it wasn't the most cleanly delivered head butt that Joe had ever seen. But it was undoubtedly one of the most effective. The top of Cassie's forehead struck Felton on the chin with enough force to snap his jaws together. Joe heard the crack of bones breaking.

Felton reeled back and fell, blood streaming from his nose and mouth, Cassie toppling after him, helpless as Sofia tumbled from his grasp. Joe dived forward, throwing his left arm under the baby as she landed, just managing to cup the back of her head before it hit the ground.

Cassie collapsed onto Felton and rolled over, howling a warning as Felton wrenched his hand from beneath her. He was still holding the gun.

Joe saw the glint of madness in his eyes and knew that all thoughts of deals had been forgotten: nothing mattered more to Felton now than simple, savage retaliation. And Joe couldn't get a clean shot at him. Cassie and Jaden were in his line of fire.

'Robert!' he shouted.

It was enough to distract Felton's attention for a split second. The mist of fury cleared as Felton forgot about Cassie and looked at Joe, and as he turned his head Joe lunged and hit him with his gun hand, clubbed him full in the face, and although Felton saw it coming there was nothing he could do to stop it. The impact drove his head back against the ground and knocked him out cold.

Joe leaned across Felton's body to grab his gun but Cassie beat him to it, stamping on Felton's hand with her heel, then using her foot to kick the gun out of his reach, all the time making raw, animal cries of desperation. Her face was bright red, her eyes crazed with fear, trapped in a place where no one could be trusted or believed, where her children might still be stolen from her.

Joe had to take her gently by the shoulders before she would look in his eyes.

'It's okay, it's okay,' he told her. 'You're safe now.'

Sixty-Five

She didn't fully believe it until Joe had picked Sofia up and soothed her as best he could while at the same time removing the tape from Cassie's mouth.

'Anyone else in the house?' he asked.

'No. We were brought here by the two men who attacked us in Brighton. They dumped us in one of the bedrooms. I heard them driving away.'

'Okay.' He realised that he no longer had his knife, but he found a little penknife in Felton's jacket and cut Cassie and Jaden free. Then he stood back as Cassie gathered both children into her arms and wept tears of joy and relief.

Joe knelt down by Felton's body and made sure there was a pulse. It was weak, but steady.

'Is he dead?' Cassie asked.

'Not quite. But I think he's got a fractured skull.'

'Good.' There was no malice in her voice; barely any emotion at all. Just a matter-of-fact statement.

'We'd better not move him. Is there any more of that tape in the house?'

He retrieved Felton's gun and offered it to Cassie, half expecting her to shrink away from it. But she took it calmly, instructing Jaden to stand behind her while she trained the gun on the unmoving body.

Joe found a roll of tape in an upstairs room and used it to bind Felton's ankles and wrists. It felt inhumane to treat an unconscious man in such a way, but if they were going to leave him here while they sought help Joe didn't want to take any chances.

While he worked, he sensed Cassie drawing up the courage to speak.

'It was my fault, wasn't it?'

'What?'

'You warned me not to make any phone calls. But I got so worried. I couldn't bear not knowing what was going on.'

Joe nodded that he understood. 'No one could have foreseen something like this.'

'How did you find us? Did you follow him here?'

'Not exactly. I managed to work it out from what he'd said to us.'

'So it was a guess?'

'Let's call it a professional deduction.'

Cassie smiled with him, but he could read the fear in her eyes: *What if you hadn't guessed it right?*

'I can see this place made the perfect staging ground for them,' Joe said.

She nodded. 'Felton was boasting that he'd bought the whole camp months ago and kept it quiet. He said he had planning permission in the bag, too.'

My island, Joe thought. For a man with as many political connections as Felton, acquiring the camp in a secret deal wouldn't have posed too much difficulty.

In a sombre voice, Cassie added: 'He also claimed that Valentin had arranged a robbery, but tried to make it look like he was one of the victims. Is that true?'

'I'm afraid so.' Joe gave her a brief account of what he knew, including Valentin's culpability and his subsequent ambush by Felton's men. Cassie was disgusted but not greatly surprised to learn of Yuri's betrayal.

'He's dead now, though?'

'A lot of people are dead. Some of them deserved it. Some didn't.' Joe sighed, thinking of Angela Weaver. Cassie had a lot more questions but he gently deflected them. This wasn't the right time to go into detail, especially with Jaden soaking up every word.

'Let's go,' he said.

He opened the back door of the Range Rover and helped the three of them climb inside. Jaden was last in and Joe stopped him for a second, crouching down to look him in the eye. Keeping his voice low, he said, 'You've been a brave man today. I'm proud of you.'

Jaden coyly shook his head.

'No, you have,' Joe told him. 'The thing is, you might need to be just as brave over the next few weeks.'

'Are more people going to hurt us?'

'No. Nothing like that. But your mum's going to need a lot of help, and a lot of love. Okay?'

Jaden was old enough to squirm at the mention of the L-word. 'Will you help her, too?' he asked. The earnest, affectionate look in his eyes was tough to bear. Joe knew it would stay with him for a long time.

'I'm sorry, Jaden. I can't.'

While they'd been talking, at least two more convoys of emergency vehicles had raced past on the other side of the perimeter fence. Joe climbed into the Range Rover and drove slowly along the access road until he reached the BMW.

Cassie said nothing as he got out and fetched the strongbox. It was only when he climbed in and put the box in the front footwell that she understood what it was, and what it signified.

She started to speak, choked up, turned it into a cough. When Joe glanced in the mirror he could see her eyes shining.

He drove out through the main gates and turned left, ignoring the instinct that urged him to leave the island right away.

Within a couple of hundred yards they found the Reach more

choked with traffic than it had ever been. There were even a few
civilian cars parked at the roadside. Insomniacs, presumably, drawn
by the sight of a fire.

'Rubberneckers,' Joe murmured, shaking his head.

From the back seat, Cassie regarded the chaos of fire and destruction and said, with bitter sadness: 'All this for a room full of gold.'

Joe parked at a safe distance, several cars back from a hurriedly erected
police cordon. The Nasenko house was a couple of hundred yards
beyond that, still looking remarkably unscathed. Flames were blazing
in the woods opposite, but hadn't yet crossed the road. There were
about twenty firefighters on the road itself, doing their utmost to hold
the fire at bay.

Joe got out of the car, then helped Cassie with the children. The
air was hot and sharp with the smell of the fire, the night sky obscured
by the spreading pall of grey smoke. Fragments of ash drifted around
them like blossom.

A familiar vehicle caught his eye, parked just inside the cordon.
Terry Fox's Hummer. It was facing the island's homes, which suggested
that someone had driven towards the fire rather than away from it.
Odd, he thought.

Then he spotted the small group clustered at the back of an ambu-
lance. Maria and the American's driver were sitting inside, receiving
treatment from a paramedic.

Cassie moved alongside Joe, followed his line of sight and said: 'Is
that Angela Weaver?'

It was one of those occasions where Joe almost had to pinch himself.
They were alive. Perhaps Oliver had done the right thing after all.

Angela and Terry were in animated conversation with two police
officers. Even from this distance Joe could tell that the police looked
taken aback by what they were hearing.

Cassie patted him on the back. 'She'll be really pleased to see you.'

Joe turned to her, his elation fading as rapidly as it had appeared.

He could see she'd mentally braced herself for what he was about to say, but that didn't make it any easier for either of them.

'I can't. I have to go.'

'Because of what you told me earlier?'

He nodded. 'My false ID's pretty good but it won't stand up to detailed scrutiny. And after something like this . . .' He waved a hand towards the devastation. 'I can't take the chance. I'm sorry.'

Cassie looked round, checked there was no one within earshot, and said, 'You really do have a price on your head?'

He smiled. He sensed another *quid pro quo* moment coming up. 'As far as I know.'

'But I still don't get it. If your wife and daughters were given new identities as well, why can't you be with them?'

'That's the complicated bit.'

'Go on.'

Joe sighed. He had never told anyone this. He had never said the words aloud, and wasn't sure he wanted to hear them now.

'My wife accepted the deal on one condition. That under no circumstances was I to be given any details about their relocation. They went off to their new lives, and I went off to mine.'

'What?' Cassie sounded appalled.

'It's safer that way. No one can target them through me.'

'But that's a terrible thing to do to someone. You're telling me that you've got no idea where they live now?'

Joe shook his head, almost embarrassed by the force of her outrage.

'I don't know where they are. I don't even know *who* they are.'

Once she had adjusted to his decision, Cassie had more questions about what she should do next. What should she tell the police?

'Tell them the truth.'

'But what do I say about you?'

'Same thing. Tell them everything you know about Joe Carter. I have another ID I can use if I have to.'

Cassie nodded slowly. Sofia was becoming fractious, drawing curious glances from one of the uniforms at the cordon; any second now he would be wandering over to ask what they were doing here.

'So I won't see you again?' she asked.

'I don't think so. No.'

She leaned forward, holding his arm while she kissed him. It was a brief, tender contact, and it warmed his heart.

Then they broke apart, and he said, 'You'd better go and tell them about Felton.' He fished in his pocket and gave her the keys to the BMW, then indicated the Range Rover. 'I'm going to borrow this for a day or two.'

Cassie didn't speak again until he'd turned away from her.

'Where are you going? I mean, I realise you can't tell me the actual place . . .'

'I don't know. I guess I'll decide when I get there.'

Joe opened the driver's door and started to climb in, but he could feel her eyes on him and knew there was more to be said. Probably one last question.

He left the door open while he started the engine. Cassie took a step towards the car and gazed at him through the windscreen, as if the existence of a barrier made it easier to say.

'Try to find them.'

Joe stared at her. It wasn't a question at all. He didn't really know what it was. A suggestion? A command? An expression of hope?

To her credit, Cassie didn't push for a response, but simply turned and led Jaden towards the police cordon. The boy only looked back once, raising his hand to wave at Joe; too entranced by the fire to be distracted for long.

It meant that neither of them got to hear Joe's reply, but that didn't matter. The important thing was that he said it.

'One day.'

Acknowledgements

Once again I owe a huge debt of gratitude to my editor, Rosie de Courcy. Thanks also to Richard Cable, Trevor Dolby, Nicola Taplin, Nick Austin and the rest of the team at Preface / Random House.

At Janklow and Nesbit, I'd like to thank my agent, Tif Loehnis, as well as Rebecca Folland, Kirsty Gordon, Tim Glister and Lucie Whitehouse.

I'm very grateful for the support of the family and friends who comprise my first readers: Tracy Brown, the Harrisons, Spencers, Deakins and Roslings. Special thanks to Claire Burrell, who provided some valuable feedback on the almost-final draft. As ever, a combination of thanks and apologies are due to Niki, James and Emily for their love and tolerance.

Finally, I should point out that certain geographical modifications were made to ensure that my fictional island of Terror's Reach could be accommodated within the real – and very beautiful – surroundings of Chichester Harbour.

Note on the Author

Tom Bale is the author of *Skin and Bones*. He lives with his family in Brighton. For more information, visit www.tombale.net.